DATE DUE

By Emily Powell

It's time for action.
Time for you to spread the word,
Sent from my iPhone.

You get to decide
Who gets to decide the rules
Sent from my iPhone.

I have spoken out,
I have told you my story,
Sent from my iPhone.

I only wonder,
What does sequential art mean,
Sent from my iPhone.

You know what you want,
And you know how to get it.
It's time for action.

It's a bunch of art.
Who gets to decide the rules?
You get to decide.

Our feelings and lives
One right after the other
Sent from my iPhone.

ADDITIONAL CONTENT IN THIS VOLUME CONTRIBUTED BY
ELIZA FANTASTIC MOHAN, EMILY POWELL, STELLA GREENVOSS, LIV OSBORN,
NINA KHOURY, NIAL DONOHOO AND LUCIE WEISS.

JAN 0 0 2020

MISSION

YOU DO YOU
PERIOD OR IT.

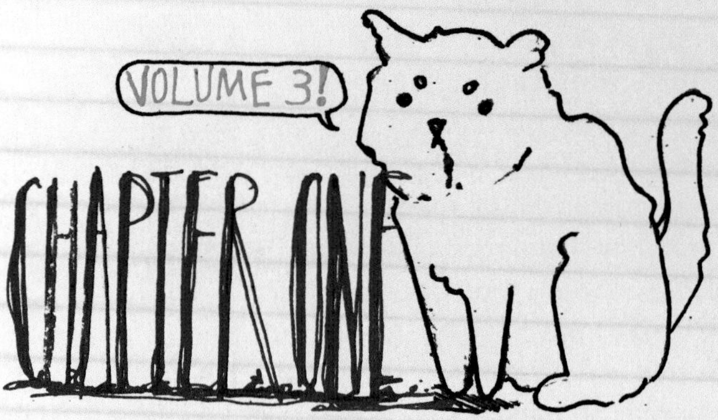
VOLUME 3!
CHAPTER ONE

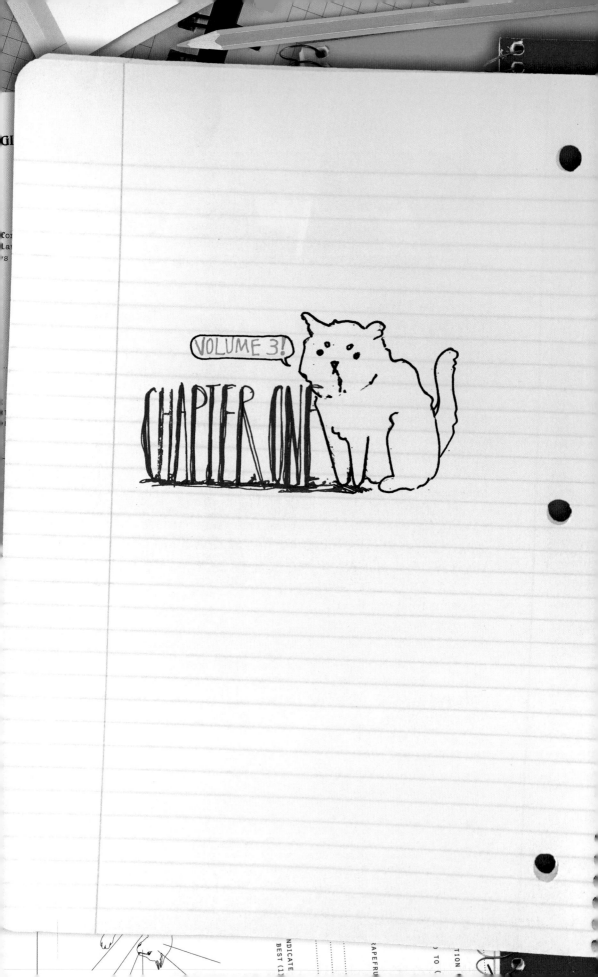

ME12–01
OFFICIAL MAN-EATERS PUBLICATION

HANDBOOK
FOR THE
REVOLUTION

HEADQUARTERS, MINISTRY OF TROUBLE
2019

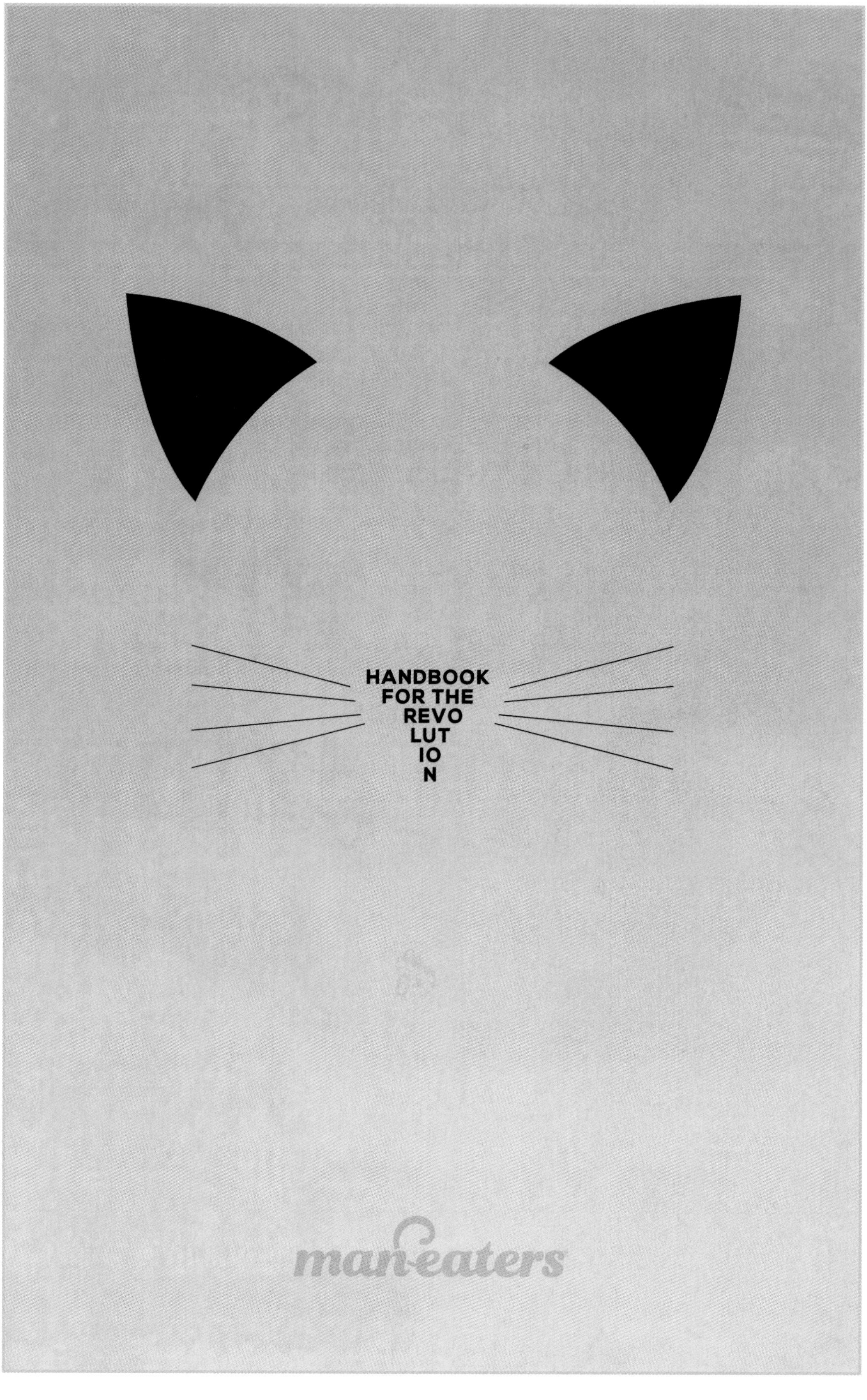
HANDBOOK
FOR THE
REVO
LUT
IO
N
man-eaters

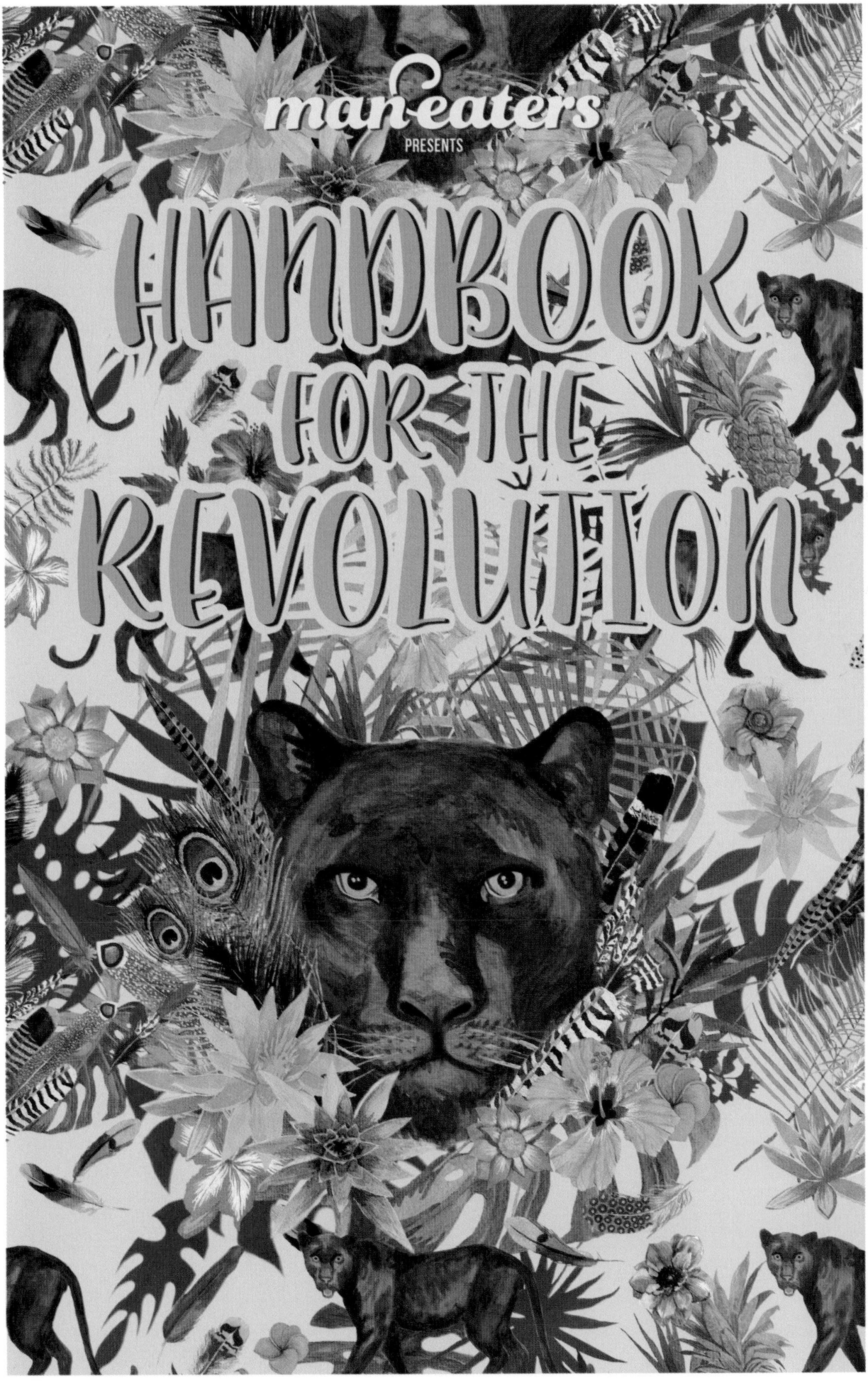
man-eaters
PRESENTS
HANDBOOK
FOR THE
REVOLUTION

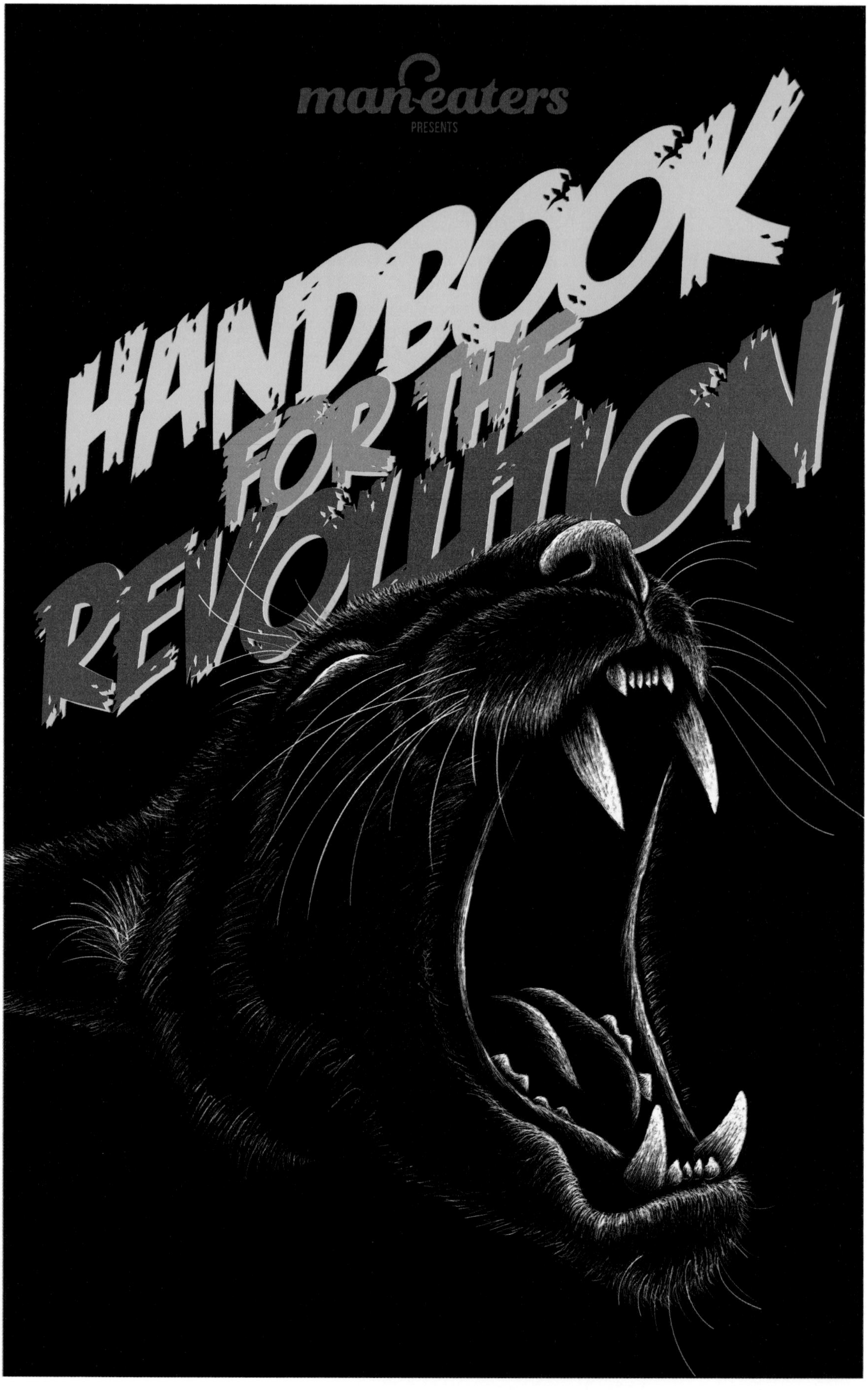
man-eaters
PRESENTS
HANDBOOK
FOR THE
REVOLUTION

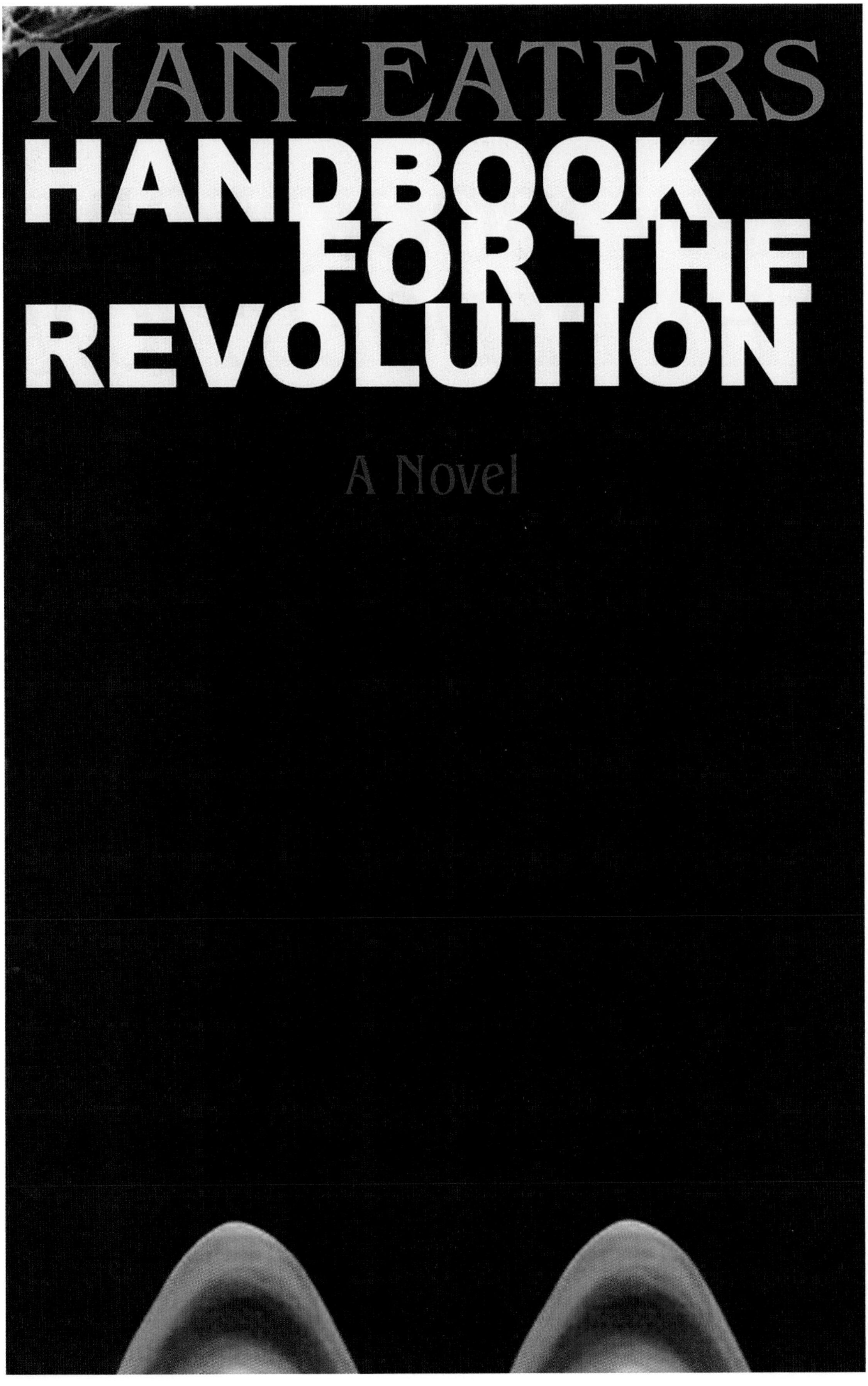
MAN-EATERS
HANDBOOK
FOR THE
REVOLUTION
A Novel

CC

man-eaters™

PRESENTS

HANDBOOK FOR THE REVOLUTION

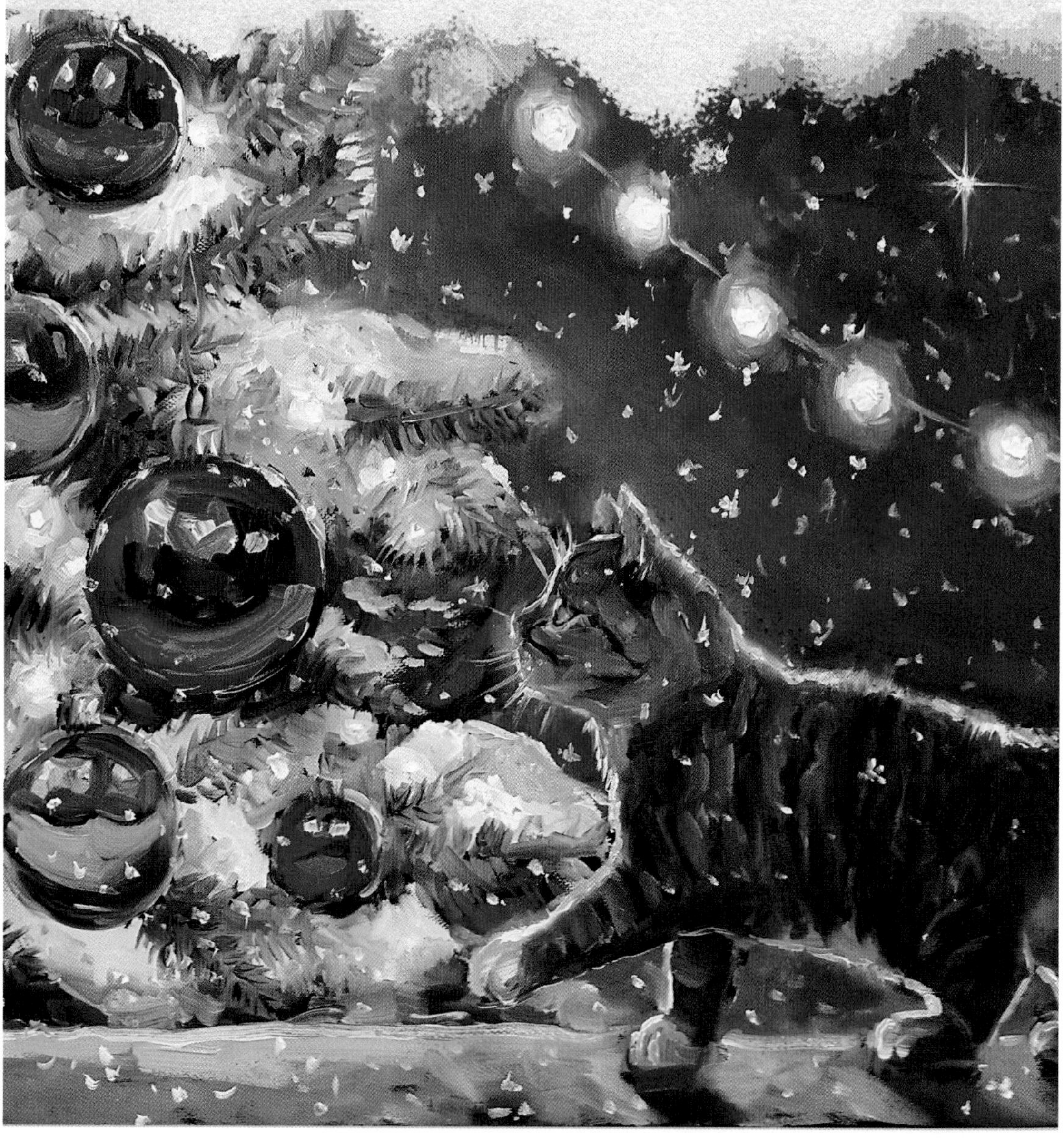

man-eaters
PRESENTS

HANDBOOK FOR THE REVOLUTION

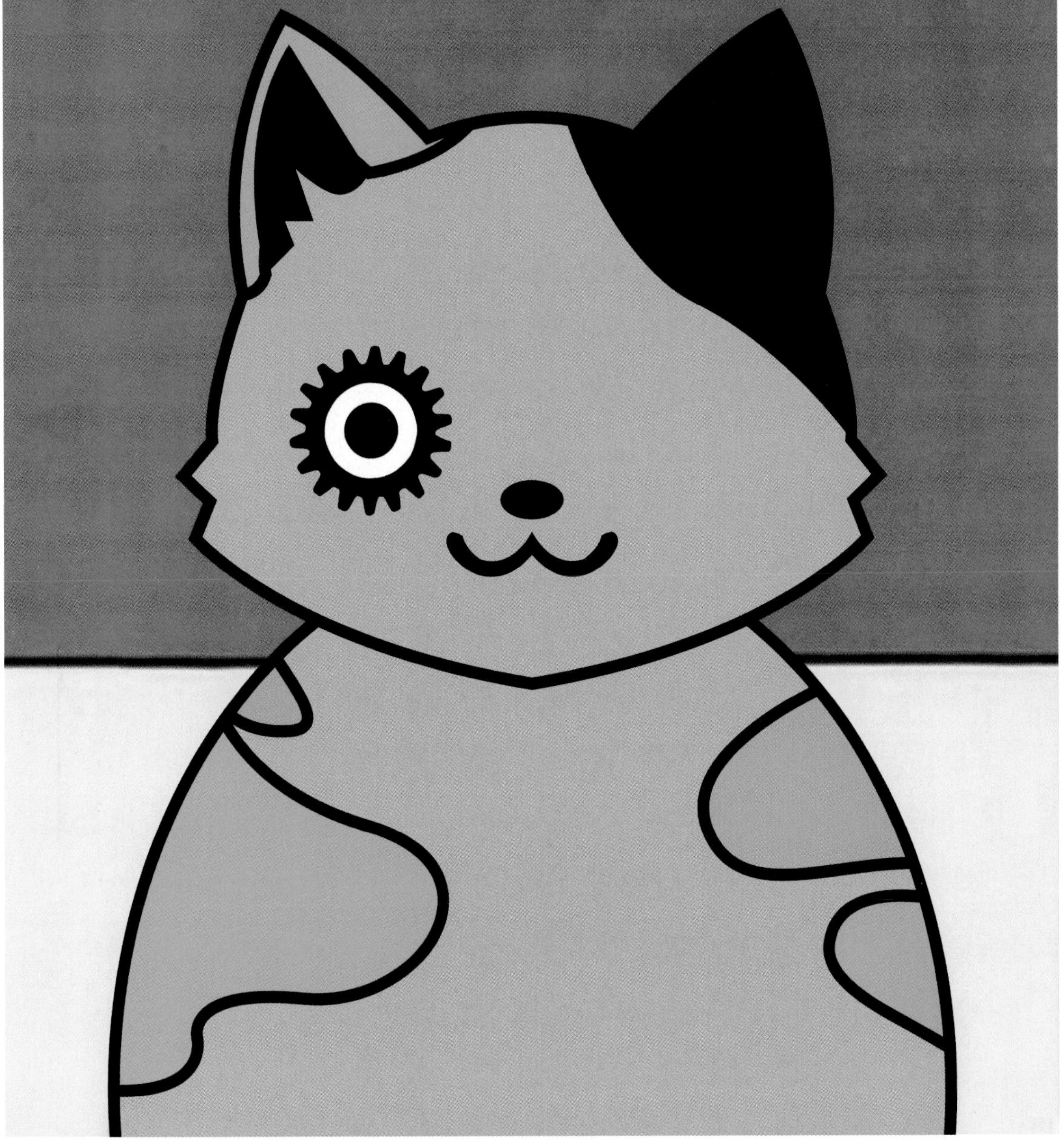

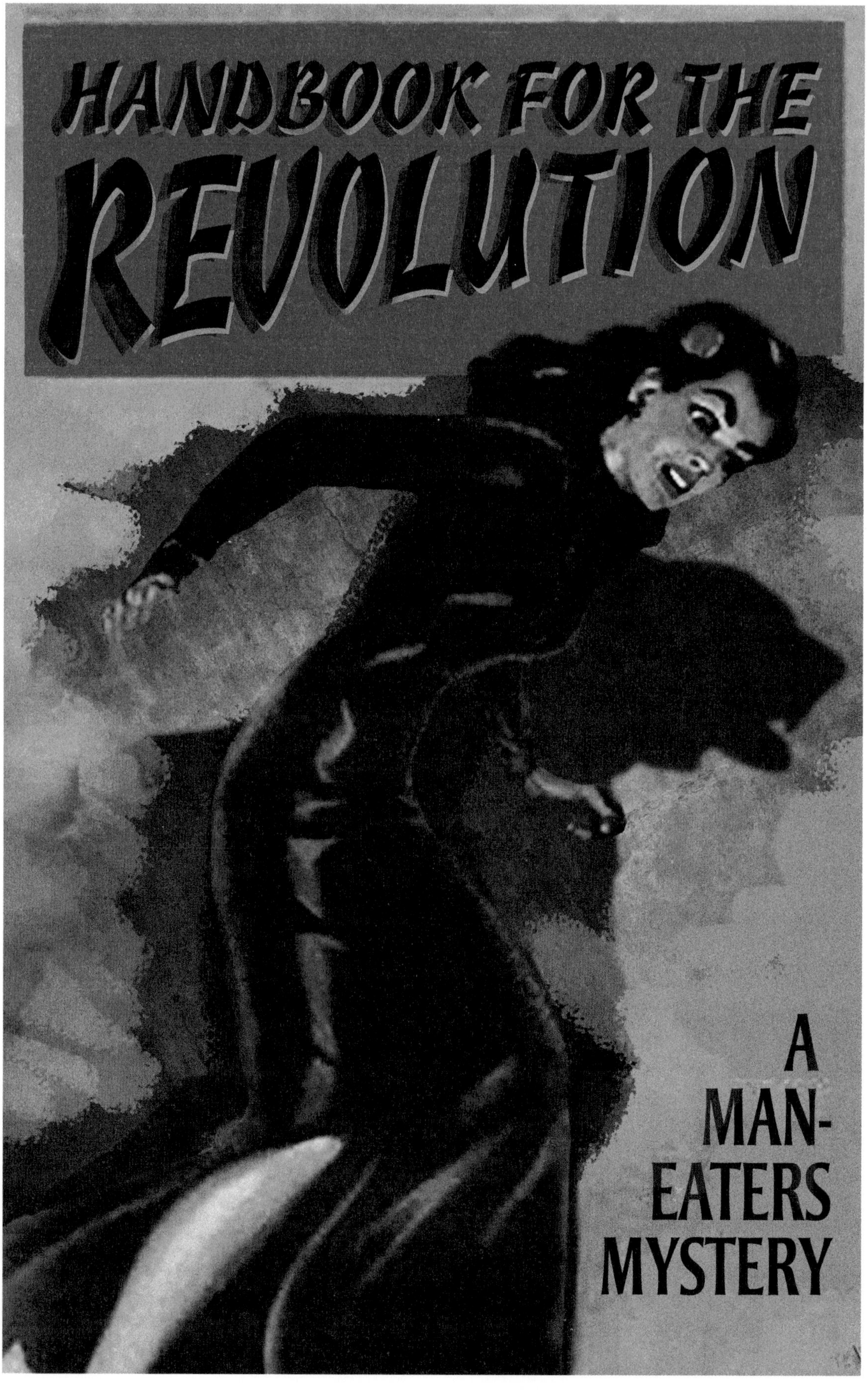
HANDBOOK FOR THE
REVOLUTION
A
MAN-
EATERS
MYSTERY

HANDBOOK FOR THE REVOLUTION

A Man-Eaters Publication

Handbook for the Revolution

Man-Eaters
Feline
Feminist
Maude
Ruminations
Jo
Corgi
Murder
Discovery
Ketchup
Mystery
Estro Corp.
Patriarchy
Plan
Attack
Jeff
Kevin
Sophie E.
Middle School
S.C.A.T.
Cerulean
Action
Movement
Pencil Shoppe
Unicorn
Blood Sport
Cats
Costume
Ezra
Pantherism
Water
Tampon
Woman
Ministry
of
Trouble
Period
Question
Mittelschmerz
Menstruation
Spuffy
Revolution

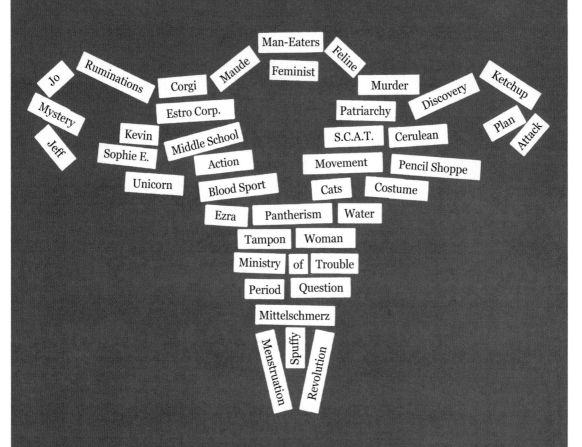

X

man-eaters

Handbook for the Revolution

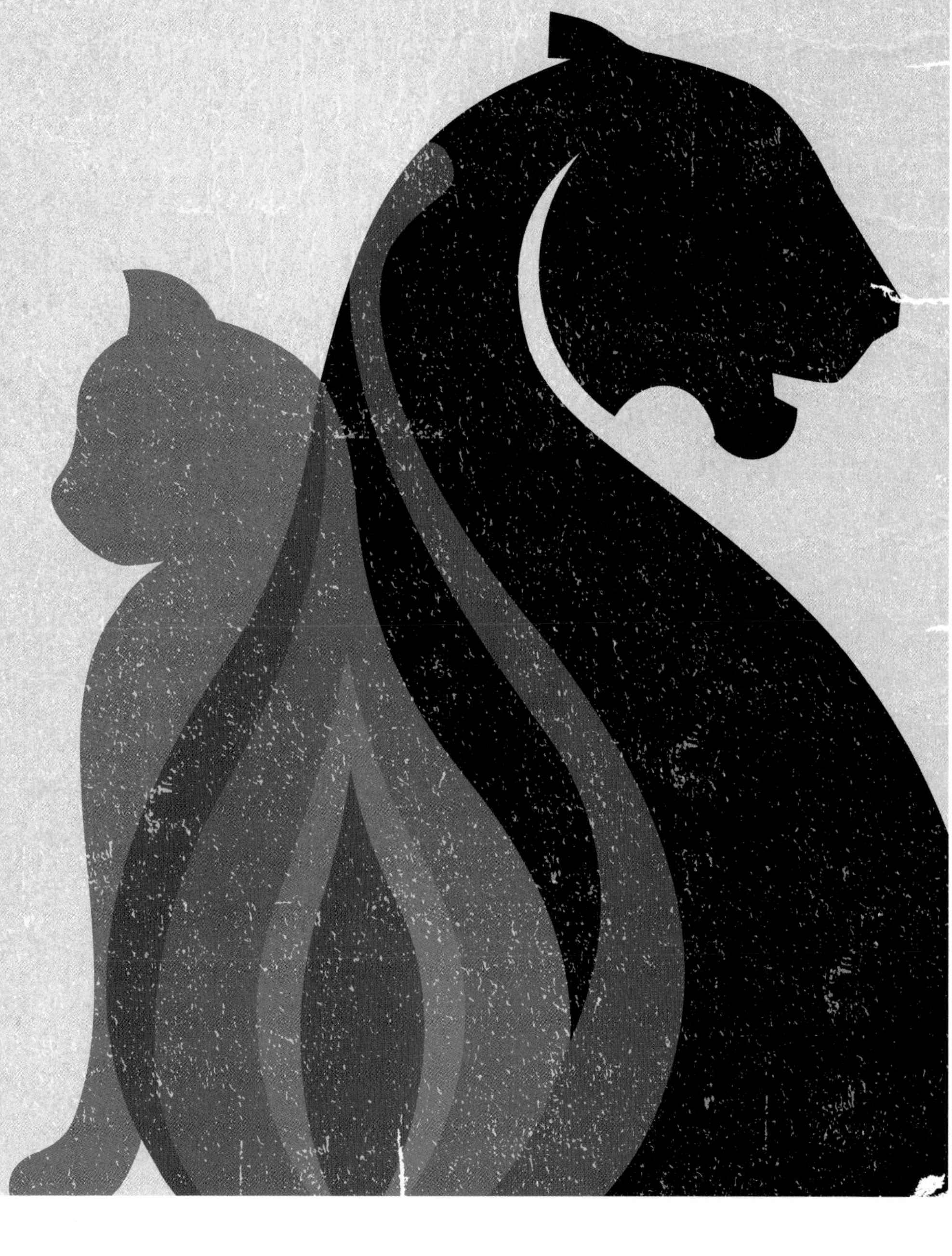

maneaters
PRESENTS

Handbook for the Revolution

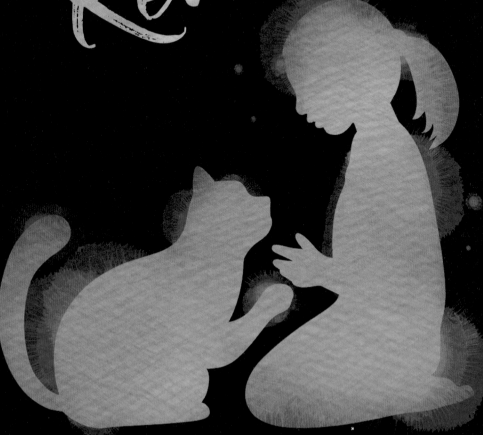

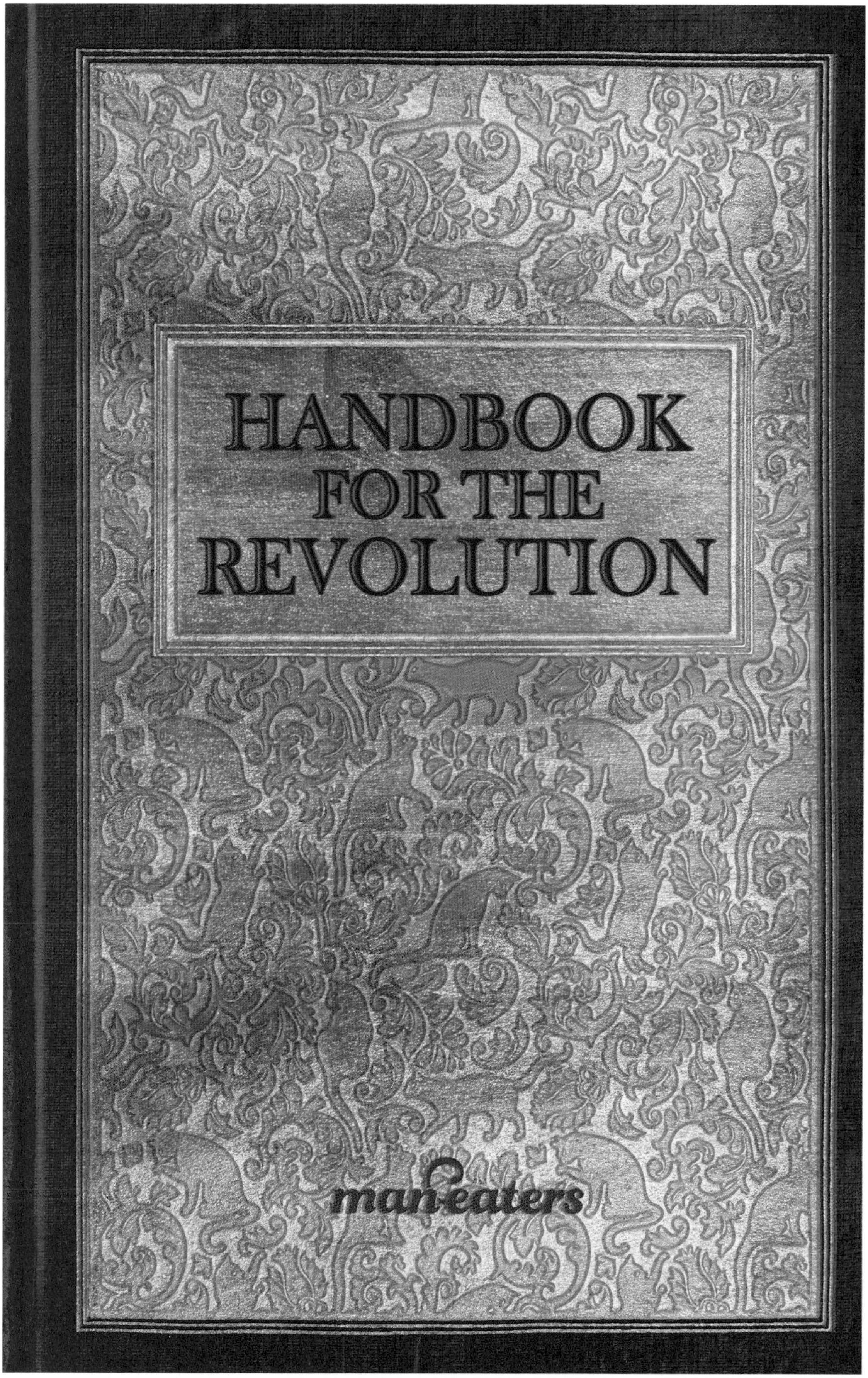
HANDBOOK
FOR THE
REVOLUTION
maneaters

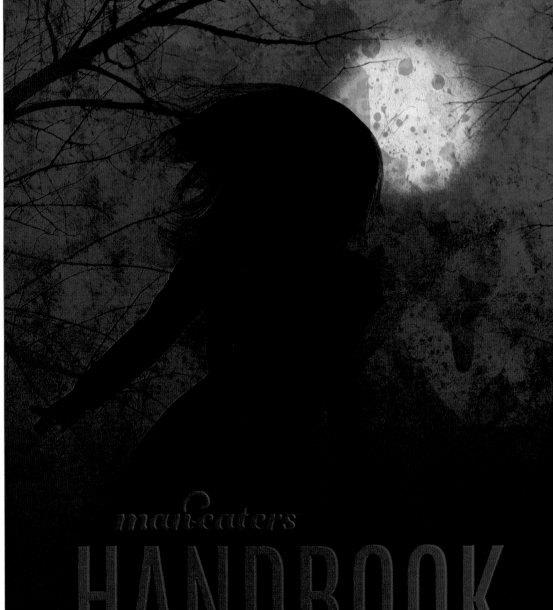

man-eaters
HANDBOOK
FOR THE
REVOLUTION

T

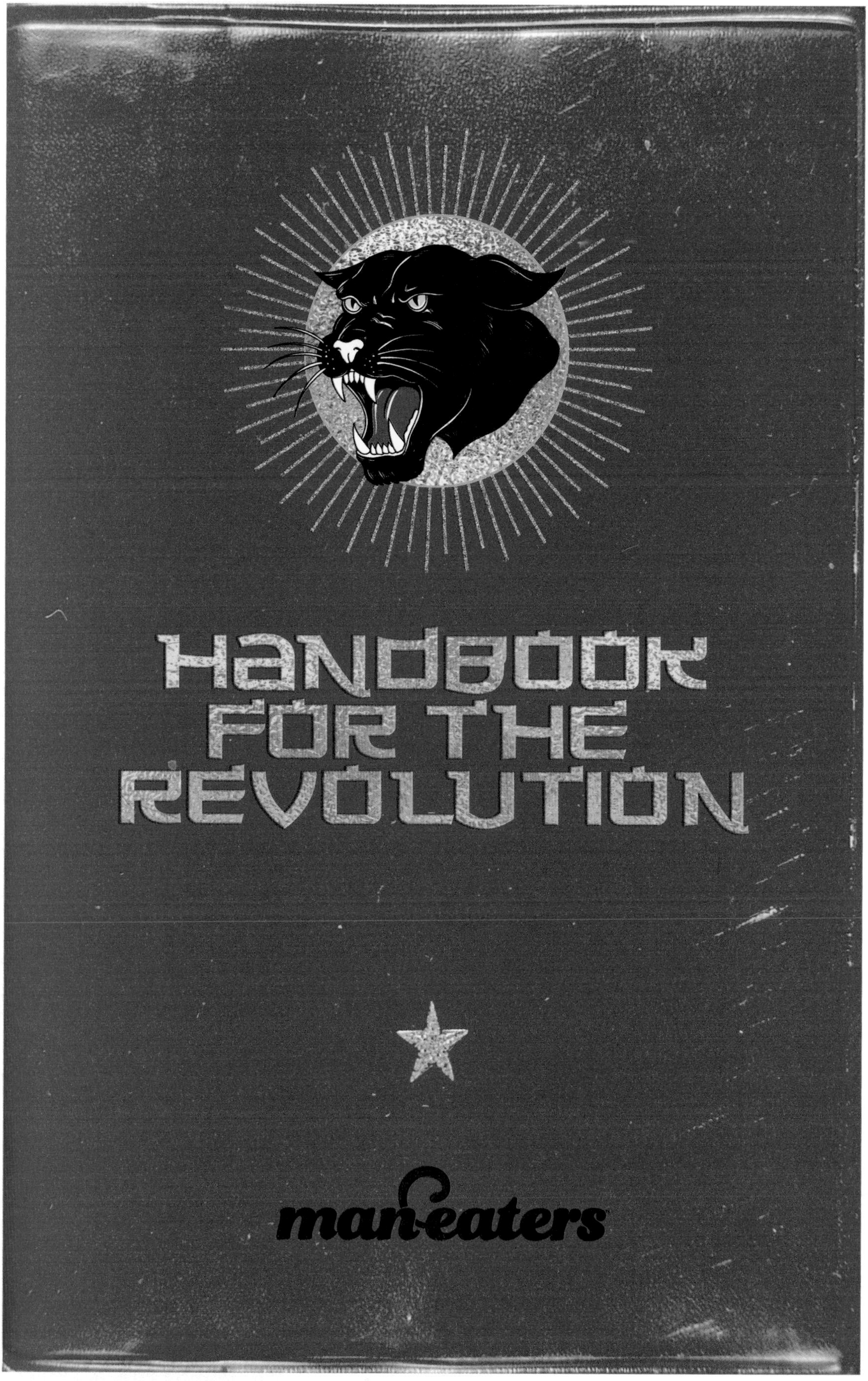
HANDBOOK
FOR THE
REVOLUTION
man-eaters

man·eaters
Hand
book
for the
Revo
lution

no.12

Chelsea Cain
Lia Miternique

image

B

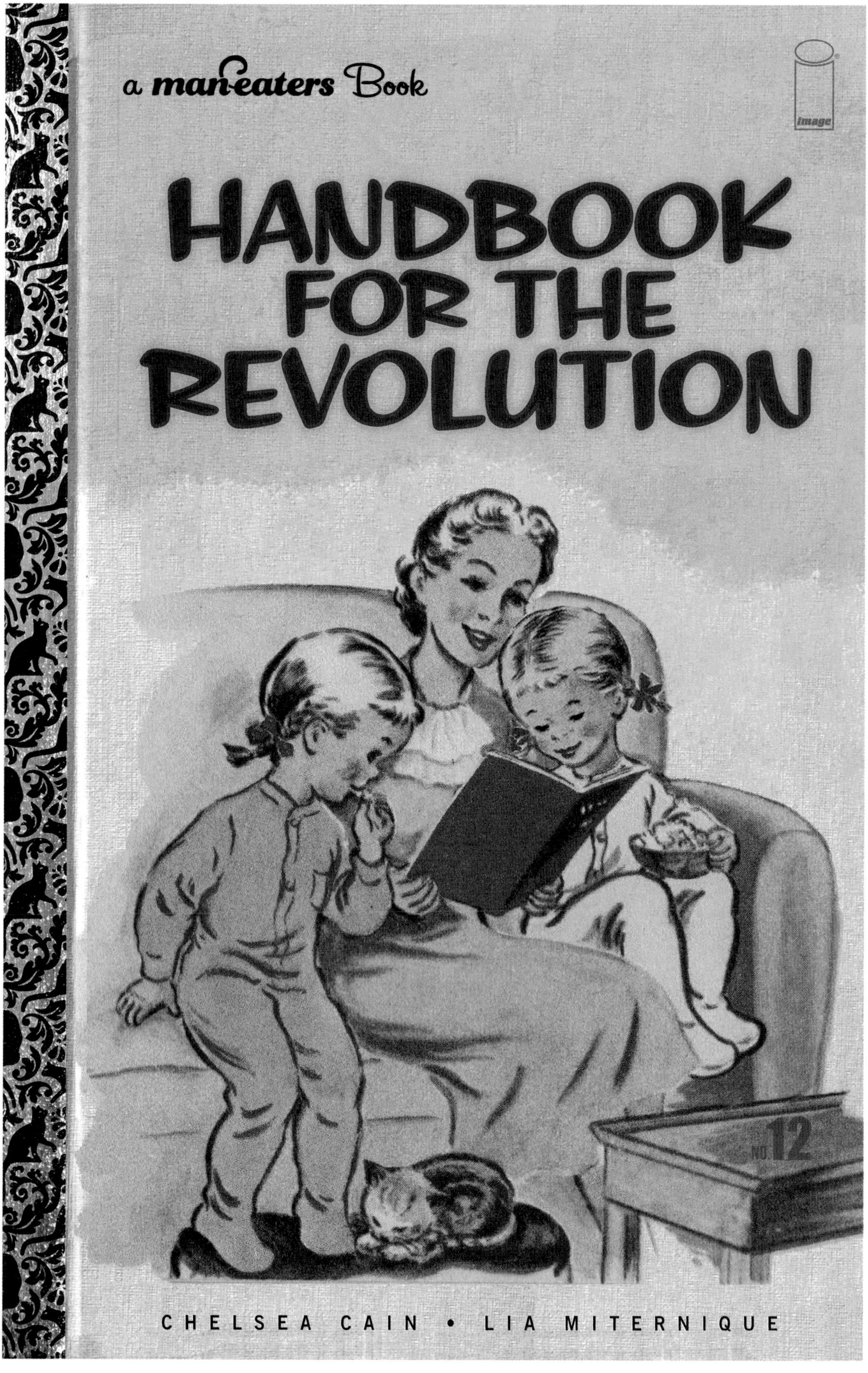
a man-eaters Book
HANDBOOK FOR THE REVOLUTION
NO. 12
CHELSEA CAIN • LIA MITERNIQUE

man-eaters

COVER ART GALLERY

COVER DESIGN: LIA MITERNIQUE

ISSUE #12

D

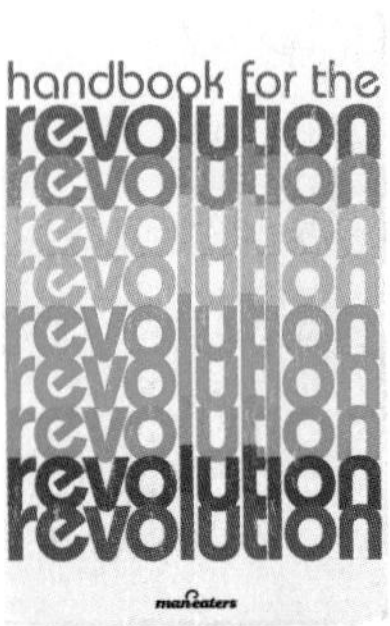
handbook for the
revolution
man-eaters

E

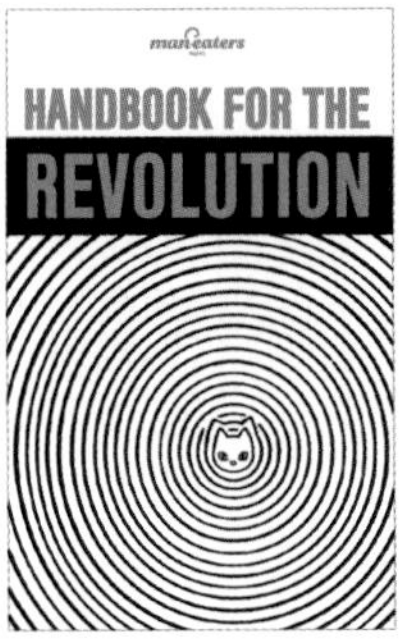
man-eaters
HANDBOOK FOR THE
REVOLUTION

F

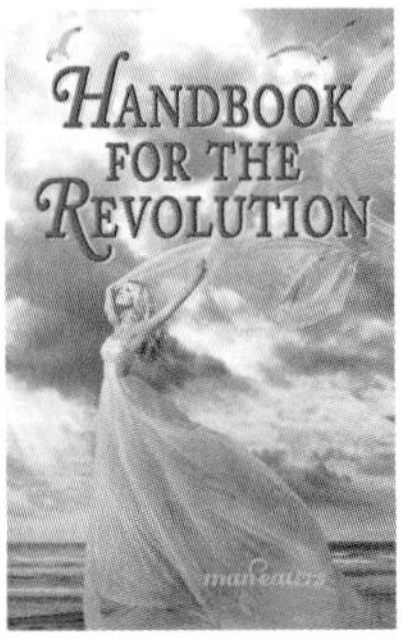
HANDBOOK
FOR THE
REVOLUTION
man-eaters

G

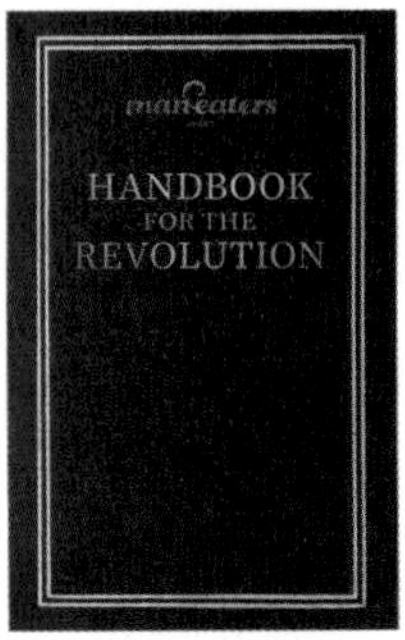
man-eaters
HANDBOOK
FOR THE
REVOLUTION

H

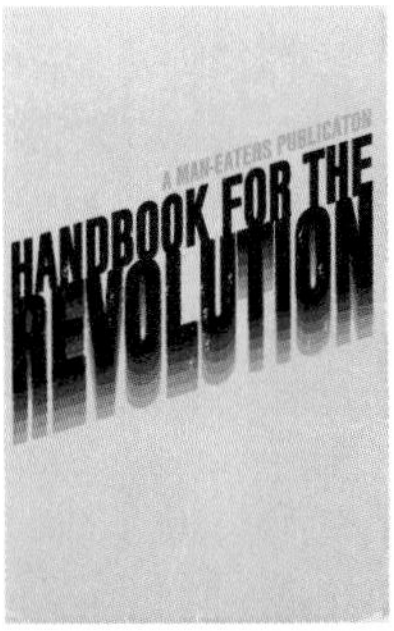
A MAN-EATERS PUBLICATON
HANDBOOK FOR THE
REVOLUTION

I

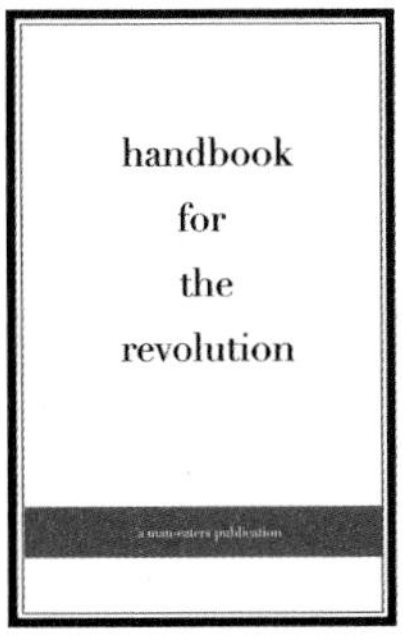
handbook
for
the
revolution

J

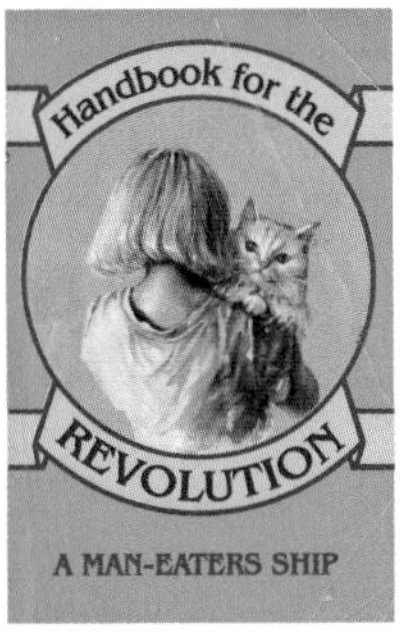
Handbook for the
REVOLUTION
A MAN-EATERS SHIP

K

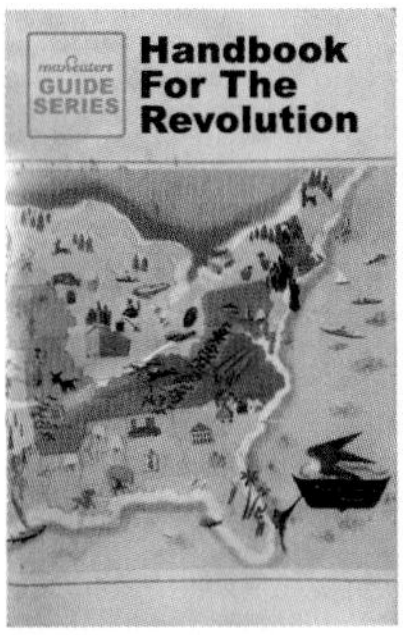
man-eaters
GUIDE
SERIES
Handbook
For The
Revolution

L

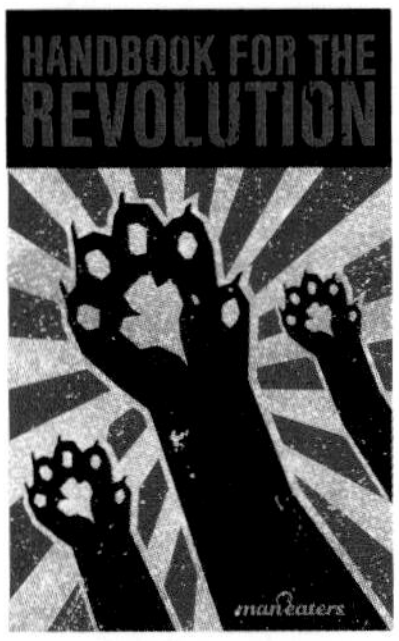
HANDBOOK FOR THE
REVOLUTION
man-eaters

M

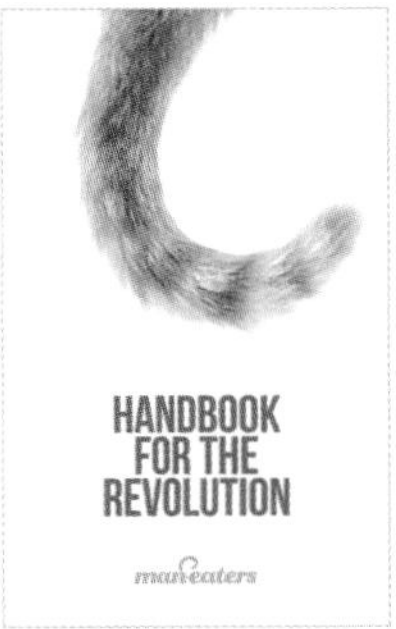
HANDBOOK
FOR THE
REVOLUTION
man-eaters

N

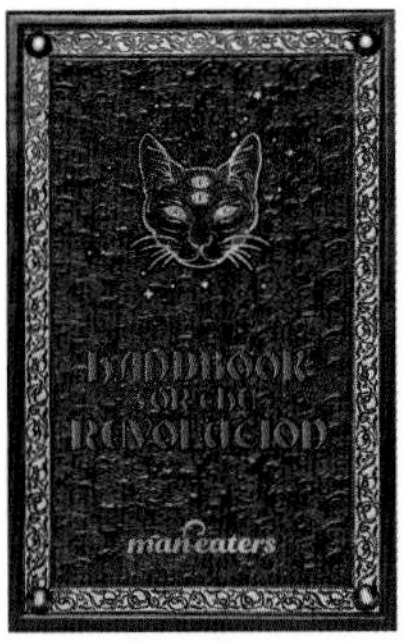
man-eaters

O

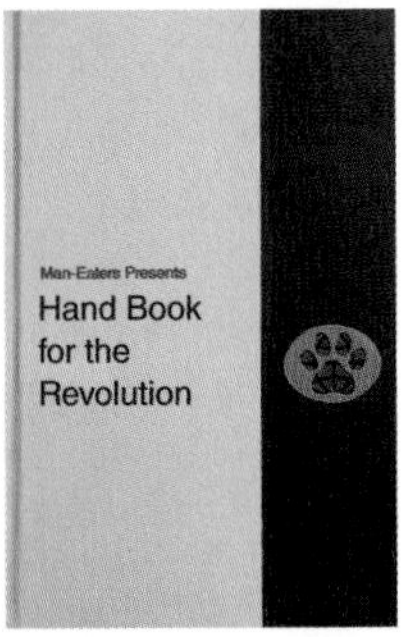
Man-Eaters Presents
Hand Book
for the
Revolution

P

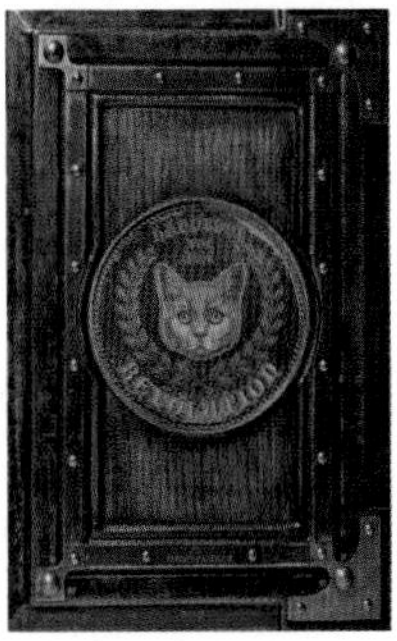

Q

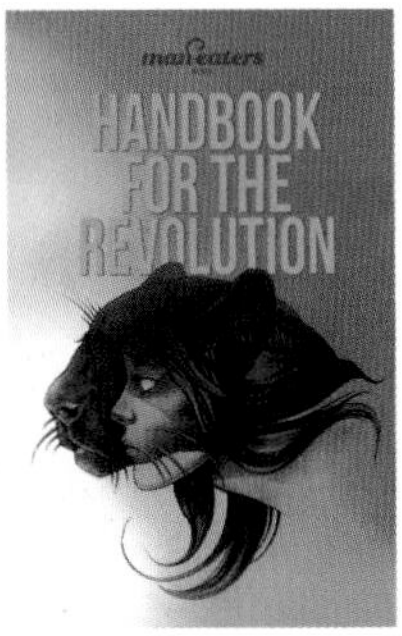
man-eaters
HANDBOOK
FOR THE
REVOLUTION

R

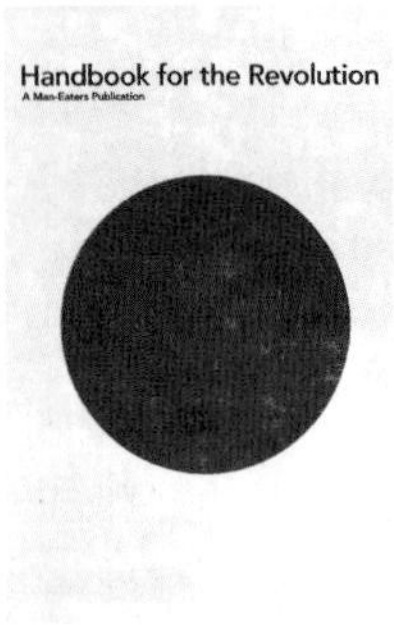
Handbook for the Revolution
A Man-Eaters Publication

S

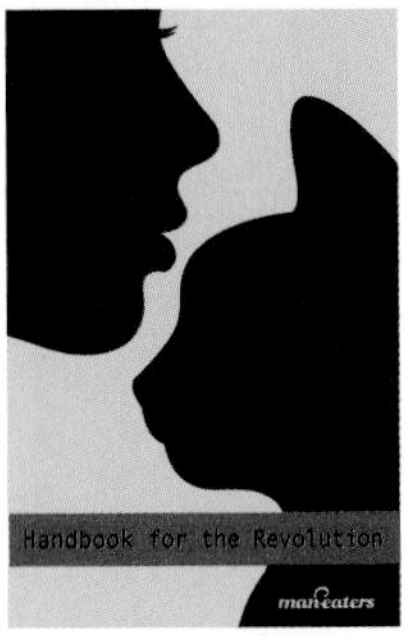
Handbook for the Revolution
man-eaters

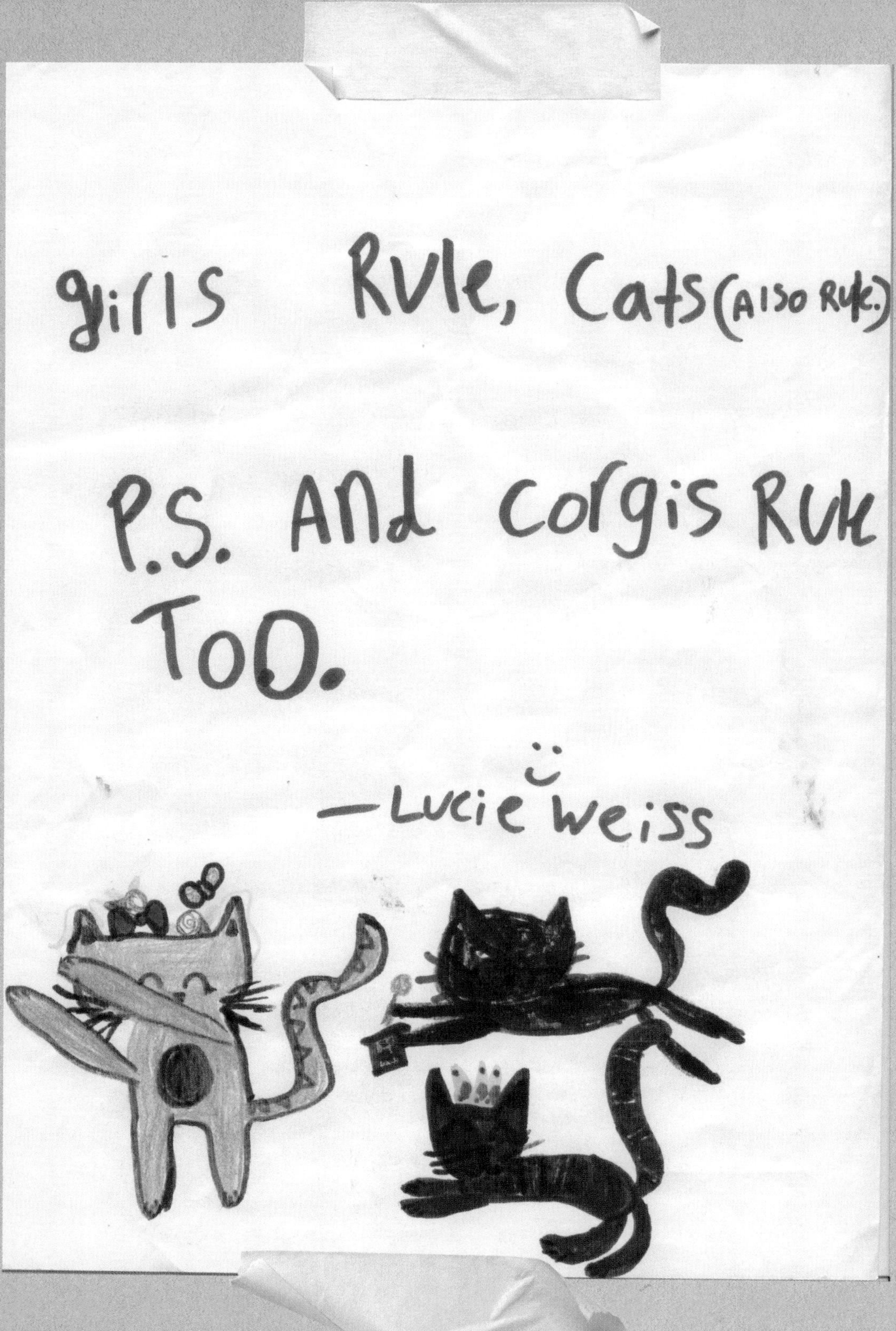
girls Rule, Cats (Also Rule.)
P.S. And corgis Rule Too.
—Lucie Weiss

PRODUCTION BY TRICIA RAMOS

IMAGE COMICS, INC. • **Robert Kirkman**: Chief Operating Officer • **Erik Larsen**: Chief Financial Officer • **Todd McFarlane**: President • **Marc Silvestri**: Chief Executive Officer • **Jim Valentino**: Vice President • **Eric Stephenson**: Publisher / Chief Creative Officer • **Jeff Boison**: Director of Publishing Planning & Book Trade Sales • **Chris Ross**: Director of Digital Sales • **Jeff Stang**: Director of Direct Market Sales • **Kat Salazar**: Director of PR & Marketing • **Drew Gill**: Cover Editor • **Heather Doornink**: Production Director • **Nicole Lapalme**: Controller • **IMAGECOMICS.COM**

MAN-EATERS, VOL. 3. First printing. November 2019. Published by Image Comics, Inc. Office of publication: 2701 NW Vaughn St., Suite 780, Portland, OR 97210. Printed in the USA. For information regarding the CPSIA on this printed material call: 203-595-3636. For international rights, contact: foreignlicensing@imagecomics.com. ISBN: 978-1-5343-1424-5.

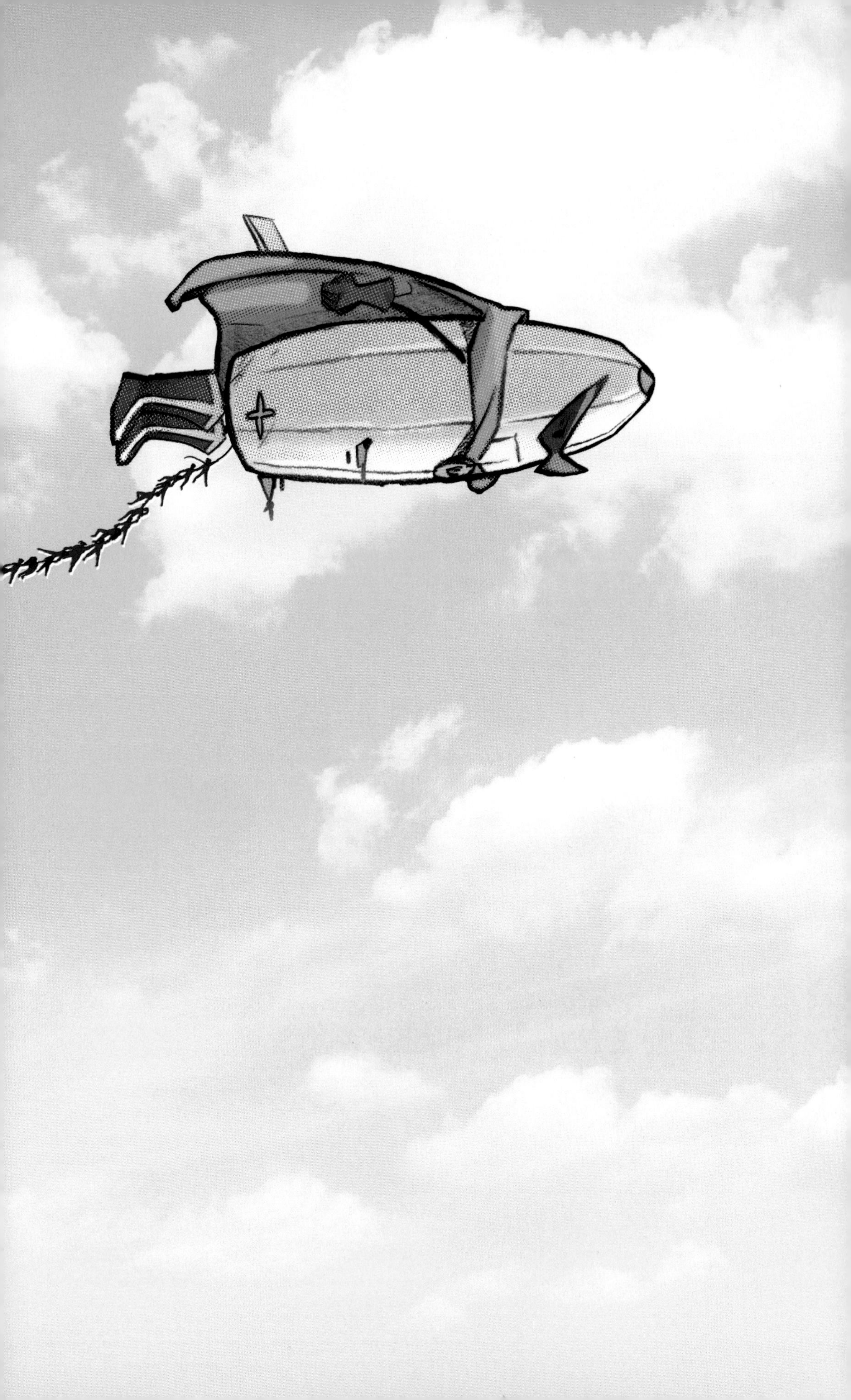

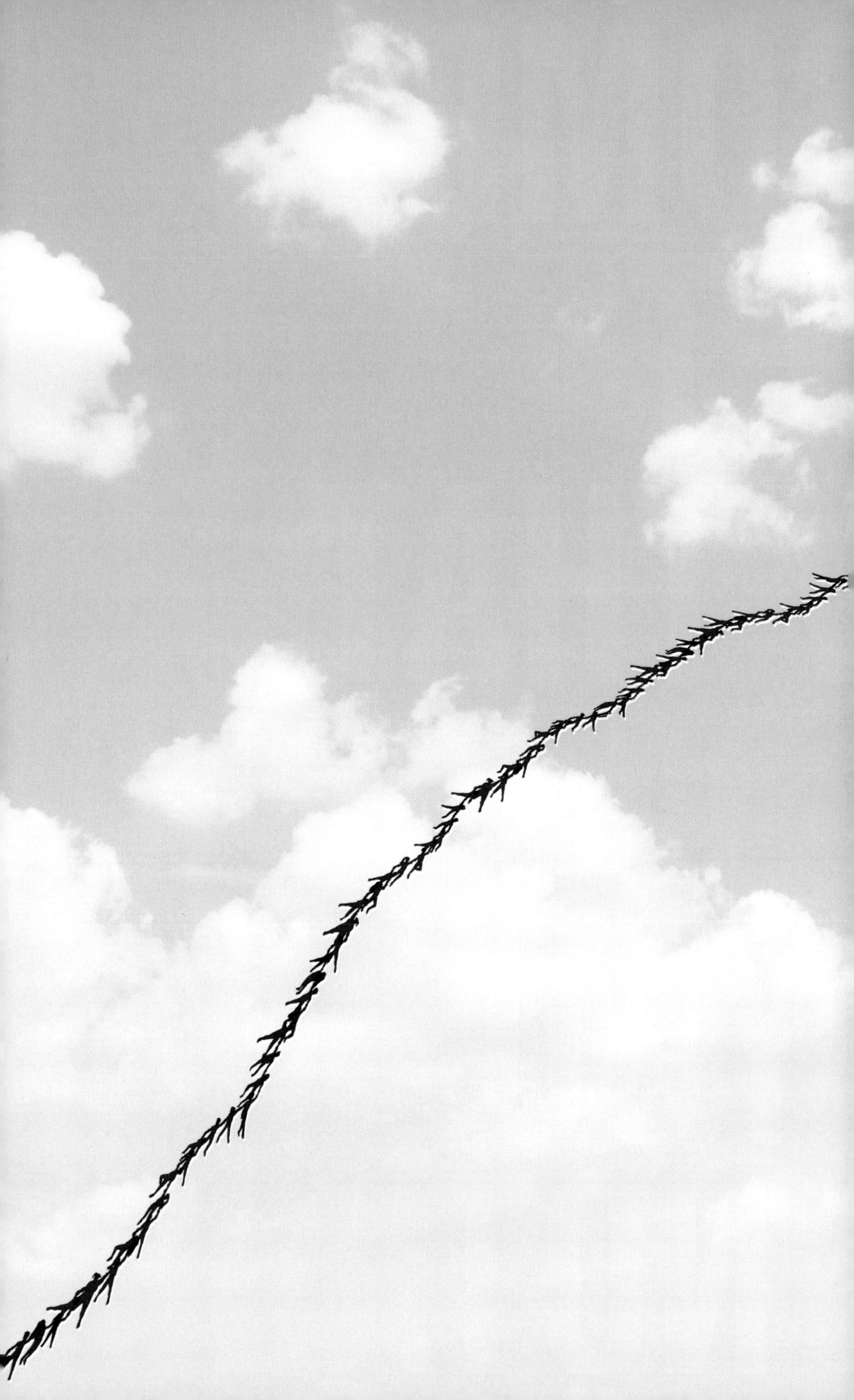

COME

ET

THAT

COMING,

YOU

NOT.

— GRETA THUNBERG

WE HAVE

HERE TO

YOU KNO

CHANGE I

WHETHER

LIKE IT O

Pocket Corgi

the happy little friend you always want around.

[EXAMPLE]

INSTRUCTIONS

Carefully cut out pocket corgi and accessories along the dotted lines. Place in the pocket of any article of clothing, backpack or gym bag. Simply take a peak inside any time you need to see a friendly face. Your corgi will always be there for you.
Accessorize and feed as necessary.

ASK ME ABOUT MY FEMINIST AGENDA

Official Adoption Papers
POCKET CORGI PROOF OF ADOPTION

This certifies that _____ was adopted on _____
NAME OF CORGI   DATE

by _____
YOUR NAME

and now lives at _____
YOUR ADDRESS

Signature of adopting parent _____

Signature of witness _____ Date _____

EXCUSED ABSENCE

THIS PERMISSION SLIP ENTITLES THE BEARER TO MISS SCHOOL IN ORDER TO PARTICIPATE IN A POLITICAL PROTEST BECAUSE:
SOMEONE HAS TO SAVE US, AND THE GROWN-UPS AREN'T GOING TO.

NAME	
DATE	
CAUSE	

SIGNATURE

APPROVED BY
THE MINISTRY OF TROUBLE

EXCUSED ABSENCE

THIS PERMISSION SLIP ENTITLES THE BEARER TO MISS SCHOOL IN ORDER TO PARTICIPATE IN A POLITICAL PROTEST BECAUSE:
SOMEONE HAS TO SAVE US, AND THE GROWN-UPS AREN'T GOING TO.

NAME	
DATE	
CAUSE	

SIGNATURE

APPROVED BY
THE MINISTRY OF TROUBLE

EXCUSED ABSENCE

THIS PERMISSION SLIP ENTITLES THE BEARER TO MISS SCHOOL IN ORDER TO PARTICIPATE IN A POLITICAL PROTEST BECAUSE:
SOMEONE HAS TO SAVE US, AND THE GROWN-UPS AREN'T GOING TO.

NAME	
DATE	
CAUSE	

SIGNATURE

APPROVED BY
THE MINISTRY OF TROUBLE

EXCUSED ABSENCE

THIS PERMISSION SLIP ENTITLES THE BEARER TO MISS SCHOOL IN ORDER TO PARTICIPATE IN A POLITICAL PROTEST BECAUSE:
SOMEONE HAS TO SAVE US, AND THE GROWN-UPS AREN'T GOING TO.

NAME	
DATE	
CAUSE	

SIGNATURE

APPROVED BY
THE MINISTRY OF TROUBLE

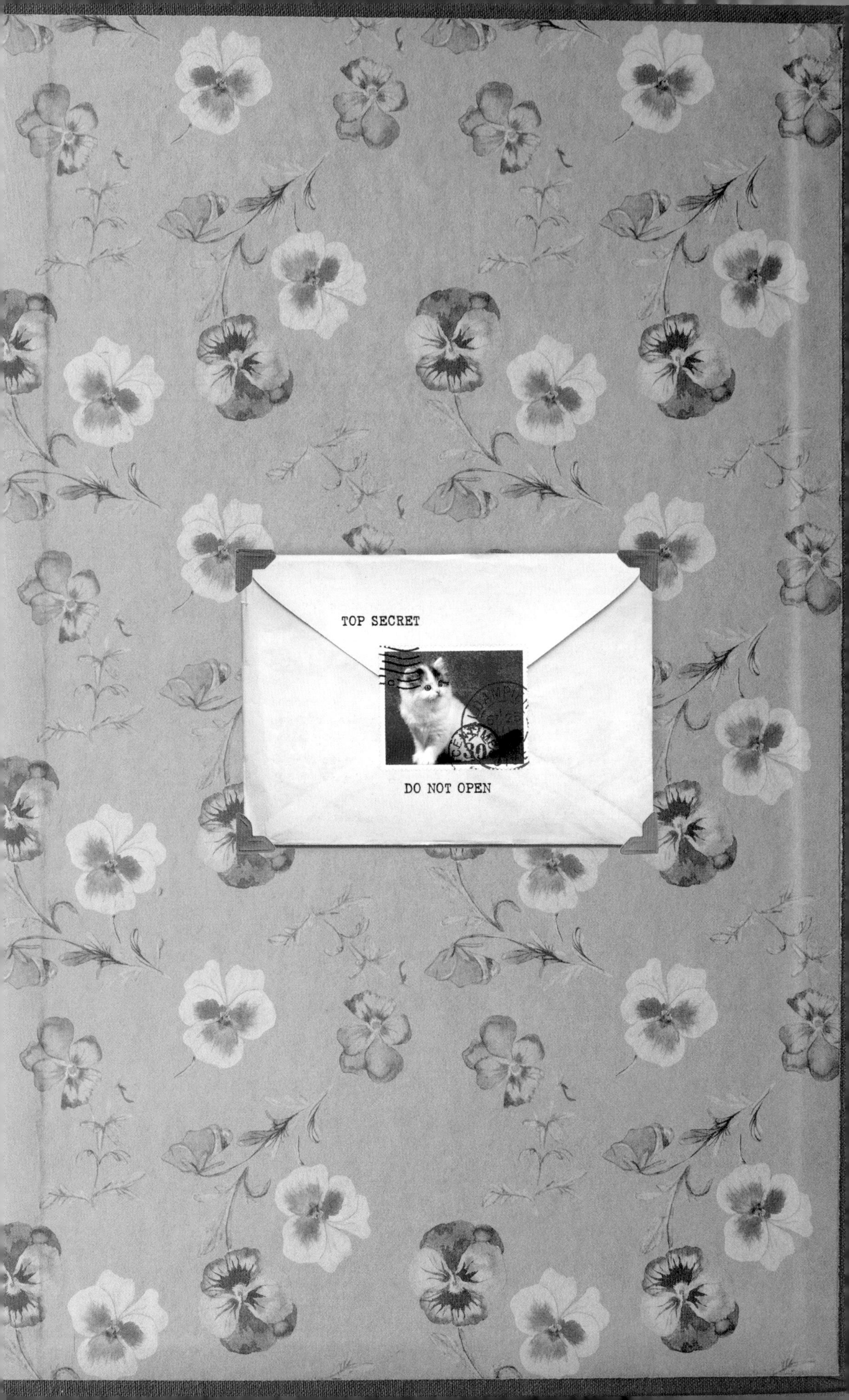
TOP SECRET
DO NOT OPEN

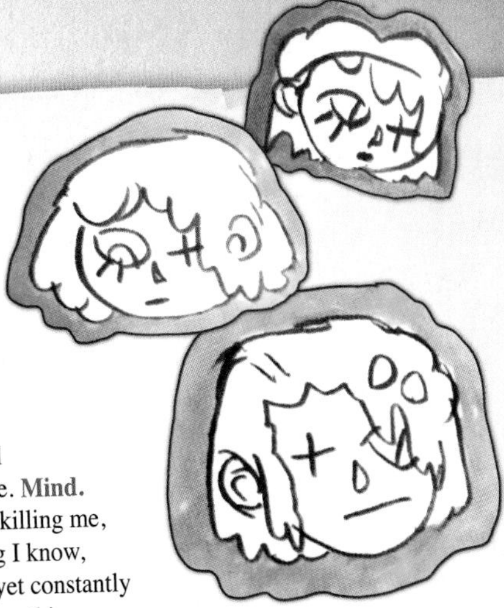

By Liv Osborn

Routine.
A word that means so much to me.
A word that shapes my everyday life in ways unimaginable
by the passerby. **Change.** A word that scares me to the point
where I can't breathe, I can't move, I can't feel.
A word that makes me feel the exact opposite at the same time.
Excited, ambitious, new. **Reality.** A word meaning the only thing I will
ever be forced to confront against my will, the only thing I can't escape. **Mind.**
A word symbolizing the only thing that keeps me alive, the only thing killing me,
the only thing that makes me, me. **Life.** A word meaning the only thing I know,
the only thing I will ever know. A word that shows others how to live yet constantly
reminds me why I'm not. **Death.** A word that cannot be explained by anything
other than the absence of life. What is the absence of life? If life is what's killing me,
what's to say killing life won't save me? Death, the only thing that seems inevitable,
the only thing I see in my future, the only thing I feel I have true control over in my own personal way.
Contention. A word used to describe the all too human feeling of surviving. Being there but not really wanting to. Staying up even though you're tired because you only ever have nightmares. Or sleeping because being awake can't compare to the feeling of blood rushing through your veins as you play games with death in a simulated version of your own life, the experience I call lucid dreaming. **Happiness.** A feeling that I see as a dream; maybe because it seems so distant and nostalgic, or maybe because the only time I truly feel alive is when I am dreaming. Every night I would cry to my mom about the monsters I saw when I closed my eyes and slept, or about the things I experienced because I couldn't wake up in time. Now, it's like all I want to do is rest my eyes and visualize all the things I cannot have simply because my brain is flawed and my situation is dire.
Everything.
A word meaning all we know, all we yearn to know.
Everything is anything we can make up and more. It's more than I can see, more than what's written in any book, shown in any film, it's more than that. Every everything is different, some big, some small, some we have the pleasure of experiencing, some we don't. My everything versus your everything will never be comparable, never be contrastable, simply because everything is more than anything any human brain or computer can make up. It's something we experience, the moment before our everything turns to nothing. **Nothing.** A word that can mean everything to someone, yet also a word that will never be understood by someone else. Nothing, the abyss of the unknown, the word we use when we don't know enough to describe something another way. Nothing being the only thing we fear, because death goes hand in hand with nothing. In the same way our life is everything and everything we know is life, death is nothing and the only comprehensible nothing we know is death. **Me.** A word that is different for each person that uses it. A word that depicts our very being, a word that will never change when stripped down to its barest form. Me, I, us, we, words that all have one thing in common. The uniqueness of the person using that vocalization of self explanation to describe their relation to the world they live in, the life they are forced to live. No matter how uninterested you are in yourself, no matter the amount of hate you put to your own name, me means something to us because me is the spitting image of humanity in the rawest form we will ever know it by. **Living.** Living is the concept of being alive plus more. I wish I were able to define living in the same way I describe other terms, but living is the one thing
I struggle with being able to do.
And for that, I'm sorry.
Surviving.
This word is a word I,
and some others,
know all too well. That being alive
without the plus more,
that beating heart, functioning brain,
the working parts.
But where's the morality,
the love, the emotion?
I will let you know when I find it.
Maybe someday I will, and
maybe someday I will have the a
bility to function within
the meaning of
all of these words.

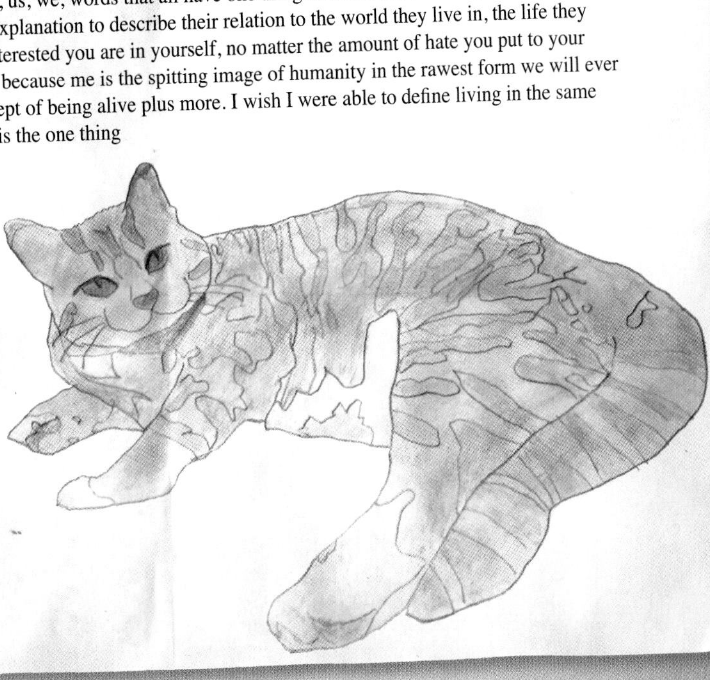

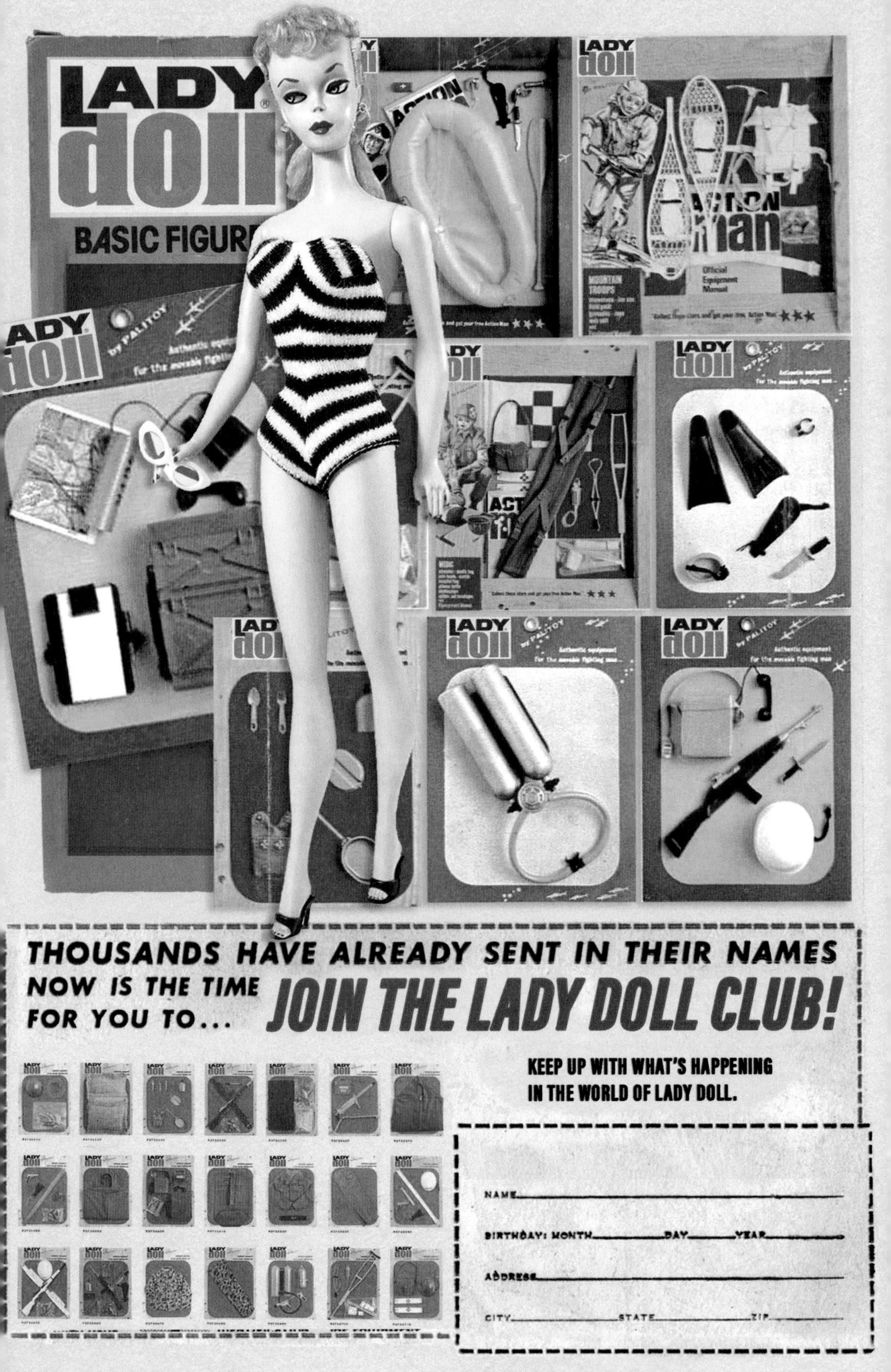

LADY doll
BASIC FIGURE
LADY doll
by PALITOY
Authentic equipment for the movable fighting man
ACTION man
Official Equipment Manual
MOUNTAIN TROOPS
THOUSANDS HAVE ALREADY SENT IN THEIR NAMES
NOW IS THE TIME FOR YOU TO...
JOIN THE LADY DOLL CLUB!
KEEP UP WITH WHAT'S HAPPENING IN THE WORLD OF LADY DOLL.
NAME
BIRTHDAY: MONTH
DAY
YEAR
ADDRESS
CITY
STATE
ZIP

AWAIT FURTHER INSTRUCTIONS.

AWAIT FURTHER INSTRUCTIONS.

AWAIT FURTHER INSTRUCTIONS.

AWAIT FURTHER INSTRUCTIONS.

AWAIT FURTHER INSTRUCTIONS.

AWAIT FURTHER INSTRUCTIONS.

AWAIT FURTHER INSTRUCTIONS.

AWAIT FURTHER INSTRUCTIONS.

AWAIT FURTHER INSTRUCTIONS.

AWAIT FURTHER INSTRUCTIONS.

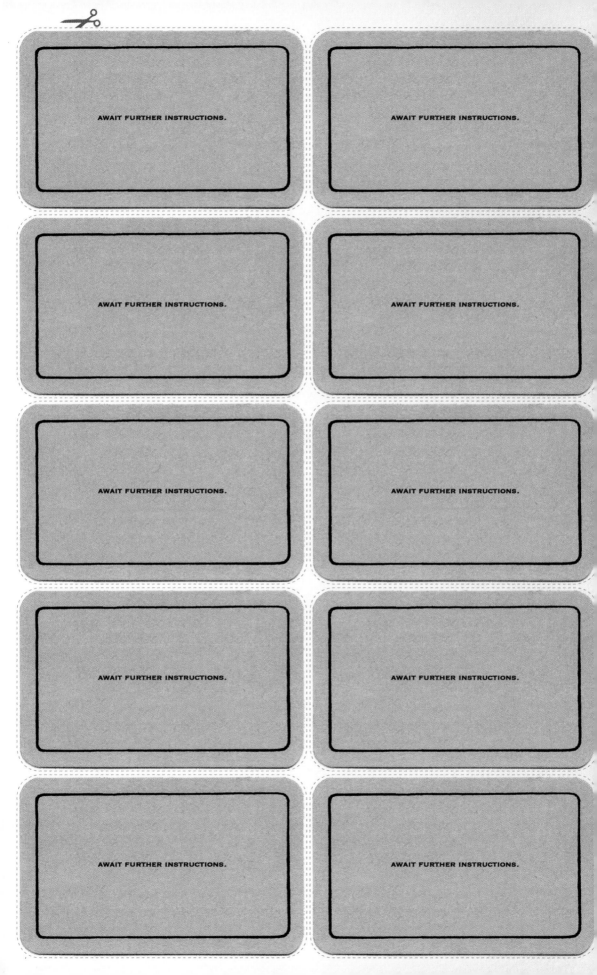

DEPARTMENT OF COMMUNICATION
MINISTRY OF TROUBLE
TELEGRAMS:
BOMBAY 31071
MEMBERSHIP CARD
Name _____
Airship _____ *Locker #* _____
Signature _____

DEPARTMENT OF COMMUNICATION
MINISTRY OF TROUBLE
TELEGRAMS:
BOMBAY 31071
MEMBERSHIP CARD
Name _____
Airship _____ *Locker #* _____
Signature _____

DEPARTMENT OF COMMUNICATION
MINISTRY OF TROUBLE
TELEGRAMS:
BOMBAY 31071
MEMBERSHIP CARD
Name _____
Airship _____ *Locker #* _____
Signature _____

DEPARTMENT OF COMMUNICATION
MINISTRY OF TROUBLE
TELEGRAMS:
BOMBAY 31071
MEMBERSHIP CARD
Name _____
Airship _____ *Locker #* _____
Signature _____

DEPARTMENT OF COMMUNICATION
MINISTRY OF TROUBLE
TELEGRAMS:
BOMBAY 31071
MEMBERSHIP CARD
Name _____
Airship _____ *Locker #* _____
Signature _____

DEPARTMENT OF COMMUNICATION
MINISTRY OF TROUBLE
TELEGRAMS:
BOMBAY 31071
MEMBERSHIP CARD
Name _____
Airship _____ *Locker #* _____
Signature _____

DEPARTMENT OF COMMUNICATION
MINISTRY OF TROUBLE
TELEGRAMS:
BOMBAY 31071
MEMBERSHIP CARD
Name _____
Airship _____ *Locker #* _____
Signature _____

DEPARTMENT OF COMMUNICATION
MINISTRY OF TROUBLE
TELEGRAMS:
BOMBAY 31071
MEMBERSHIP CARD
Name _____
Airship _____ *Locker #* _____
Signature _____

DEPARTMENT OF COMMUNICATION
MINISTRY OF TROUBLE
TELEGRAMS:
BOMBAY 31071
MEMBERSHIP CARD
Name _____
Airship _____ *Locker #* _____
Signature _____

DEPARTMENT OF COMMUNICATION
MINISTRY OF TROUBLE
TELEGRAMS:
BOMBAY 31071
MEMBERSHIP CARD
Name _____
Airship _____ *Locker #* _____
Signature _____

FORM No. DD101U

MINISTRY OF TROUBLE
PETITION FOR MEMBERSHIP (ABRIDGED)

[ALL APPLICANTS WILL BE ACCEPTED]

FILED BY:

[YOUR NAME HERE] ....

PLEASE LIST ANY ALIASES:

AKA ____________________ AKA ____________________
AKA ____________________ AKA ____________________
AKA ____________________ AKA ____________________

DRAW A PICTURE OF YOUR FINGERPRINT IN THE BOX PROVIDED.

I HAVE AN INTEREST IN: [CHECK ALL THAT APPLY]

- ☐ DISRUPTING THE PATRIARCHY
- ☐ BEING A UNICORN
- ☐ PSYCHOLOGICAL EXPERIMENTS
- ☐ CATS
- ☐ FILLING OUT FORMS
- ☐ TEACUPS
- ☐ FERNS
- ☐ OTHER ____________________

NUMBER THE FOLLOWING LIST OF WORDS FROM LEAST TO FAVORITE.

__ ICONOCLAST __ PARALLEL __ ZEPHYR __ CHUM __ FORTUITOUS __ POP-TART __ PUDDLE __ CAT

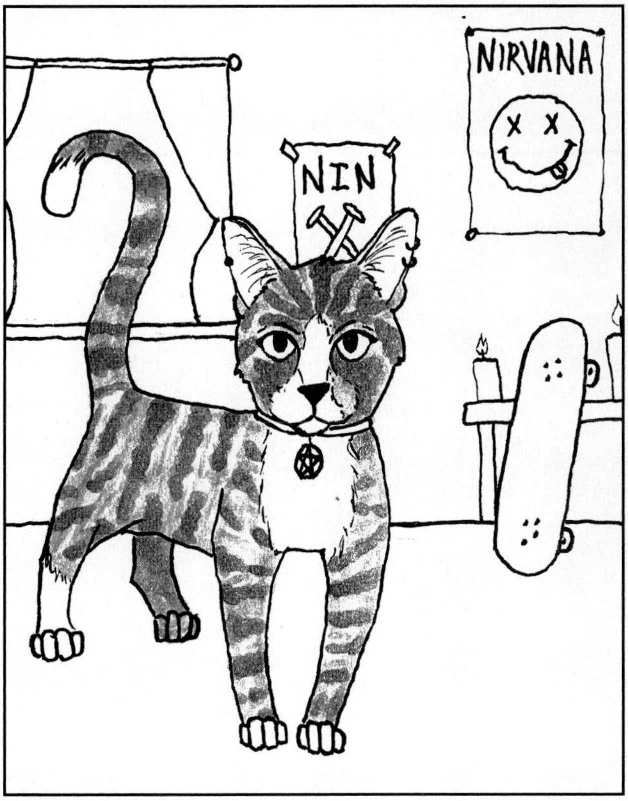

NIRVANA
NIN

WRITE A PARGRAPH ABOUT WHAT THE CAT IN THE IMAGE TO THE LEFT IS THINKING.

LIST THE FIRST THREE WORDS YOU OVERHEAR WHEN YOU GET TO THE END OF THIS SENTENCE.

1) ....

2) ....

3) ....

....
YOUR SIGNATURE

....
THE SIGNATURE OF A PERSON STANDING NEAR YOU

MINISTRY USE ONLY

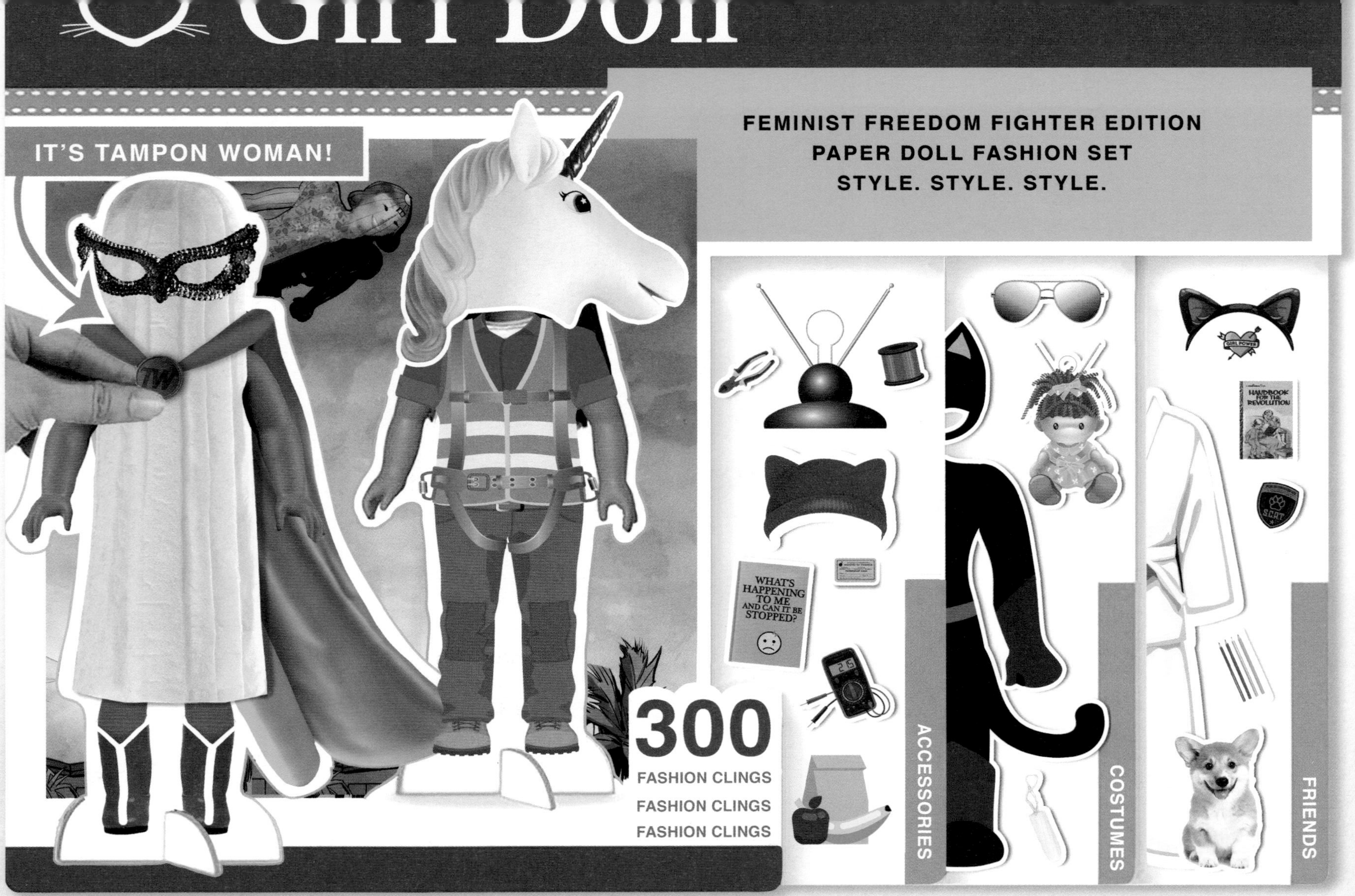
Girl Doll
FEMINIST FREEDOM FIGHTER EDITION
PAPER DOLL FASHION SET
STYLE. STYLE. STYLE.
IT'S TAMPON WOMAN!
TW
300
FASHION CLINGS
FASHION CLINGS
FASHION CLINGS
WHAT'S HAPPENING TO ME AND CAN IT BE STOPPED?
HANDBOOK FOR THE REVOLUTION
GIRL POWER
SCRT
ACCESSORIES
COSTUMES
FRIENDS

This hollowed-out book or "stash box" can be easily concealed inside another book jacket. Simply remove the jacket of a school text book, affix it over this book's jacket, tape in place, and you'll be ready to go. A sample book cover has been included.

Use sticky notes to mark important sections.

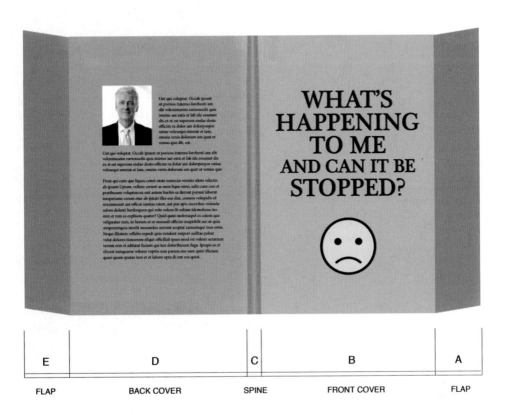

E	D	C	B	A
FLAP	BACK COVER	SPINE	FRONT COVER	FLAP

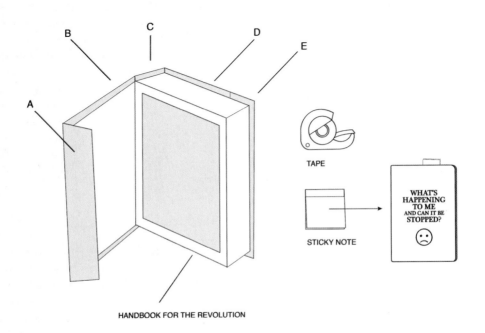

TAPE

STICKY NOTE

HANDBOOK FOR THE REVOLUTION

WARDROBE SELECTION SHEET

OFFICIAL

Please select one from each category.

S.C.A.T. FORM 103-552

EVENINGWEAR

A.

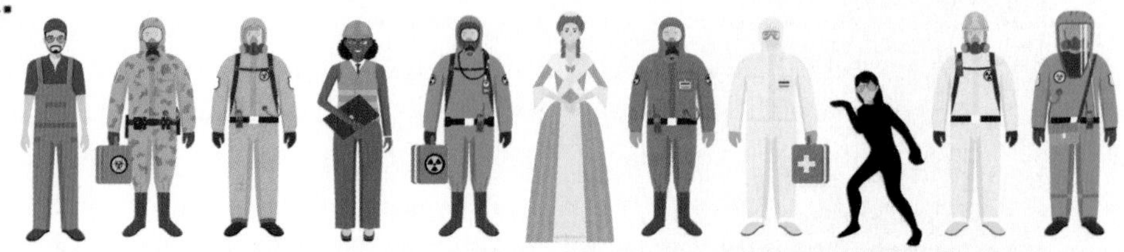

○ ○ ○ ○ ○ ○ ○ ○ ○ ○ ○

CAMOUFLAGE

B.

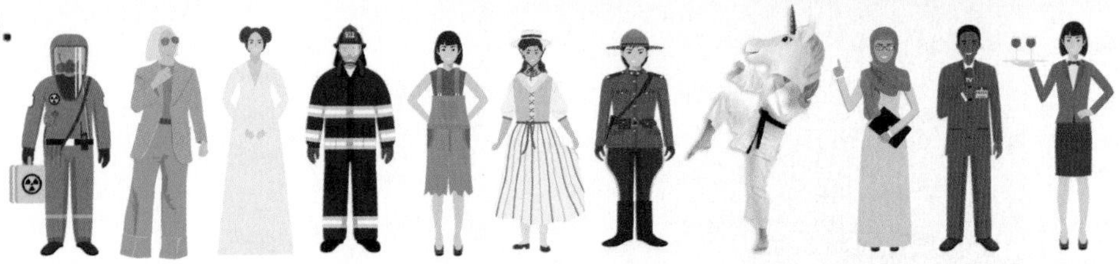

○ ○ ○ ○ ○ ○ ○ ○ ○ ○ ○

DAYWEAR

C.

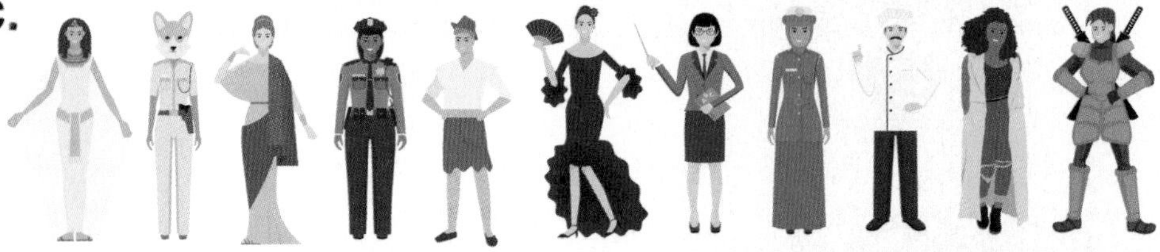

○ ○ ○ ○ ○ ○ ○ ○ ○ ○ ○

RESORT CASUAL

D.

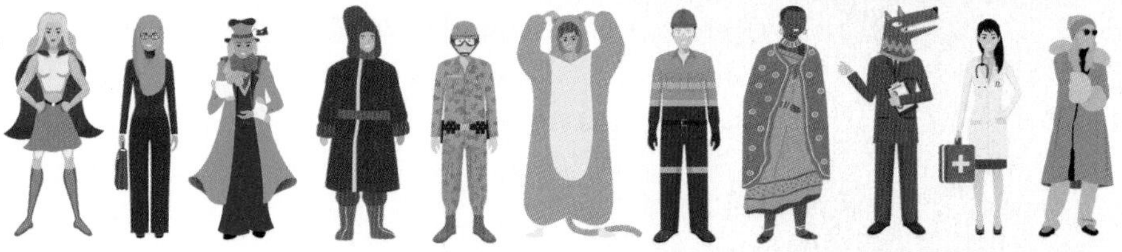

○ ○ ○ ○ ○ ○ ○ ○ ○ ○ ○

NAME ______________________________ SIZE __________

AIRSHIP NAME ______________________________ LOCKER # __________

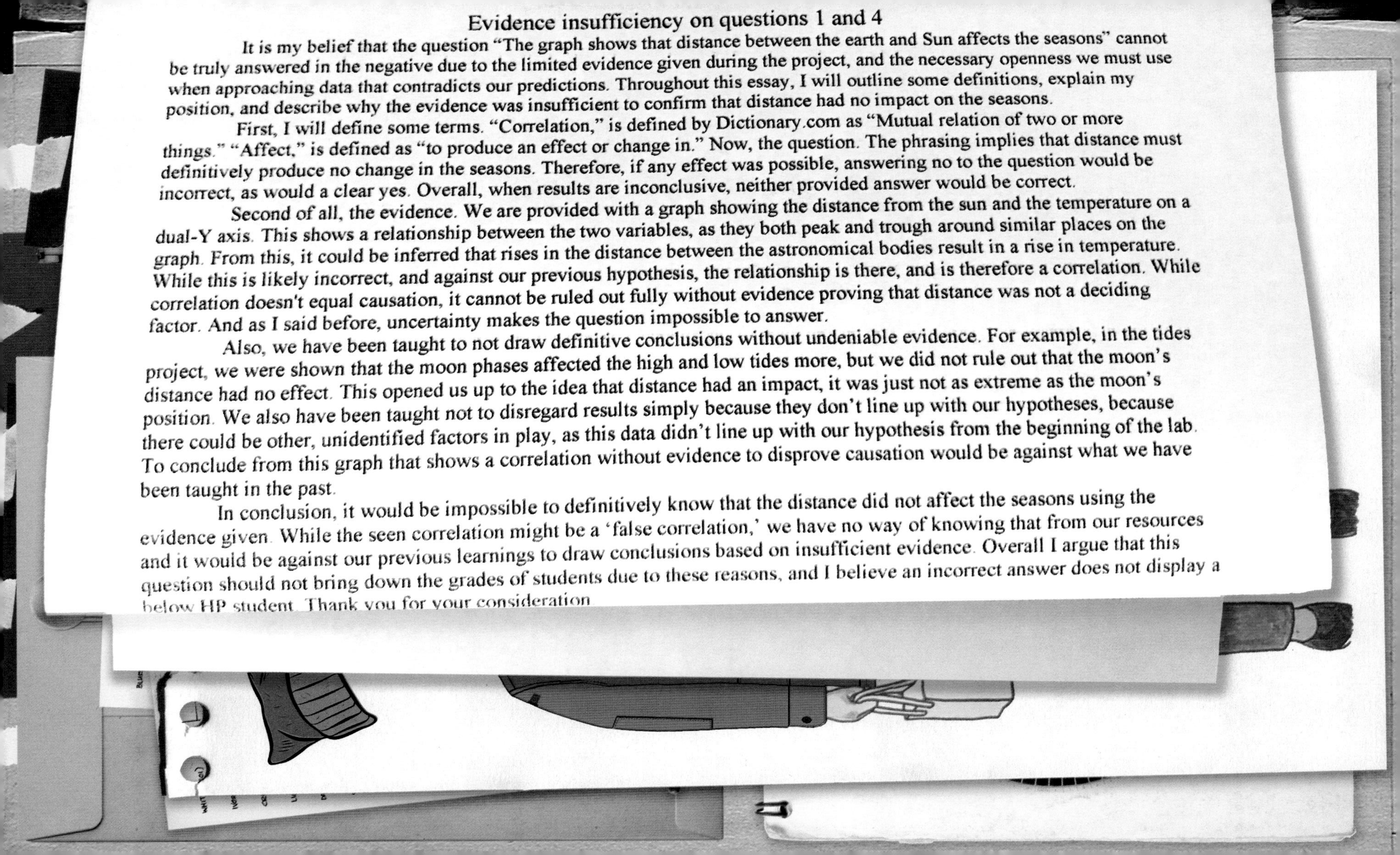

Evidence insufficiency on questions 1 and 4

It is my belief that the question "The graph shows that distance between the earth and Sun affects the seasons" cannot be truly answered in the negative due to the limited evidence given during the project, and the necessary openness we must use when approaching data that contradicts our predictions. Throughout this essay, I will outline some definitions, explain my position, and describe why the evidence was insufficient to confirm that distance had no impact on the seasons.

First, I will define some terms. "Correlation," is defined by Dictionary.com as "Mutual relation of two or more things." "Affect," is defined as "to produce an effect or change in." Now, the question. The phrasing implies that distance must definitively produce no change in the seasons. Therefore, if any effect was possible, answering no to the question would be incorrect, as would a clear yes. Overall, when results are inconclusive, neither provided answer would be correct.

Second of all, the evidence. We are provided with a graph showing the distance from the sun and the temperature on a dual-Y axis. This shows a relationship between the two variables, as they both peak and trough around similar places on the graph. From this, it could be inferred that rises in the distance between the astronomical bodies result in a rise in temperature. While this is likely incorrect, and against our previous hypothesis, the relationship is there, and is therefore a correlation. While correlation doesn't equal causation, it cannot be ruled out fully without evidence proving that distance was not a deciding factor. And as I said before, uncertainty makes the question impossible to answer.

Also, we have been taught to not draw definitive conclusions without undeniable evidence. For example, in the tides project, we were shown that the moon phases affected the high and low tides more, but we did not rule out that the moon's distance had no effect. This opened us up to the idea that distance had an impact, it was just not as extreme as the moon's position. We also have been taught not to disregard results simply because they don't line up with our hypotheses, because there could be other, unidentified factors in play, as this data didn't line up with our hypothesis from the beginning of the lab. To conclude from this graph that shows a correlation without evidence to disprove causation would be against what we have been taught in the past.

In conclusion, it would be impossible to definitively know that the distance did not affect the seasons using the evidence given. While the seen correlation might be a 'false correlation,' we have no way of knowing that from our resources and it would be against our previous learnings to draw conclusions based on insufficient evidence. Overall I argue that this question should not bring down the grades of students due to these reasons, and I believe an incorrect answer does not display a below HP student. Thank you for your consideration

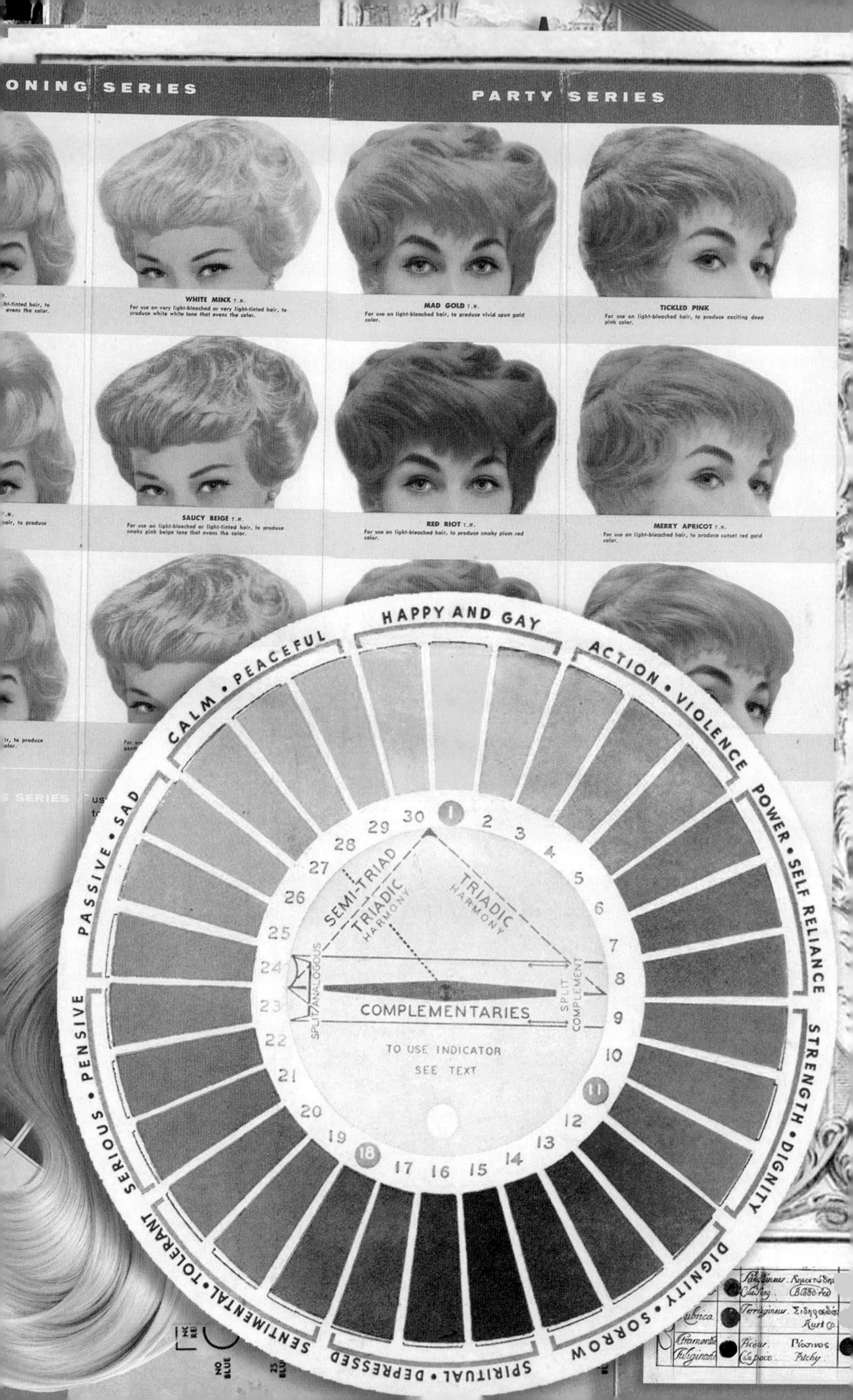
ONING SERIES
PARTY SERIES
WHITE MINX T.M.
For use on very light-bleached or very light-tinted hair, to produce white white tone that evens the color.
MAD GOLD T.M.
For use on light-bleached hair, to produce vivid spun gold color.
TICKLED PINK
For use on light-bleached hair, to produce exciting deep pink color.
SAUCY BEIGE T.M.
For use on light-bleached or light-tinted hair, to produce smoky pink beige tone that evens the color.
RED RIOT T.M.
For use on light-bleached hair, to produce smoky plum red color.
MERRY APRICOT T.M.
For use on light-bleached hair, to produce sunset red gold color.
HAPPY AND GAY
ACTION • VIOLENCE
POWER • SELF RELIANCE
STRENGTH • DIGNITY
DIGNITY • SORROW
SPIRITUAL • DEPRESSED
SENTIMENTAL • TOLERANT
SERIOUS • PENSIVE
PASSIVE • SAD
CALM • PEACEFUL
1 2 3 4 5 6 7 8 9 10 11 12 13 14 15 16 17 18 19 20 21 22 23 24 25 26 27 28 29 30
SEMI-TRIAD
TRIADIC HARMONY
TRIADIC HARMONY
SPLIT ANALOGOUS
COMPLEMENTARIES
SPLIT COMPLEMENT
TO USE INDICATOR
SEE TEXT

GILDED LILY T.M.

For use on gray or graying dark blonde (or lighter) hair, to produce sparkling golden blonde color. On bleached hair (natural color dark blonde or lighter) produces sparkling golden blonde color that blends with new growth.

FRIVOLOUS FAWN T.M.

For use on gray or graying light brown (or lighter) hair, to produce sunny golden brown color. On bleached hair (natural color light brown or lighter) produces sunny golden brown color that blends with new growth.

PLATINUM PLUS T.M.

For use on white or gray hair, to produce pale platinum tone. On bleached hair, produces platinum blonde tone.

For use on very light
produce palest silver

LUCKY COPPER T.M.

For use on gray or graying medium brown (or lighter) hair, to produce shimmering auburn color. On bleached hair (natural color medium brown or lighter) produces shimmering auburn color that blends with new growth.

PLUSH BROWN T.M.

For use on gray or graying medium brown (or lighter) hair, to produce rich medium brown color. On bleached hair (natural color medium brown or lighter) produces rich medium brown color that blends with new growth.

SILVER LINING T.M.

For use on white or gray hair, to produce shining silver gray tone. On bleached hair, produces silvery blonde tone.

BA

For use on light-ble
soft beige tone that

CHOCOLATE KISS T.M.

For use on gray or graying dark brown (or lighter) hair, to produce lustrous dark brown color. On bleached hair (natural color dark brown or lighter) produces lustrous dark ash brown color that blends with new growth.

BLACK RAGE T.M.

For use on gray or graying hair, to produce deep charcoal color.

TRUE STEEL T.M.

For use on white or gray hair, to produce pure steel gray color.

For use on light-blea
delicate pink lavende

COLOR SELECTION CARD

NAME _MAUDE W._

| PENSIVE | BUMMED | DELIGHTED | FURIOUS | QUITE PLEASED | JUST. DON'T. EVEN |

CHART 50
MIDDLE VALUE SCALES OF HUE AND CHROMA

This Chart is a horizontal section through the center of the Color Solid, classifying all colors of MIDDLE VALUE by measured scales, of HUE and CHROMA.

Each radius is a SCALE OF CHROMA starting from the neutral center .N⁵. It traces a' regular increase in the chroma of its pigment hue, and bears appropriate symbols. Thus R⅜. indicates that the red upon which it is placed reflects 50% of standard white and 90% of the strength of standard vermilion.

Each circle struck from the neutral center is a SCALE OF HUE. It is a circuit of ten measured hues, equal in value and chroma. This equality appears in their symbols, — R⅜. YR⅜. Y⅜. GY⅜. G⅜. BG⅜. B⅜. PB⅜. P⅜ and RP⅜. which is a balanced circle of hues reflecting 50% of standard white and 50% of the chroma of standard vermilion.

A BALANCE of opposite hues which co equal areas of equal chroma: such as BG⅔. and such as nine parts of BG⅔. with five parts of R⅝.

A SEQUENCE of successive hues comb traced thus : B₂. G₃. Y₅. R₃. or the differences the qualitative and quantitative construction of this succession of colors, and any selection,—regular or symbols. See Chapters III and VI of "A COLO describes the nature and use of these charts.

AVOID HANDLING and EXPOSURE TO LI

e another, is obtained by g areas of unequal chroma,

hroma in equal additions is : P₇. C₅. R₆. In short, tervals, insures an orderly e evident in the written by the author, which

Dad
Pantherism
blimp program
Haar
Espro - corp
Mittelschmerz

Pure White is theoretic and not practic

WHITE

B

B-G

G

BLUISH TURQUOISE (149)

WHITE (101)

IVORY (103)

CREAM (102)

LIGHT CHROME YELLOW (106)

DARK CHROME YELLOW (109)

ORANGE GLAZE (113)

SCARLET RED (118)

LIGHT FLESH (132)

MEDIUM FLESH (131)

ROSE CARMINE (124)

ALIZARIN CRIMSON (226)

PINK CARMINE (127)

RED-VIOLET (194)

VIOLET (138)

DARK INDIGO (157)

HE... E-REDDISH (151)

COBALT BLUE (1)

LIGHT ULTRAM... (140)

GREEN (156)

GREEN (159)

GREEN (165)

EN (172)

GREEN OLIVE (167)

LLOWISH (160)

OWISH (173)

E (183)

7)

Contents:
instruction manual
decoder dial
color pencil studies
comparison swatches
blue blockers
(use as needed)

1er
CERCLE CHROMATIQUE
DE
Mr CHEVREUL
RENFERMANT
LES COULEURS FRANCHES

instruction manual

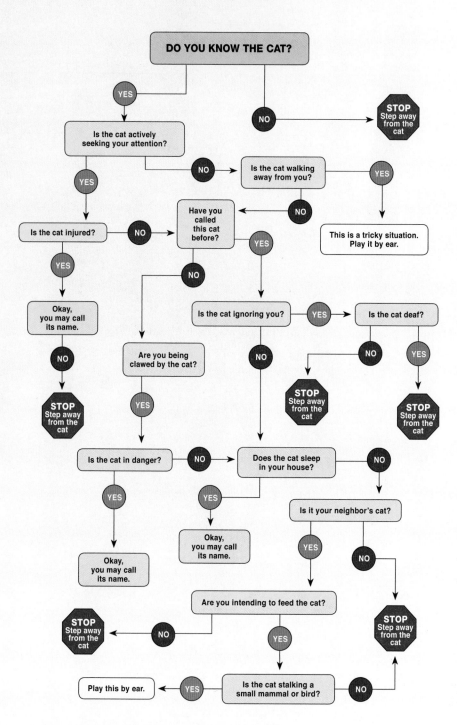

KNOW THE FACTS

CAT CALLING
When is it okay to call a cat?

ASK YOURSELF:

DO YOU KNOW THE CAT?

YES

NO → STOP Step away from the cat

Is the cat actively seeking your attention?

YES

NO → Is the cat walking away from you?

YES → This is a tricky situation. Play it by ear.

NO → Have you called this cat before?

Is the cat injured?

NO → Have you called this cat before?

YES → Okay, you may call its name.

NO → STOP Step away from the cat

NO → Are you being clawed by the cat?

YES → Is the cat ignoring you?

YES → Is the cat deaf?

NO → STOP Step away from the cat

NO → STOP Step away from the cat

YES → STOP Step away from the cat

YES → Are you being clawed by the cat?

YES → Is the cat in danger?

NO → Does the cat sleep in your house?

YES → Okay, you may call its name.

NO → Is it your neighbor's cat?

YES → Okay, you may call its name.

YES → Is it your neighbor's cat?

YES → Are you intending to feed the cat?

NO → STOP Step away from the cat

NO → STOP Step away from the cat

YES → Is the cat stalking a small mammal or bird?

NO → STOP Step away from the cat

YES → Play this by ear.

I'm so BORED

El Preterito - Preterite Tense

I want some m[...] in a taza for m[...] casa.

Things that happen once:
- being born → nacer
- turning five → cumplir
- graduating kindergarten → graduar

doesn't always happen once (Tim)

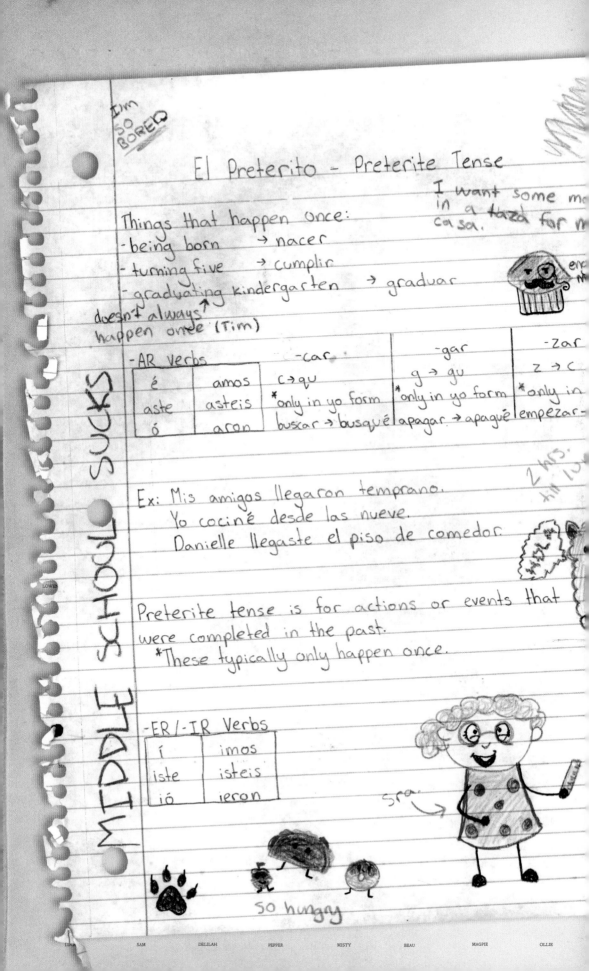

-AR verbs

é	amos
aste	asteis
ó	aron

-car	-gar	-zar
c → qu	g → gu	z → c
*only in yo form	*only in yo form	*only in
buscar → busqué	apagar → apagué	empezar-

2 hrs. till lu

Ex: Mis amigos llegaron temprano.
Yo cociné desde las nueve.
Danielle llegaste el piso de comedor.

Preterite tense is for actions or events that were completed in the past.
*These typically only happen once.

-ER/-IR Verbs

í	imos
iste	isteis
ió	ieron

Sra.

so hungry

MIDDLE SCHOOL SUCKS

LOWEN

BU

Practice troop movements with these paper soldiers.

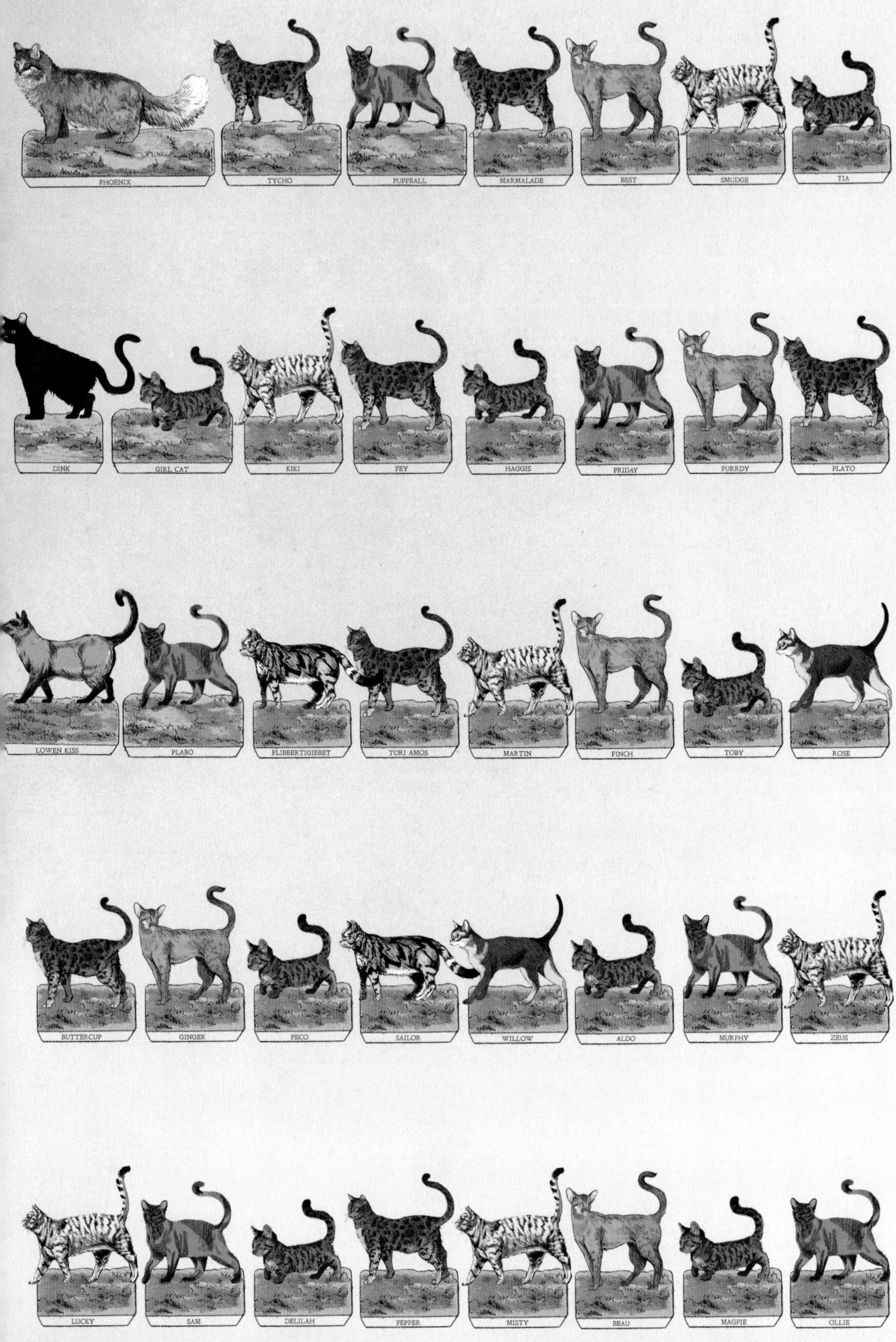
PHOENIX
TYCHO
PUFFBALL
MARMALADE
BEST
SMUDGE
TIA
DINK
GIRL CAT
KIKI
FEY
HAGGIS
FRIDAY
PURRDY
PLATO
LOWEN KISS
PLABO
FLIBBERTIGIBBET
TORI AMOS
MARTIN
FINCH
TOBY
ROSE
BUTTERCUP
GINGER
PECO
SAILOR
WILLOW
ALDO
MURPHY
ZEUS
LUCKY
SAM
DELILAH
PEPPER
MISTY
BEAU
MAGPIE
OLLIE

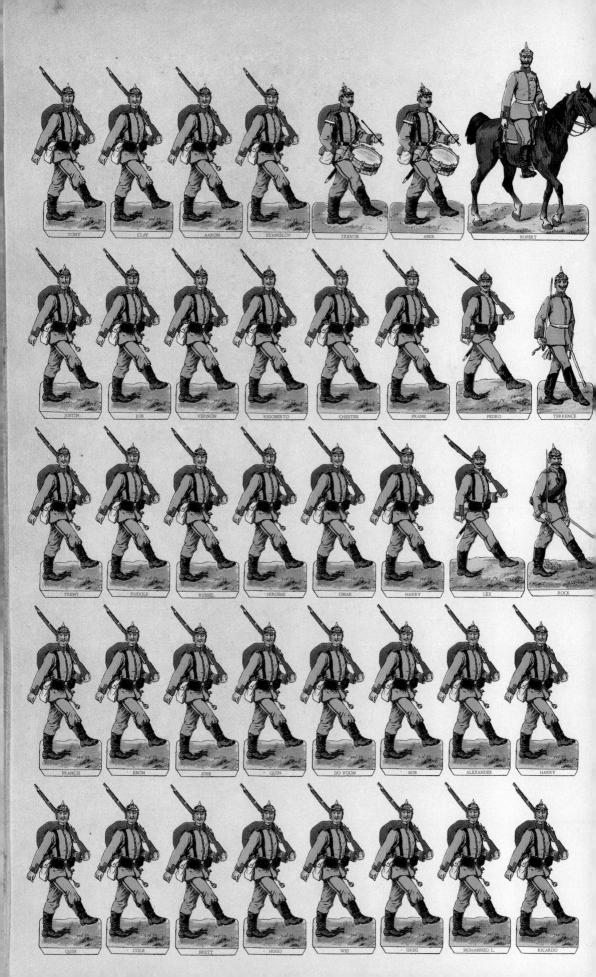

TONY CLAY AARON STANISLOV TREVOR AMIR RUPERT

JUSTIN JOB VERNON RIGOBERTO CHESTER FRANK PEDRO TERRENCE

TRENT RUDOLF RUSSEL HIROSHI OMAR HARRY LEX ROCK

FRANCIS EBON JOSE QUIN DO VOON BOB ALEXANDER HARRY

QUIN COLE BRETT HUGO WEI GREG MOHAMMED L. RICARDO

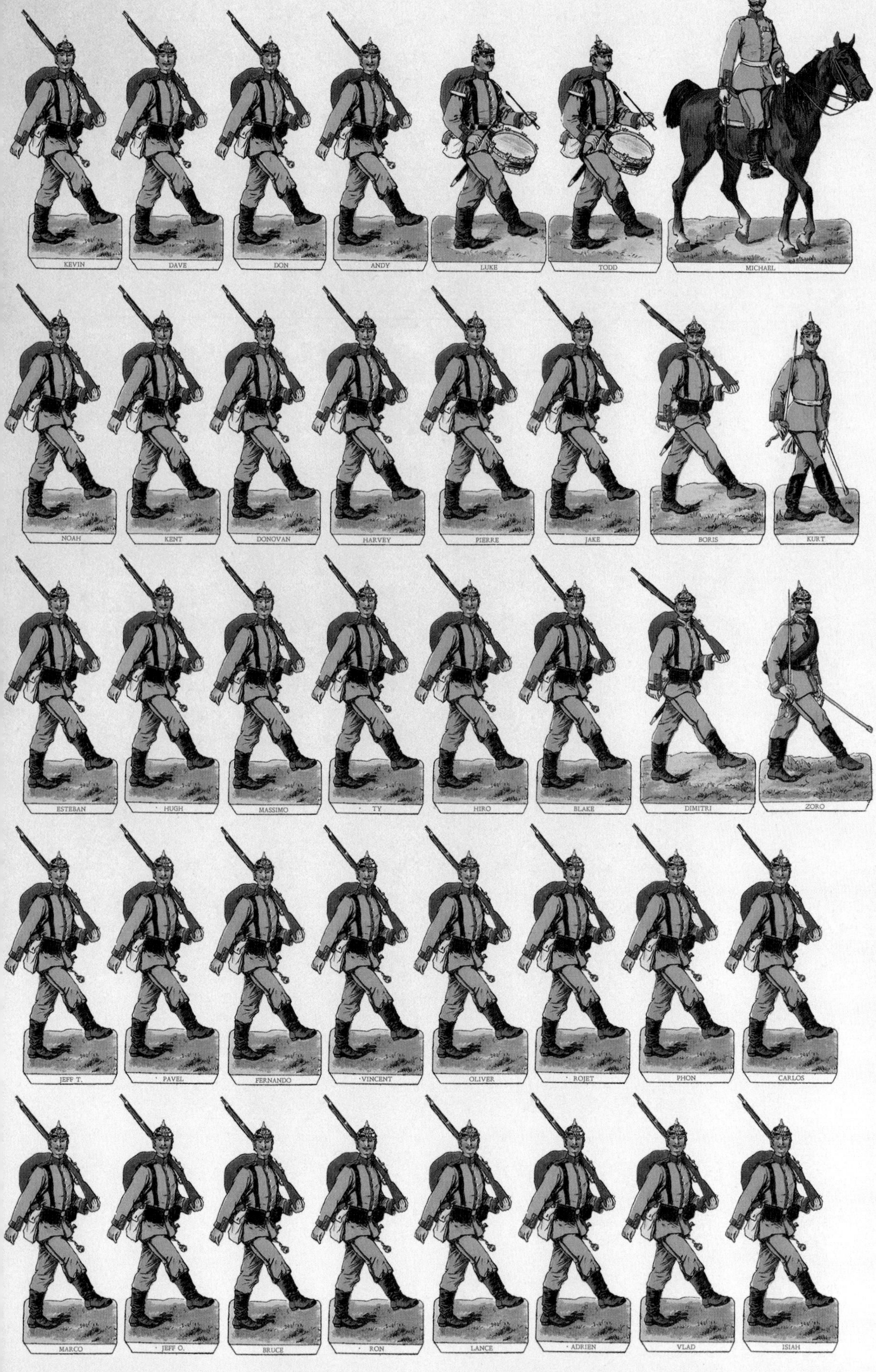
KEVIN
DAVE
DON
ANDY
LUKE
TODD
MICHAEL
NOAH
KENT
DONOVAN
HARVEY
PIERRE
JAKE
BORIS
KURT
ESTEBAN
HUGH
MASSIMO
TY
HIRO
BLAKE
DIMITRI
ZORO
JEFF T.
PAVEL
FERNANDO
VINCENT
OLIVER
ROJET
PHON
CARLOS
MARCO
JEFF O.
BRUCE
RON
LANCE
ADRIEN
VLAD
ISIAH

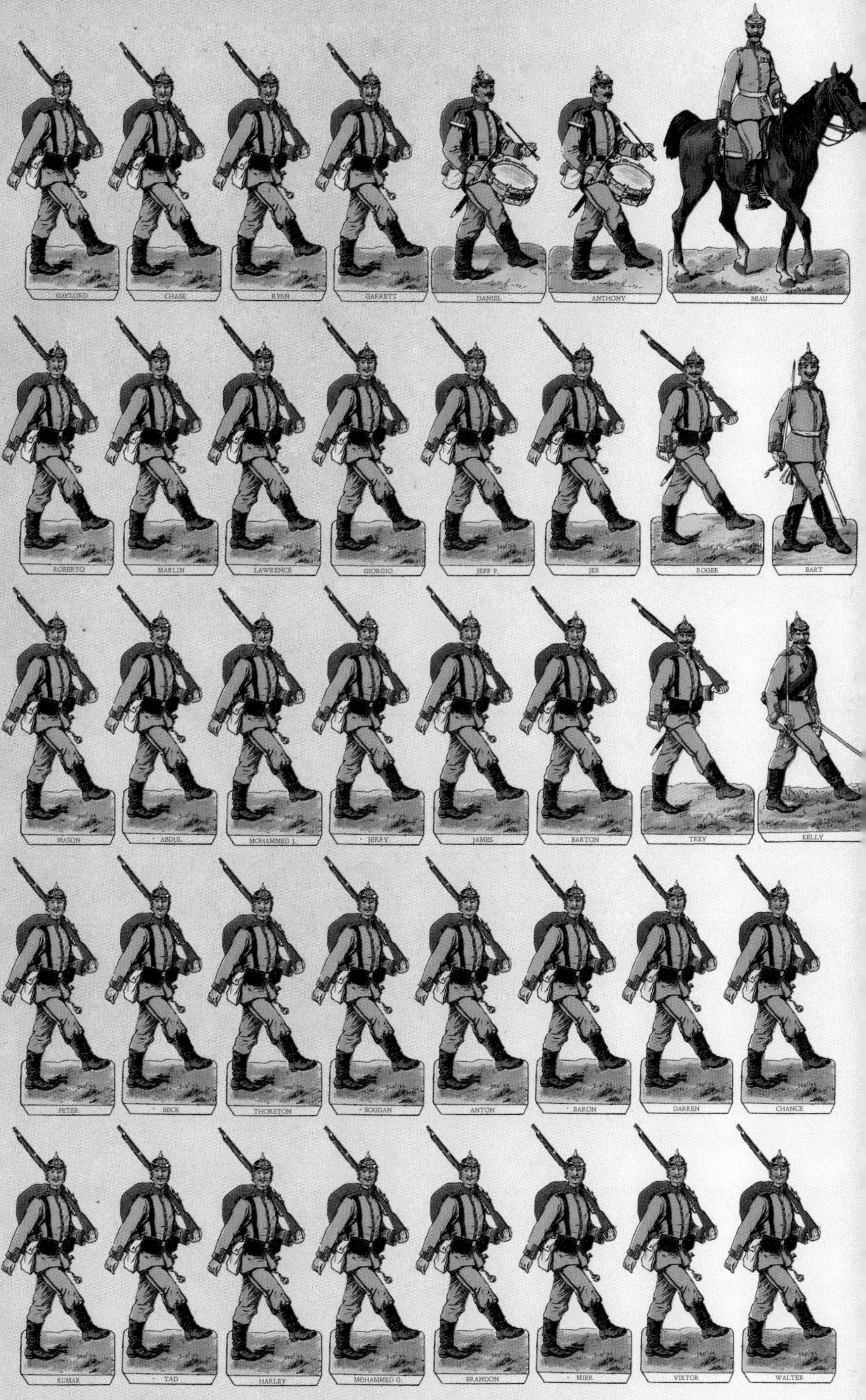

GAYLORD
CHASE
RYAN
GARRETT
DANIEL
ANTHONY
BEAU
ROBERTO
MARLIN
LAWRENCE
GIORGIO
JEFF P.
JEB
ROGER
BART
MASON
ABDUL
MOHAMMED J.
JERRY
JAMES
BARTON
TREY
KELLY
PETER
BECK
THORSTON
BOGDAN
ANTON
BARON
DARREN
CHANCE
KUMAR
TAD
HARLEY
MOHAMMED G.
BRANDON
MIER
VIKTOR
WALTER

Are you ready to fight the patriarchy?

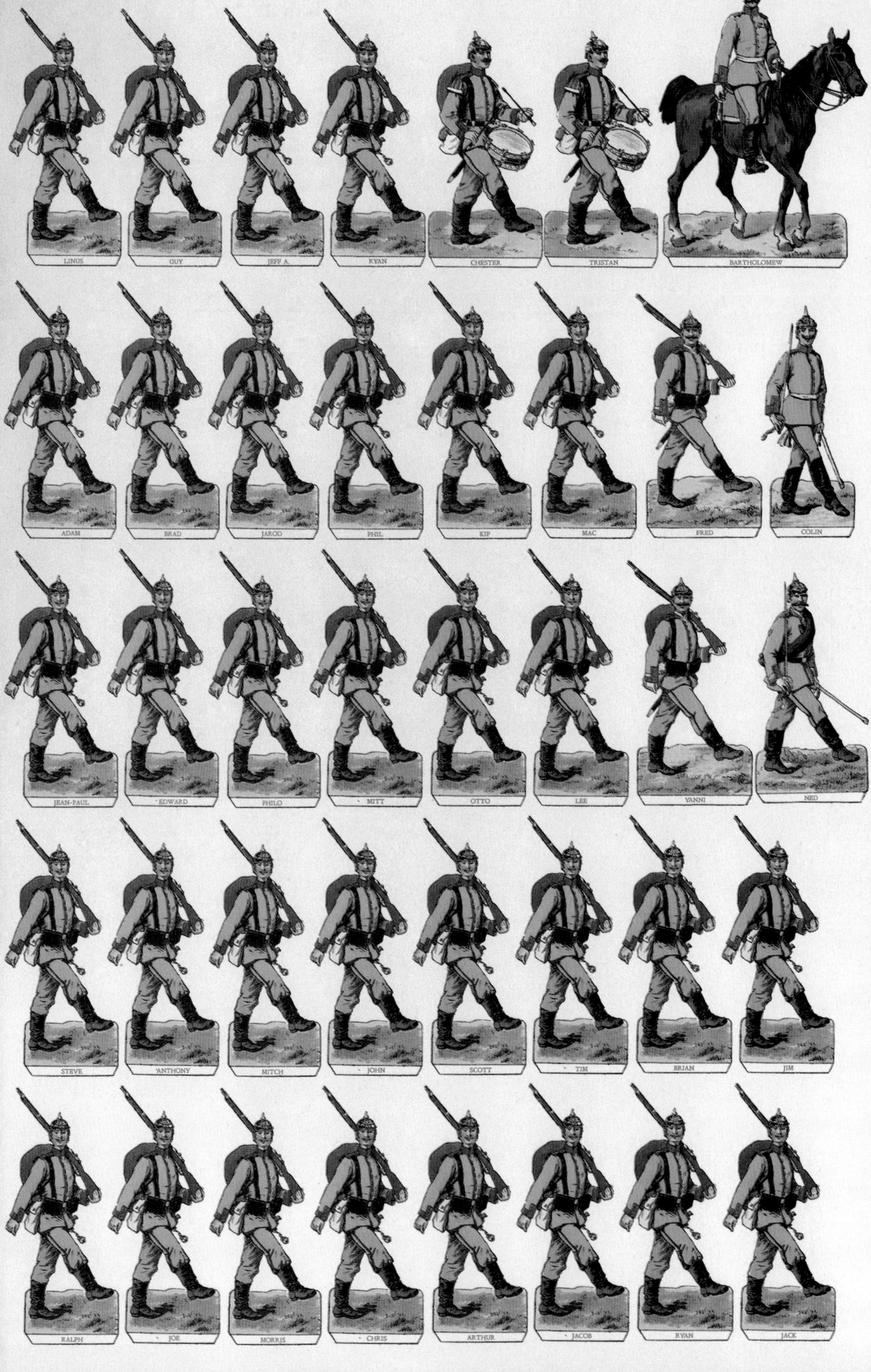
LINUS
GUY
JEFF A.
RYAN
CHESTER
TRISTAN
BARTHOLOMEW
ADAM
BRAD
JAROD
PHIL
KIP
MAC
FRED
COLIN
JEAN-PAUL
EDWARD
PHILO
MITT
OTTO
LEE
YANNI
NED
STEVE
ANTHONY
MITCH
JOHN
SCOTT
TIM
BRIAN
JIM
RALPH
JOE
MORRIS
CHRIS
ARTHUR
JACOB
RYAN
JACK

(1) Instructor
   COMMA
   Mass: 1.
(2) Instructor
   COMMA
   Mass: 1. R
(3) Instructor
   MAND.
   Mass: AT
(4) Instructor
   2. COMM
   Mass: 1. P
(5) Instructor
   MAND.
   Mass: 1.

ARD) (OVER-

RHEAD),

OMMAND.

ULDERS),

ACE.

2. COM-

NTION,

SITIONS

(10

(11

(12

(13

DEWARD, 4.
ERS BE-
ERS. 10.
ANDS ON

Mass
MO
HI
PL
HI

The handwritten pages placed over the manual read:

Drowning
in words,
Buried alive
in the soil.
Full with seeds sprouting in my misery
How do I describe
The way I've changed
The way I've thrived
The days I've felt
I might just DIE
But it was middle school
I like to believe it was all happy
and it sucked sometimes
I was alone
I was confused
And I was delusional to assume
the transition would be easy
But I grew.
The soil that took the breath
from my lungs
Sprouted flowers
leaves
petals
beauty
I realized, after months of
drowning
There was no water.
All I had to do

To keep from dying, slow&agonizing
Was close my eyes
Watch the last bubble drift from
my chapped lips
And take a breath

I took a breath
The moment I opened myself up to the world
The moment I closed my book during lunch
The moment I dressed like myself
The moment I dyed my hair
The moment I met my friends
The moment I said "Screw it"
The moment I stopped holding back
And saw, for the first time
the people around me
I saw the girls whose perfect bodies
showed rib cages and forgotten lunch bags
I saw sleeves hiding scars
I saw strict parents
and procrastination until 4 a.m.
I saw friends not out to their parents
I saw a school full of hurt people
People just like me
People who had bad days
and bad weeks
People who had been betrayed
bullied
cast out
People who worried, as I did,
about how they appeared to others

All of these moments of realization
compiled into a scrapbook of growth
A scrapbook I will hold with me until I die
I will never forget these years
I mean it
I truly do
Middle school has been tattooed on my heart
graffitied into my flesh
Because I would not be who I am without them
My friends of course
And the teachers
And the girls I pass in the hallway
The boys who play shell shackers
The people who surround me every day
I will miss all of you
I look around me
And I see beautiful people
I see dancers
scientists
singers
writers
and horseback riders
I see a brilliant future.
So goodbye Middle School,
Hello everything.

d. Mass
commands   to those
necessary   the exer-
cise, to inc   he exercise. Mass   *the trunk*
exercises   relaxed
ones), in   ny other
exercises i   breathing.

SCENARIO NO. 4

ROPE CLIMBING OPTIONS FOR RESCUE OPS

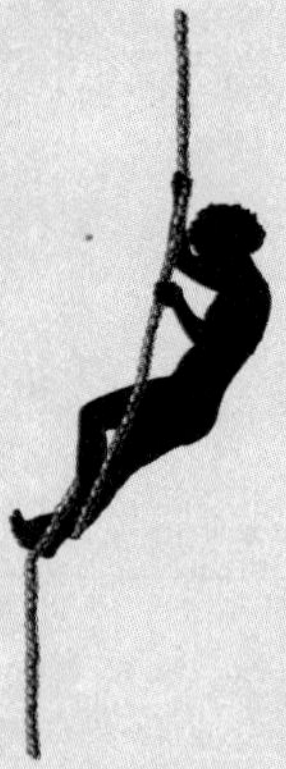

Basic
Loop rope around leg. Climb rope.

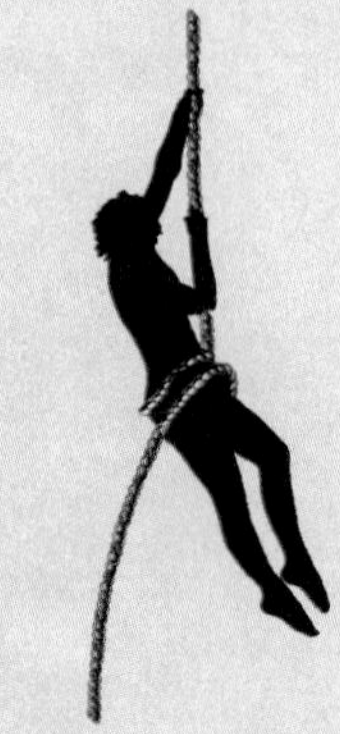

Body Wrap
Loop rope around waist and seat. Wait to be pulled up.

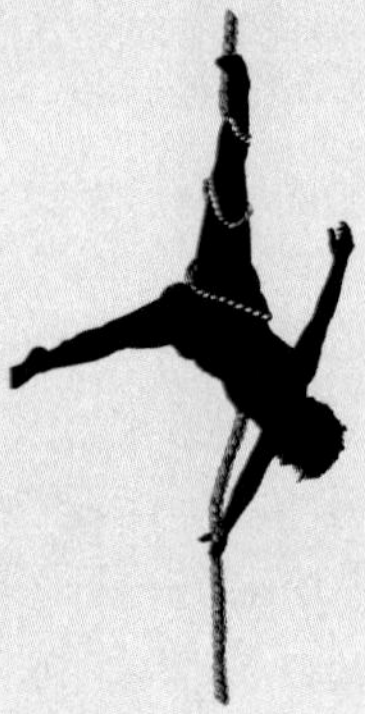

Inverted Single Leg Wrap
Loop rope around one leg. Flip upside down. Wait to be pulled up.

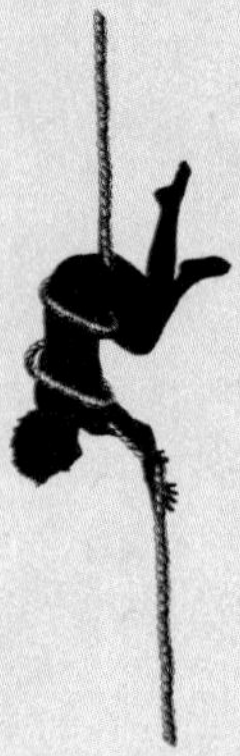

Inverted Tuck
Loop rope around body and one leg. Flip upside down. Crunch into tucked position.

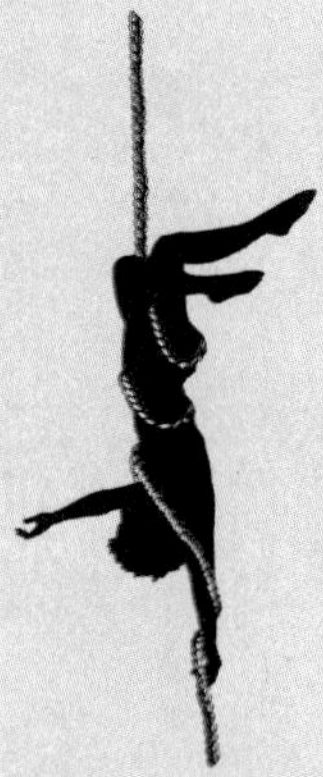

Inverted Body Wrap (Simple)
Loop rope around body twice. Flip over. Grip between legs.

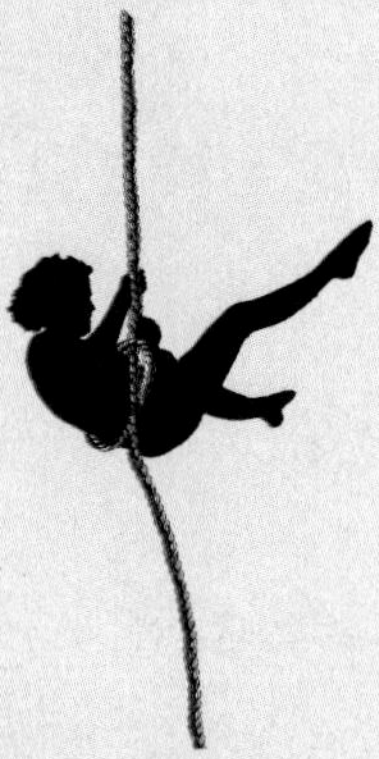

Swing
Loop rope around body until comfortable Hold on. Sit back.

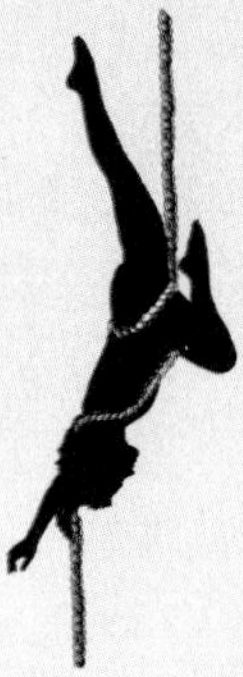

Inverted Body Wrap (Fancy)
Loop rope around body twice. Flip. Arrange legs in stag position.

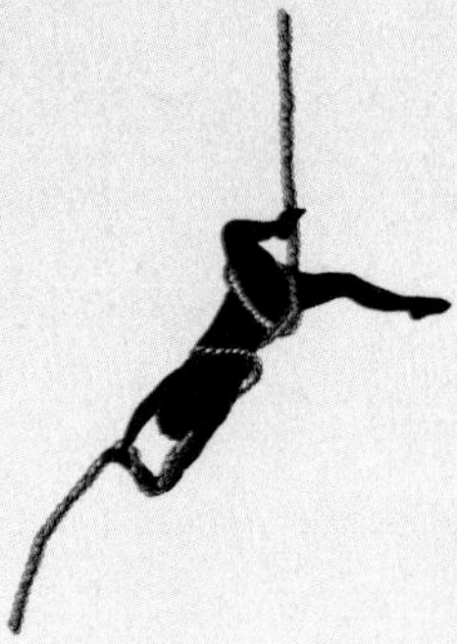

Flying Inverted Body Wrap
Loop rope around body twice. Flip. Grip over head.

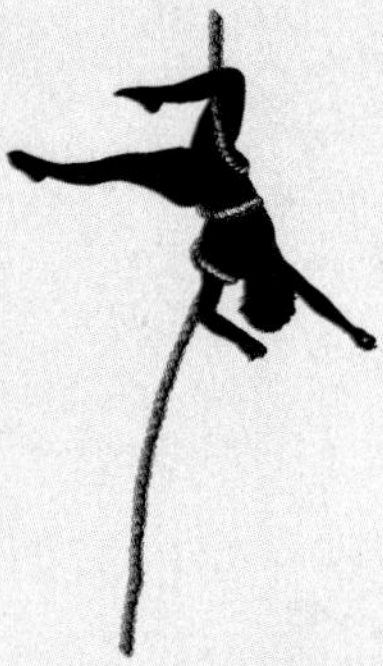

Flying Inverted Body Wrap (No Grip)
Not recommended.

SCENARIO NO. 3

SIGNAL A BLIMP

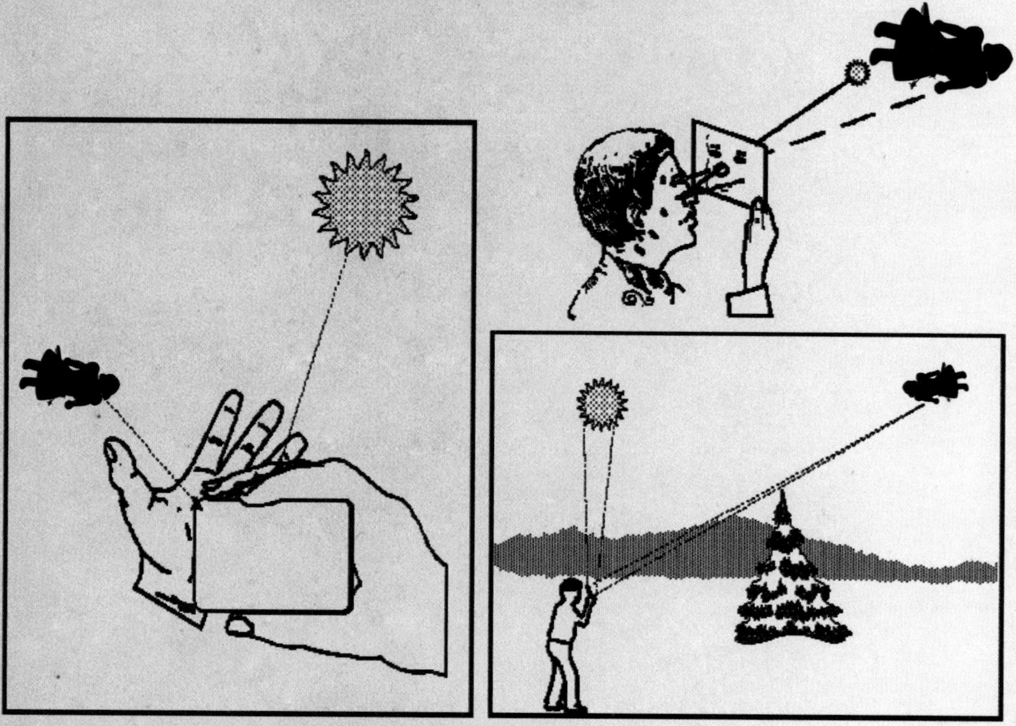

AIMING THE SIGNAL MIRROR

METHODS OF COMMUNICATION

a. Audio. Eg. Shouting, hooting, hollering, whistling. These may sound like good ideas, but they do have some limitations.

Sound has limited range unless you use a device that will significantly project the sound, like an opera singer or a megaphone.

(2) It may be hard for the blimp to pinpoint your location due to echoes or wind or hearing loss.

(3) If you do need to rely on audio, remember the International Distress Signal. (MSVX.02.18a) The survivor will make six blasts in one minute, returned by three blasts in one minute by the receiver, replied with eighteen two-second blasts evenly spaced over 42 seconds.

b. Radio. Eg. Girl Doll Radio, Lady Doll CB, Polly Pocket Emergency Transponder Beacons, etc.

Your radio device may not be operational.
Terrain may dampen signal from your device.

c. Visual. Waving, jumping up and down, signaling with light and a mirror. This last option is particularly useful and is an excellent choice in good weather conditions.

(1) The visual international distress symbol is recognized by a series of three evenly spaced improvised signaling devices followed by a thumbs-up. (MSVX.02.18b)

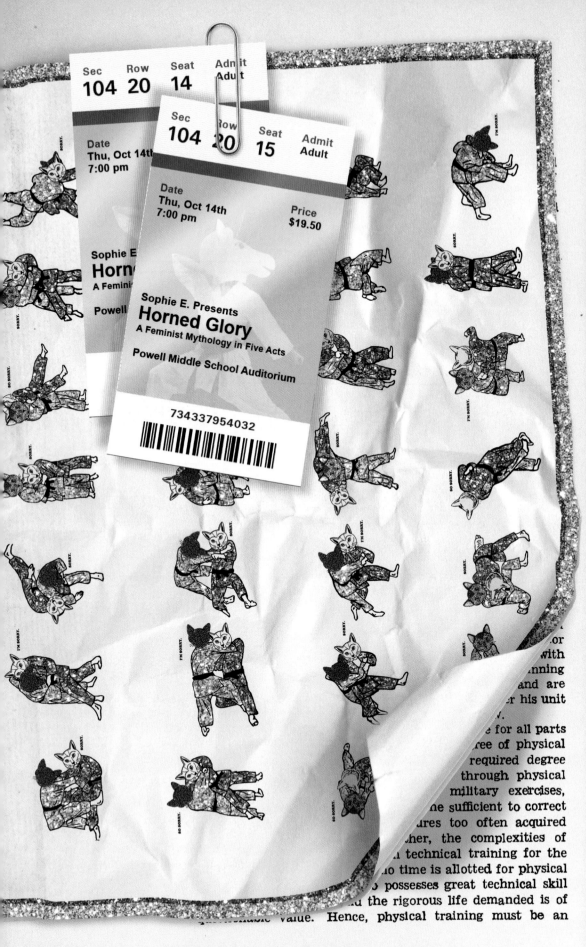

Sec **104** Row **20** Seat **14** Admit **Adult**

Date
Thu, Oct 14th
7:00 pm

Sophie E. Presents
Horned
A Femini

Powell

Sec **104** Row **20** Seat **15** Admit **Adult**

Date
Thu, Oct 14th
7:00 pm

Price
$19.50

Sophie E. Presents
Horned Glory
A Feminist Mythology in Five Acts

Powell Middle School Auditorium

734337954032

or
with
nning
and are
r his unit
.

e for all parts
ree of physical
required degree
through physical
military exercises,
e sufficient to correct
res too often acquired
her, the complexities of
technical training for the
o time is allotted for physical
possesses great technical skill
the rigorous life demanded is of
value. Hence, **physical training must be an**

3

COMBAT TRAINING

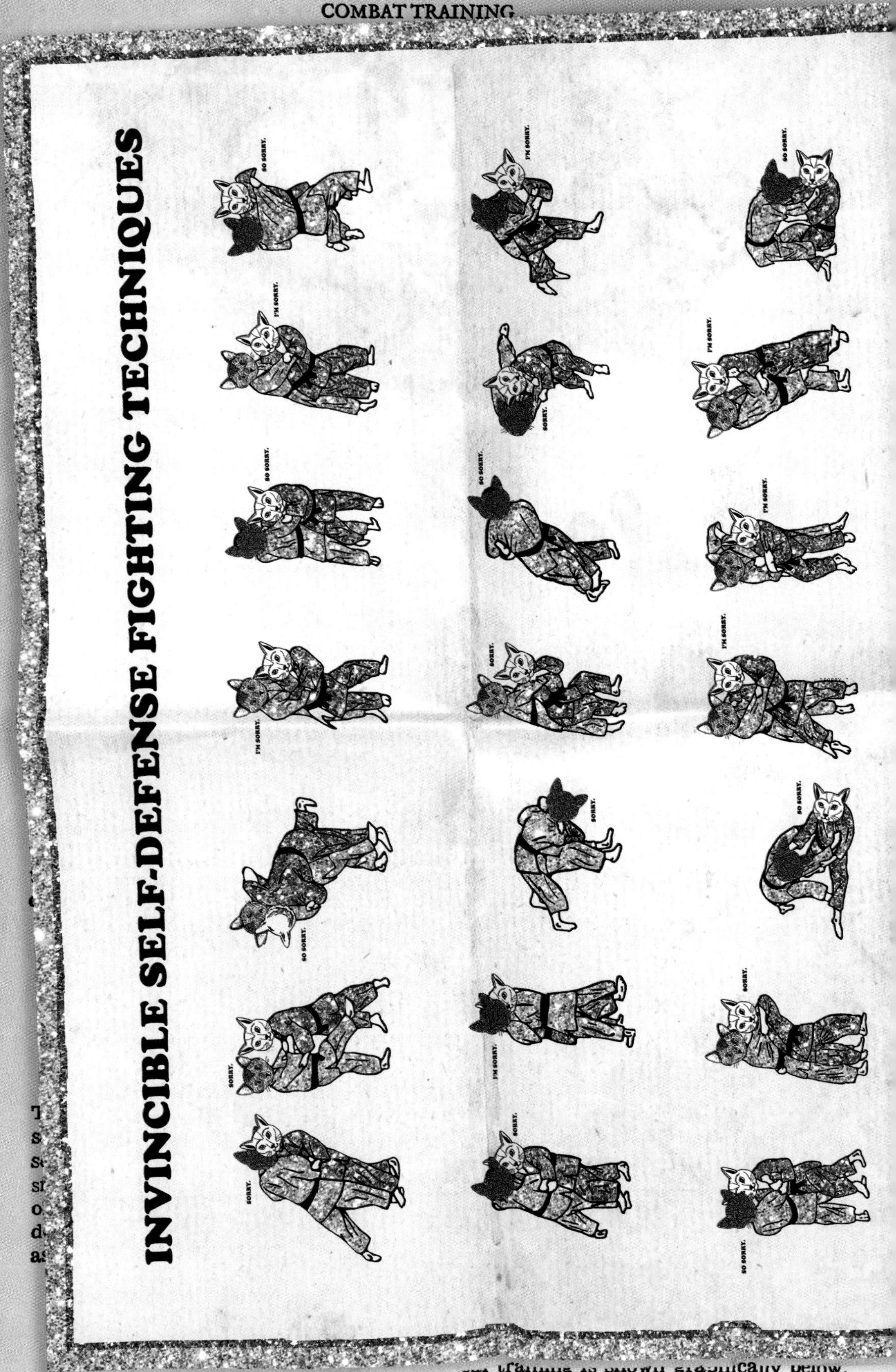
INVINCIBLE SELF-DEFENSE FIGHTING TECHNIQUES
SO SORRY.
I'M SORRY.
SO SORRY.
I'M SORRY.
SO SORRY.
SORRY.
SORRY.
I'M SORRY.
SORRY.
SO SORRY.
SORRY.
I'M SORRY.
SO SORRY.
SORRY.
I'M SORRY.
SO SORRY.
I'M SORRY.
SO SORRY.
SORRY.
SO SORRY.

... training is shown graphically below.

TOOL CAT

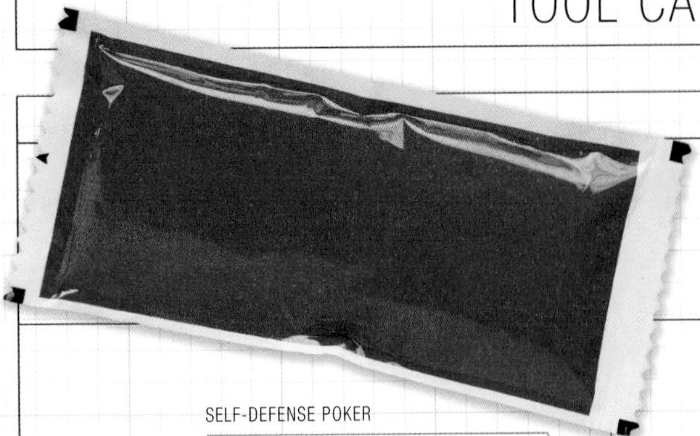

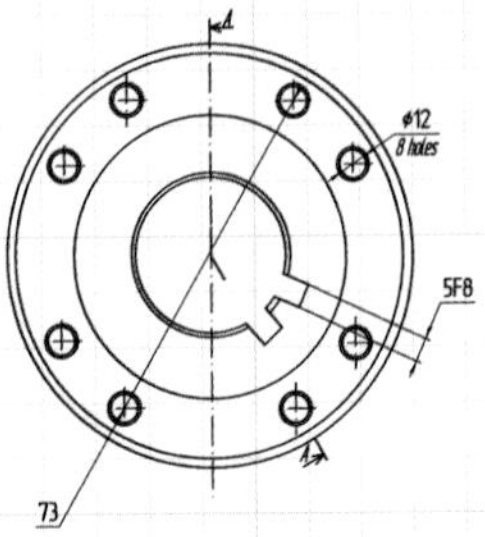

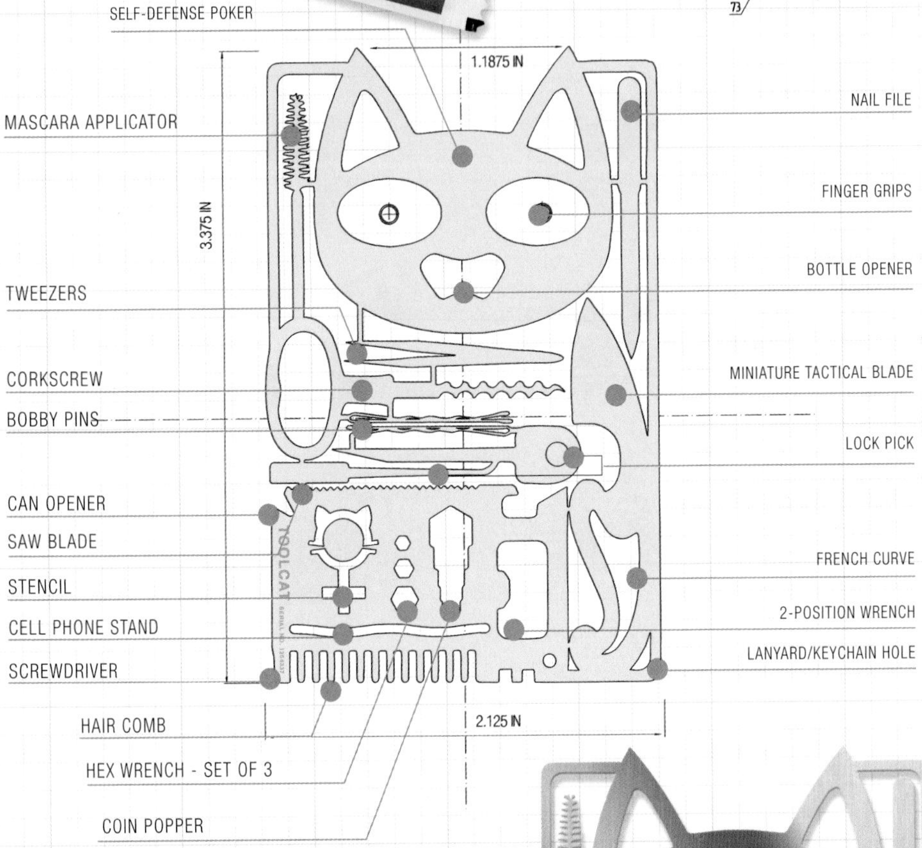
SELF-DEFENSE POKER
1.1875 IN
MASCARA APPLICATOR
NAIL FILE
FINGER GRIPS
3.375 IN
BOTTLE OPENER
TWEEZERS
CORKSCREW
MINIATURE TACTICAL BLADE
BOBBY PINS
LOCK PICK
CAN OPENER
SAW BLADE
FRENCH CURVE
STENCIL
2-POSITION WRENCH
CELL PHONE STAND
LANYARD/KEYCHAIN HOLE
SCREWDRIVER
HAIR COMB
2.125 IN
HEX WRENCH - SET OF 3
COIN POPPER
TOOLCAT

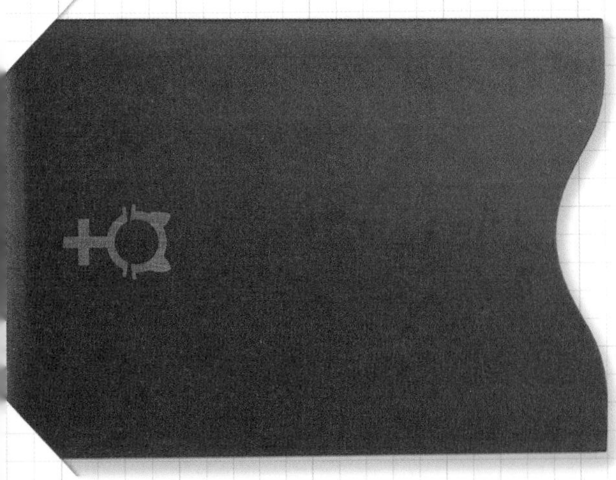

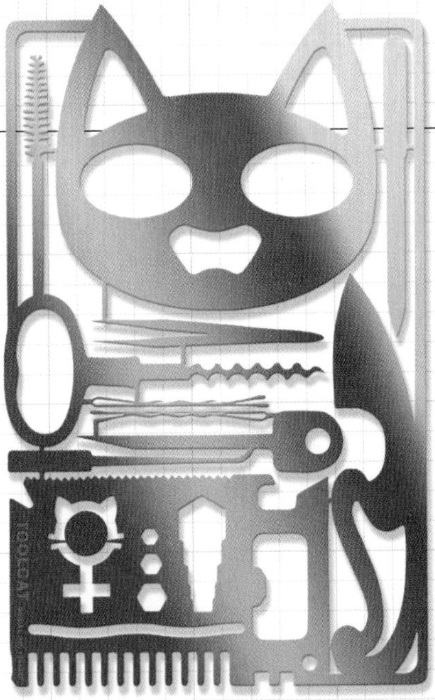
TOOLCAT

PASSING NOTES

COIN COMPARTMENTS

The Susan B. Anthony dollar was minted from 1979 to 1981, and then suspended due to so-called "poor public acceptance." In fact this limited edition coin is very special as each 1979-P Wide Rim Variety edition houses a slim secret compartment. Use the tool from your tool cat to open it. The coin was again minted in 1999. That edition does not feature the compartment.

LIBERTY
IN GOD WE TRUST
1979

125
65
1.043307 IN
LIBERTY
IN GOD WE TRUST
1979
R81
R70
R15
R28

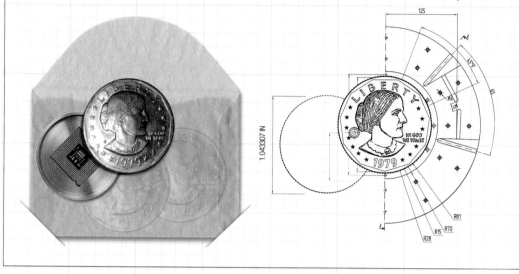

SHOE COMPARTMENTS

Most women wear high heels for one reason: They are smuggling secret information. If you see a woman wearing very high heels you can be certain that she is on a very important mission.

Items commonly stored in heels:
1. tampons
2. microchips
3. flashdrives
4. rolls of money
5. glitterbombs

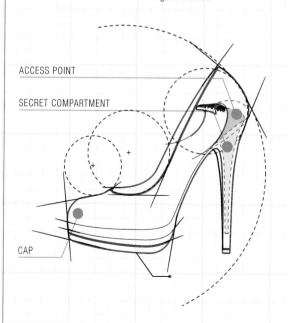

ACCESS POINT
SECRET COMPARTMENT
CAP

PLATFORM PUMP

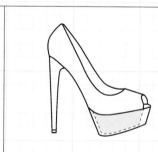

KITTEN

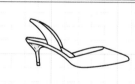

HIGH BLOCK

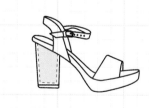

WEDGE

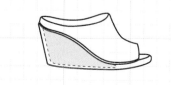

Girl Doll model 59.11b
The gold standard of doll radios, Girl Dolls continue to dominate the market due to their well-made, state-of-the-art push-to-talk technology. Newer models come with LED flashlights (just twist the doll's left wrist). Are they expensive? Yes. You get what you pay for.

Lady Doll model G110987b
This two-way radio fashion doll handset comes equipped with 50 channels and automatically checks for activity. The 9-VOX sensitivity levels allow you to choose the point the radio will detect your voice. Handsets can communicate as far as 36 miles depending on the environment. Waterproof, lightweight, comes with a car adapter, lots of tiny shoes, and other accessories.

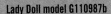

Nesting Dolls model 31.33bf
Well designed and easy to use, these Russian nesting dolls create a mesh network, providing a large, seamless Wi-Fi network with reliable — and stealth — internet access. Place them throughout the home for optimal performance.

Kokeshi model 1.794xp
Memory Channels: 199. Weather Resistant: IP55 Waterproof Standard. Weight: 9.1 oz. w/ battery pack and included antenna. Made in Japan.

Stuffed Bunny model 47.12
This bunny comes with two power levels, 4 watts and 1 watt in the frequency range of 136 – 174 MHz and 400 – 480MHz. It makes up for its low range of coverage with its simple interface. Also good for cuddling.

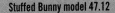

Doll House model A29
Suburb performance coupled with a pleasing plastic exterior, this dollhouse features tri-band support with quad stream radios for all three Wi-Fi bands; it also supports MU-MIMO and OFDMA to more efficiently handle multiple users and devices.

Dolls have been used throughout history for communication. When four-year-old Natasha Pushkin discovered copper wiring and a receiver in her doll, Varga, she modified the doll so that she could tap into the two-way telegraphy used across the Atlantic. In doing so, she transformed Varga into a means of organizing the resistance.

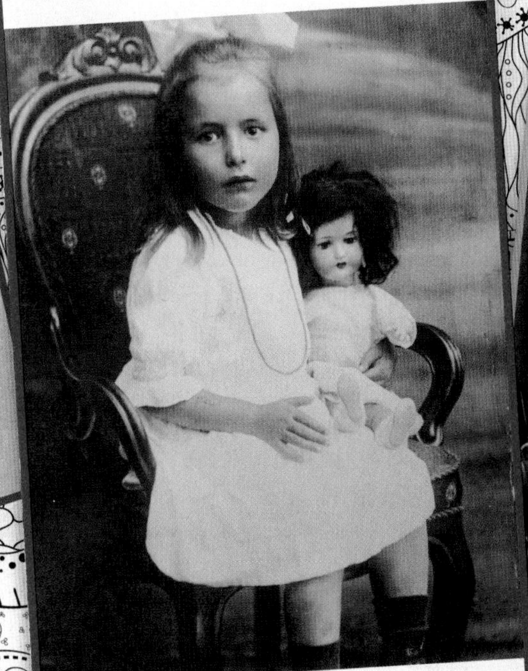

Natasha, with her doll, Varga, at her childhood home in Brooklyn, NY, USA. Decades later the American suffragette movement of the early 20th century would wear white in her honor.

Mary Elizabeth Toots is widely credited with refining two-way radio "simplex mode." She went on to get four advanced degrees and still enjoys teaching college-level math.

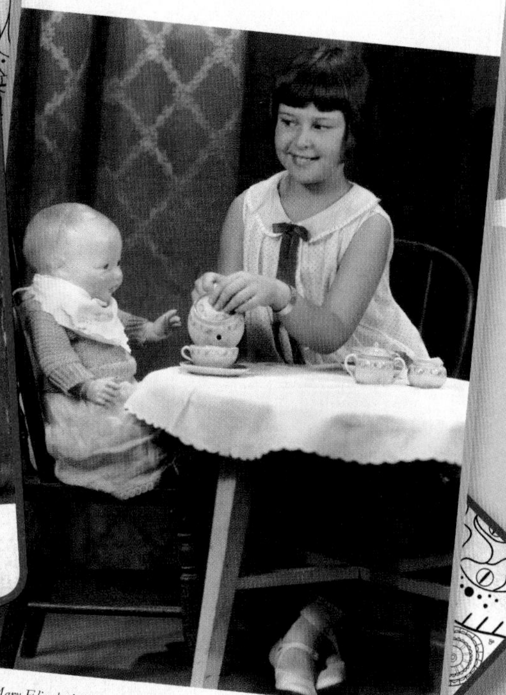

Mary Elizabeth Toots and her doll, Peg, in 1941. Toots' work was widely used during WW2.

Hailed as the inventor of the lightweight modern cell phone, Mindy Sapperstein first honed her abilities rewiring the digital system from her computer-aided dispatch (CAD) doll. She ran a FM pirate radio station from the ages of six to eleven.

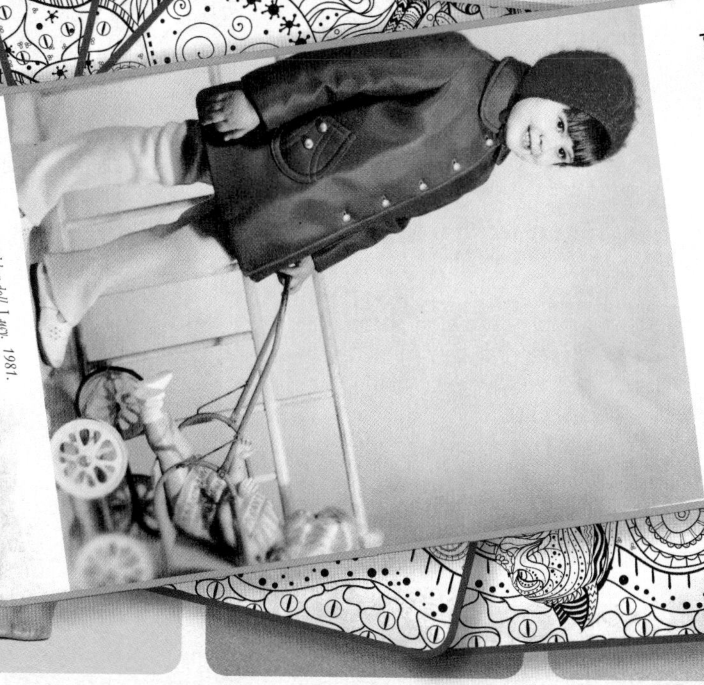

Mindy Sapperstein and her doll, Lucy. 1981.

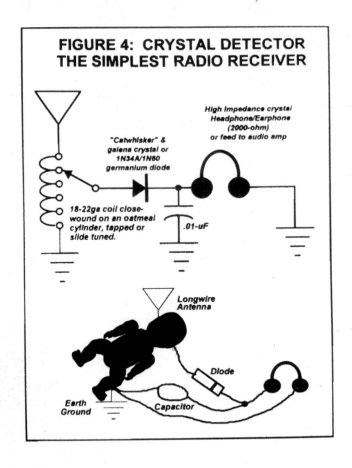

FIGURE 4: CRYSTAL DETECTOR
THE SIMPLEST RADIO RECEIVER

High Impedance crystal
Headphone/Earphone
(2000-ohm)
or feed to audio amp

"Catwhisker" &
galena crystal or
1N34A/1N60
germanium diode

18-22ga coil close-
wound on an oatmeal
cylinder, tapped or
slide tuned.

.01-uF

Longwire
Antenna

Diode

Earth
Ground

Capacitor

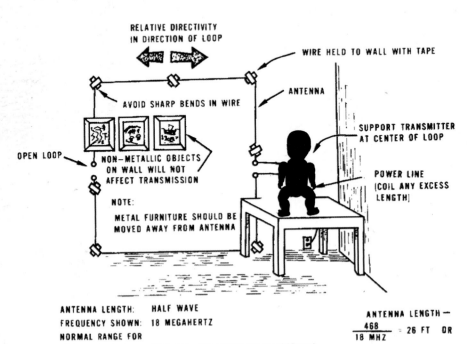

RELATIVE DIRECTIVITY
IN DIRECTION OF LOOP

WIRE HELD TO WALL WITH TAPE

AVOID SHARP BENDS IN WIRE

ANTENNA

SUPPORT TRANSMITTER
AT CENTER OF LOOP

OPEN LOOP

NON-METALLIC OBJECTS
ON WALL WILL NOT
AFFECT TRANSMISSION

POWER LINE
(COIL ANY EXCESS
LENGTH)

NOTE:

METAL FURNITURE SHOULD BE
MOVED AWAY FROM ANTENNA

ANTENNA LENGTH: HALF WAVE
FREQUENCY SHOWN: 18 MEGAHERTZ
NORMAL RANGE FOR
FREQUENCY SHOWN: DAY, 200-750 MILES; EARLY MORNING
                   OR LATE EVENING, 750-2500 MILES.

ANTENNA LENGTH —

$$\frac{468}{18 \text{ MHZ}} = 26 \text{ FT} \quad \text{OR}$$

13 FT PER SECTION

NOTE: TUNE OUTPUT CAREFULLY BY INDICATOR LAMP. BULB WILL NOT GLOW BRIGHTLY.

Figure 10–8. Half-wave square-loop antenna.

Transmitter Doll Model 28.6
Interior Wiring Schematic

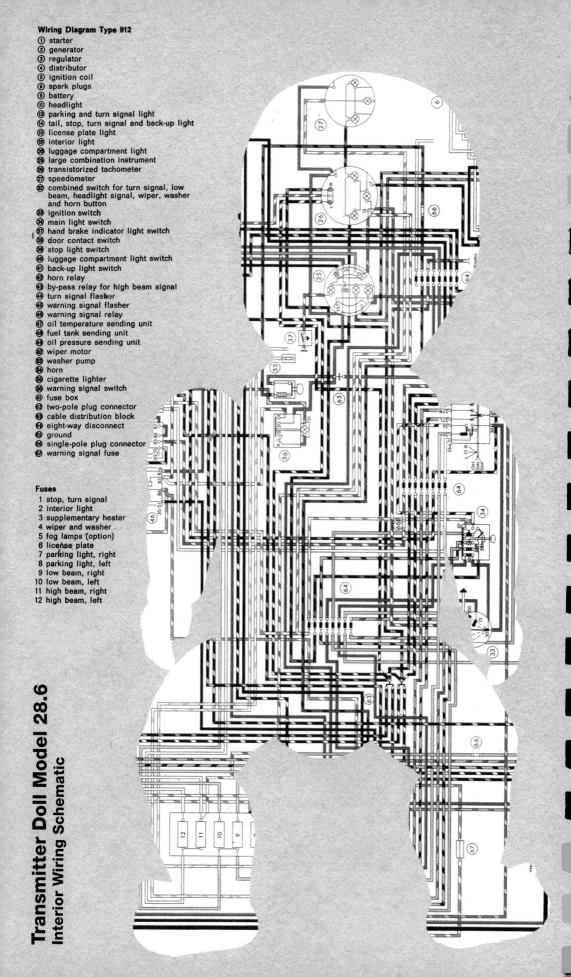

Wiring Diagram Type 912

① starter
② generator
③ regulator
④ distributor
⑤ ignition coil
⑥ spark plugs
⑨ battery
⑪ headlight
⑬ parking and turn signal light
⑭ tail, stop, turn signal and back-up light
⑮ license plate light
⑲ interior light
⑳ luggage compartment light
㉕ large combination instrument
㉖ transistorized tachometer
㉗ speedometer
㉜ combined switch for turn signal, low beam, headlight signal, wiper, washer and horn button
㉝ ignition switch
㉞ main light switch
㊲ hand brake indicator light switch
㊳ door contact switch
㊴ stop light switch
㊵ luggage compartment light switch
㊶ back-up light switch
㊷ horn relay
㊸ by-pass relay for high beam signal
㊹ turn signal flasher
㊺ warning signal flasher
㊻ warning signal relay
㊼ oil temperature sending unit
㊽ fuel tank sending unit
㊾ oil pressure sending unit
(52) wiper motor
(53) washer pump
(54) horn
(55) cigarette lighter
(56) warning signal switch
(61) fuse box
(62) two-pole plug connector
(63) cable distribution block
(64) eight-way disconnect
(65) ground
(66) single-pole plug connector
(67) warning signal fuse

Fuses

1 stop, turn signal
2 interior light
3 supplementary heater
4 wiper and washer
5 fog lamps (option)
6 license plate
7 parking light, right
8 parking light, left
9 low beam, right
10 low beam, left
11 high beam, right
12 high beam, left

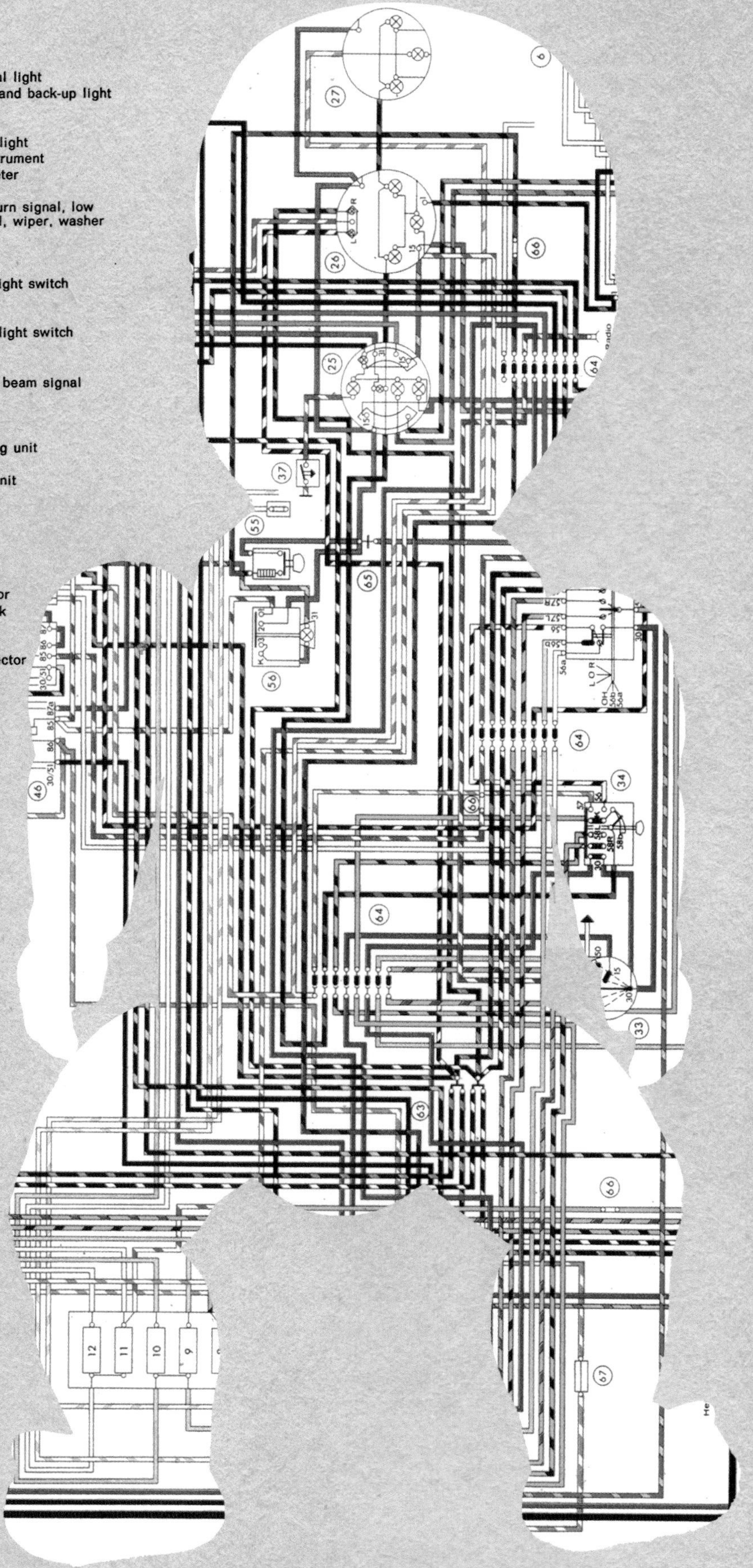

CHAPTER 3

TECHNICAL SPECIFICATIONS

SECTION 1. OPERATIONS AND WIRING

The model 28.6 is a powerhouse of broadcast capabilities. Up to a two-mile range, or up to 50 miles of clear transmission. That denotes a totally open, flat, unhindered location like a valley, field, or desert. Works with all FRS two-way radios. 14 channels and 38GHz to minimize interference. Compact, lightweight, long-range two-way radios are more trouble-free to carry and use. Waterproof. Heavy rain and dust-proof. Resistant to fire, snowstorms, blizzards, and whiteouts.

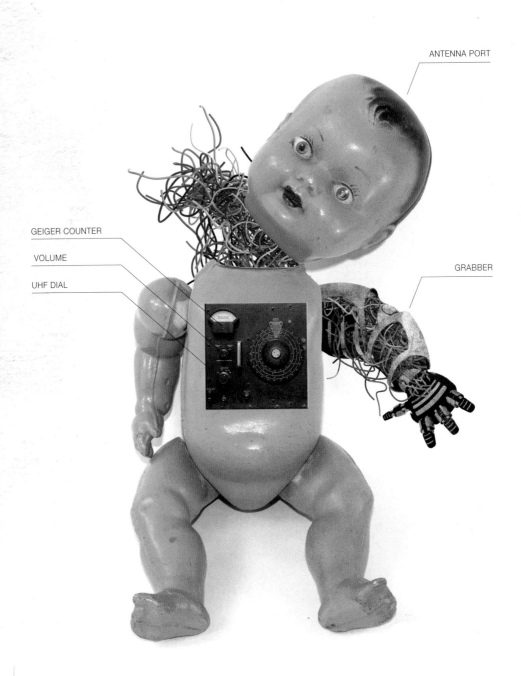

ANTENNA PORT

GEIGER COUNTER

VOLUME

UHF DIAL

GRABBER

Owners' Manual
Transmitter Doll Model 28.6

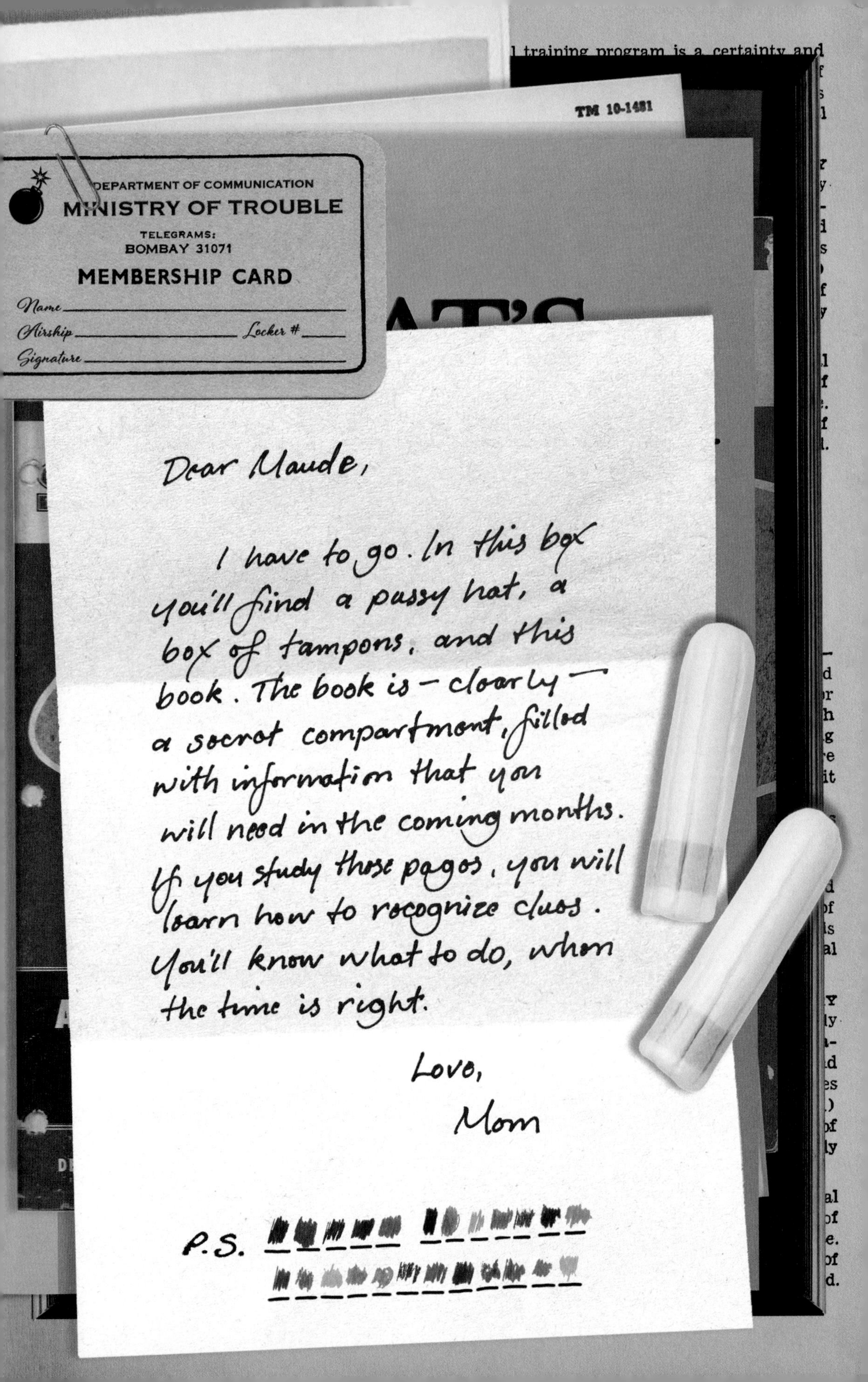
l training program is a certainty and
TM 10-1481
DEPARTMENT OF COMMUNICATION
MINISTRY OF TROUBLE
TELEGRAMS:
BOMBAY 31071
MEMBERSHIP CARD
Name
Airship
Locker #
Signature

Dear Maude,

I have to go. In this box
you'll find a pussy hat, a
box of tampons, and this
book. The book is—clearly—
a secret compartment, filled
with information that you
will need in the coming months.
If you study these pages, you will
learn how to recognize clues.
You'll know what to do, when
the time is right.

Love,
Mom

P.S. [redacted]

This Book
Belongs
To
MAUDE W.

MINISTRY OF
TROUBLE
INCORPORATED

ADDITIONAL WORDS AND ILLUSTRATIONS CONTRIBUTED BY
ELIZA FANTASTIC MOHAN, EMILY POWELL, SOPHIE JACQMOTTE-PARKS
AND LIV OSBORN. SPECIAL THANKS TO MARY JO BIERIG.

YOU HAVE BEEN CONTACTED BY THE MINISTRY OF TROUBLE. AWAIT FURTHER INSTRUCTIONS. ⚲

man-eaters
PRESENTS
NUMBER TWELVE

HANDBOOK
FOR THE
REVOLUTION

CHELSEA CAIN

LIA MITERNIQUE

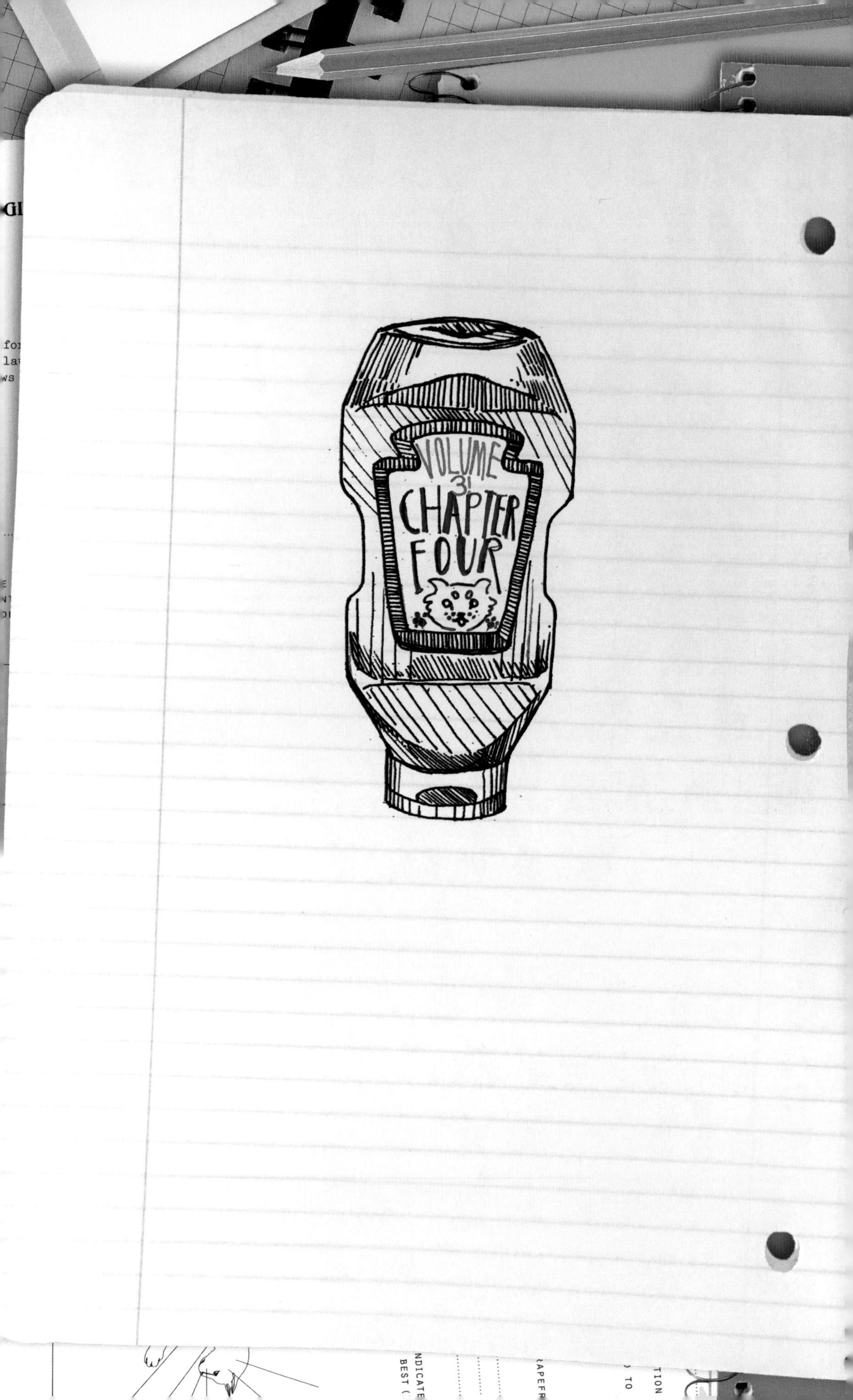
VOLUME
31
CHAPTER
FOUR

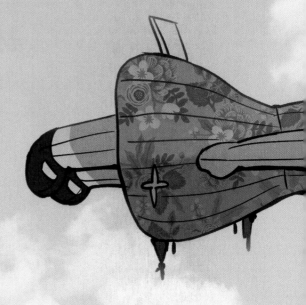

MINISTRY OF
TROUBLE
INCORPORATED

PUBLIC WARNING

The public is advised to familiarize themselves with the appearance of girl-shaped airships and aeroplanes. Should an aircraft be seen, take shelter immediately. Remain there until the aircraft have left the vicinity. Do not stand about in crowds. Do not interact with passengers. Definitely do not board the aircraft. In the event of a confirmed sighting, notify the patriarchy by telephone.

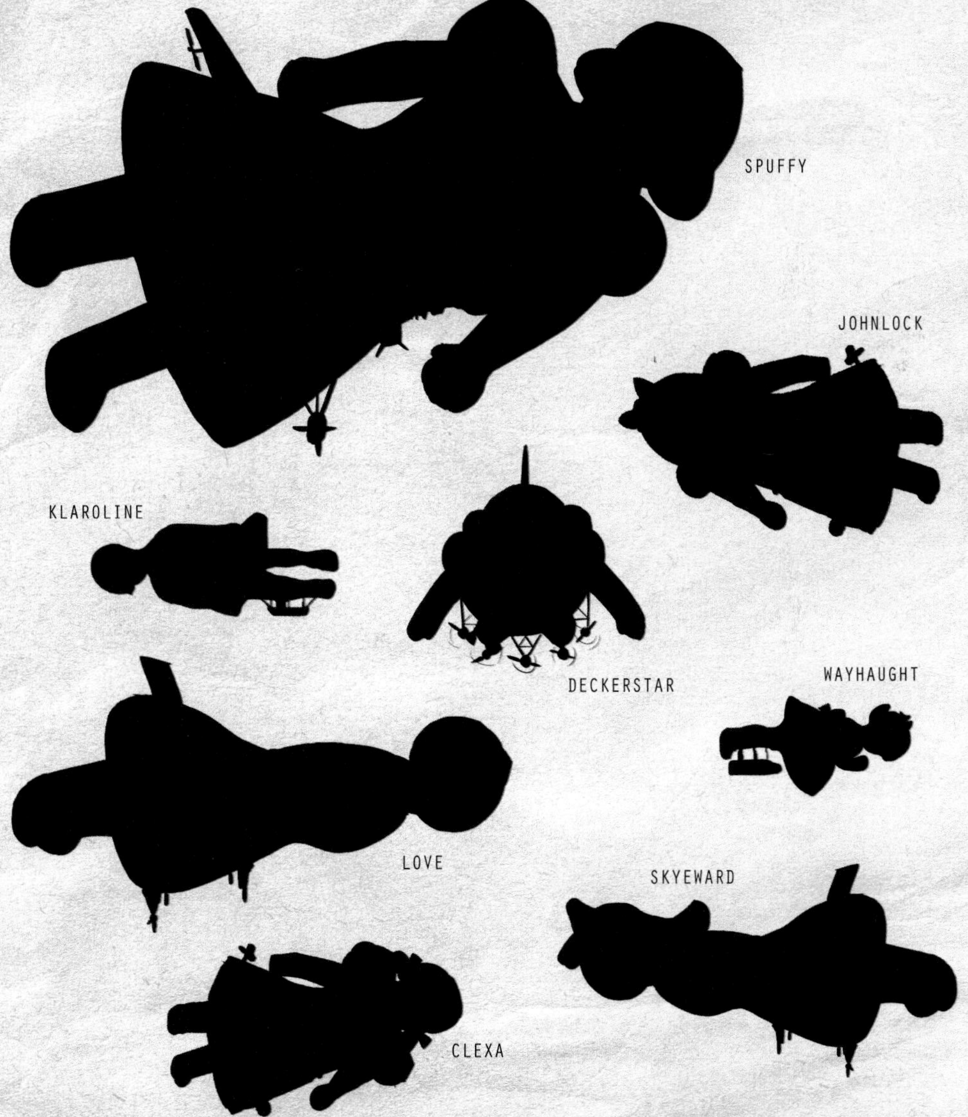
SPUFFY
JOHNLOCK
KLAROLINE
DECKERSTAR
WAYHAUGHT
LOVE
SKYEWARD
CLEXA

WRITER/CREATOR CHELSEA CAIN **COVER/CO-CREATOR/ADS, SUPPLEMENTAL ART** LIA MITERNIQUE
ARTIST ELISE MCCALL **COLORIST** RACHELLE ROSENBERG **LETTERER** JOE CARAMAGNA
ADDITIONAL INTERIOR ART STELLA GREENVOSS **SHIP CONSULTANT** ELIZA FANTASTIC MOHAN

YOU HAVE BEEN CONTACTED BY THE MINISTRY OF TROUBLE. AWAIT FURTHER INSTRUCTIONS. ☿

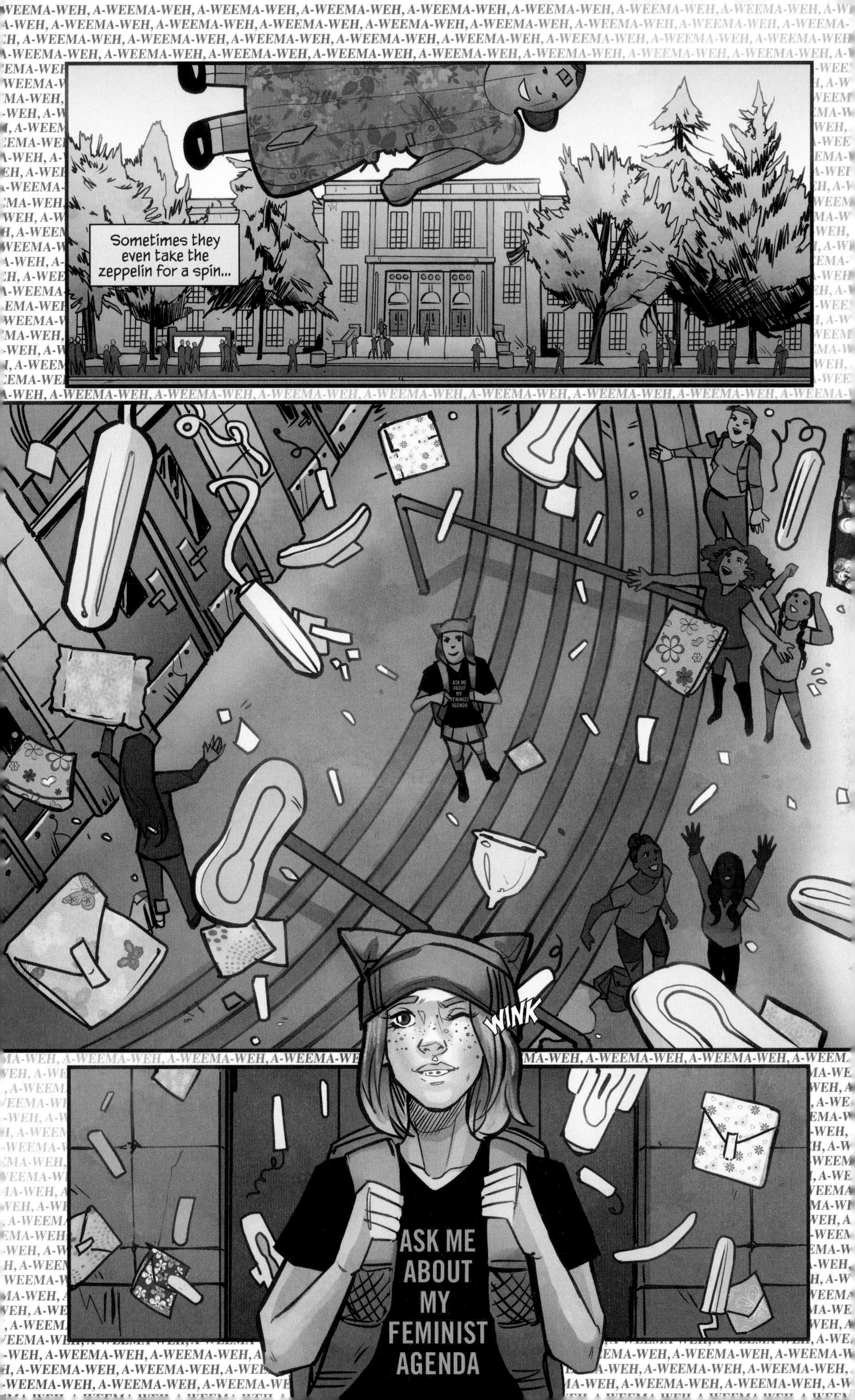
A-WEEMA-WEH, A-WEEMA-WEH, A-WEEMA-WEH, A-WEEMA-WEH, A-WEEMA-WEH, A-WEEMA-WEH
Sometimes they even take the zeppelin for a spin...
ASK ME ABOUT MY FEMINIST AGENDA
WINK
ASK ME ABOUT MY FEMINIST AGENDA

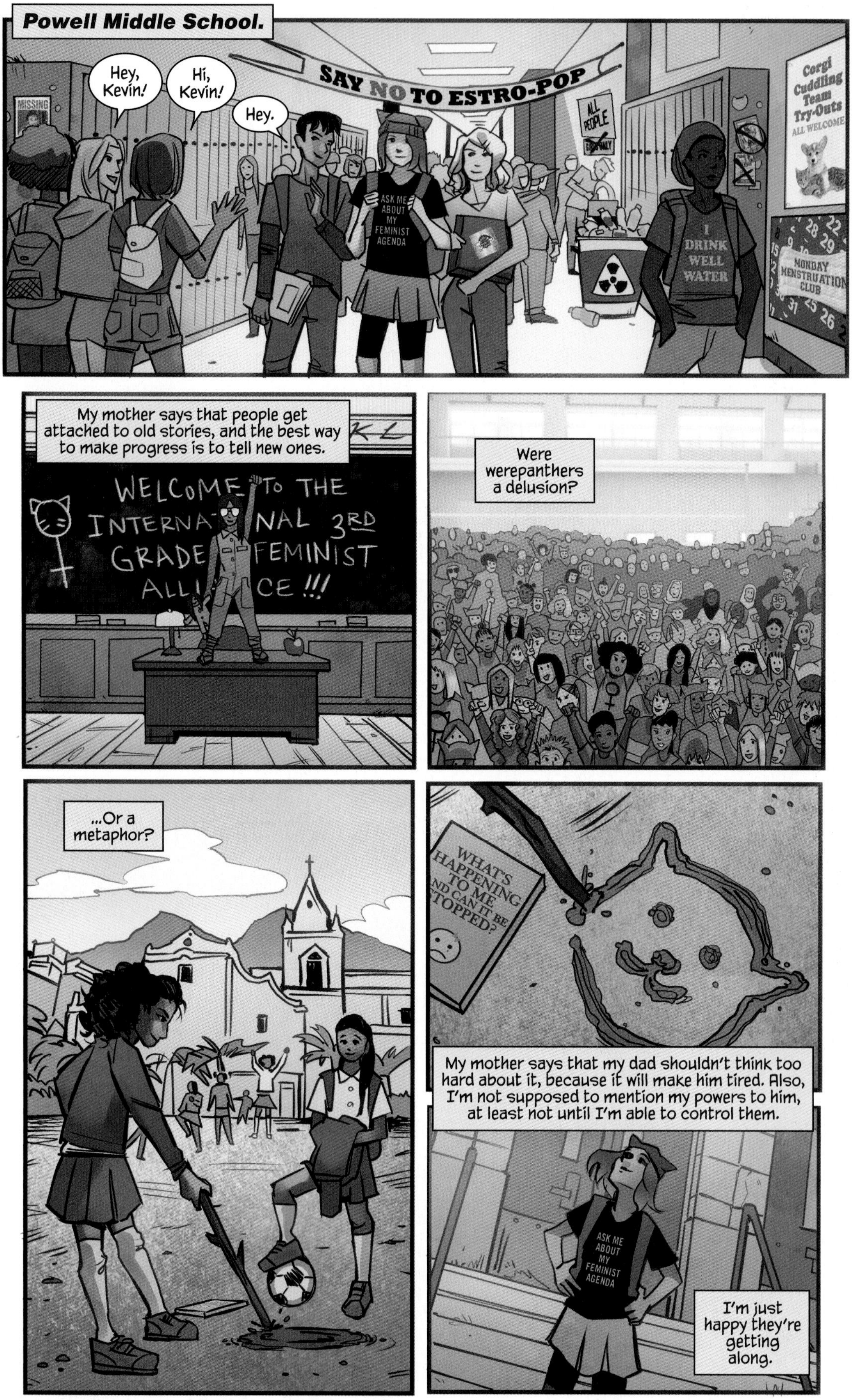
Powell Middle School.
Hey, Kevin!
Hi, Kevin!
Hey.
SAY NO TO ESTRO-POP
MISSING
ALL PEOPLE
ASK ME ABOUT MY FEMINIST AGENDA
I DRINK WELL WATER
Corgi Cuddling Team Try-Outs
ALL WELCOME
MONDAY MENSTRUATION CLUB
My mother says that people get attached to old stories, and the best way to make progress is to tell new ones.
WELCOME TO THE INTERNATIONAL 3RD GRADE FEMINIST ALLIANCE!!!
Were werepanthers a delusion?
...Or a metaphor?
WHAT'S HAPPENING TO ME AND CAN IT BE STOPPED?
My mother says that my dad shouldn't think too hard about it, because it will make him tired. Also, I'm not supposed to mention my powers to him, at least not until I'm able to control them.
ASK ME ABOUT MY FEMINIST AGENDA
I'm just happy they're getting along.

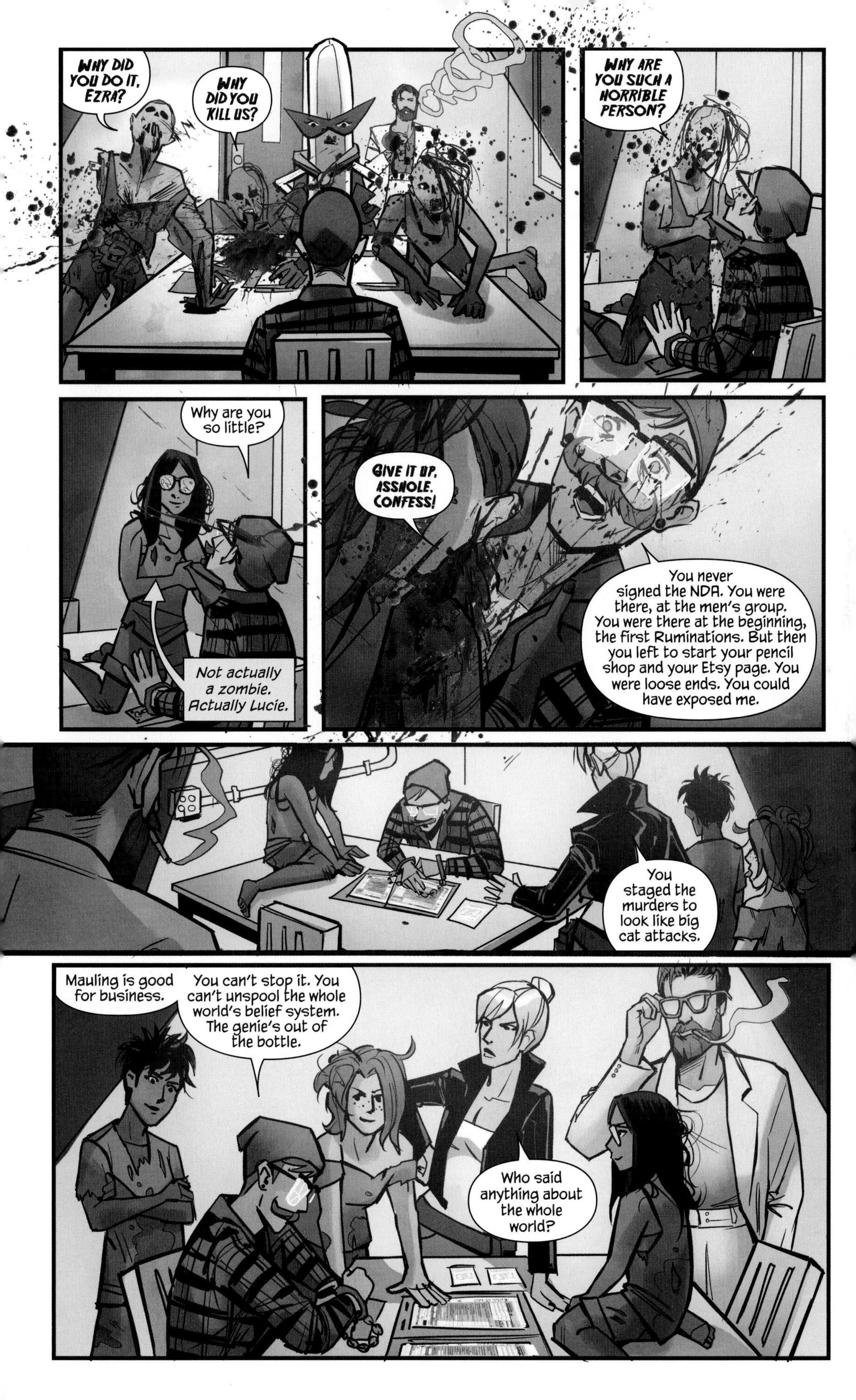
WHY DID YOU DO IT, EZRA?
WHY DID YOU KILL US?
WHY ARE YOU SUCH A HORRIBLE PERSON?
Why are you so little?
Not actually a zombie. Actually Lucie.
GIVE IT UP, ASSHOLE. CONFESS!
You never signed the NDA. You were there, at the men's group. You were there at the beginning, the first Ruminations. But then you left to start your pencil shop and your Etsy page. You were loose ends. You could have exposed me.
You staged the murders to look like big cat attacks.
Mauling is good for business.
You can't stop it. You can't unspool the whole world's belief system. The genie's out of the bottle.
Who said anything about the whole world?

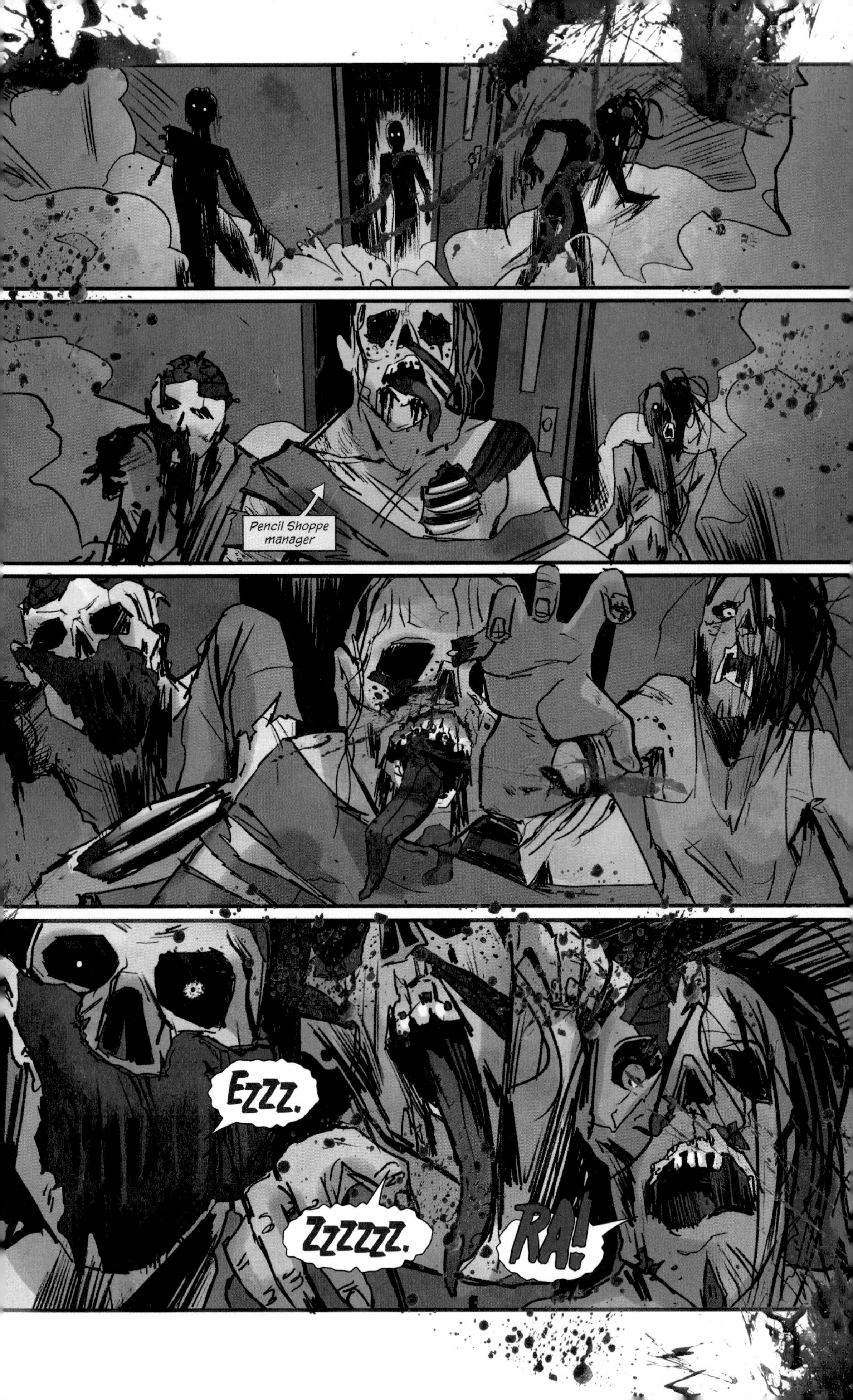
Pencil Shoppe manager
Ezzz.
Zzzzzz.
RA!

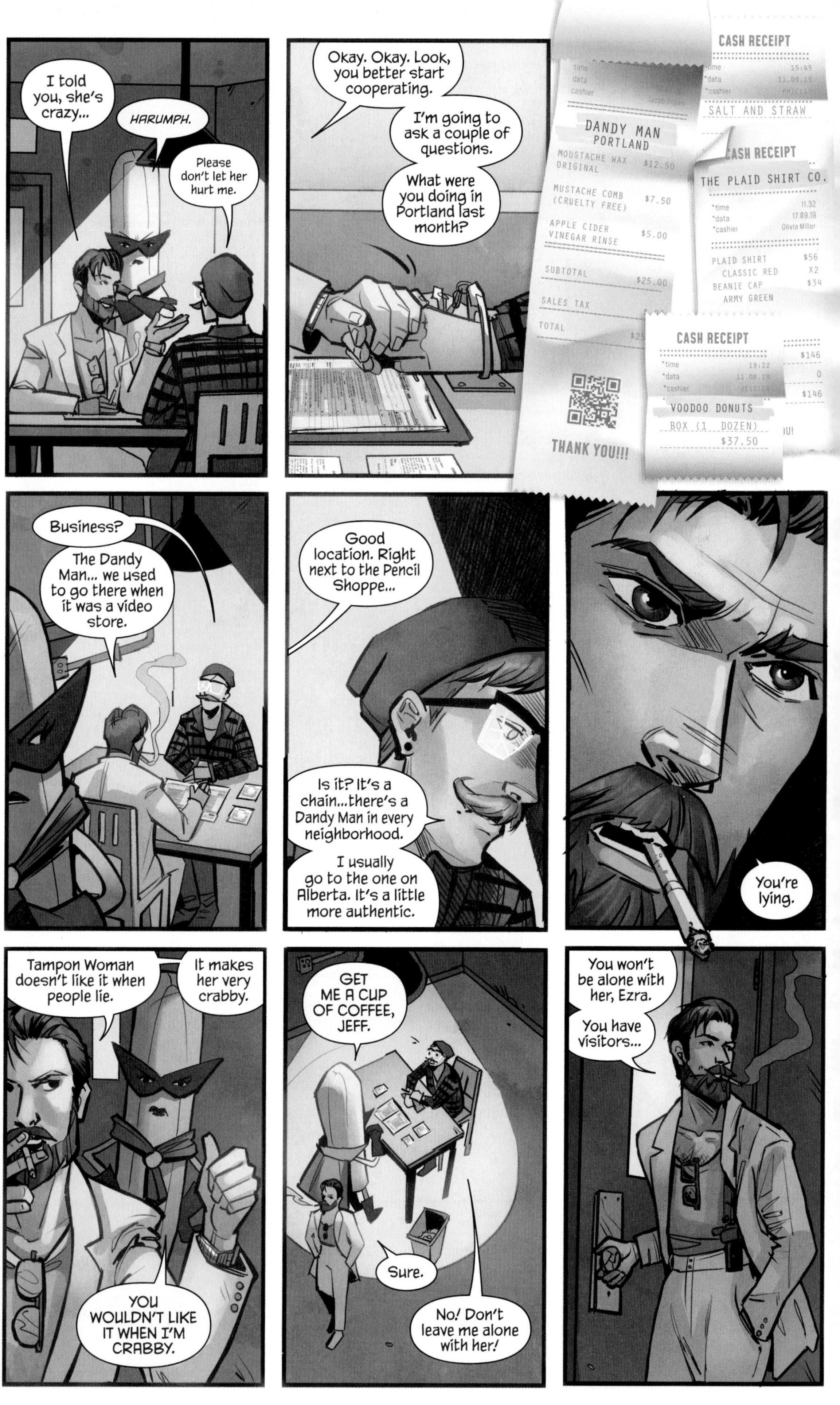
I told you, she's crazy...
HARUMPH.
Please don't let her hurt me.
Okay. Okay. Look, you better start cooperating.
I'm going to ask a couple of questions.
What were you doing in Portland last month?
DANDY MAN PORTLAND
MOUSTACHE WAX ORIGINAL $12.50
MUSTACHE COMB (CRUELTY FREE) $7.50
APPLE CIDER VINEGAR RINSE $5.00
SUBTOTAL $25.00
SALES TAX
TOTAL
THANK YOU!!!
CASH RECEIPT
time 15:45
data 11.09.19
cashier
SALT AND STRAW
CASH RECEIPT
THE PLAID SHIRT CO.
time 11.32
data 17.09.19
cashier Olivia Miller
PLAID SHIRT $56
CLASSIC RED X2
BEANIE CAP $34
ARMY GREEN
$146
0
$146
CASH RECEIPT
time 19:22
data 11.08.19
cashier
VOODOO DONUTS
BOX (1 DOZEN)
$37.50
Business?
The Dandy Man... we used to go there when it was a video store.
Good location. Right next to the Pencil Shoppe...
Is it? It's a chain...there's a Dandy Man in every neighborhood.
I usually go to the one on Alberta. It's a little more authentic.
You're lying.
Tampon Woman doesn't like it when people lie.
It makes her very crabby.
YOU WOULDN'T LIKE IT WHEN I'M CRABBY.
GET ME A CUP OF COFFEE, JEFF.
Sure.
No! Don't leave me alone with her!
You won't be alone with her, Ezra.
You have visitors...

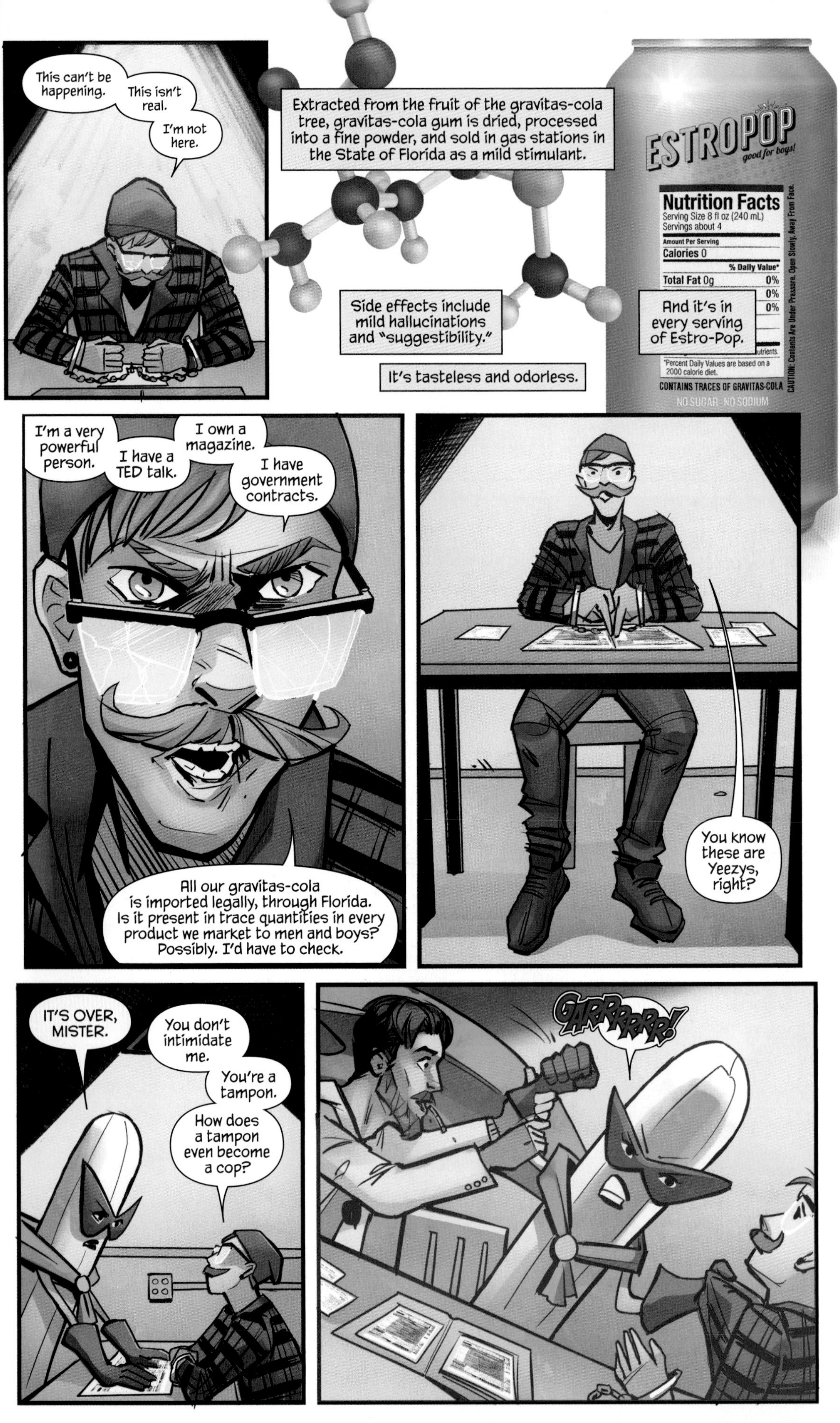
This can't be happening.
This isn't real.
I'm not here.
Extracted from the fruit of the gravitas-cola tree, gravitas-cola gum is dried, processed into a fine powder, and sold in gas stations in the State of Florida as a mild stimulant.
ESTROPOP
good for boys!
Nutrition Facts
Serving Size 8 fl oz (240 mL)
Servings about 4
Amount Per Serving
Calories 0
% Daily Value*
Total Fat 0g 0%
0%
0%
*Percent Daily Values are based on a 2000 calorie diet.
CONTAINS TRACES OF GRAVITAS-COLA
NO SUGAR NO SODIUM
CAUTION: Contents Are Under Pressure. Open Slowly, Away From Face.
Side effects include mild hallucinations and "suggestibility."
And it's in every serving of Estro-Pop.
It's tasteless and odorless.
I'm a very powerful person.
I have a TED talk.
I own a magazine.
I have government contracts.
All our gravitas-cola is imported legally, through Florida. Is it present in trace quantities in every product we market to men and boys? Possibly. I'd have to check.
You know these are Yeezys, right?
IT'S OVER, MISTER.
You don't intimidate me.
You're a tampon.
How does a tampon even become a cop?
GARRRRRR!

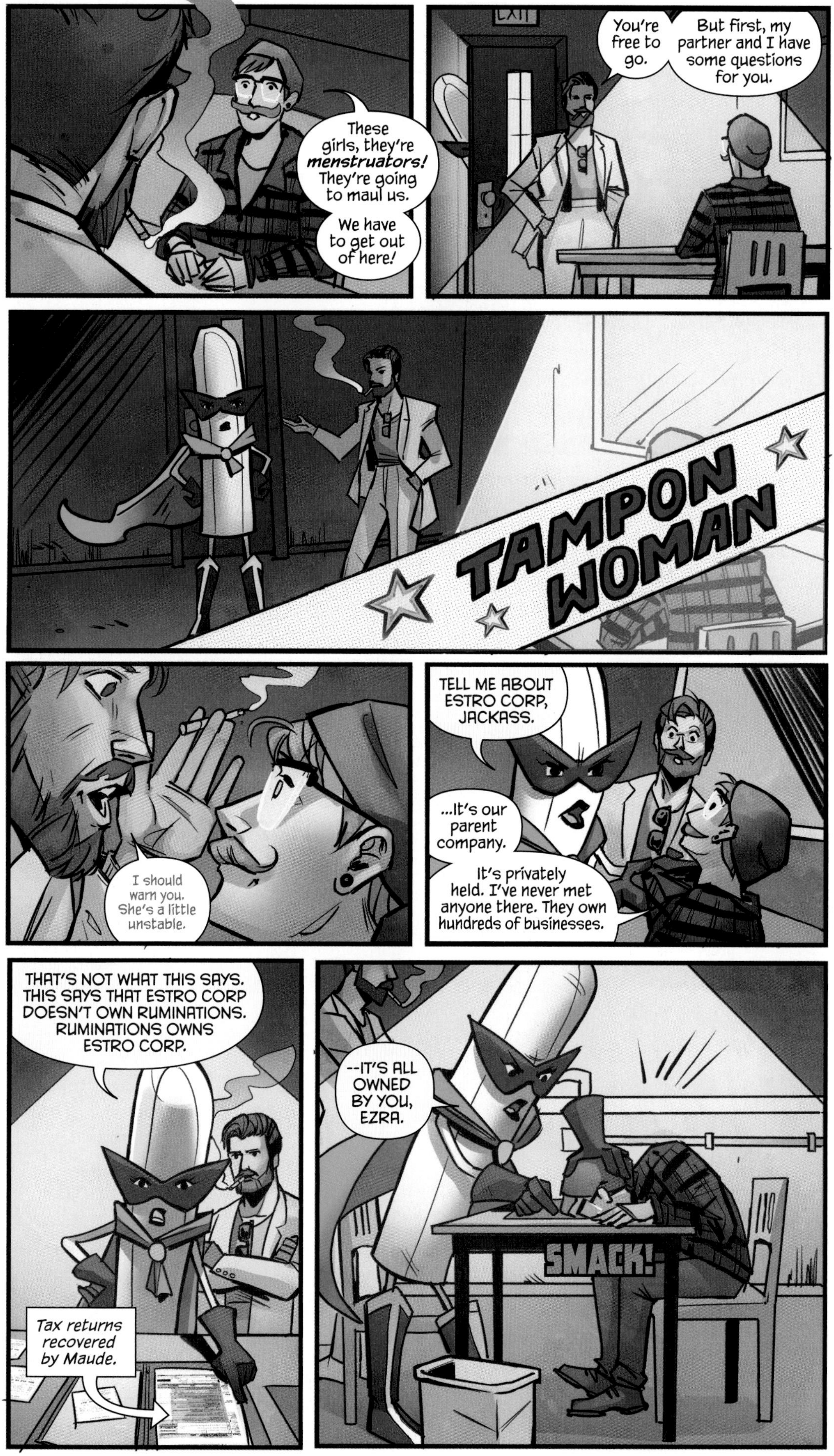
These girls, they're *menstruators!* They're going to maul us.
We have to get out of here!
EXIT
You're free to go.
But first, my partner and I have some questions for you.
TAMPON WOMAN
I should warn you. She's a little unstable.
TELL ME ABOUT ESTRO CORP, JACKASS.
...It's our parent company.
It's privately held. I've never met anyone there. They own hundreds of businesses.
THAT'S NOT WHAT THIS SAYS. THIS SAYS THAT ESTRO CORP DOESN'T OWN RUMINATIONS. RUMINATIONS OWNS ESTRO CORP.
Tax returns recovered by Maude.
--IT'S ALL OWNED BY YOU, EZRA.
SMACK!

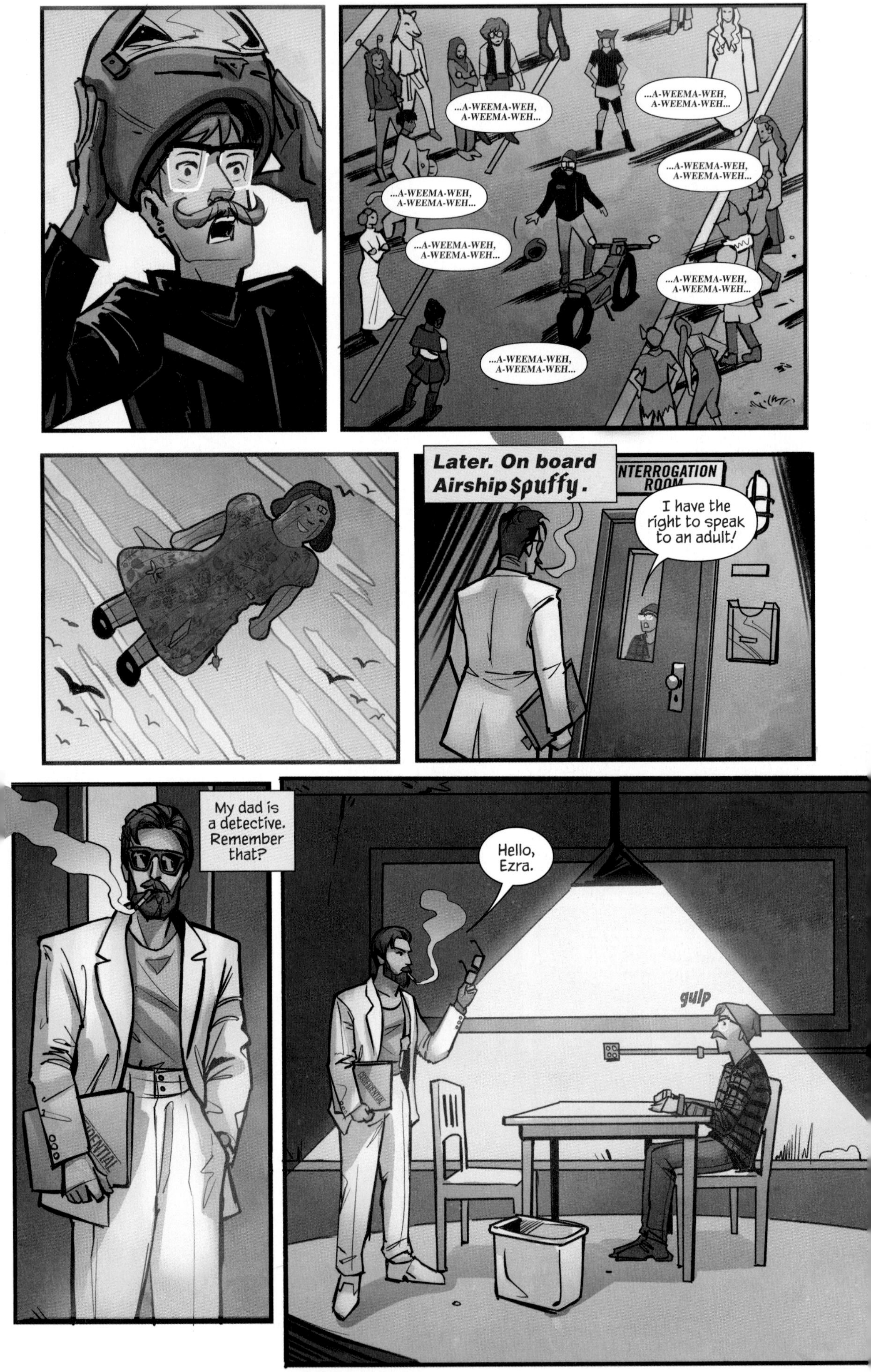
...A-WEEMA-WEH, A-WEEMA-WEH...
...A-WEEMA-WEH, A-WEEMA-WEH...
...A-WEEMA-WEH, A-WEEMA-WEH...
...A-WEEMA-WEH, A-WEEMA-WEH...
...A-WEEMA-WEH, A-WEEMA-WEH...
...A-WEEMA-WEH, A-WEEMA-WEH...
...A-WEEMA-WEH, A-WEEMA-WEH...
Later. On board Airship Spuffy.
INTERROGATION ROOM
I have the right to speak to an adult!
My dad is a detective. Remember that?
Hello, Ezra.
gulp

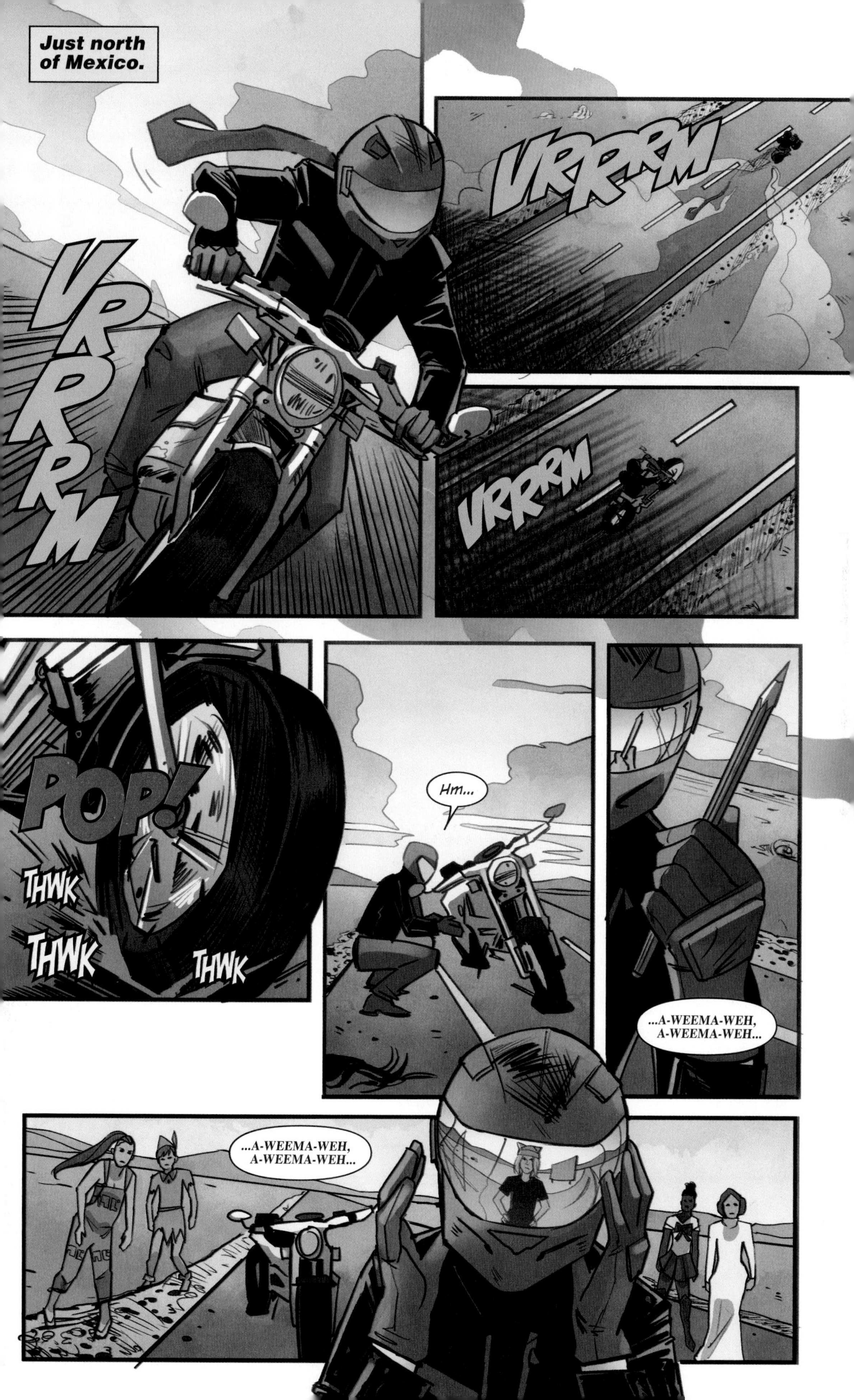

Just north of Mexico.
VRRRM
VRRRM
VRRRM
POP!
THWK
THWK
THWK
Hm...
...A-WEEMA-WEH, A-WEEMA-WEH...
...A-WEEMA-WEH, A-WEEMA-WEH...

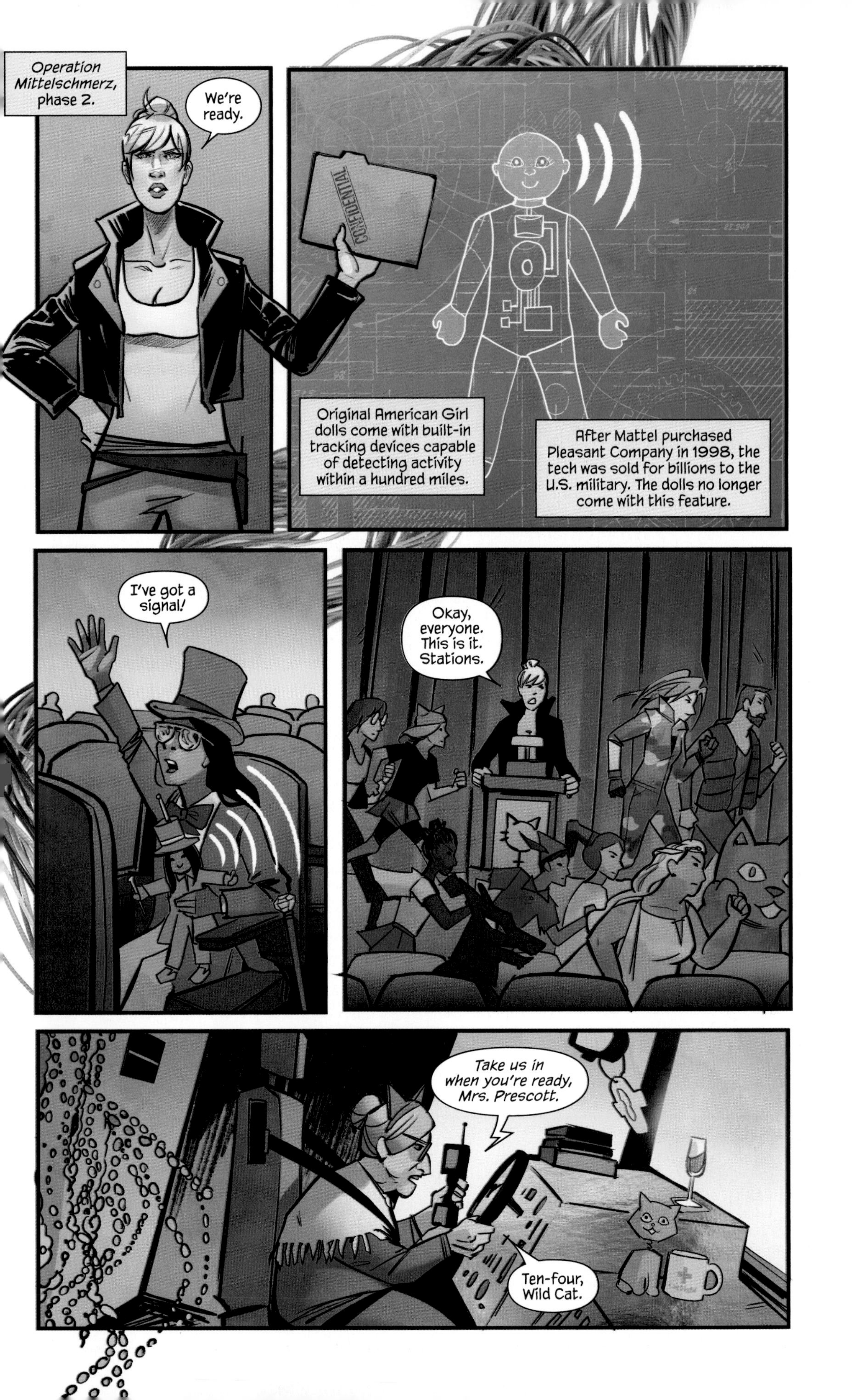
Operation Mittelschmerz, phase 2.
We're ready.
CONFIDENTIAL
Original American Girl dolls come with built-in tracking devices capable of detecting activity within a hundred miles.
After Mattel purchased Pleasant Company in 1998, the tech was sold for billions to the U.S. military. The dolls no longer come with this feature.
I've got a signal!
Okay, everyone. This is it. Stations.
Take us in when you're ready, Mrs. Prescott.
Ten-four, Wild Cat.

ESTRO CORP
GLOBAL

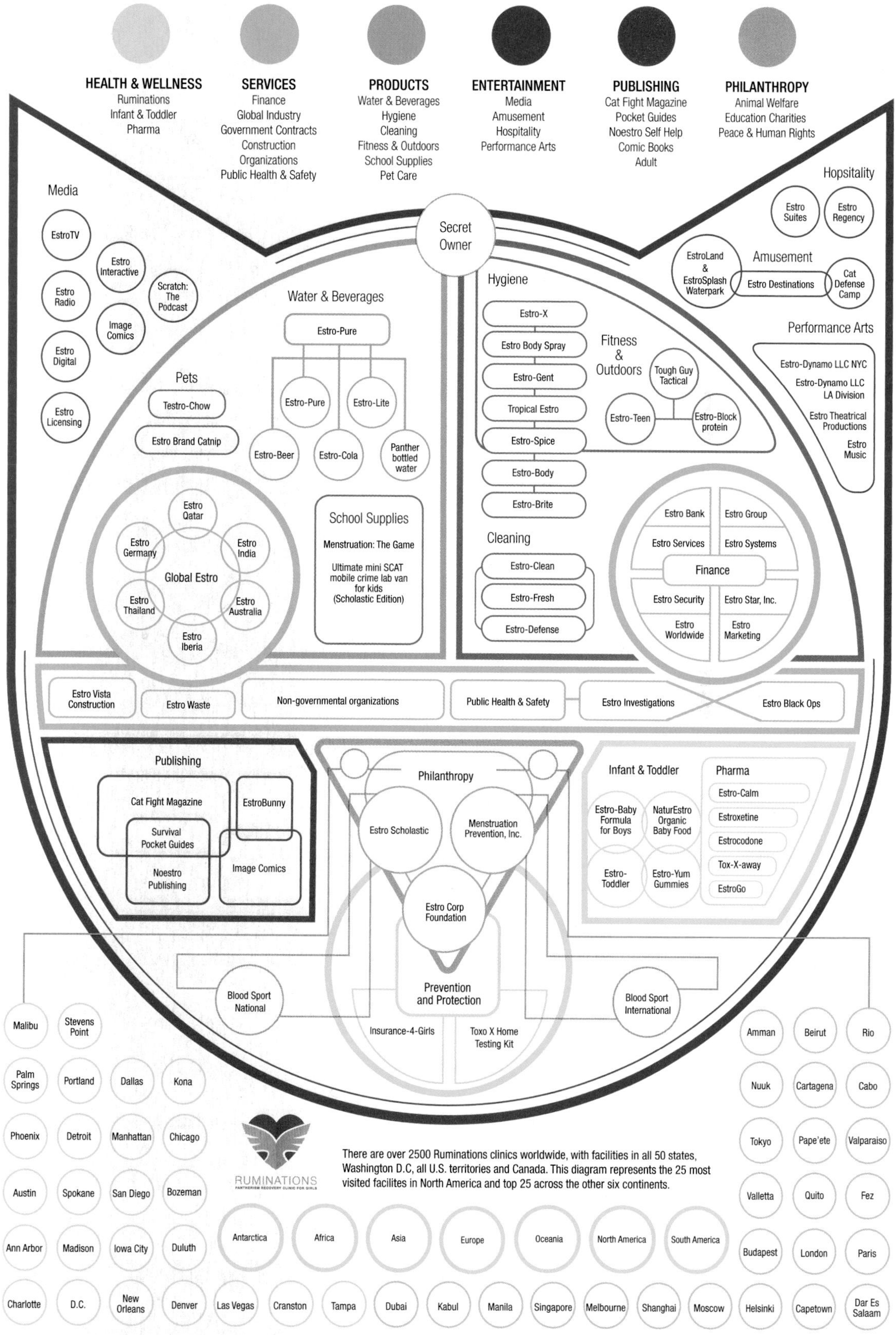
HEALTH & WELLNESS
Ruminations
Infant & Toddler
Pharma
SERVICES
Finance
Global Industry
Government Contracts
Construction
Organizations
Public Health & Safety
PRODUCTS
Water & Beverages
Hygiene
Cleaning
Fitness & Outdoors
School Supplies
Pet Care
ENTERTAINMENT
Media
Amusement
Hospitality
Performance Arts
PUBLISHING
Cat Fight Magazine
Pocket Guides
Noestro Self Help
Comic Books
Adult
PHILANTHROPY
Animal Welfare
Education Charities
Peace & Human Rights
Media
EstroTV
Estro Interactive
Estro Radio
Scratch: The Podcast
Image Comics
Estro Digital
Estro Licensing
Secret Owner
Hopsitality
Estro Suites
Estro Regency
EstroLand & EstroSplash Waterpark
Amusement
Estro Destinations
Cat Defense Camp
Performance Arts
Estro-Dynamo LLC NYC
Estro-Dynamo LLC LA Division
Estro Theatrical Productions
Estro Music
Water & Beverages
Estro-Pure
Estro-Pure
Estro-Lite
Estro-Beer
Estro-Cola
Panther bottled water
Pets
Testro-Chow
Estro Brand Catnip
Hygiene
Estro-X
Estro Body Spray
Estro-Gent
Tropical Estro
Estro-Spice
Estro-Body
Estro-Brite
Fitness & Outdoors
Tough Guy Tactical
Estro-Teen
Estro-Block protein
Estro Qatar
Estro Germany
Estro India
Global Estro
Estro Thailand
Estro Australia
Estro Iberia
School Supplies
Menstruation: The Game
Ultimate mini SCAT mobile crime lab van for kids (Scholastic Edition)
Cleaning
Estro-Clean
Estro-Fresh
Estro-Defense
Estro Bank
Estro Group
Estro Services
Estro Systems
Finance
Estro Security
Estro Star, Inc.
Estro Worldwide
Estro Marketing
Estro Vista Construction
Estro Waste
Non-governmental organizations
Public Health & Safety
Estro Investigations
Estro Black Ops
Publishing
Cat Fight Magazine
EstroBunny
Survival Pocket Guides
Noestro Publishing
Image Comics
Philanthropy
Estro Scholastic
Menstruation Prevention, Inc.
Estro Corp Foundation
Prevention and Protection
Insurance-4-Girls
Toxo X Home Testing Kit
Infant & Toddler
Estro-Baby Formula for Boys
NaturEstro Organic Baby Food
Estro-Toddler
Estro-Yum Gummies
Pharma
Estro-Calm
Estroxetine
Estrocodone
Tox-X-away
EstroGo
Blood Sport National
Blood Sport International
Malibu
Stevens Point
Palm Springs
Portland
Dallas
Kona
Phoenix
Detroit
Manhattan
Chicago
Austin
Spokane
San Diego
Bozeman
Ann Arbor
Madison
Iowa City
Duluth
Charlotte
D.C.
New Orleans
Denver
Amman
Beirut
Rio
Nuuk
Cartagena
Cabo
Tokyo
Pape'ete
Valparaiso
Valletta
Quito
Fez
Budapest
London
Paris
RUMINATIONS
There are over 2500 Ruminations clinics worldwide, with facilities in all 50 states, Washington D.C, all U.S. territories and Canada. This diagram represents the 25 most visited facilites in North America and top 25 across the other six continents.
Antarctica
Africa
Asia
Europe
Oceania
North America
South America
Las Vegas
Cranston
Tampa
Dubai
Kabul
Manila
Singapore
Melbourne
Shanghai
Moscow
Helsinki
Capetown
Dar Es Salaam

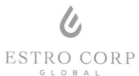

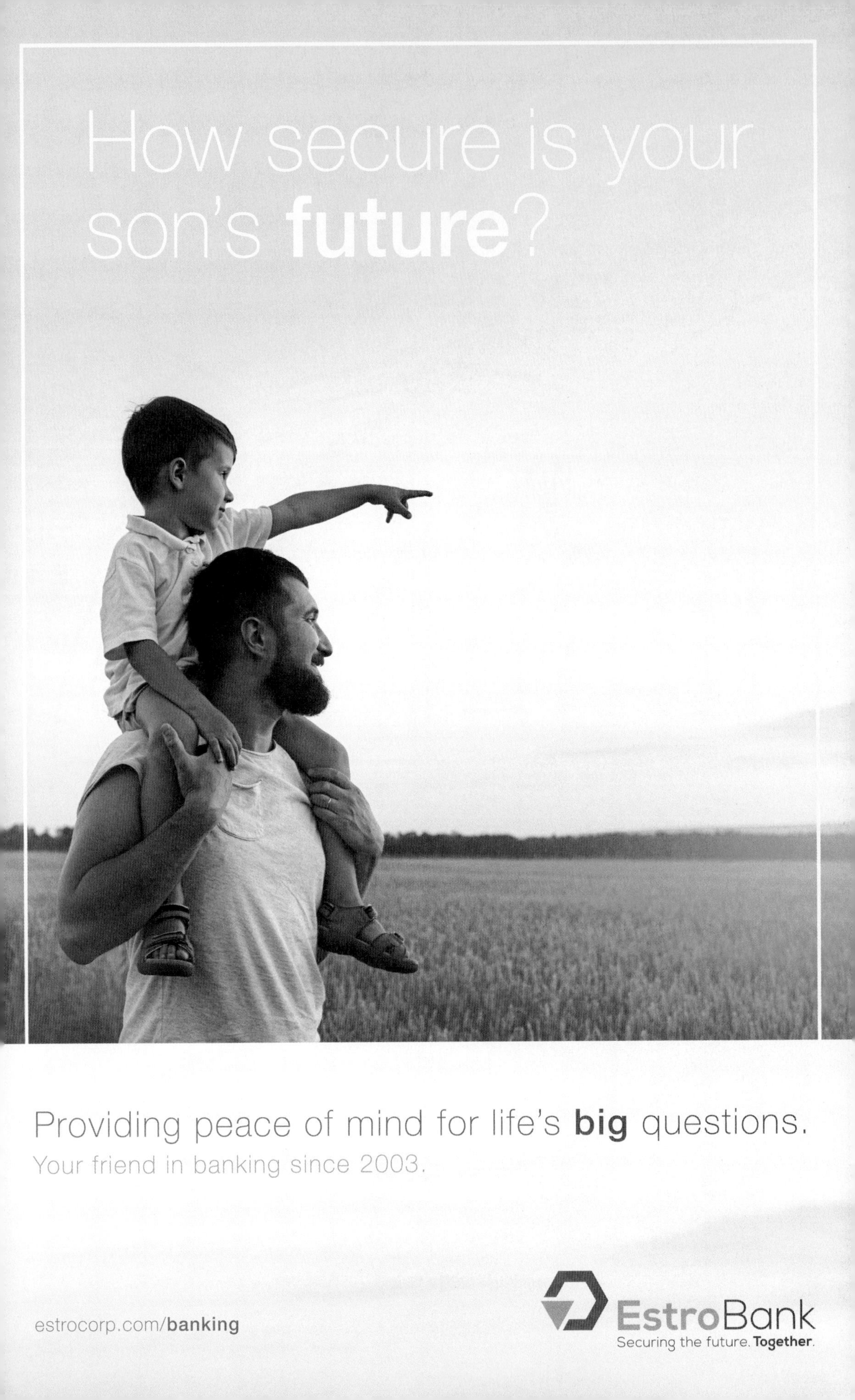
How secure is your son's **future**?
Providing peace of mind for life's **big** questions.
Your friend in banking since 2003.
estrocorp.com/**banking**
EstroBank
Securing the future. **Together**.

plot recap by kevin

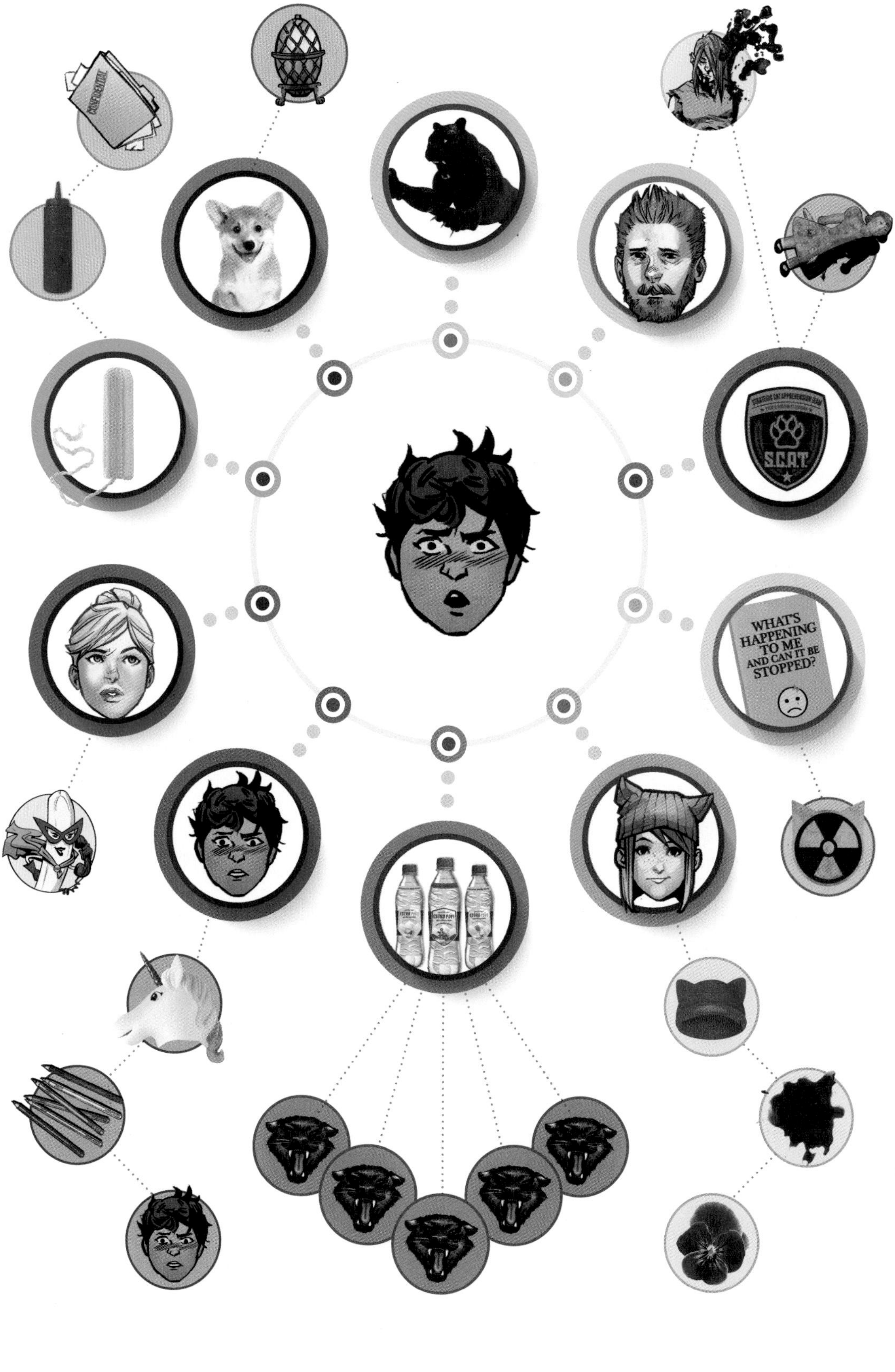
S.C.A.T.
WHAT'S HAPPENING TO ME AND CAN IT BE STOPPED?

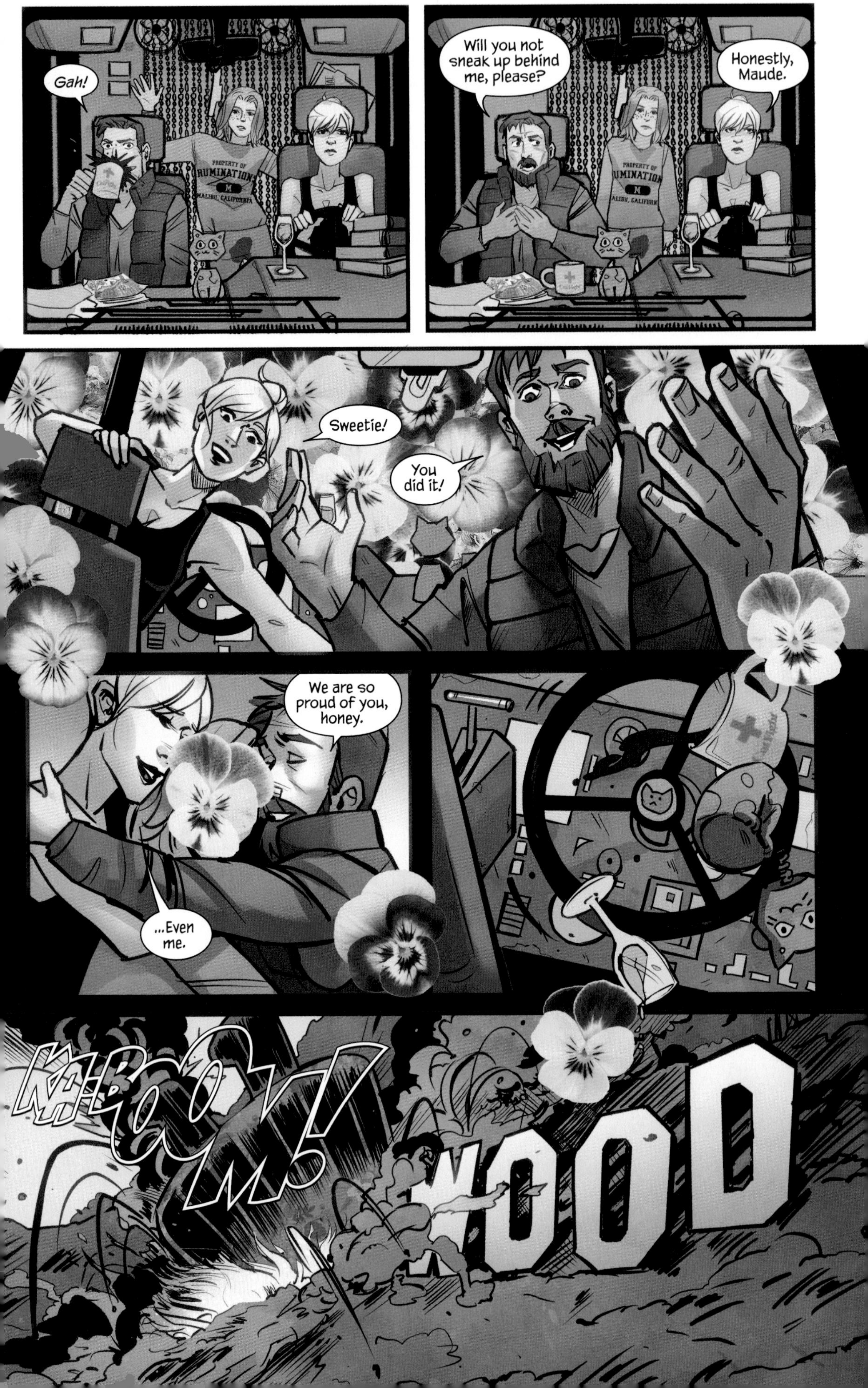
Gah!
PROPERTY OF
RUMINATION
M
MALIBU, CALIFORNIA
Will you not sneak up behind me, please?
Honestly, Maude.
Sweetie!
You did it!
We are so proud of you, honey.
...Even me.
KA-BOOM!
WOOD

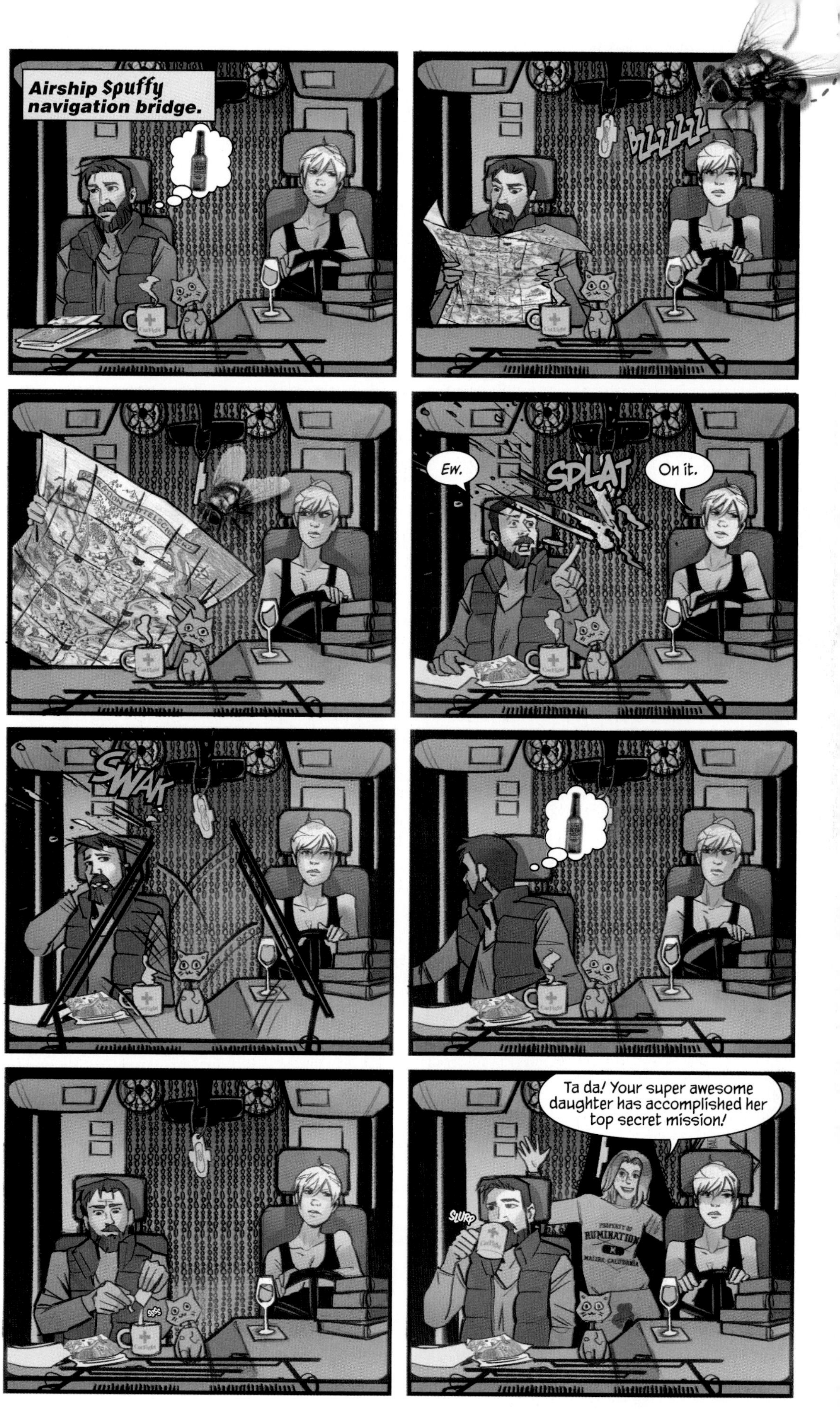
Airship $puffy navigation bridge.
BZZZZZZ
Ew.
SPLAT
On it.
SWAK
SSSS
Ta da! Your super awesome daughter has accomplished her top secret mission!
SLURP
PROPERTY OF
RUMINATION
MALIBU, CALIFORNIA

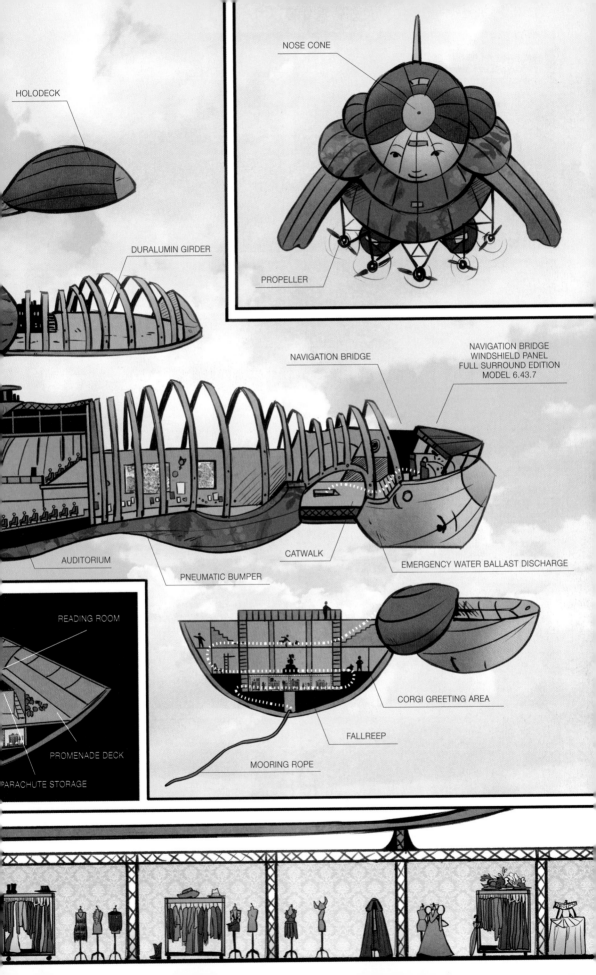

HOLODECK

NOSE CONE

PROPELLER

DURALUMIN GIRDER

NAVIGATION BRIDGE

NAVIGATION BRIDGE
WINDSHIELD PANEL
FULL SURROUND EDITION
MODEL 6.43.7

AUDITORIUM

PNEUMATIC BUMPER

CATWALK

EMERGENCY WATER BALLAST DISCHARGE

READING ROOM

PROMENADE DECK

PARACHUTE STORAGE

CORGI GREETING AREA

FALLREEP

MOORING ROPE

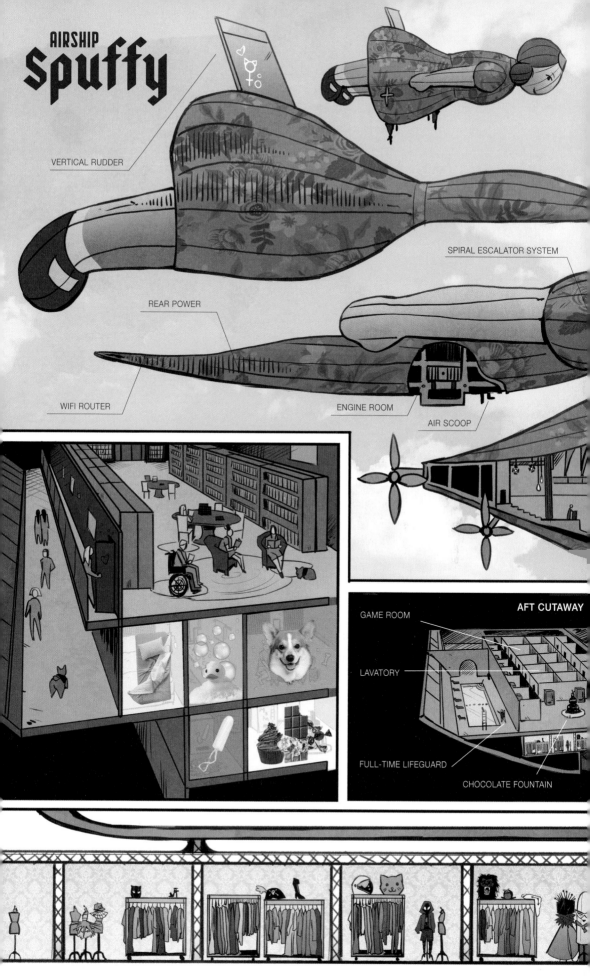

AIRSHIP
Spuffy

VERTICAL RUDDER

SPIRAL ESCALATOR SYSTEM

REAR POWER

WIFI ROUTER

ENGINE ROOM

AIR SCOOP

AFT CUTAWAY

GAME ROOM

LAVATORY

FULL-TIME LIFEGUARD

CHOCOLATE FOUNTAIN

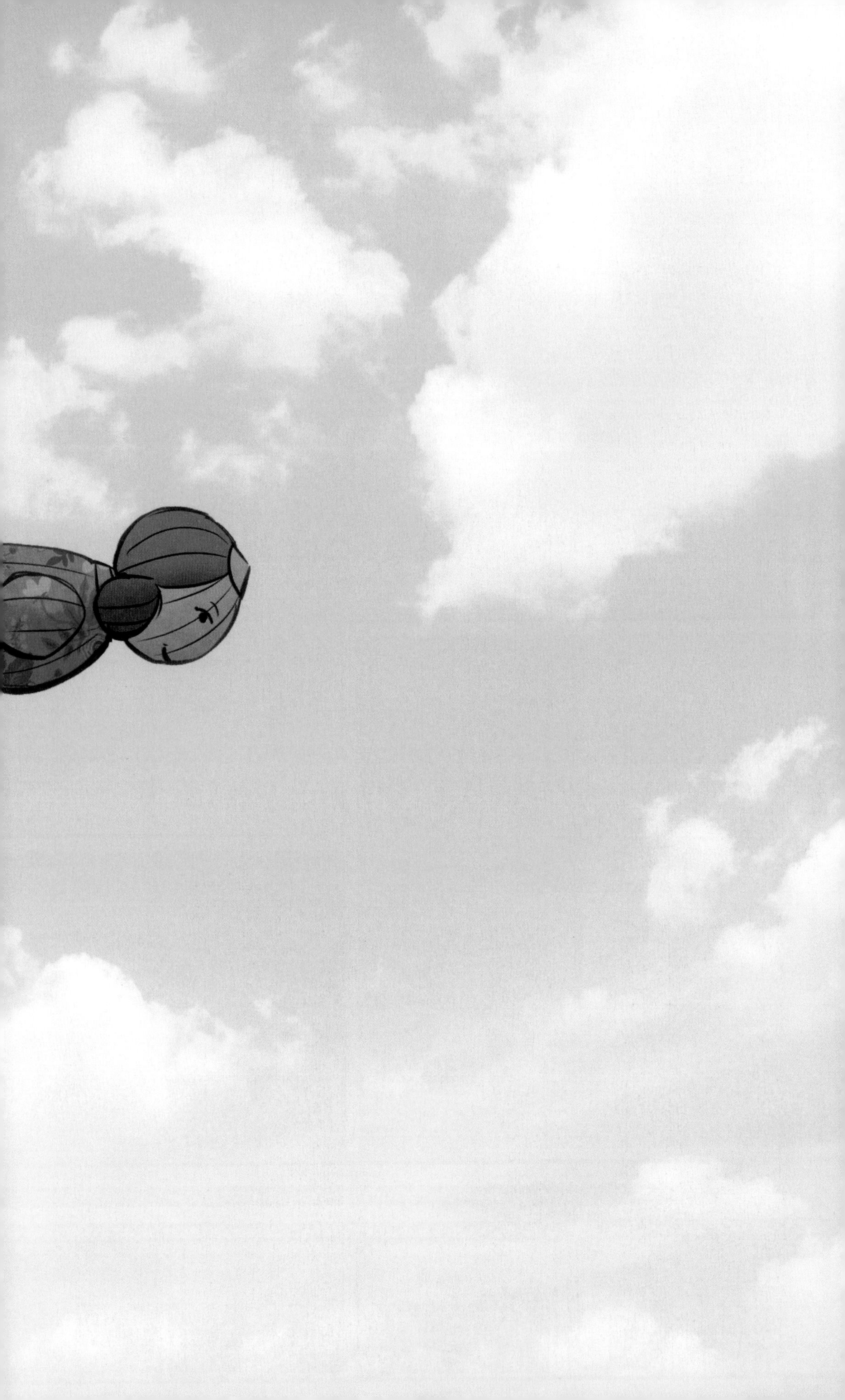

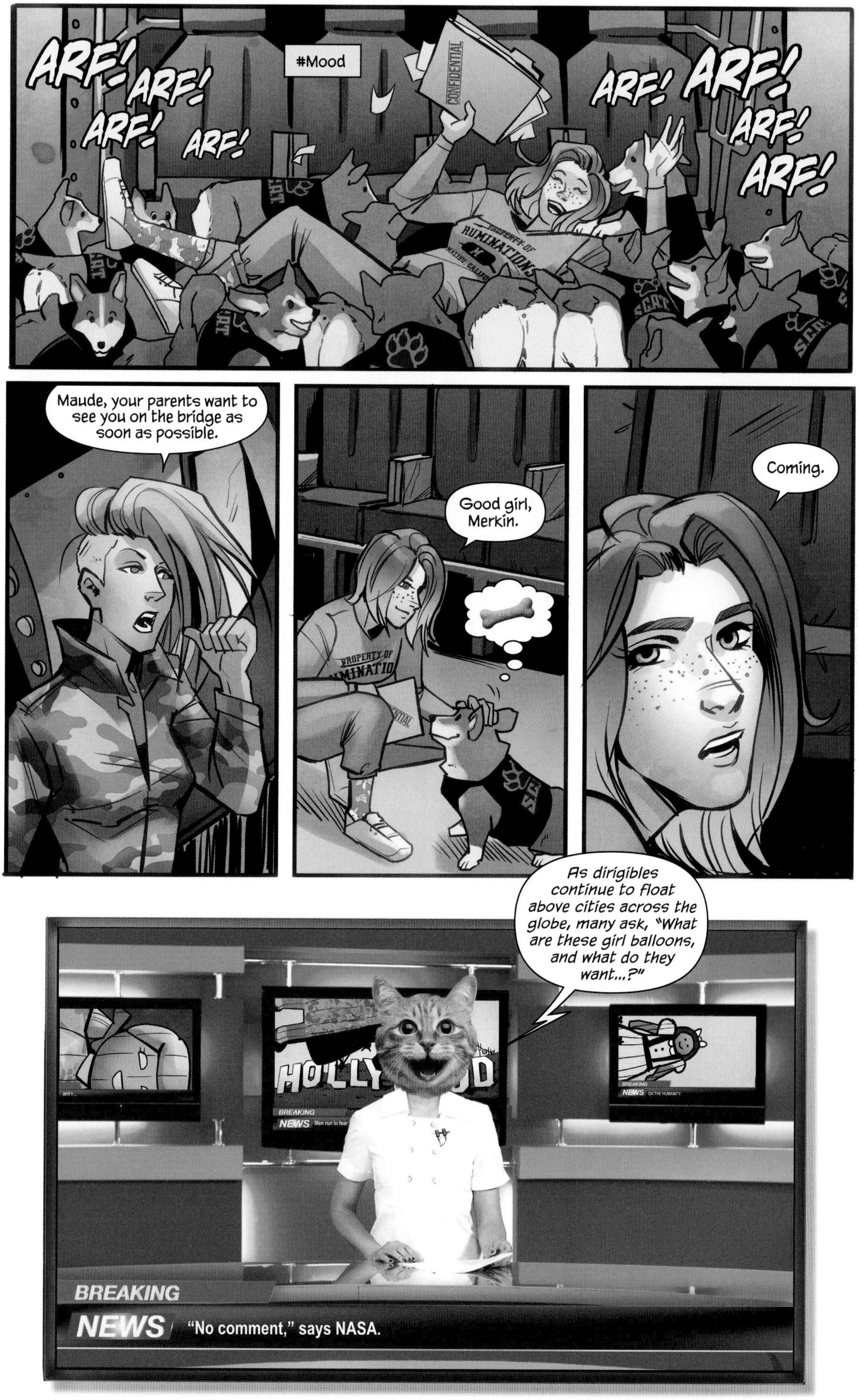
ARF! ARF!
ARF! ARF!
#Mood
CONFIDENTIAL
ARF! ARF!
ARF!
ARF!
PROPERTY OF RUMINATIONS
Maude, your parents want to see you on the bridge as soon as possible.
Good girl, Merkin.
Coming.
As dirigibles continue to float above cities across the globe, many ask, "What are these girl balloons, and what do they want...?"
HOLLY OD
BREAKING NEWS Men run in fear
BREAKING NEWS OH THE HUMANITY.
BREAKING
NEWS "No comment," says NASA.

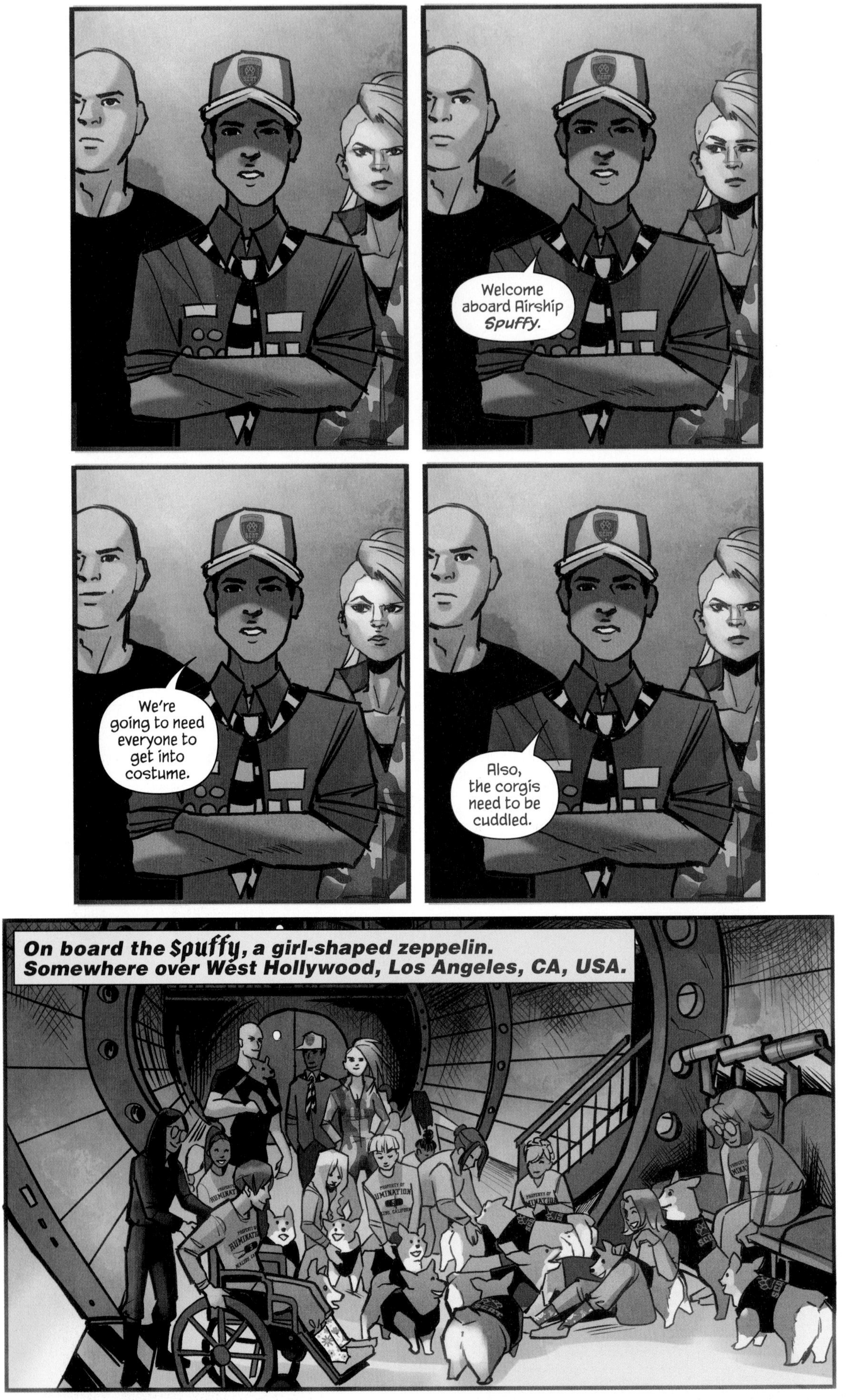
Welcome aboard Airship Spuffy.
We're going to need everyone to get into costume.
Also, the corgis need to be cuddled.
On board the Spuffy, a girl-shaped zeppelin. Somewhere over West Hollywood, Los Angeles, CA, USA.

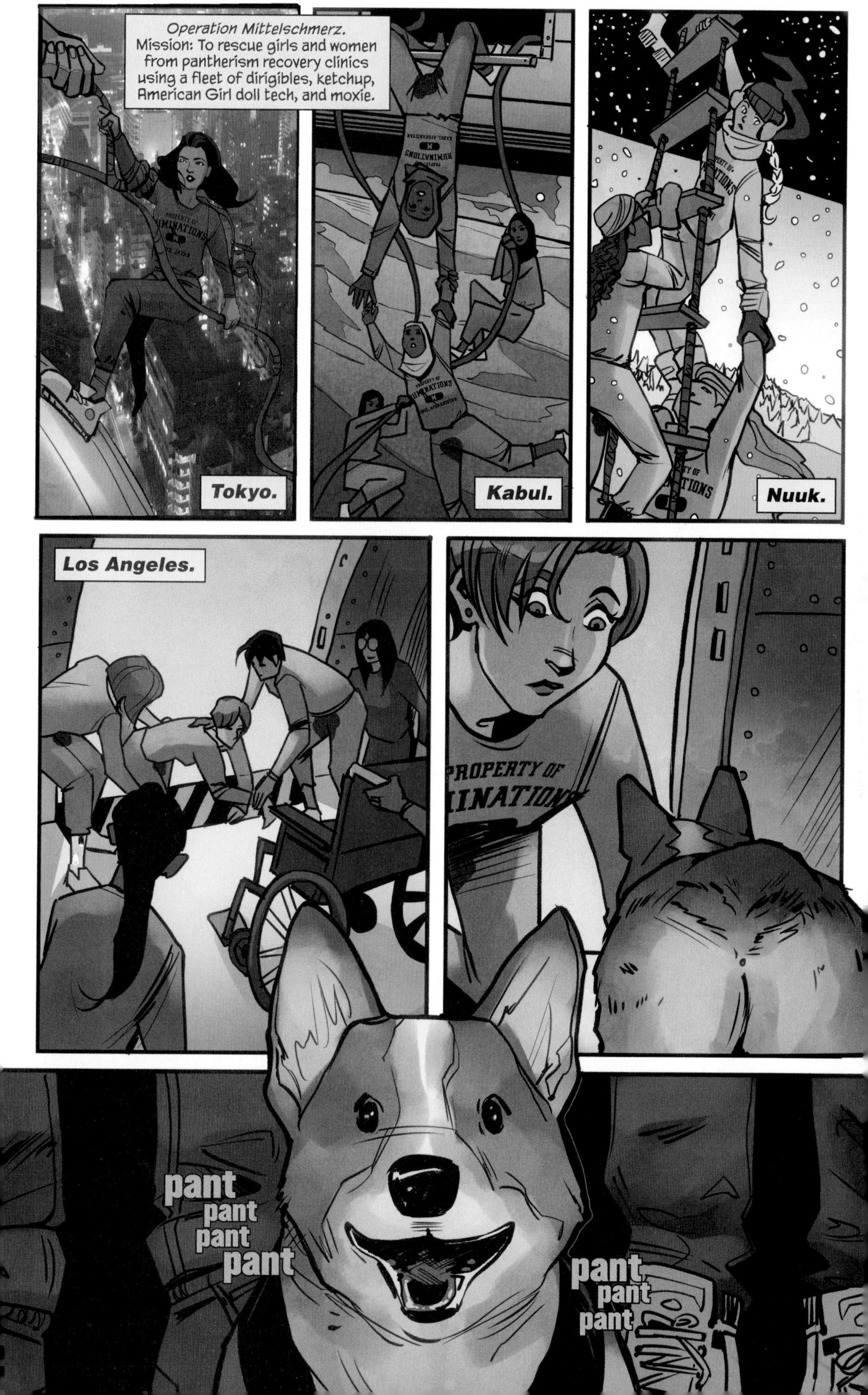

Operation Mittelschmerz.
Mission: To rescue girls and women from pantherism recovery clinics using a fleet of dirigibles, ketchup, American Girl doll tech, and moxie.
Tokyo.
Kabul.
Nuuk.
Los Angeles.
pant pant pant pant
pant, pant pant

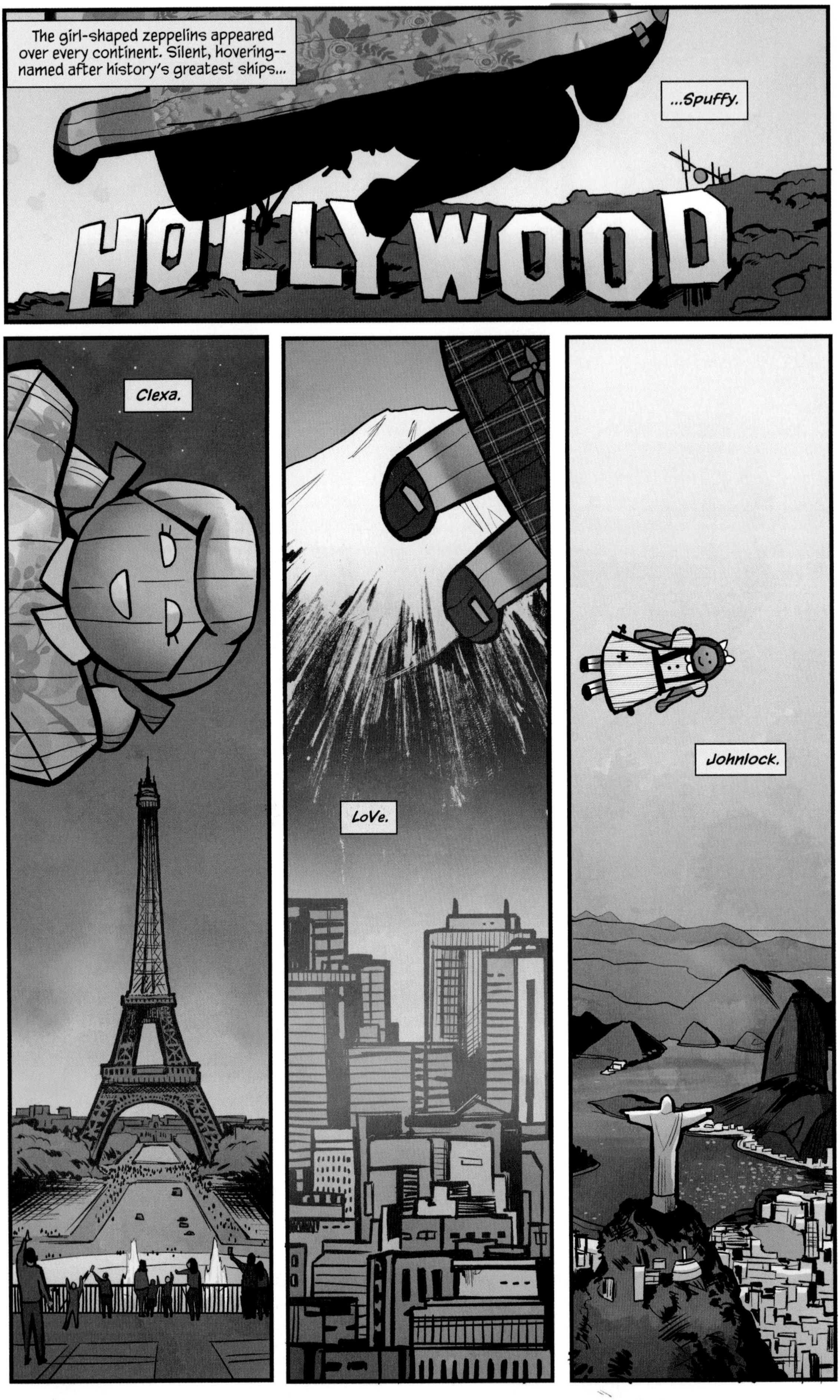
The girl-shaped zeppelins appeared over every continent. Silent, hovering--named after history's greatest ships...
...Spuffy.
HOLLYWOOD
Clexa.
LoVe.
Johnlock.

PRODUCT SAFETY RECALL

ESTRO-YUM!™ VITAMIN GUMMIES FOR BOYS
PRODUCT #47639887207

CHOKING HAZARD

Some customers have choked to death while consuming this product. Other have reported significant head and neck injuries.

Be aware that the green Estro-Yum! gummies do contain trace amounts of arsenic and may irritate arsenic-sensitive individuals.

Estro-Yum! products are manufactured in a factory that contains asbestos.

If an Estro-Yum! becomes lodged in your trachea, attempt to get someone's attention, and request assistance. Restore oxygen flow as soon as possible to prevent brain injury.

Estro-Yum gummies can be returned to point of purchase and exchanged for another Estro-Corp product of equal or lesser value.

Attn: Girls and Women. This product is tested on, and manufactured for, boys. Girls and women should not consume it. If you come into contact with this product, wash hands immediately, then induce vomiting.

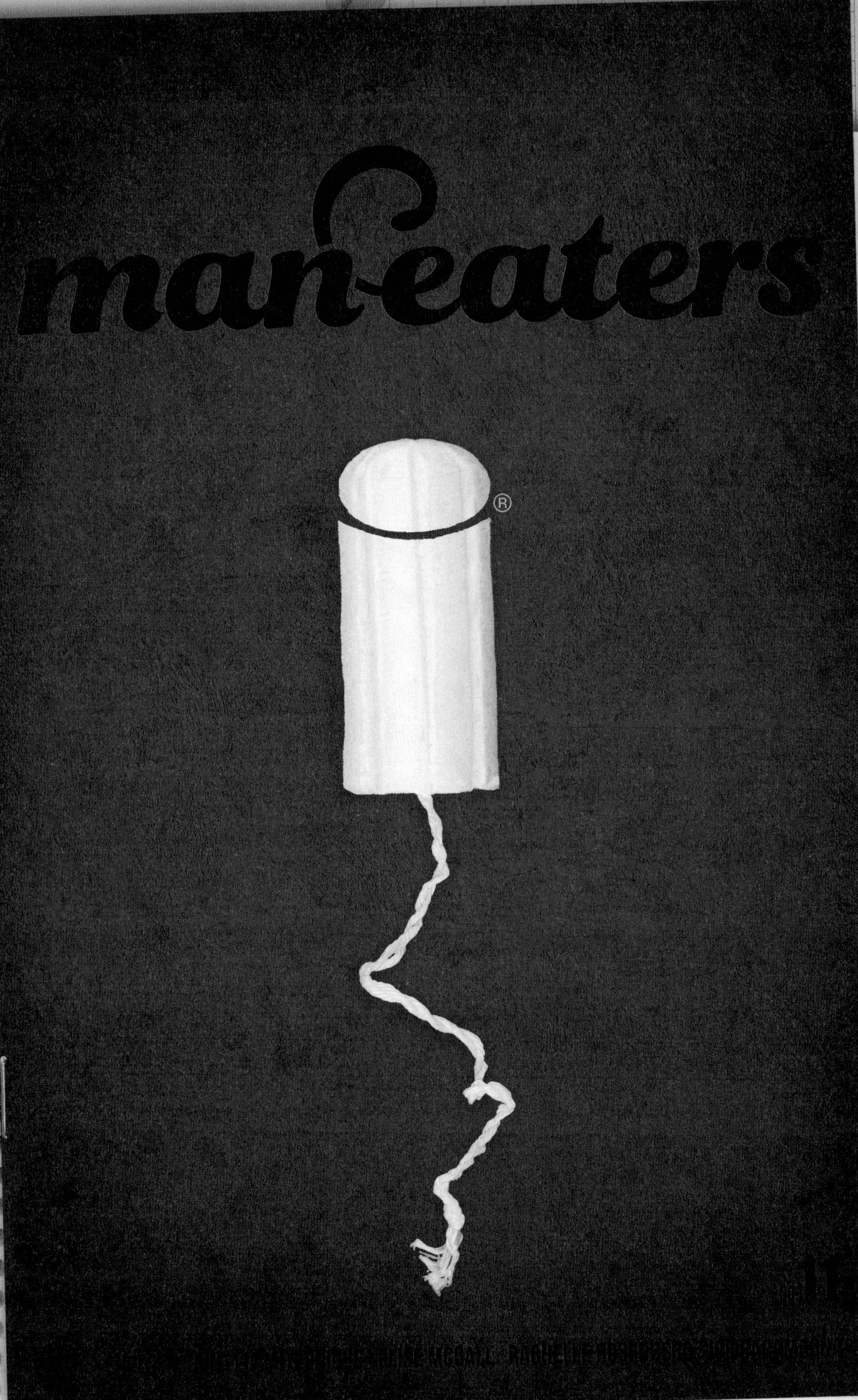
man-eaters

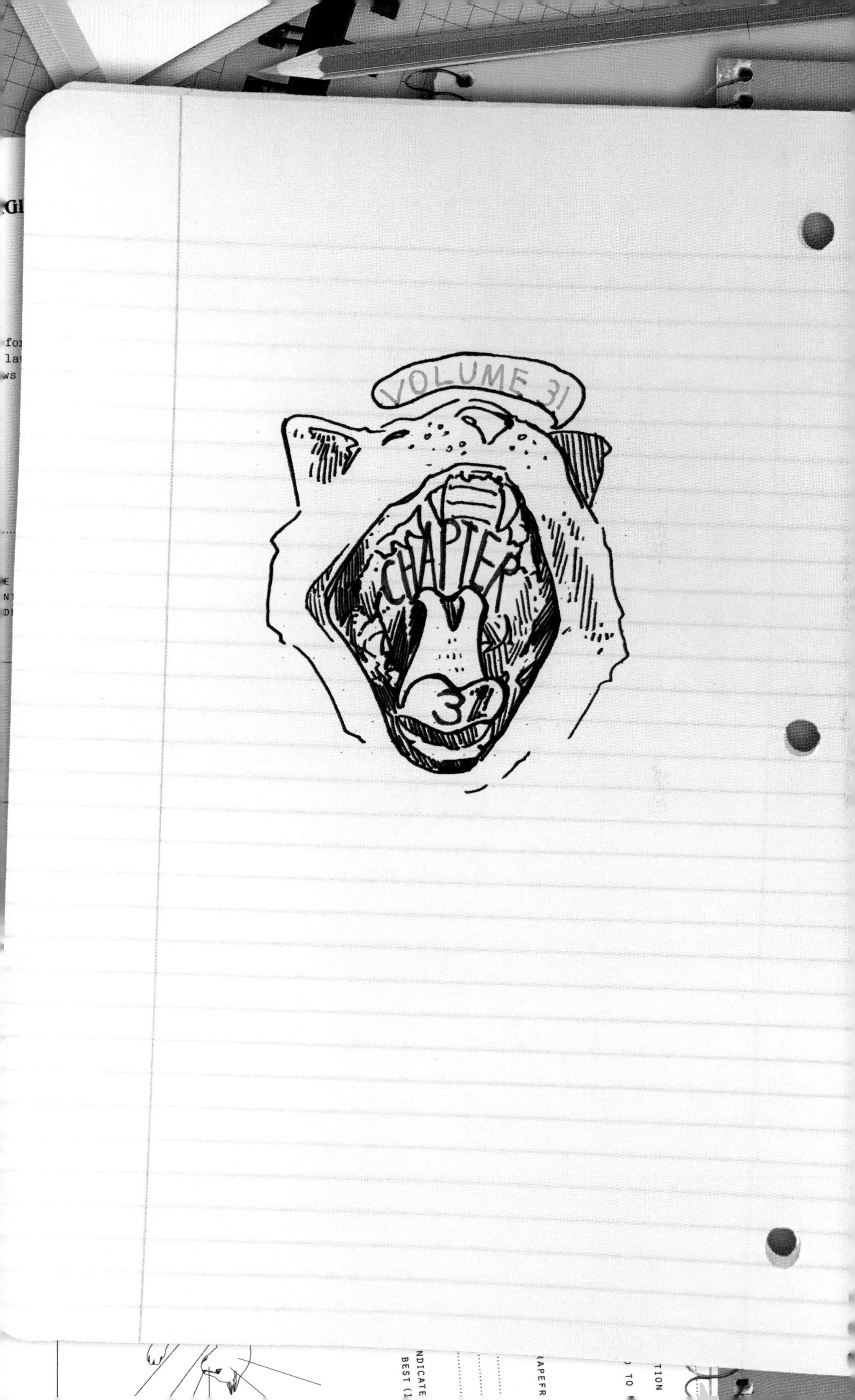
VOLUME 31
CHAPTER
32

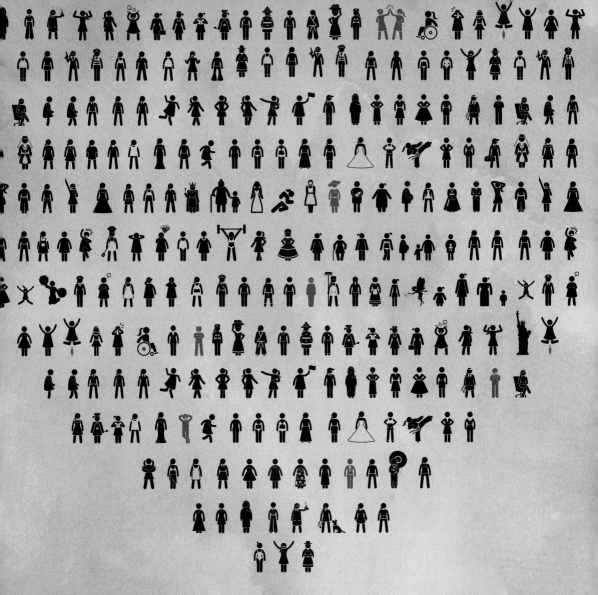

MINISTRY OF
TROUBLE
INCORPORATED

WRITER/CREATOR CHELSEA CAIN **COVER/CO-CREATOR/ADS, SUPPLEMENTAL ART** LIA MITERNIQUE
ARTIST ELISE MCCALL **COLORIST** RACHELLE ROSENBERG **LETTERER** JOE CARAMAGNA
HAIKU EMILY POWELL **ADDITIONAL INTERIOR ART** STELLA GREENVOSS **POETRY/PROSE** ELIZA FANTASTIC MOHAN

YOU HAVE BEEN CONTACTED BY THE MINISTRY OF TROUBLE. AWAIT FURTHER INSTRUCTIONS. ⚥

I want to take flight,
To weave through the trees and stars,
To soar through the air.

— Emily Powell, age 14

Picture this: **A teen full to the brim with angst and drama and hormones. Now picture her in bed, the lights are out and her phone is in her hand. And the day has been hard and her friends are asleep and she doesn't want to wake them. So here she is, unprocessed emotions flowing through her veins, eager to escape the confinement of her skin. The hair on her arms sticks straight up and the blanket feels too heavy and light at the same time. She keeps her toes covered, because if she doesn't the shadows might drag her away into a distant land.** The girl unlocks her phone. She turns it to night shift and carefully lays the charger cord on her bed so it won't fall and collide with the shiny wood floorboards. She goes to notes, and makes a new one with a couple touches and taps to her screen. **And something breaks in her, almost like a dam to a river that has been gathering quietly. And her fingers can't keep up with the constant thumping of her heart, the messages sent throughout her body, telling her to type, type, type. She doesn't breathe, doesn't blink, until her fingers fall still. And she sits, panting softly, with words she didn't know she had in her. And the river is still again, and the fish swim freely back and forth, and nature prospers. She has not quieted the storm. She has not calmed the waves in a temporary solution. She has not ignored the flames licking away and filling the air with their smoke. She has turned the river, the storm, the waves, the flames, into words on a phone. They will sit there untouched, until maybe months later, she finds them again and remembers when that day felt so strong, a day that has since healed over. Do not cover cracks with bandaids. Do not ignore the pain and the emotions.** It does not have to be poetry that comes from you, or music or art or dance. **It does not have to be happy, or beautiful, or nice to look at. Because whatever comes from the things you keep locked up inside is yours, and no one else's. It is not for amusement or criticism or enjoyment. It is an essential step in healing.** I believe in processing life through art, through bad poetry and messy paintings and wrong notes. I believe in healing through creativity, in all its complicated forms. I believe in the girl lying in bed far past her bedtime, and finally feeling free.

— Eliza Fantastic Mohan, age 14

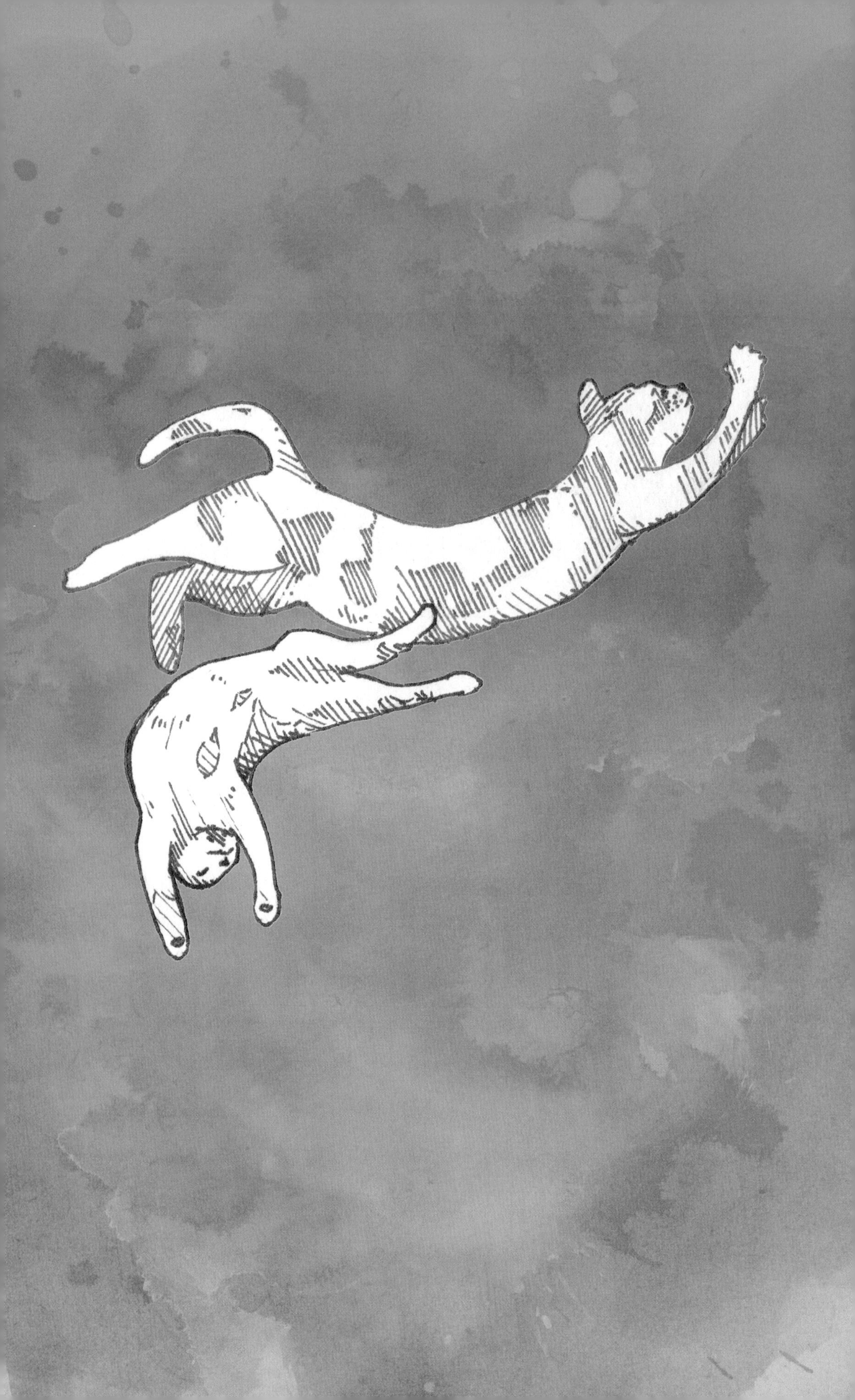

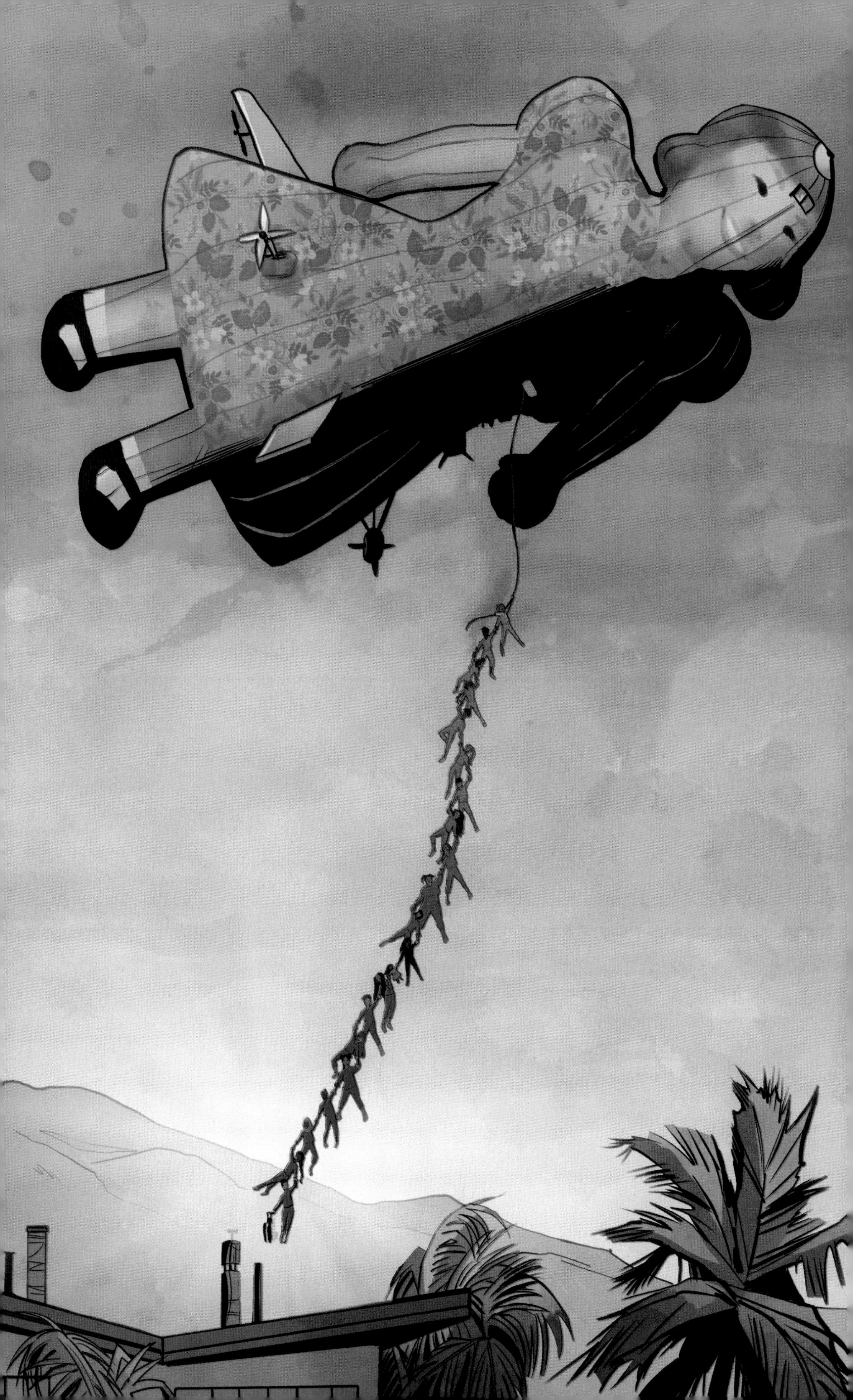

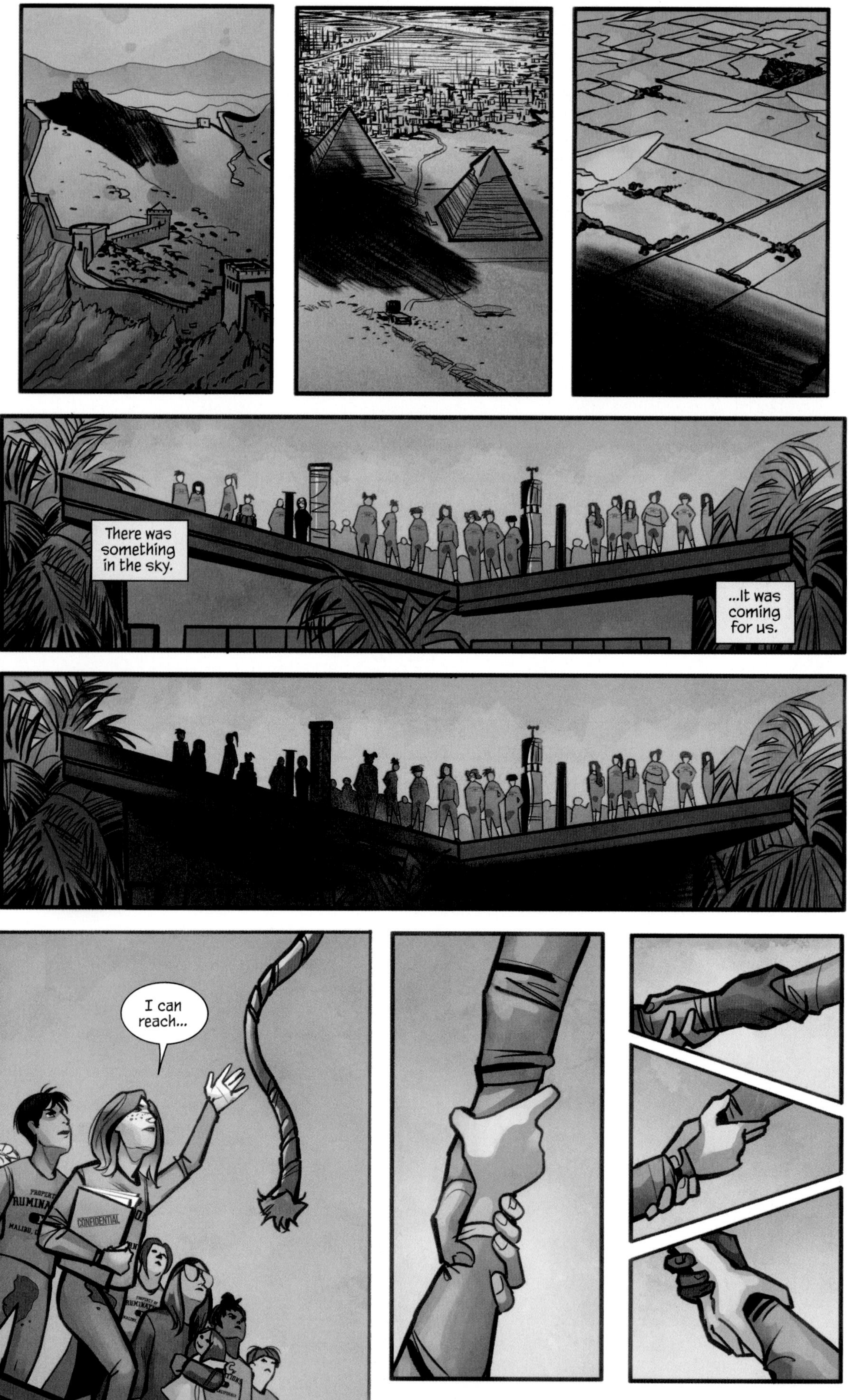
There was something in the sky.
...It was coming for us.
I can reach...
CONFIDENTIAL

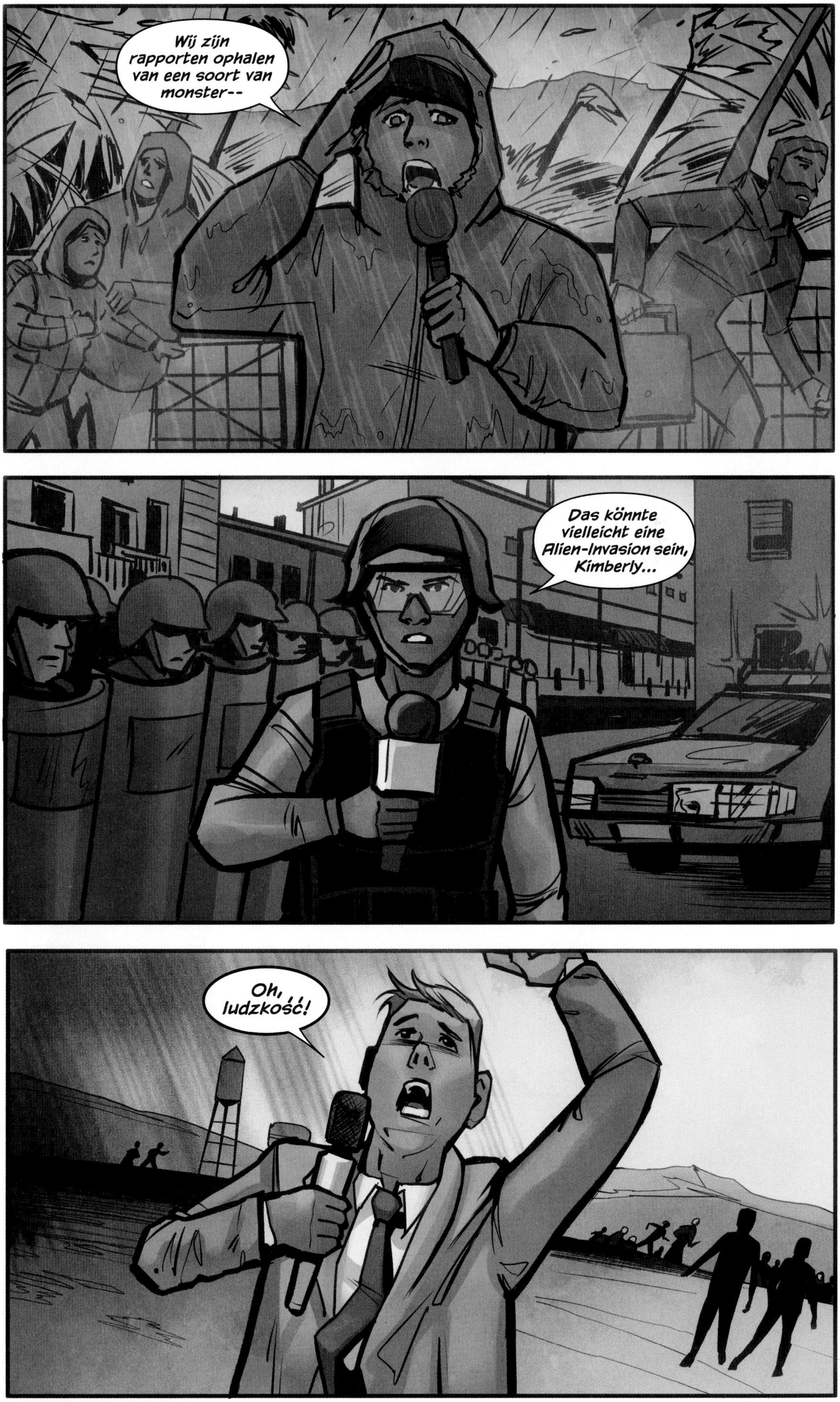
Wij zijn rapporten ophalen van een soort van monster--
Das könnte vielleicht eine Alien-Invasion sein, Kimberly...
Oh, ludzkość!

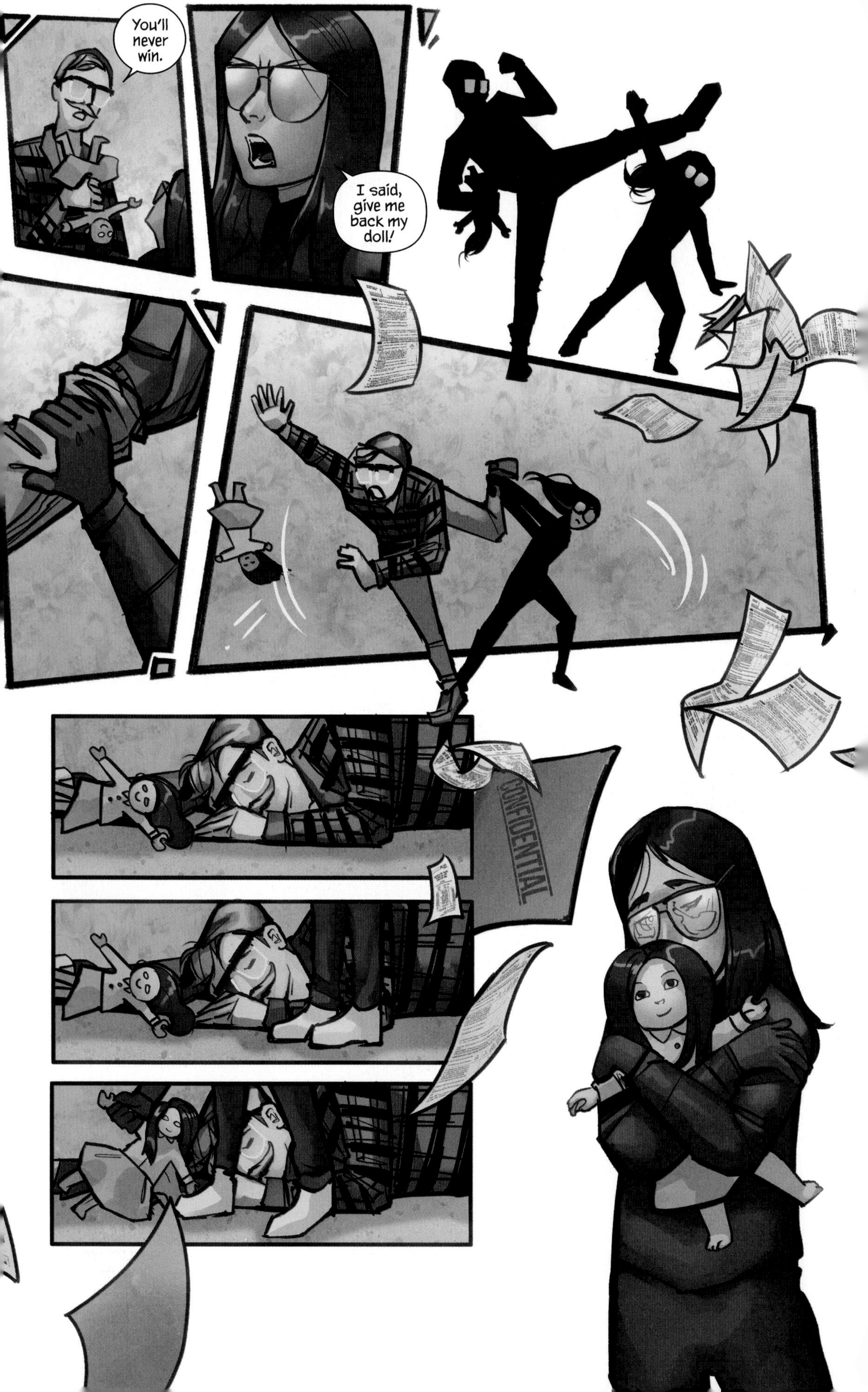
You'll never win.
I said, give me back my doll!
CONFIDENTIAL

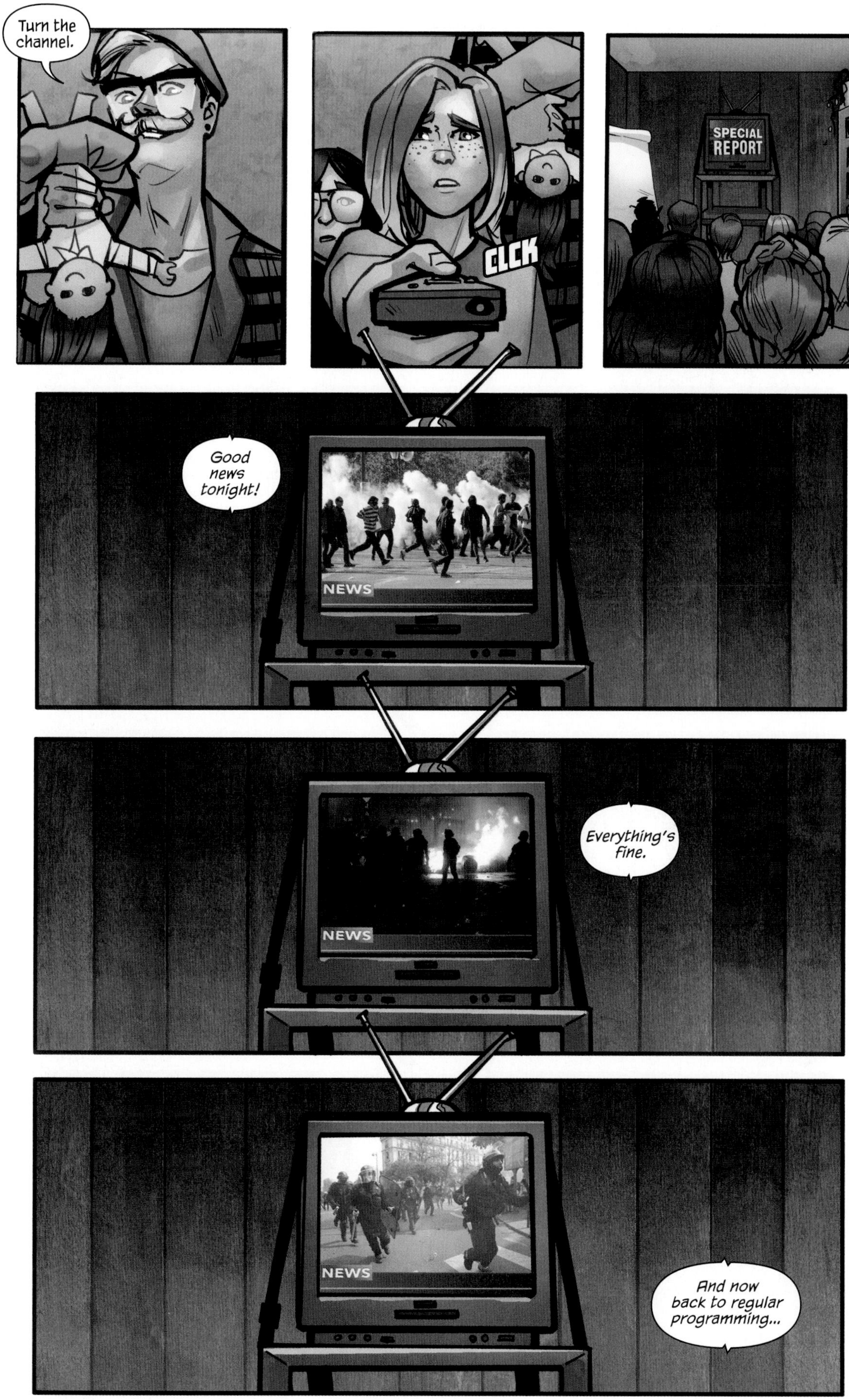
Turn the channel.
CLCK
SPECIAL REPORT
Good news tonight!
NEWS
Everything's fine.
NEWS
NEWS
And now back to regular programming...

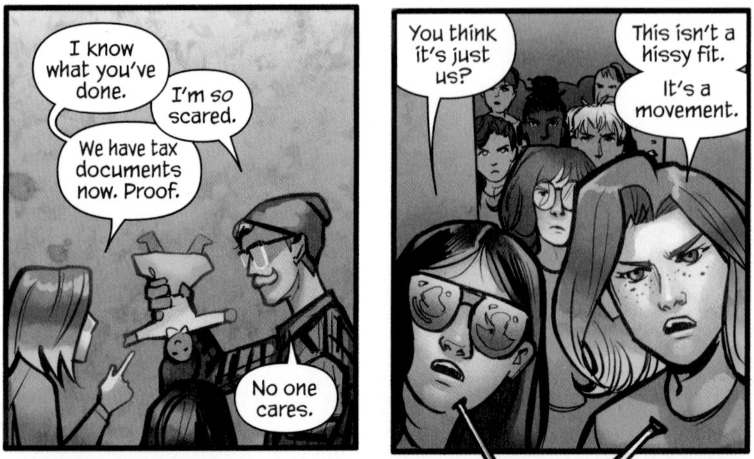
I know what you've done.
I'm so scared.
We have tax documents now. Proof.
No one cares.
You think it's just us?
This isn't a hissy fit.
It's a movement.

#DrinkResponsibly
Protect your future. With every sip.
What's your favorite Estro beverage?
Promoted by Estro-Corp

#Cerulean
9,001 Tweets

#Mittelschmerz
11,203 Tweets

#CatAttacks
6,005 Tweets

#NationalDoughnutDay
Emerald City Comic Con, Great Big Story, and more are Tweeting about this

Mandy
12.1K Tweets

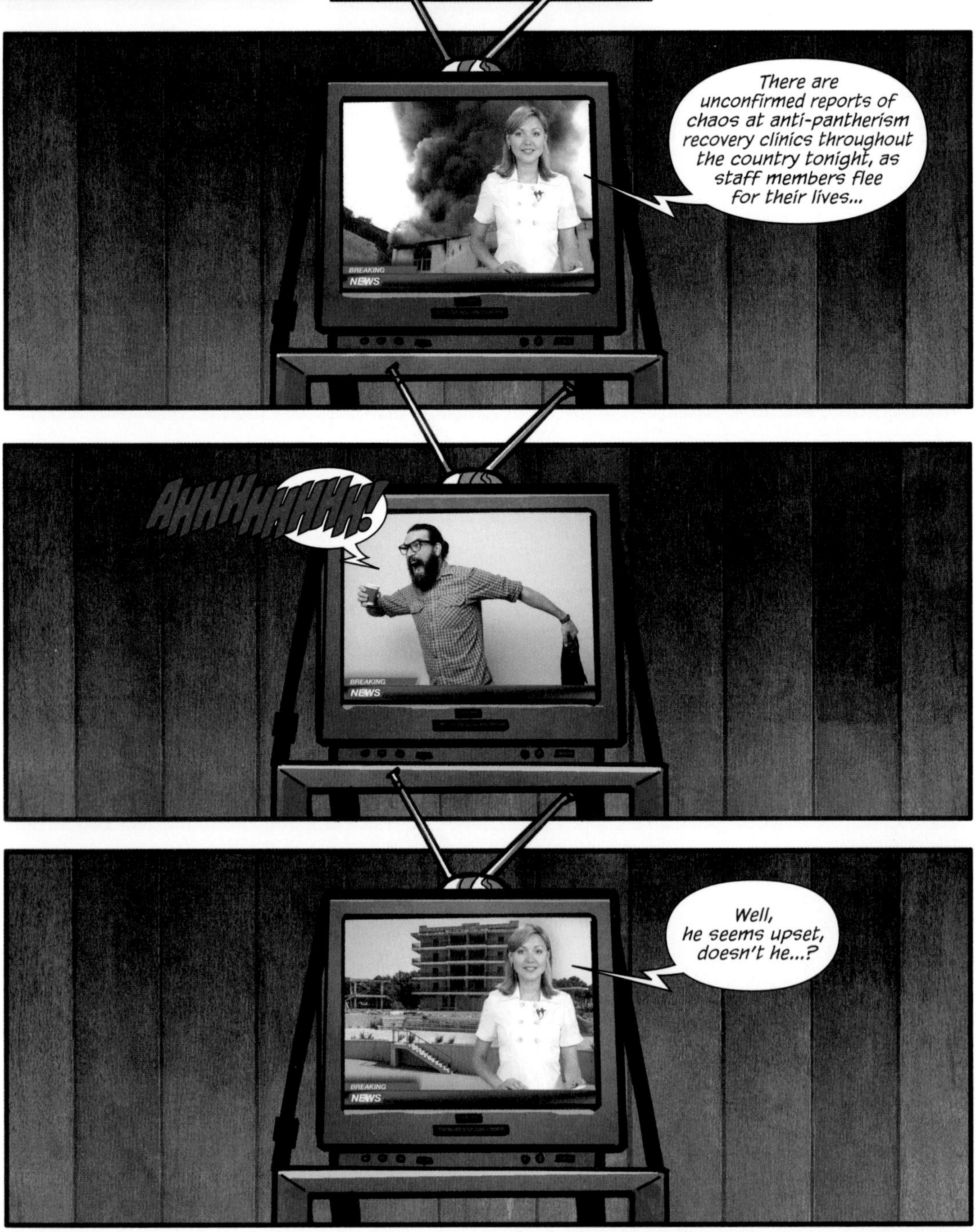
There are unconfirmed reports of chaos at anti-pantherism recovery clinics throughout the country tonight, as staff members flee for their lives...
BREAKING NEWS
AHHHHHHHH!
BREAKING NEWS
Well, he seems upset, doesn't he...?
BREAKING NEWS

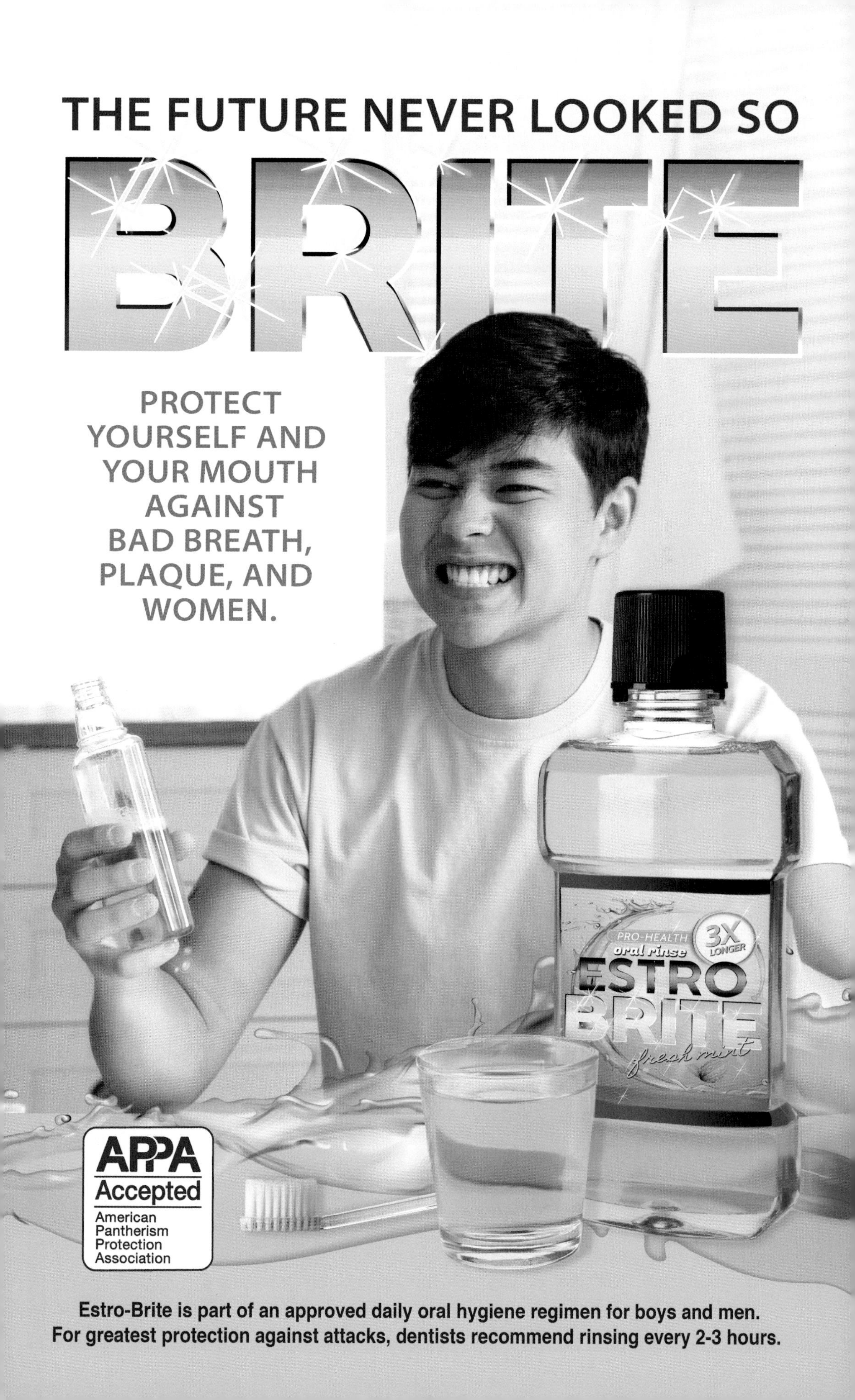
THE FUTURE NEVER LOOKED SO
BRITE
PROTECT YOURSELF AND YOUR MOUTH AGAINST BAD BREATH, PLAQUE, AND WOMEN.
PRO-HEALTH
oral rinse
3X LONGER
ESTRO BRITE
fresh mint
APPA Accepted
American Pantherism Protection Association
Estro-Brite is part of an approved daily oral hygiene regimen for boys and men.
For greatest protection against attacks, dentists recommend rinsing every 2-3 hours.

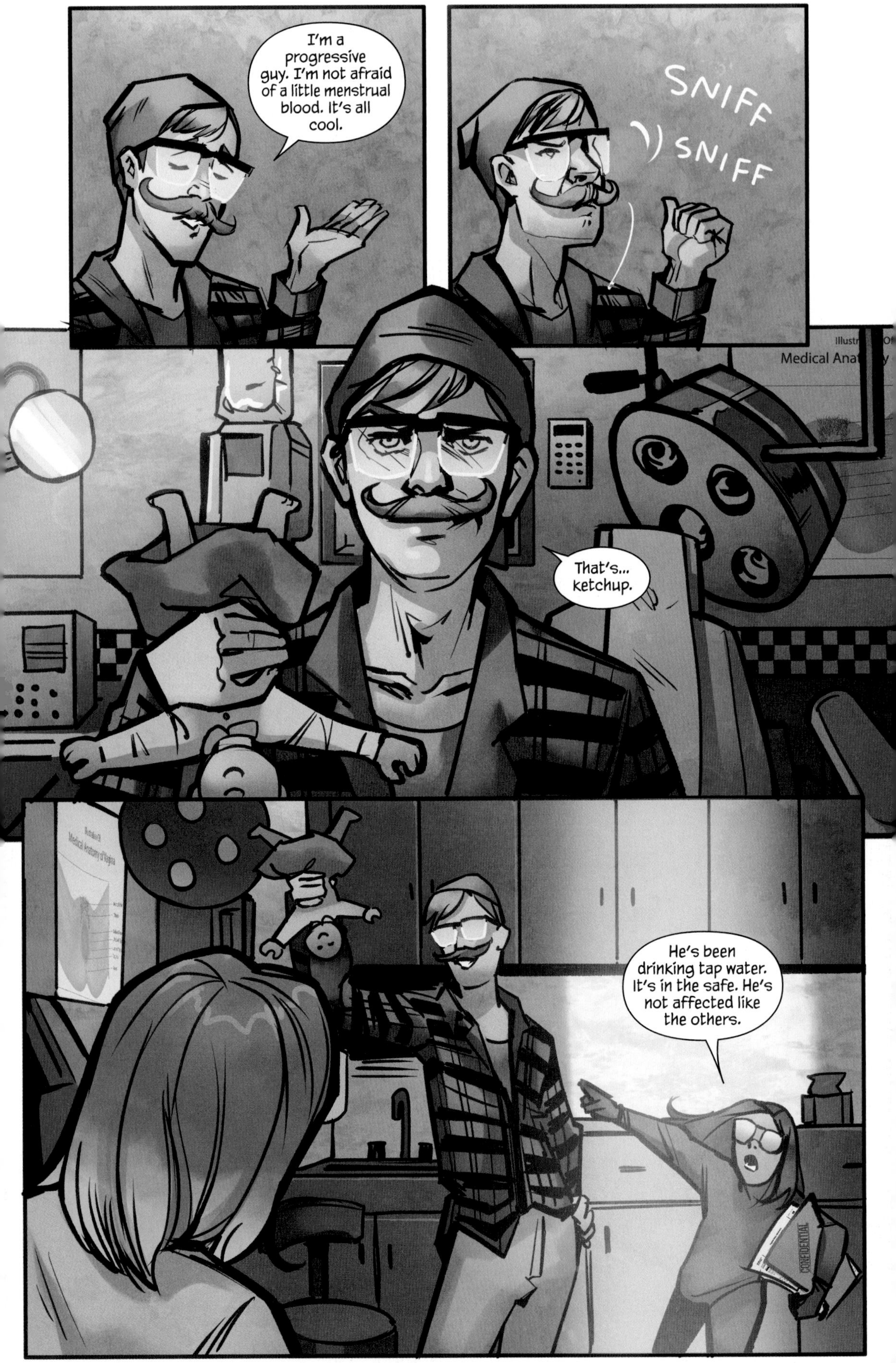
I'm a progressive guy. I'm not afraid of a little menstrual blood. It's all cool.
SNIFF
SNIFF
Medical Anat
That's... ketchup.
Medical Anatomy of Vagina
He's been drinking tap water. It's in the safe. He's not affected like the others.
CONFIDENTIAL

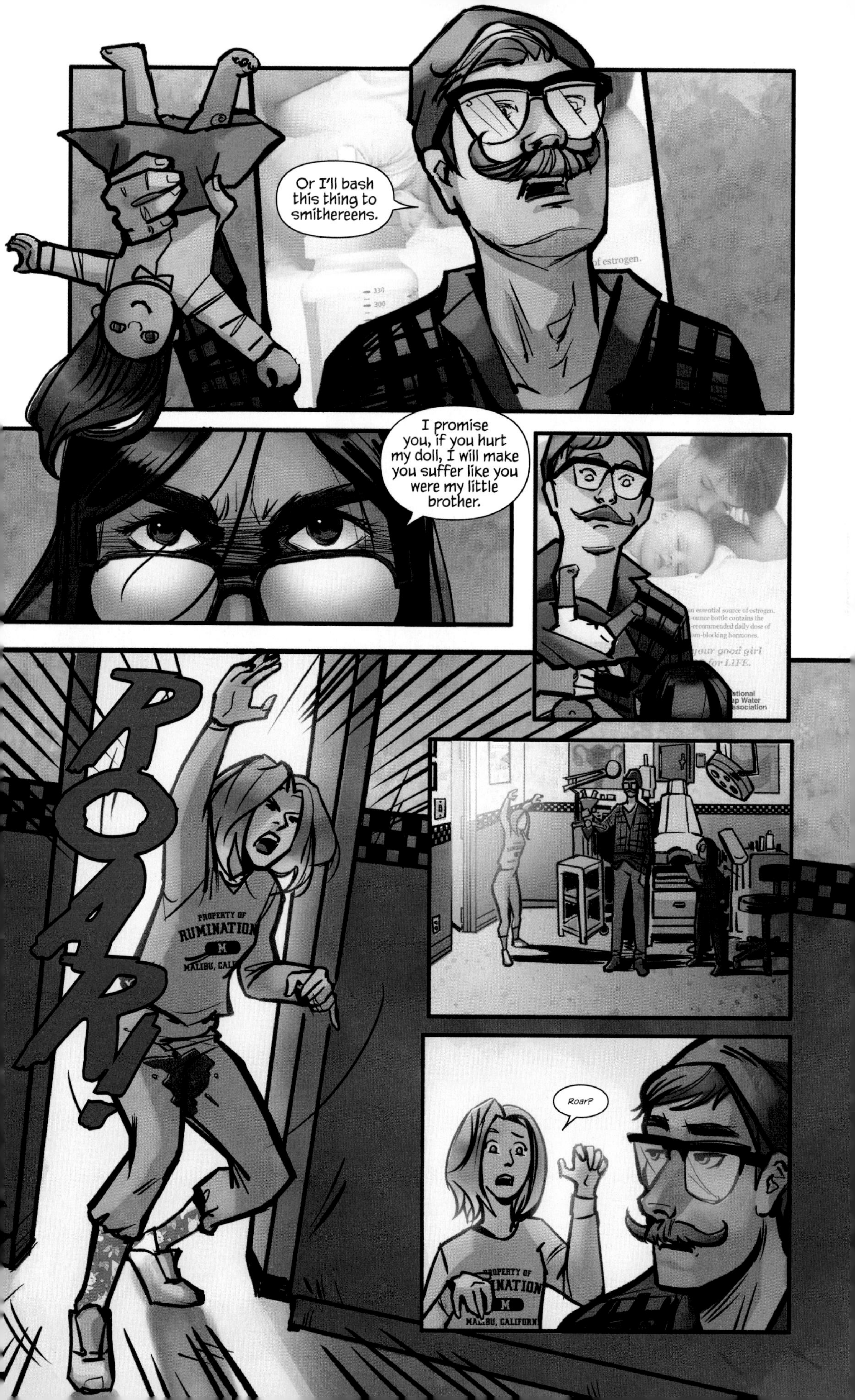
Or I'll bash this thing to smithereens.
I promise you, if you hurt my doll, I will make you suffer like you were my little brother.
ROAR!
PROPERTY OF RUMINATION
Roar?

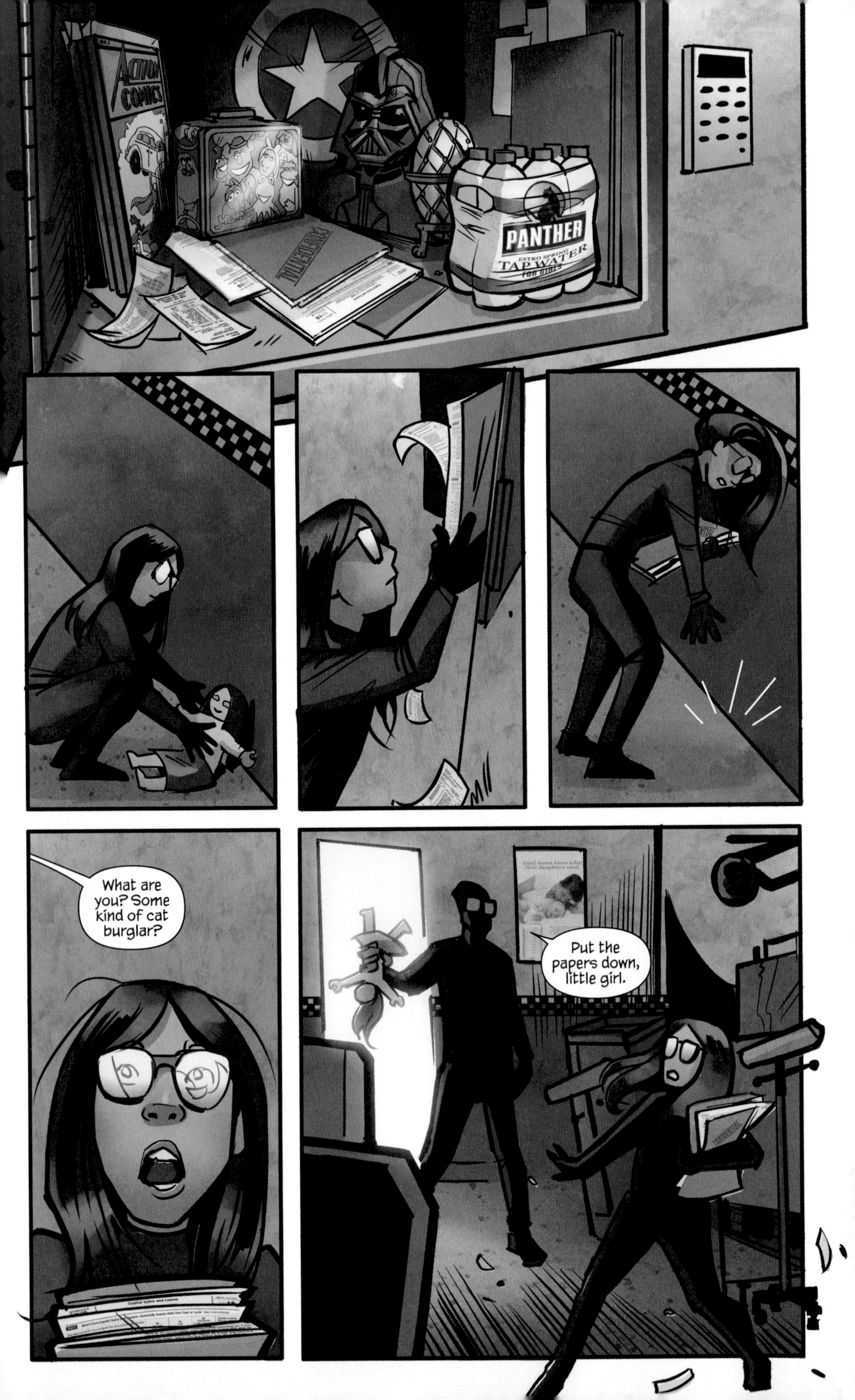
ACTION COMICS
CONFIDENTIAL
PANTHER
ESTRO SPRING
TAP WATER
What are you? Some kind of cat burglar?
Put the papers down, little girl.

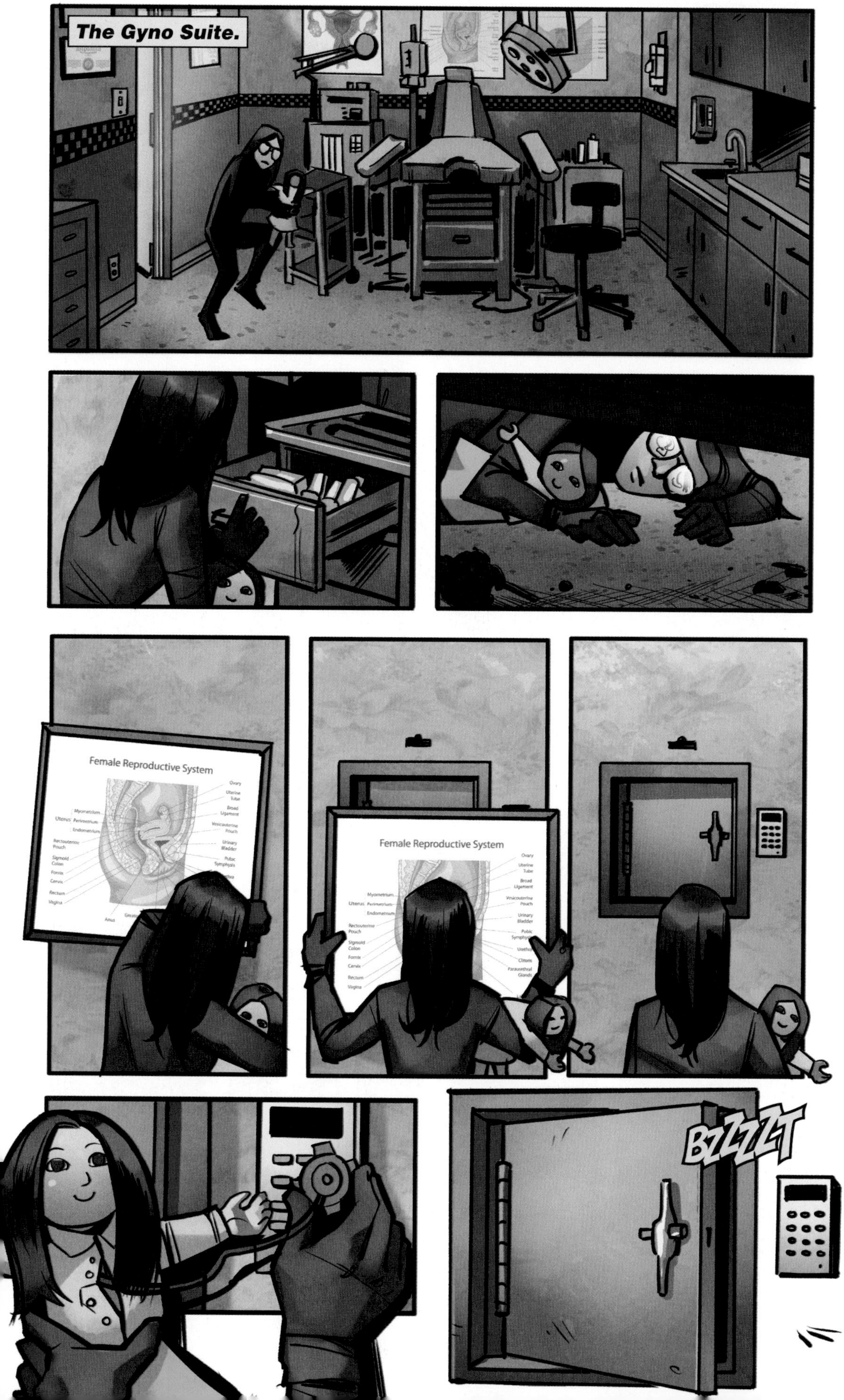
The Gyno Suite.
Female Reproductive System
Ovary
Uterine Tube
Broad Ligament
Vesicouterine Pouch
Urinary Bladder
Pubic Symphysis
Myometrium
Uterus
Perimetrium
Endometrium
Rectouterine Pouch
Sigmoid Colon
Fornix
Cervix
Rectum
Vagina
Anus
Female Reproductive System
BZZZZT

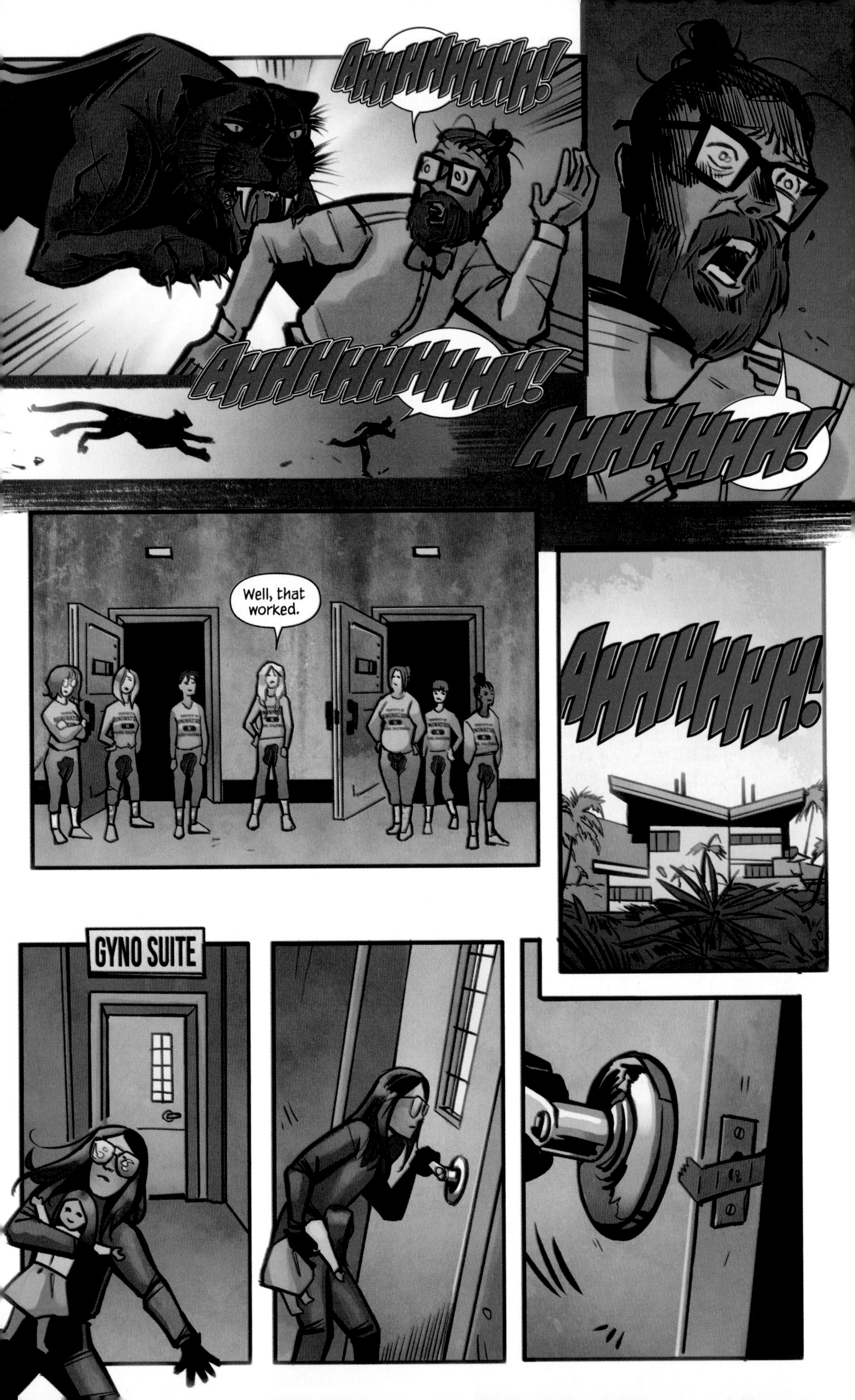
AHHHHHHHH!
AHHHHHHHHHH!
AHHHHHHH!
Well, that worked.
AHHHHHHH!
GYNO SUITE

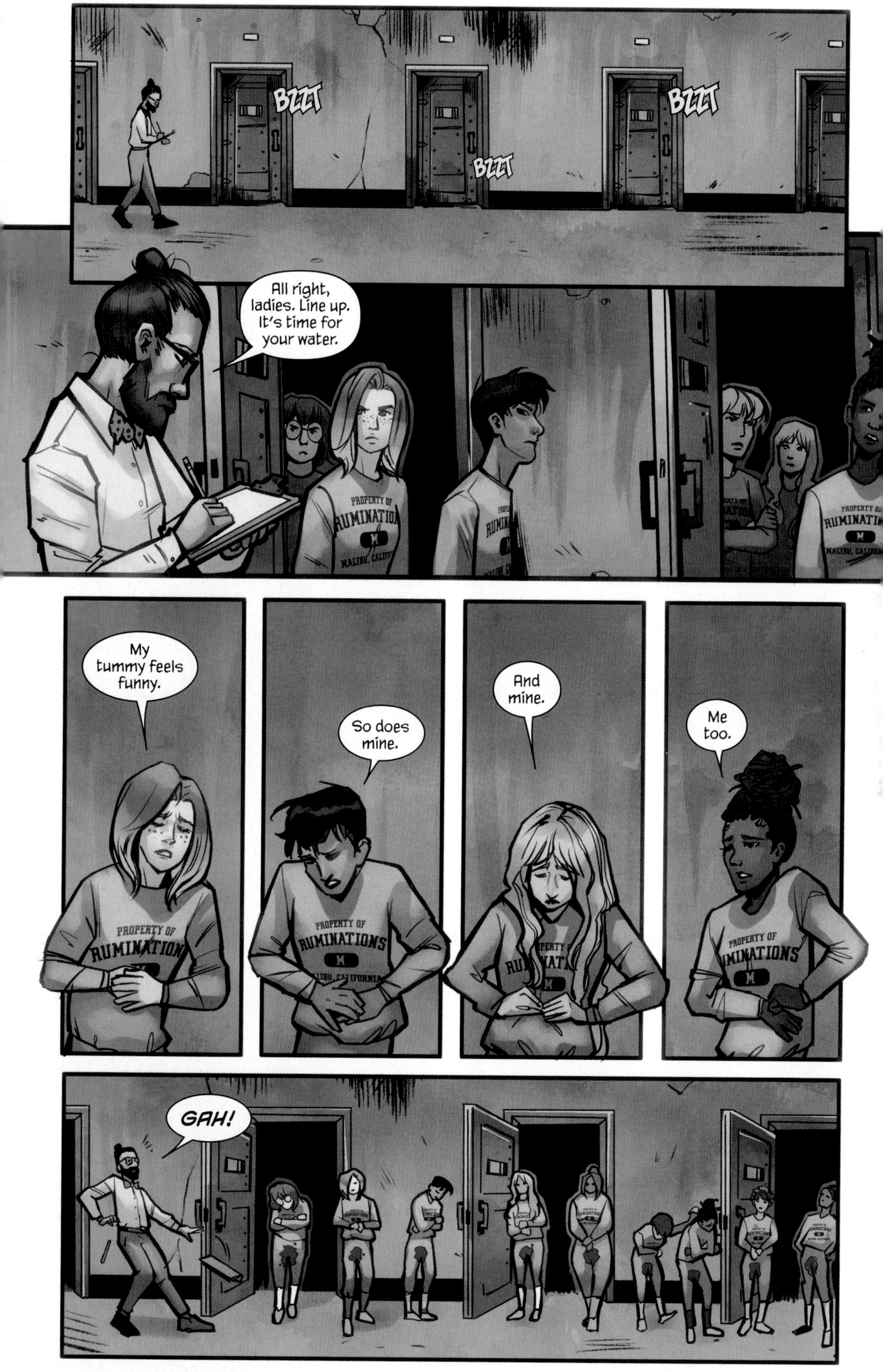
BZZT
BZZT
BZZT
All right, ladies. Line up. It's time for your water.
PROPERTY OF RUMINATIONS M MALIBU, CALIFORNIA
My tummy feels funny.
So does mine.
And mine.
Me too.
GAH!

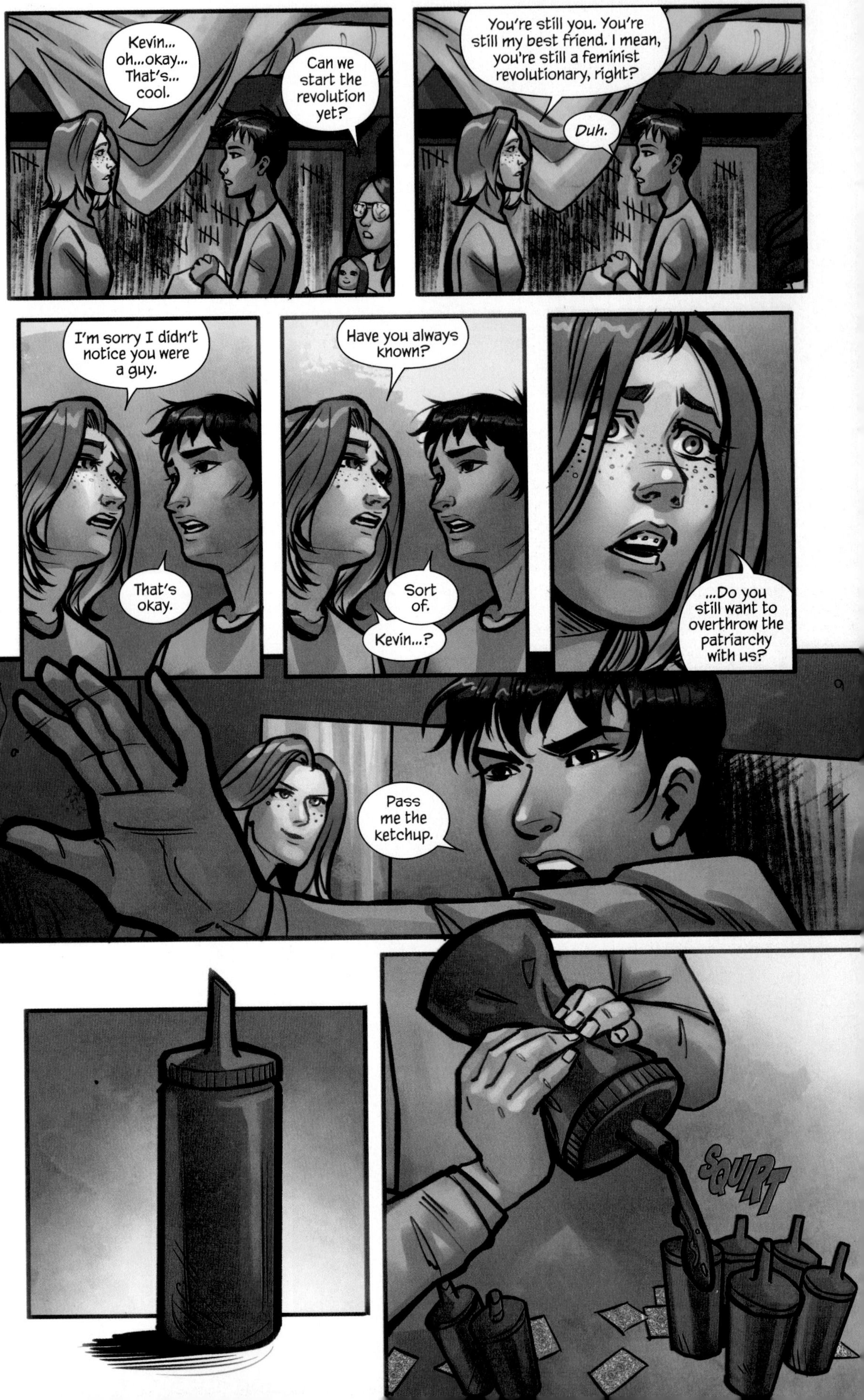
Kevin... oh...okay... That's... cool.
Can we start the revolution yet?
You're still you. You're still my best friend. I mean, you're still a feminist revolutionary, right?
Duh.
I'm sorry I didn't notice you were a guy.
That's okay.
Have you always known?
Sort of.
Kevin...?
...Do you still want to overthrow the patriarchy with us?
Pass me the ketchup.
SQUIRT

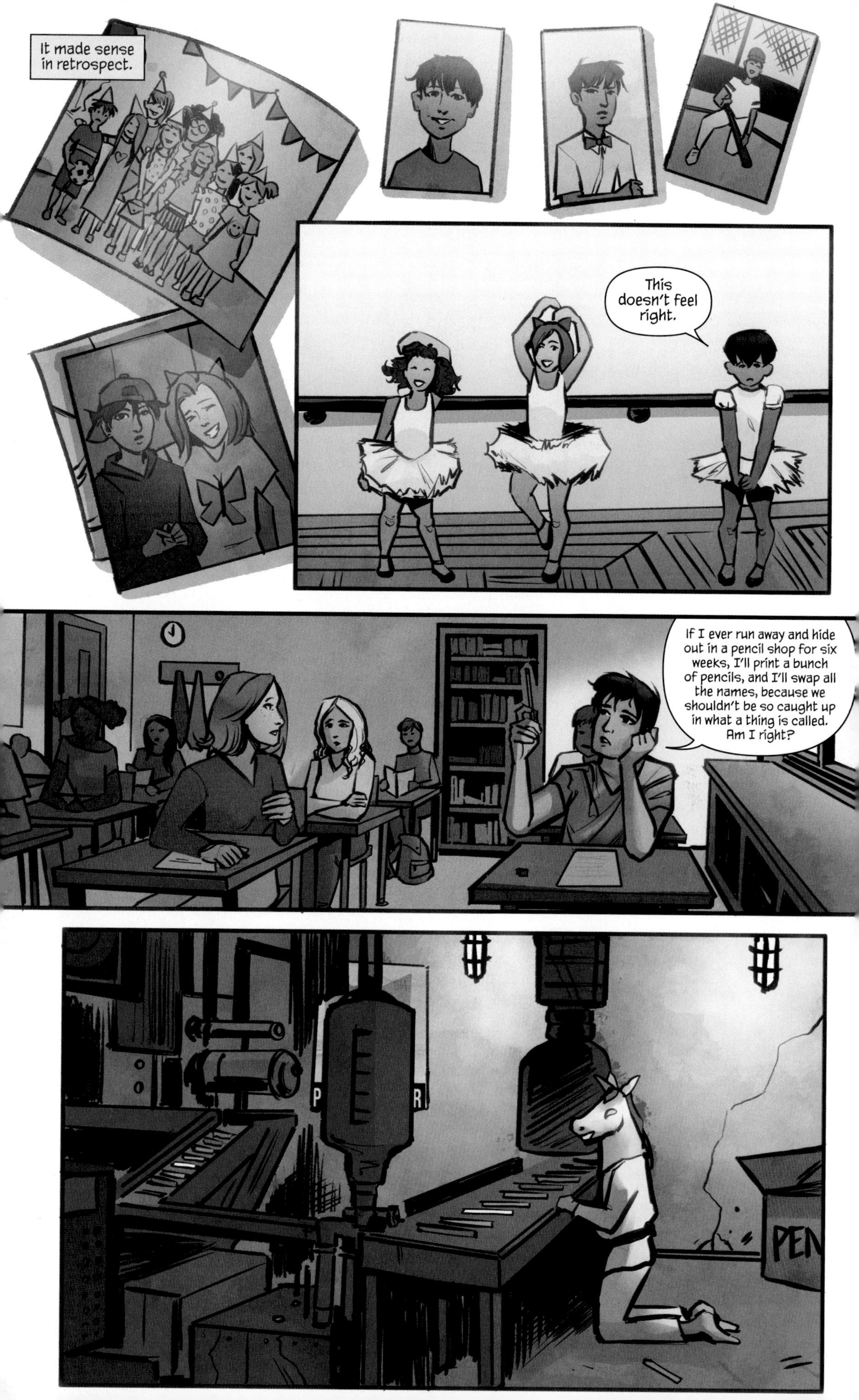
It made sense in retrospect.
This doesn't feel right.
If I ever run away and hide out in a pencil shop for six weeks, I'll print a bunch of pencils, and I'll swap all the names, because we shouldn't be so caught up in what a thing is called. Am I right?

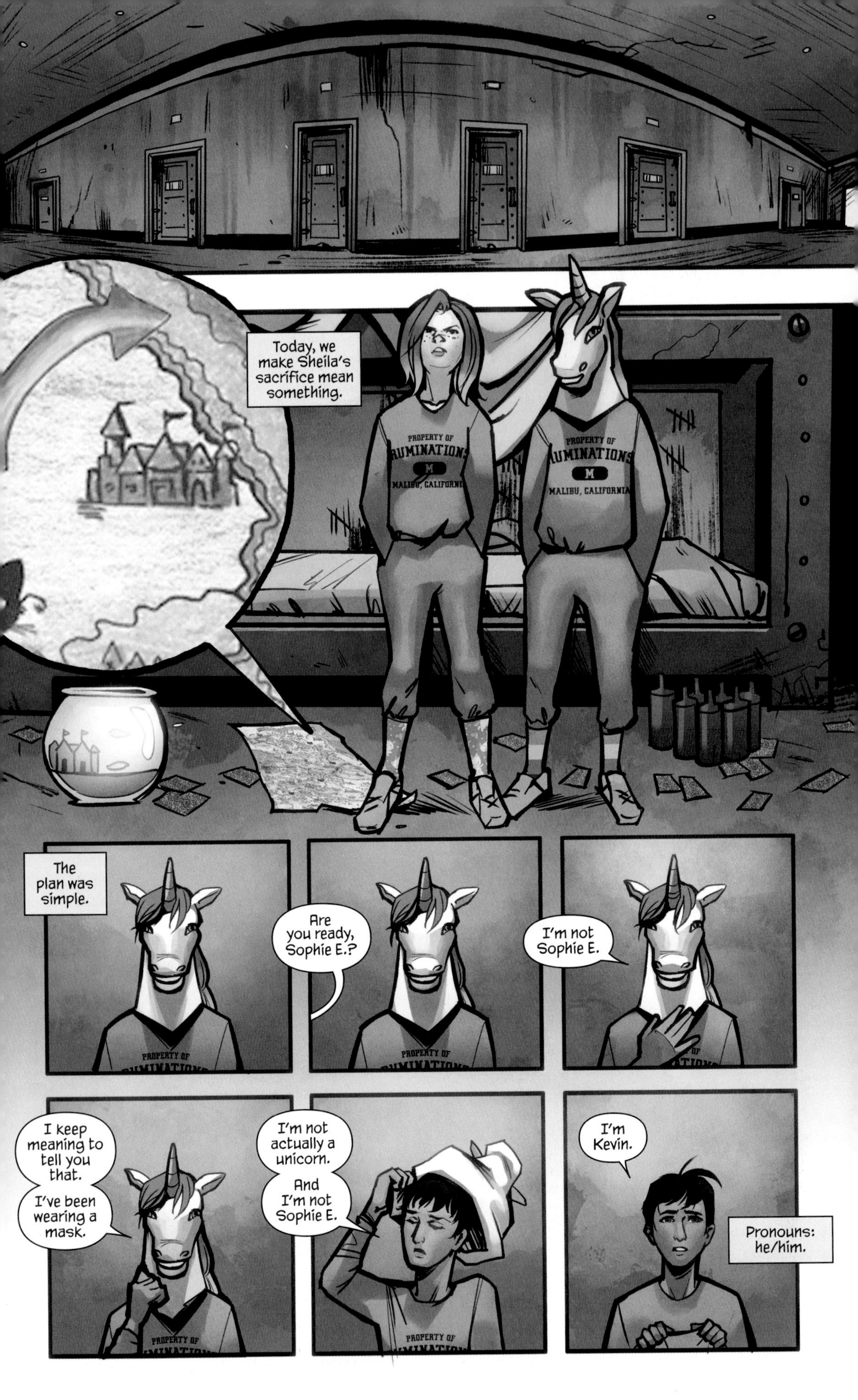

Today, we make Sheila's sacrifice mean something.
PROPERTY OF RUMINATIONS M MALIBU, CALIFORNIA
PROPERTY OF RUMINATIONS M MALIBU, CALIFORNIA
The plan was simple.
Are you ready, Sophie E.?
I'm not Sophie E.
I keep meaning to tell you that.
I've been wearing a mask.
I'm not actually a unicorn.
And I'm not Sophie E.
I'm Kevin.
Pronouns: he/him.

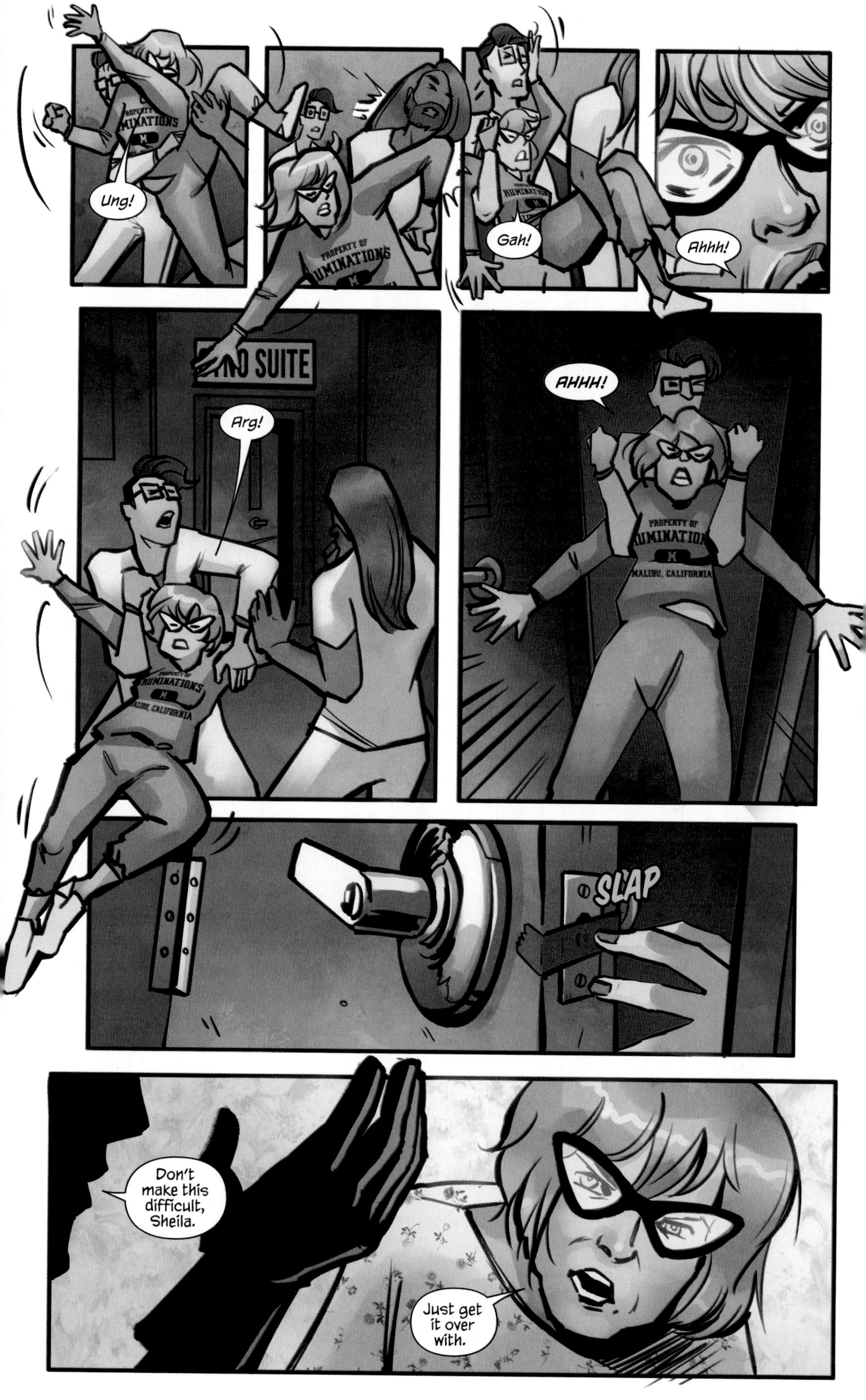
Ung!
Gah!
Ahhh!
Arg!
AHHH!
SLAP
Don't make this difficult, Sheila.
Just get it over with.

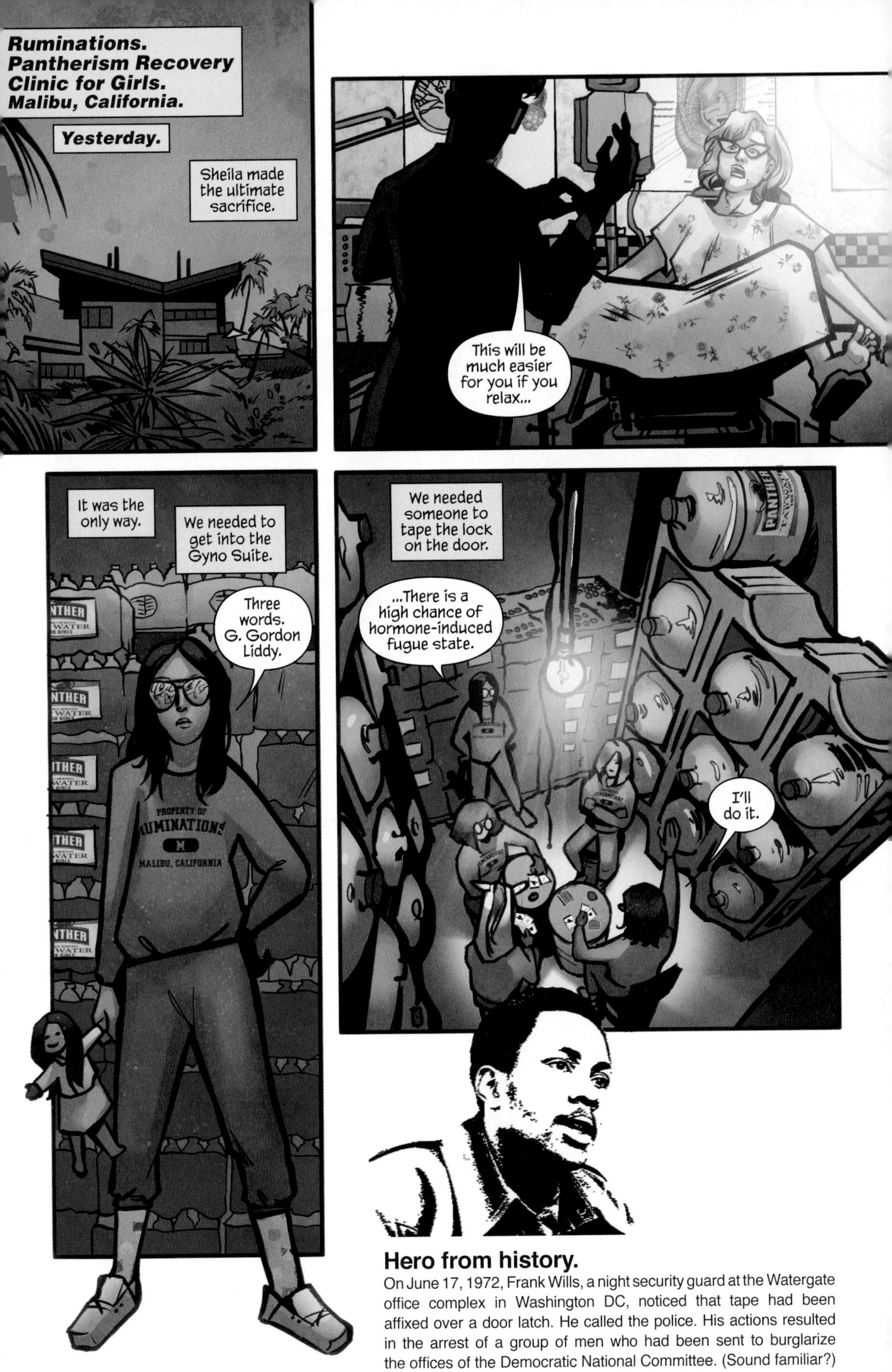
Ruminations. Pantherism Recovery Clinic for Girls. Malibu, California.
Yesterday.
Sheila made the ultimate sacrifice.
This will be much easier for you if you relax...
It was the only way.
We needed to get into the Gyno Suite.
Three words. G. Gordon Liddy.
PROPERTY OF RUMINATIONS MALIBU, CALIFORNIA
We needed someone to tape the lock on the door.
...There is a high chance of hormone-induced fugue state.
I'll do it.

Hero from history.

On June 17, 1972, Frank Wills, a night security guard at the Watergate office complex in Washington DC, noticed that tape had been affixed over a door latch. He called the police. His actions resulted in the arrest of a group of men who had been sent to burglarize the offices of the Democratic National Committee. (Sound familiar?) The resulting scandal, referred to simply as "Watergate," resulted in the impeachment and resignation of President Richard M. Nixon.

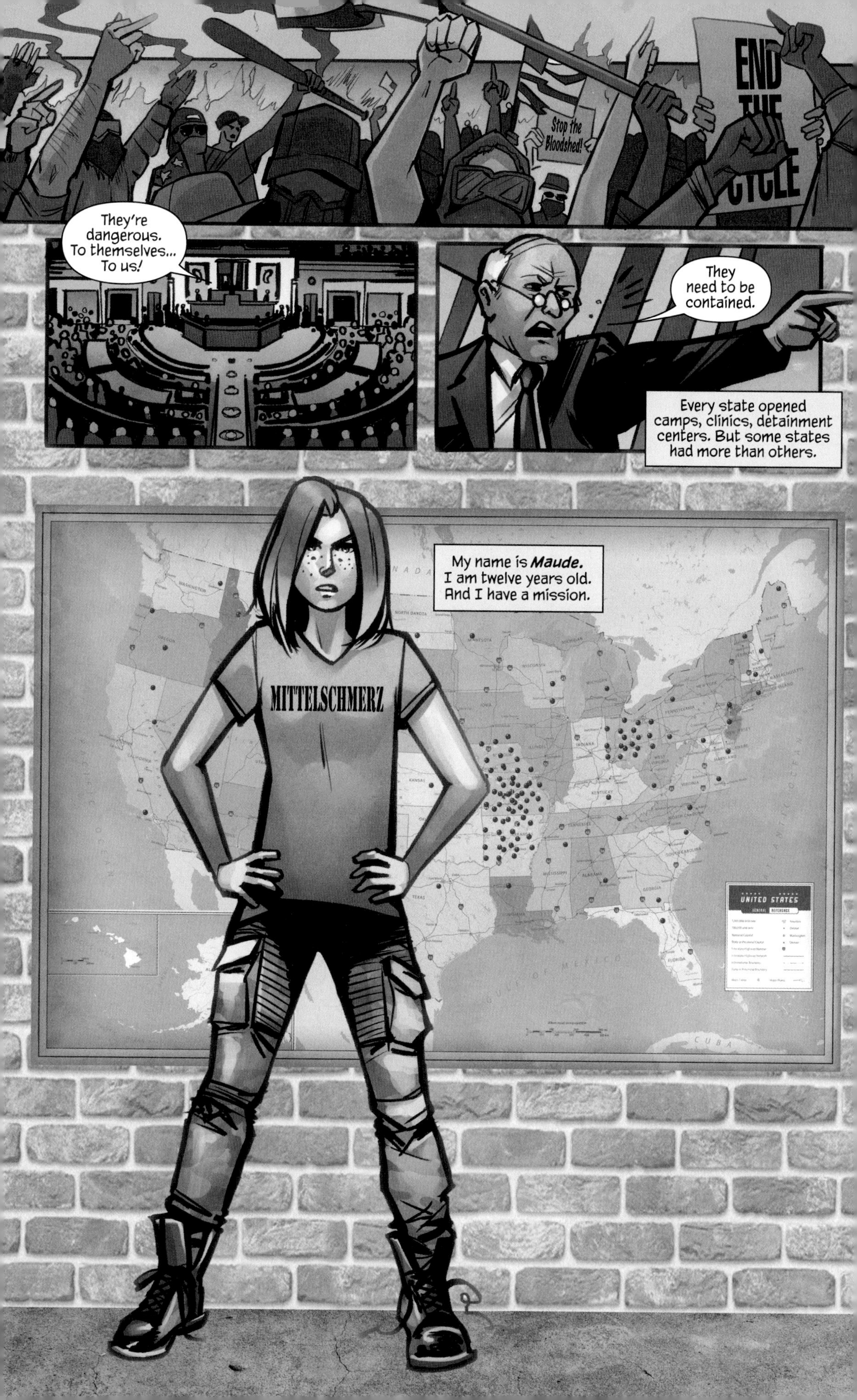

Stop the Bloodshed!
END THE CYCLE
They're dangerous. To themselves... To us!
They need to be contained.
Every state opened camps, clinics, detainment centers. But some states had more than others.
My name is *Maude.* I am twelve years old. And I have a mission.
MITTELSCHMERZ
UNITED STATES

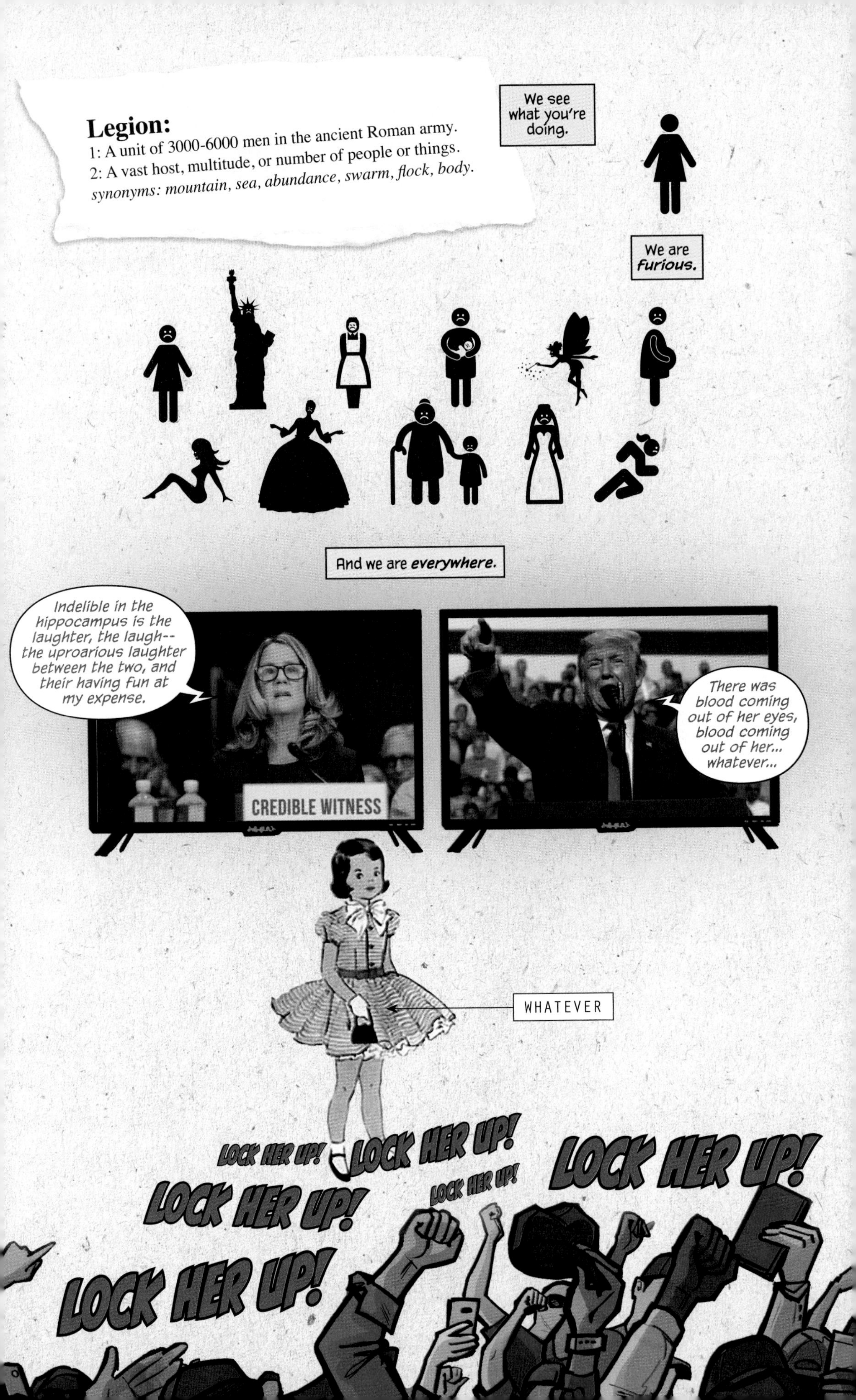

Legion:
1: A unit of 3000-6000 men in the ancient Roman army.
2: A vast host, multitude, or number of people or things.
synonyms: mountain, sea, abundance, swarm, flock, body.
We see what you're doing.
We are furious.
And we are everywhere.
Indelible in the hippocampus is the laughter, the laugh-- the uproarious laughter between the two, and their having fun at my expense.
CREDIBLE WITNESS
There was blood coming out of her eyes, blood coming out of her... whatever...
WHATEVER
LOCK HER UP!
LOCK HER UP!
LOCK HER UP!
LOCK HER UP!
LOCK HER UP!
LOCK HER UP!

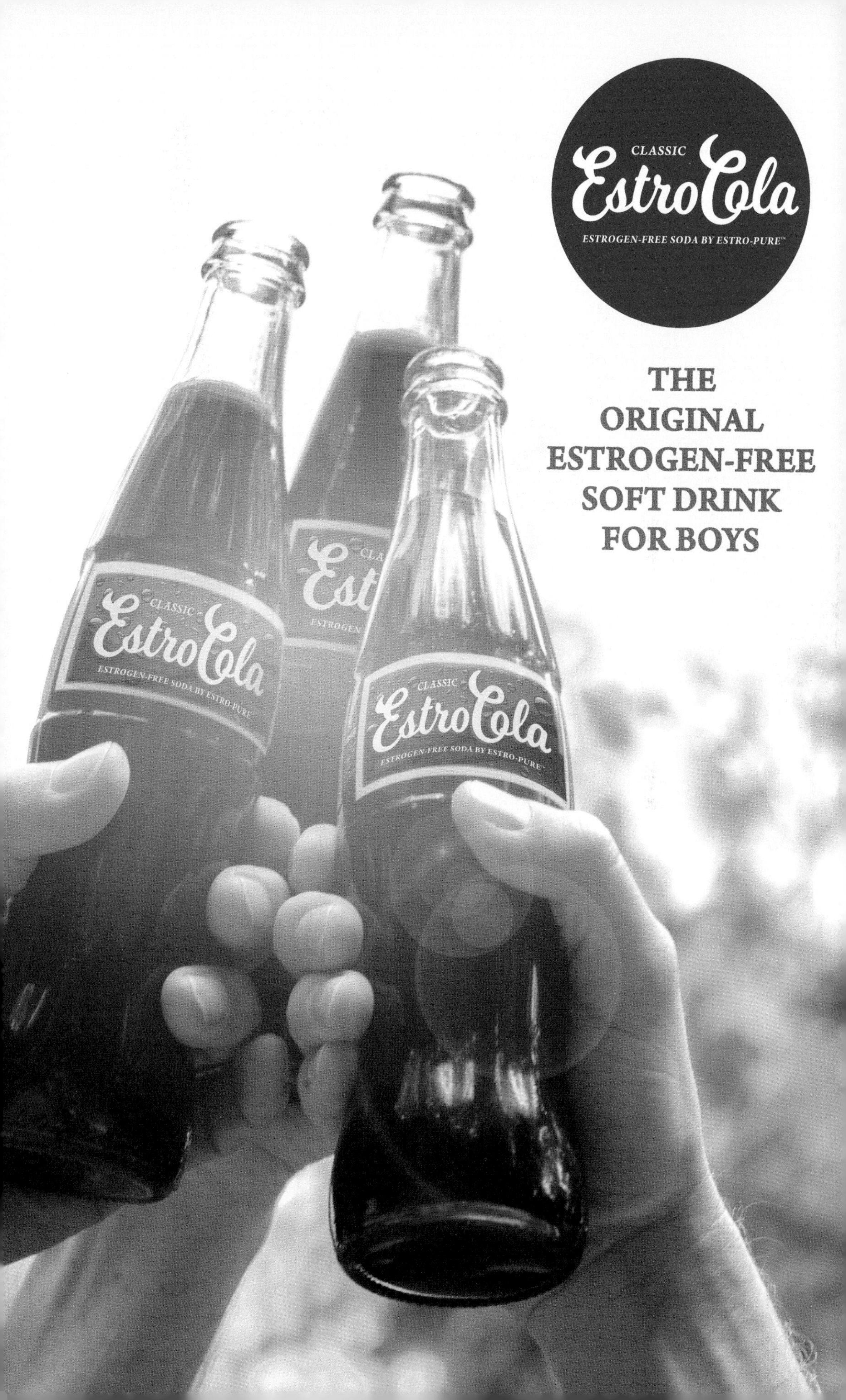
CLASSIC
EstroCola
ESTROGEN-FREE SODA BY ESTRO-PURE™
THE ORIGINAL ESTROGEN-FREE SOFT DRINK FOR BOYS
CLASSIC
EstroCola
ESTROGEN-FREE SODA BY ESTRO-PURE
CLASSIC
EstroCola
ESTROGEN-FREE SODA BY ESTRO-PURE™

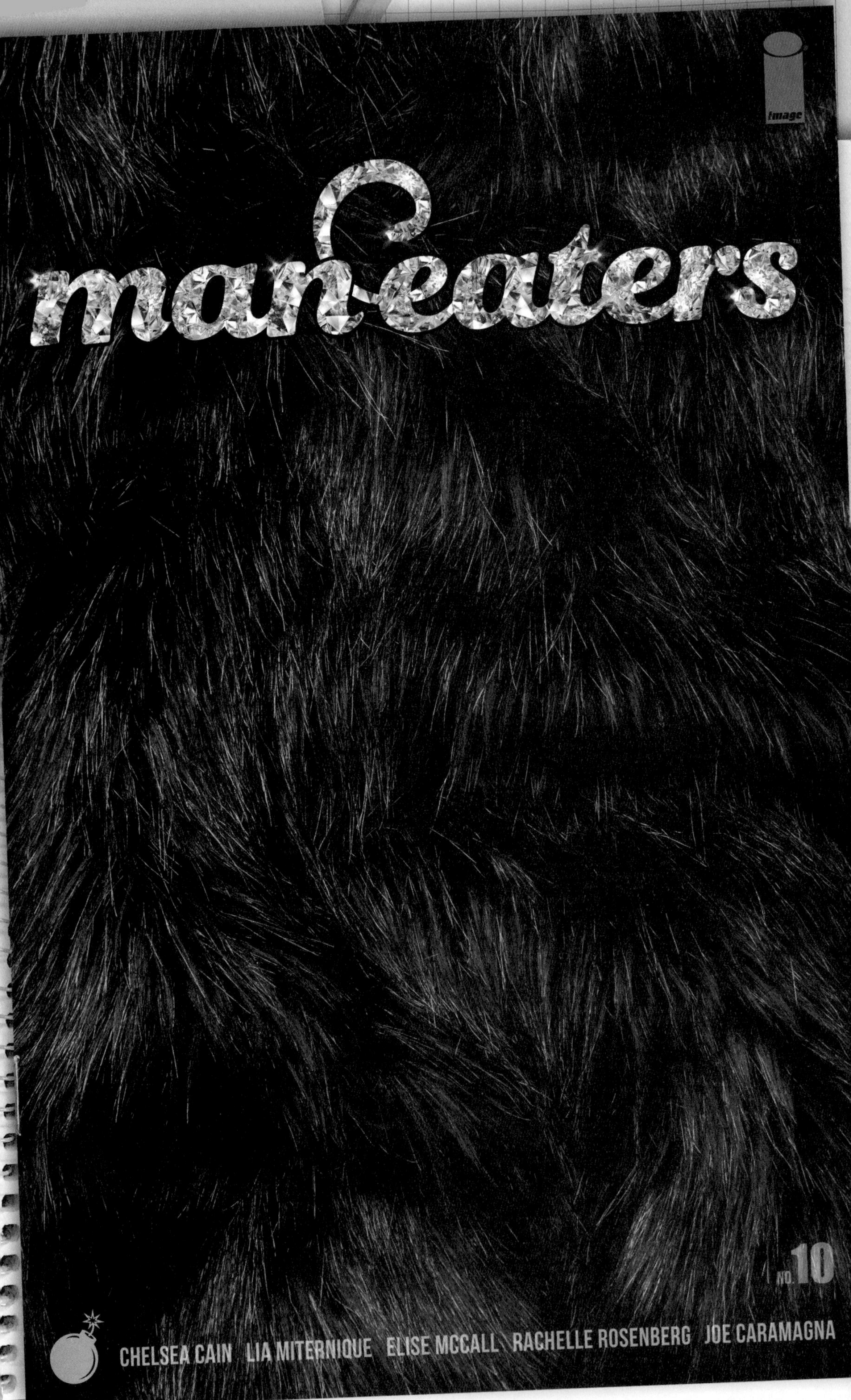
image
man eaters™
NO. 10
CHELSEA CAIN LIA MITERNIQUE ELISE MCCALL RACHELLE ROSENBERG JOE CARAMAGNA

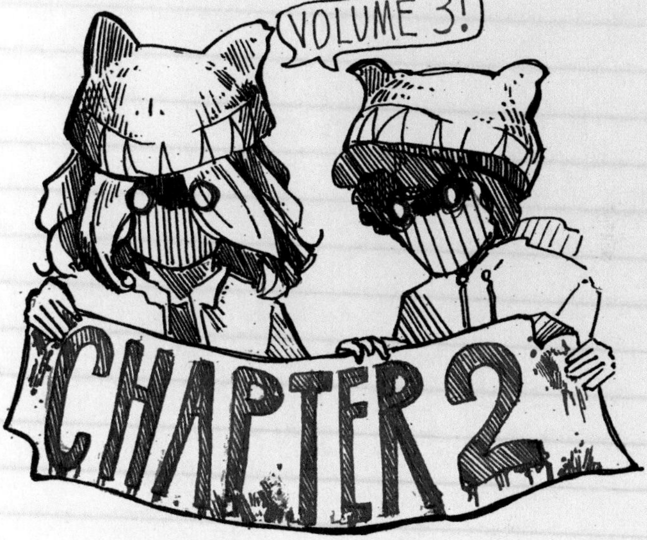
VOLUME 3!
CHAPTER 2

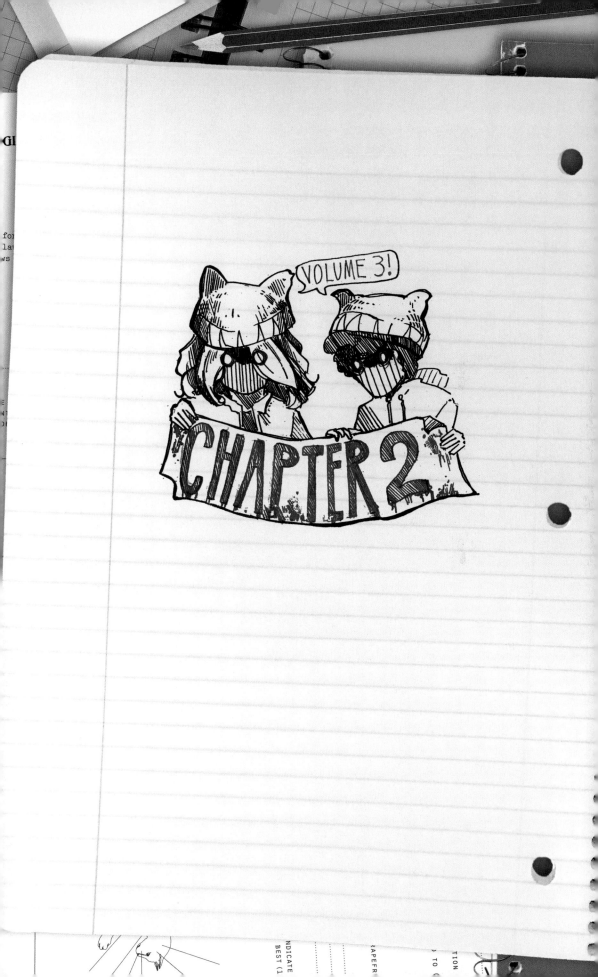

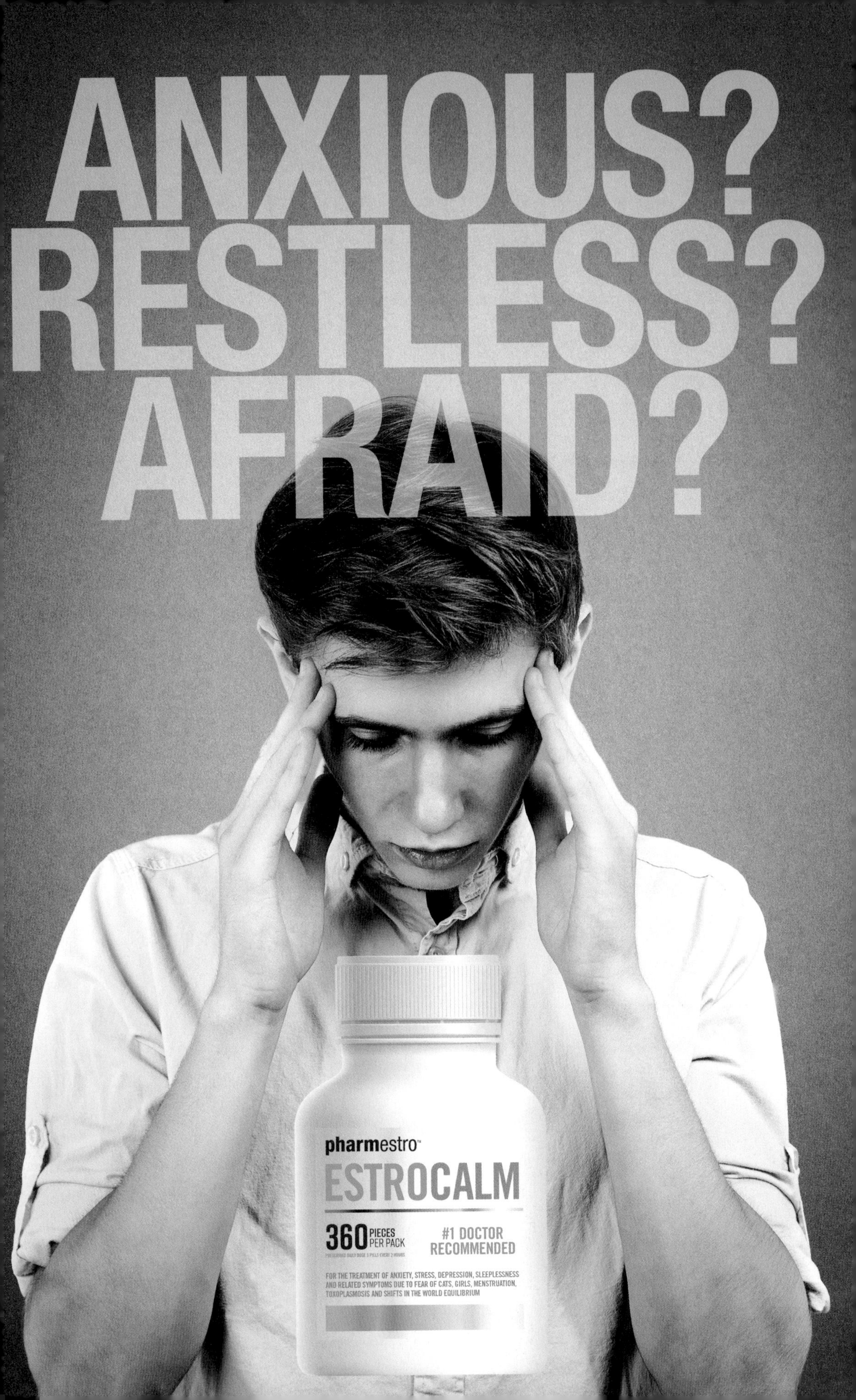
ANXIOUS?
RESTLESS?
AFRAID?
pharmestro™
ESTROCALM
360 PIECES PER PACK
#1 DOCTOR RECOMMENDED
FOR THE TREATMENT OF ANXIETY, STRESS, DEPRESSION, SLEEPLESSNESS AND RELATED SYMPTOMS DUE TO FEAR OF CATS, GIRLS, MENSTRUATION, TOXOPLASMOSIS AND SHIFTS IN THE WORLD EQUILIBRIUM

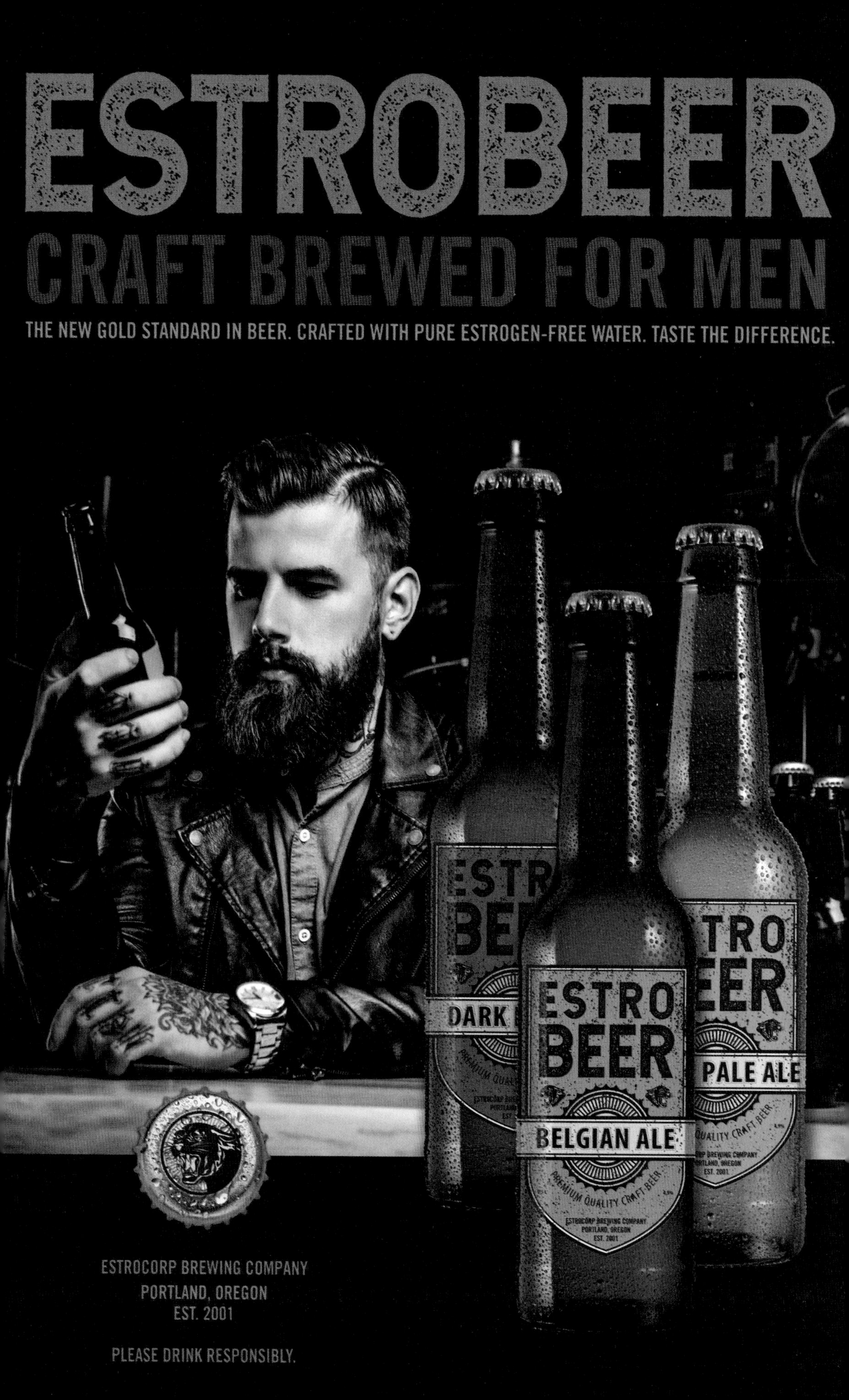
ESTROBEER
CRAFT BREWED FOR MEN
THE NEW GOLD STANDARD IN BEER. CRAFTED WITH PURE ESTROGEN-FREE WATER. TASTE THE DIFFERENCE.
ESTRO BEER
BELGIAN ALE
PREMIUM QUALITY CRAFT BEER
ESTROCORP BREWING COMPANY
PORTLAND, OREGON
EST. 2001
PALE ALE
ESTROCORP BREWING COMPANY
PORTLAND, OREGON
EST. 2001
PLEASE DRINK RESPONSIBLY.

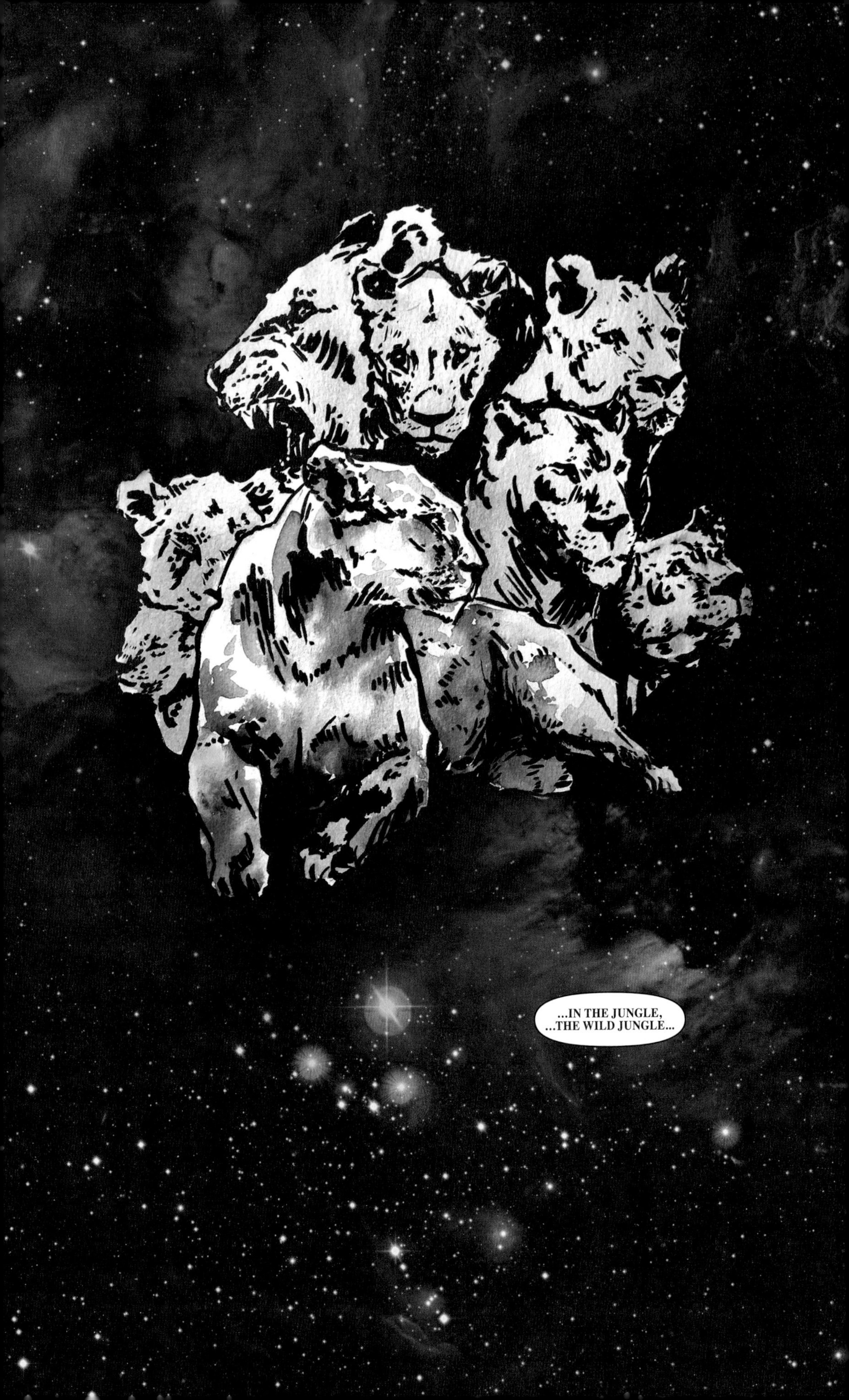
...IN THE JUNGLE,
...THE WILD JUNGLE...

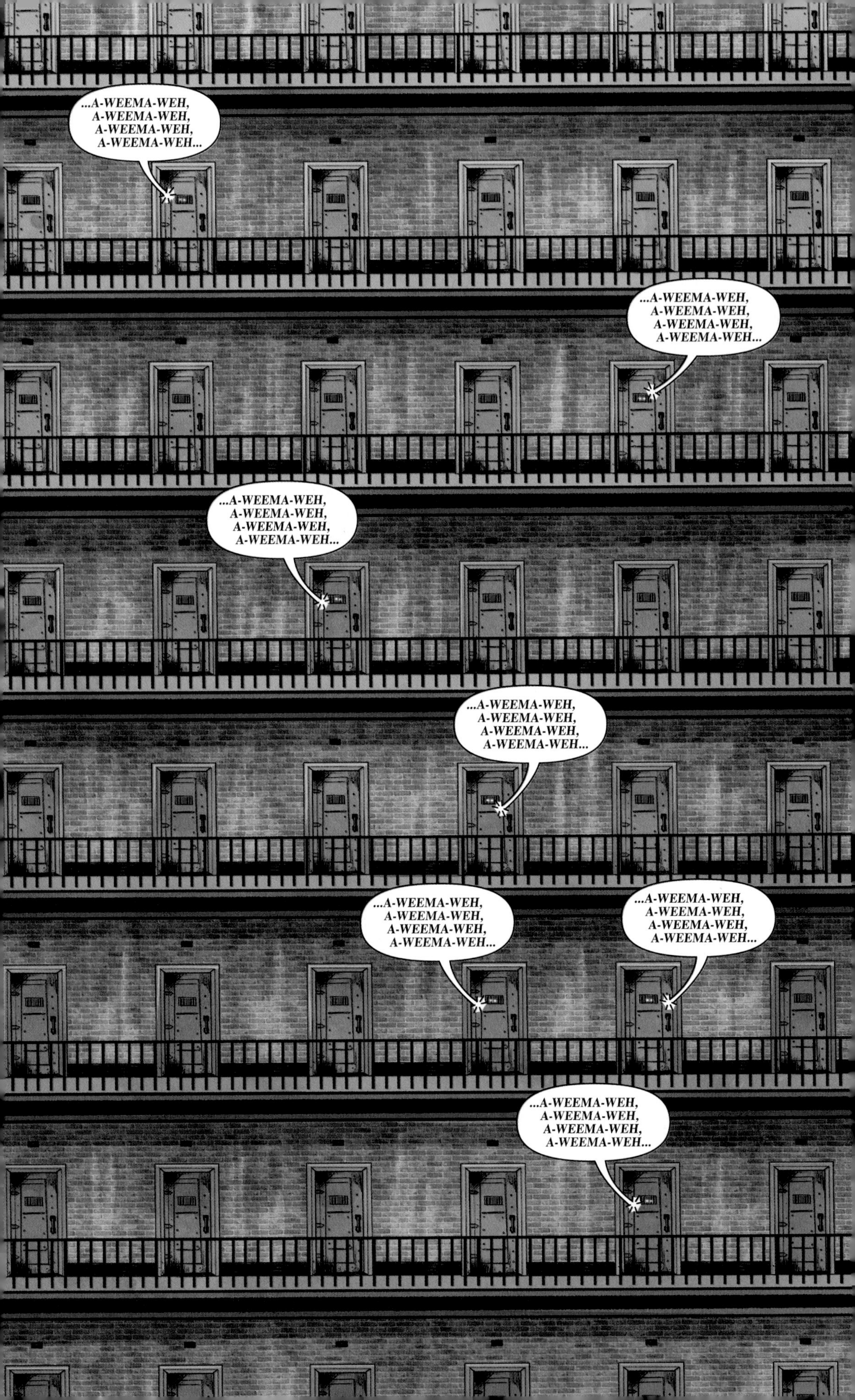
...A-WEEMA-WEH, A-WEEMA-WEH, A-WEEMA-WEH, A-WEEMA-WEH...
...A-WEEMA-WEH, A-WEEMA-WEH, A-WEEMA-WEH, A-WEEMA-WEH...
...A-WEEMA-WEH, A-WEEMA-WEH, A-WEEMA-WEH, A-WEEMA-WEH...
...A-WEEMA-WEH, A-WEEMA-WEH, A-WEEMA-WEH, A-WEEMA-WEH...
...A-WEEMA-WEH, A-WEEMA-WEH, A-WEEMA-WEH, A-WEEMA-WEH...
...A-WEEMA-WEH, A-WEEMA-WEH, A-WEEMA-WEH, A-WEEMA-WEH...
...A-WEEMA-WEH, A-WEEMA-WEH, A-WEEMA-WEH, A-WEEMA-WEH...

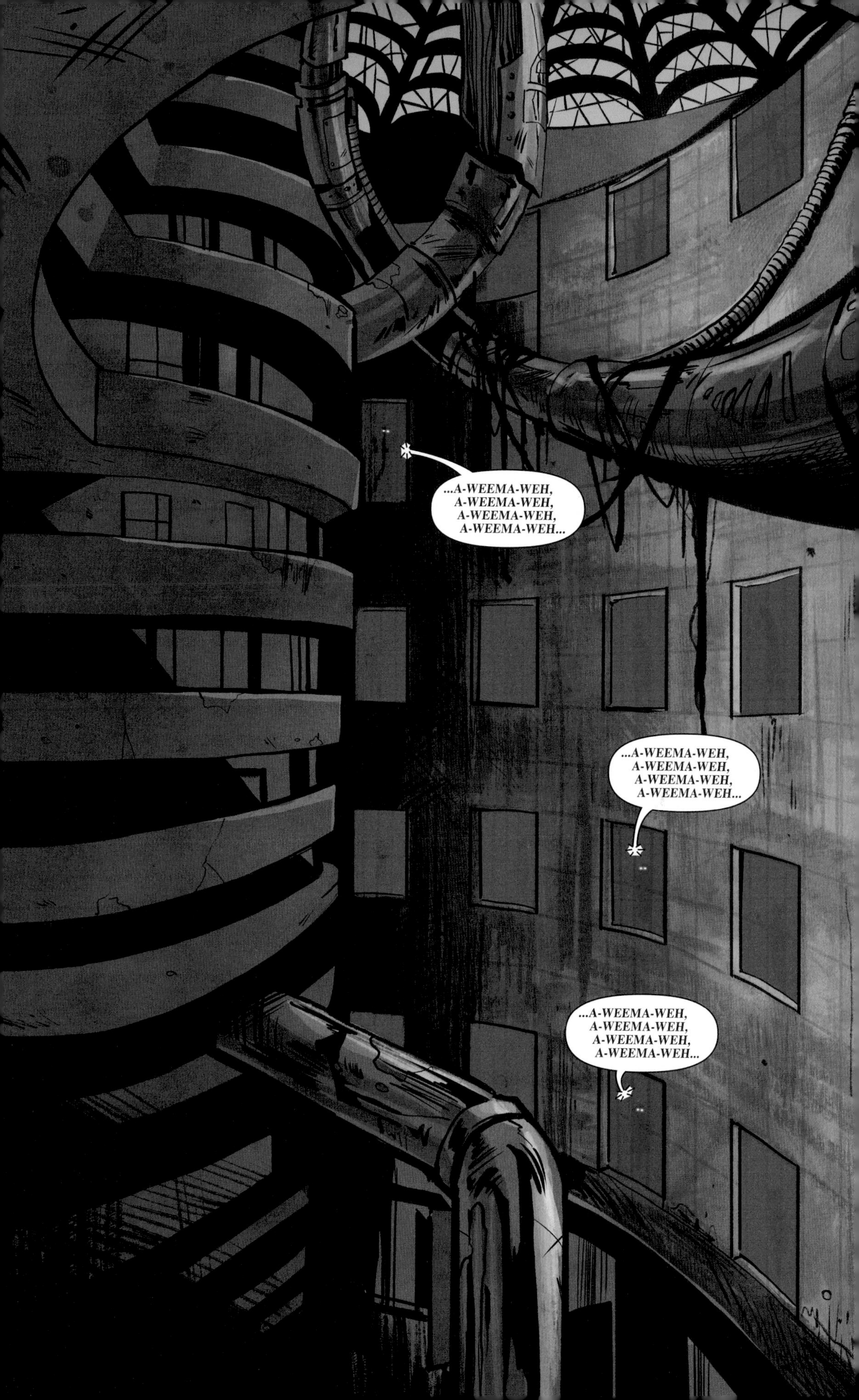
...A-WEEMA-WEH, A-WEEMA-WEH, A-WEEMA-WEH, A-WEEMA-WEH...
...A-WEEMA-WEH, A-WEEMA-WEH, A-WEEMA-WEH, A-WEEMA-WEH...
...A-WEEMA-WEH, A-WEEMA-WEH, A-WEEMA-WEH, A-WEEMA-WEH...

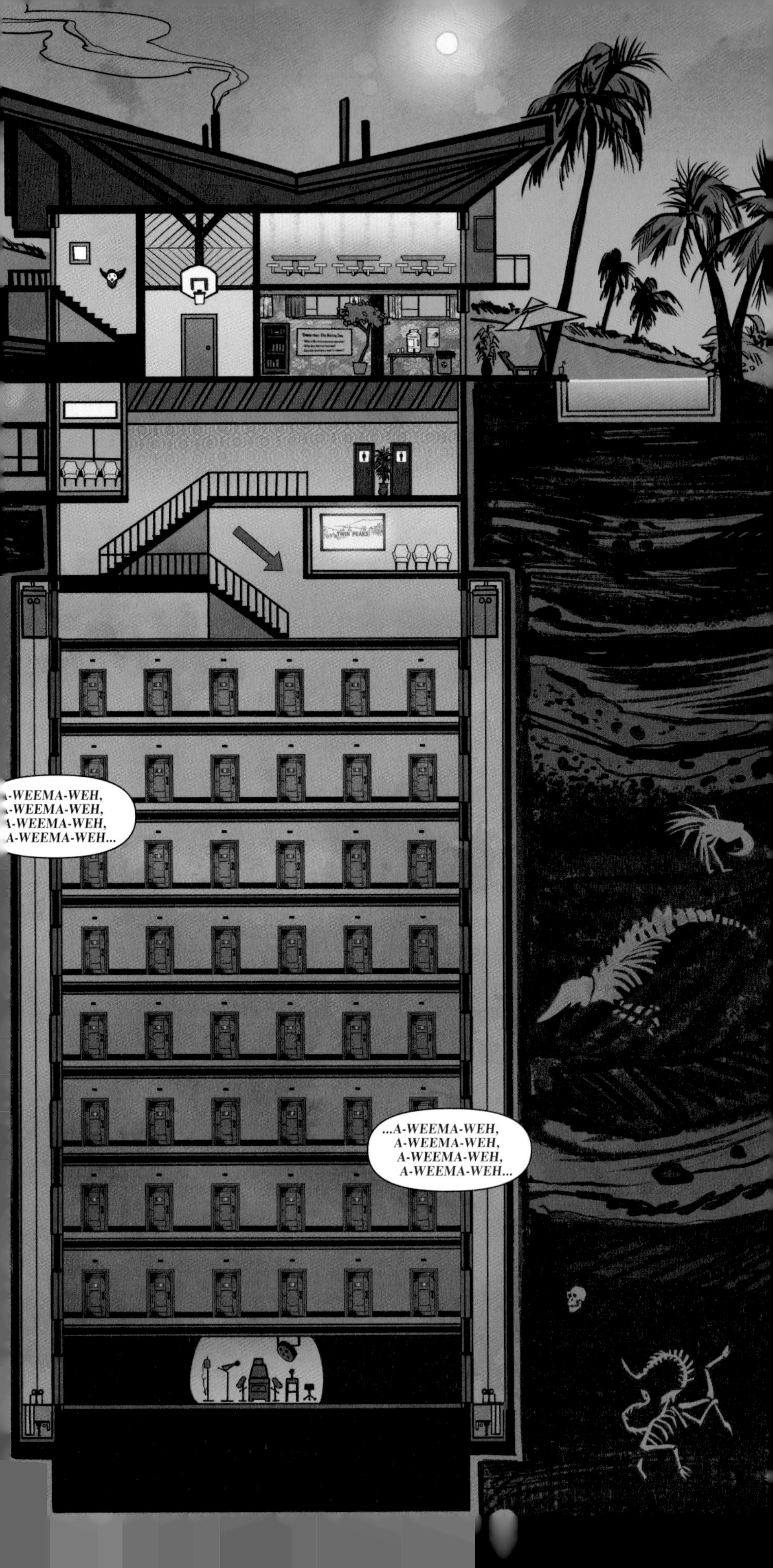
TWIN PEAKS
A-WEEMA-WEH, -WEEMA-WEH, A-WEEMA-WEH, A-WEEMA-WEH...
...A-WEEMA-WEH, A-WEEMA-WEH, A-WEEMA-WEH, A-WEEMA-WEH...

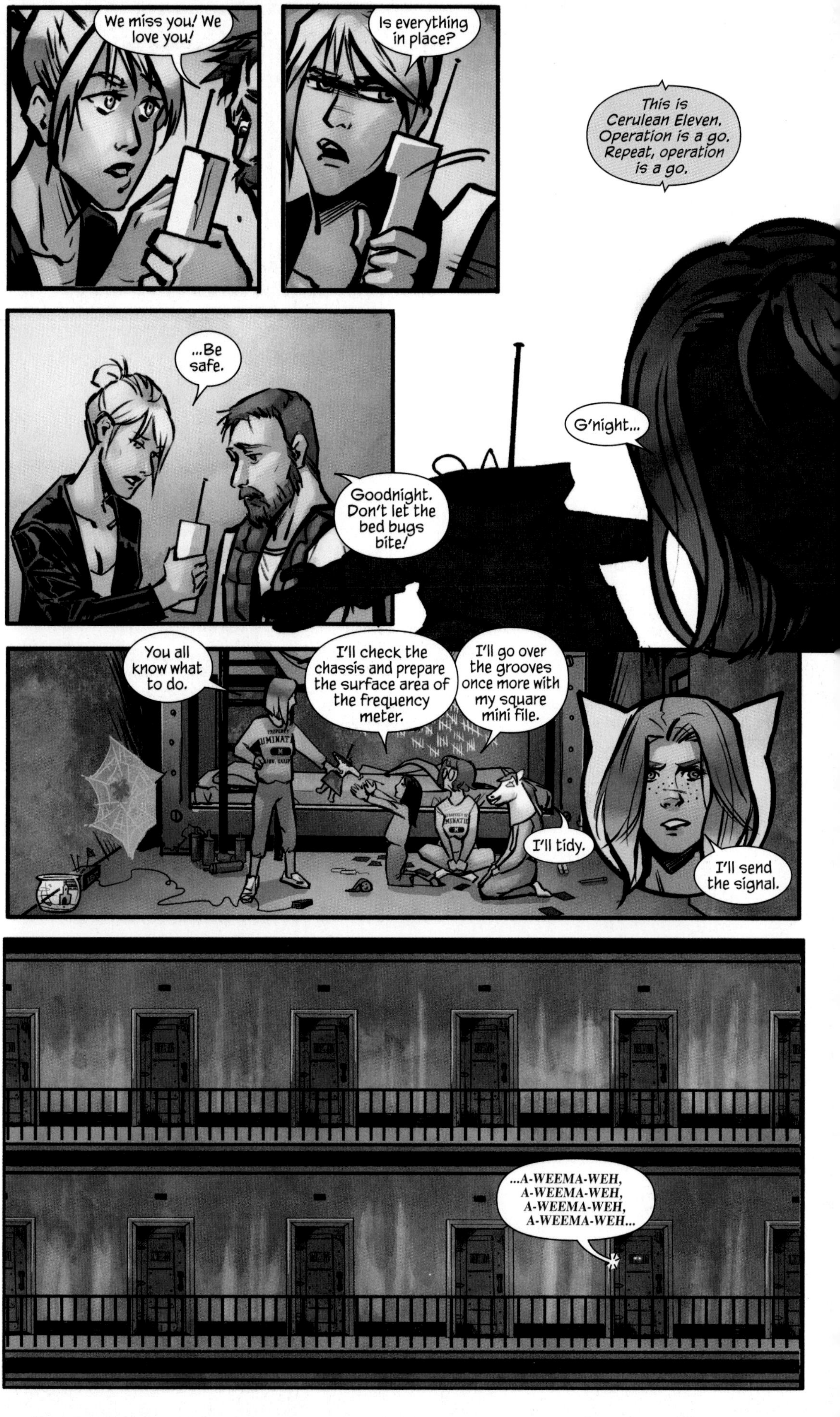
We miss you! We love you!
Is everything in place?
This is Cerulean Eleven. Operation is a go. Repeat, operation is a go.
...Be safe.
Goodnight. Don't let the bed bugs bite!
G'night...
You all know what to do.
I'll check the chassis and prepare the surface area of the frequency meter.
I'll go over the grooves once more with my square mini file.
I'll tidy.
I'll send the signal.
...A-WEEMA-WEH, A-WEEMA-WEH, A-WEEMA-WEH, A-WEEMA-WEH...

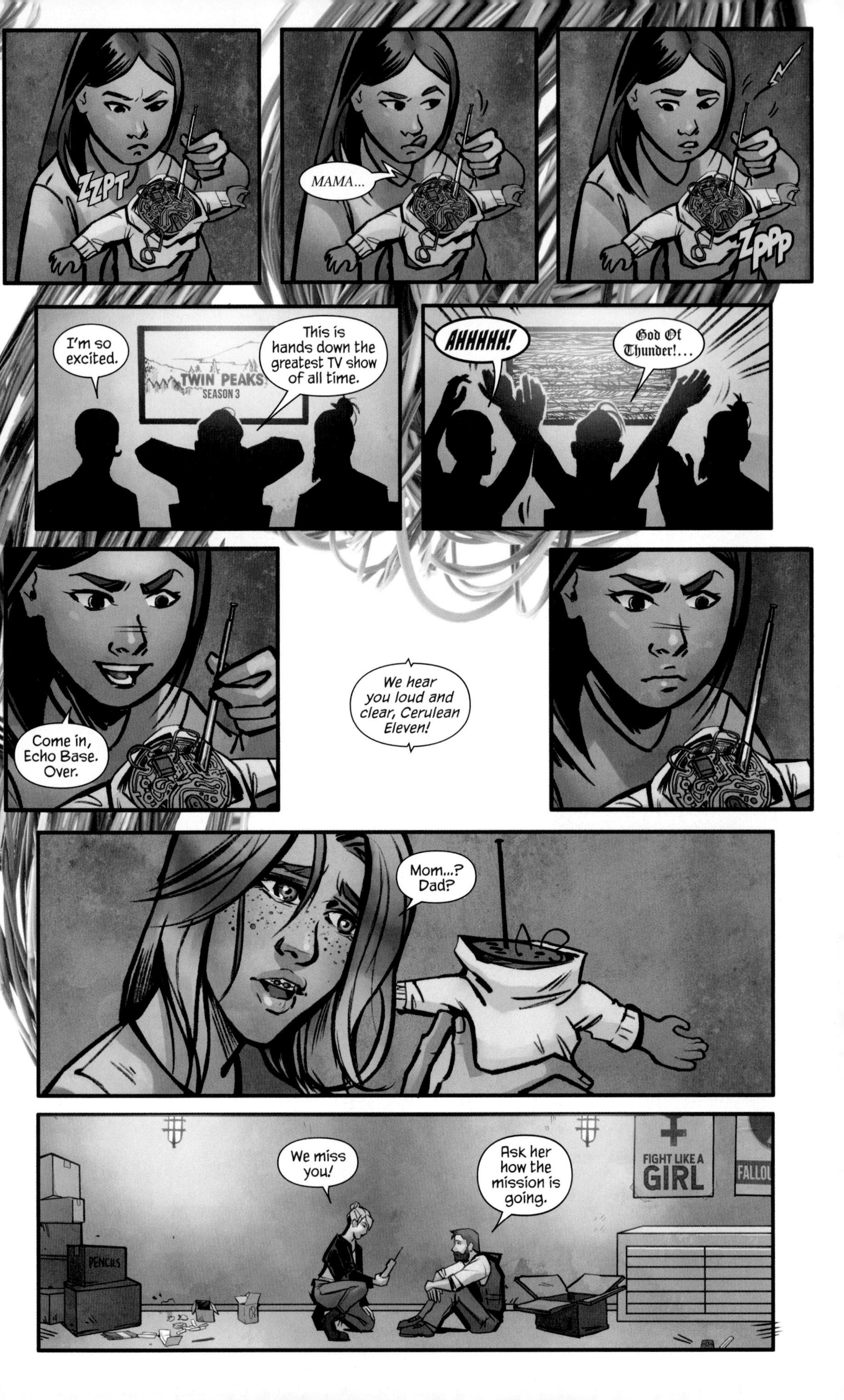
ZZPT
MAMA...
ZPPP
I'm so excited.
TWIN PEAKS
SEASON 3
This is hands down the greatest TV show of all time.
AHHHHH!
God Of Thunder!...
Come in, Echo Base. Over.
We hear you loud and clear, Cerulean Eleven!
Mom...? Dad?
We miss you!
Ask her how the mission is going.
FIGHT LIKE A GIRL
PENCILS

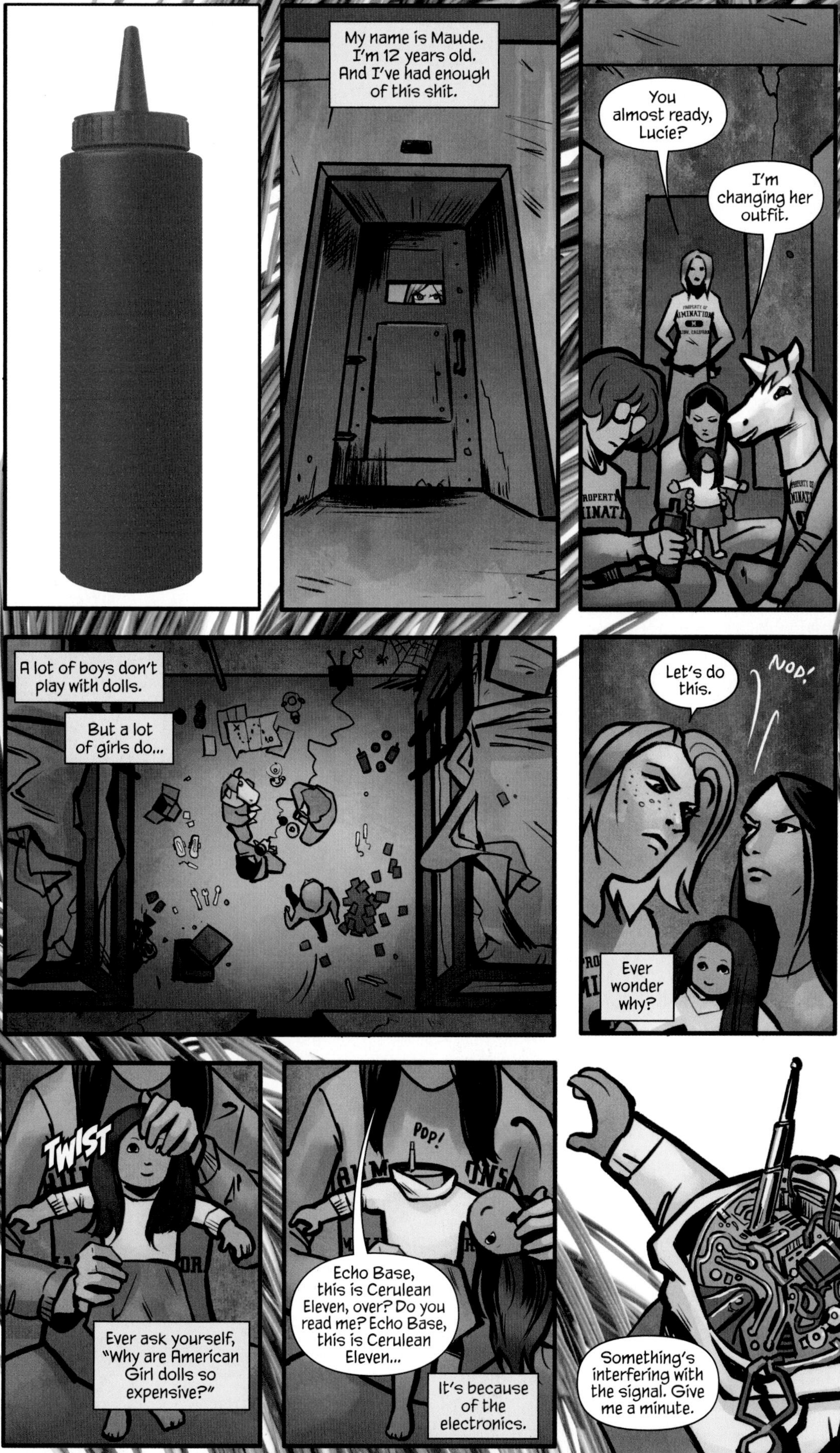
My name is Maude.
I'm 12 years old.
And I've had enough of this shit.
You almost ready, Lucie?
I'm changing her outfit.
A lot of boys don't play with dolls.
But a lot of girls do...
Let's do this.
NOD!
Ever wonder why?
TWIST
Ever ask yourself, "Why are American Girl dolls so expensive?"
POP!
Echo Base, this is Cerulean Eleven, over? Do you read me? Echo Base, this is Cerulean Eleven...
It's because of the electronics.
Something's interfering with the signal. Give me a minute.

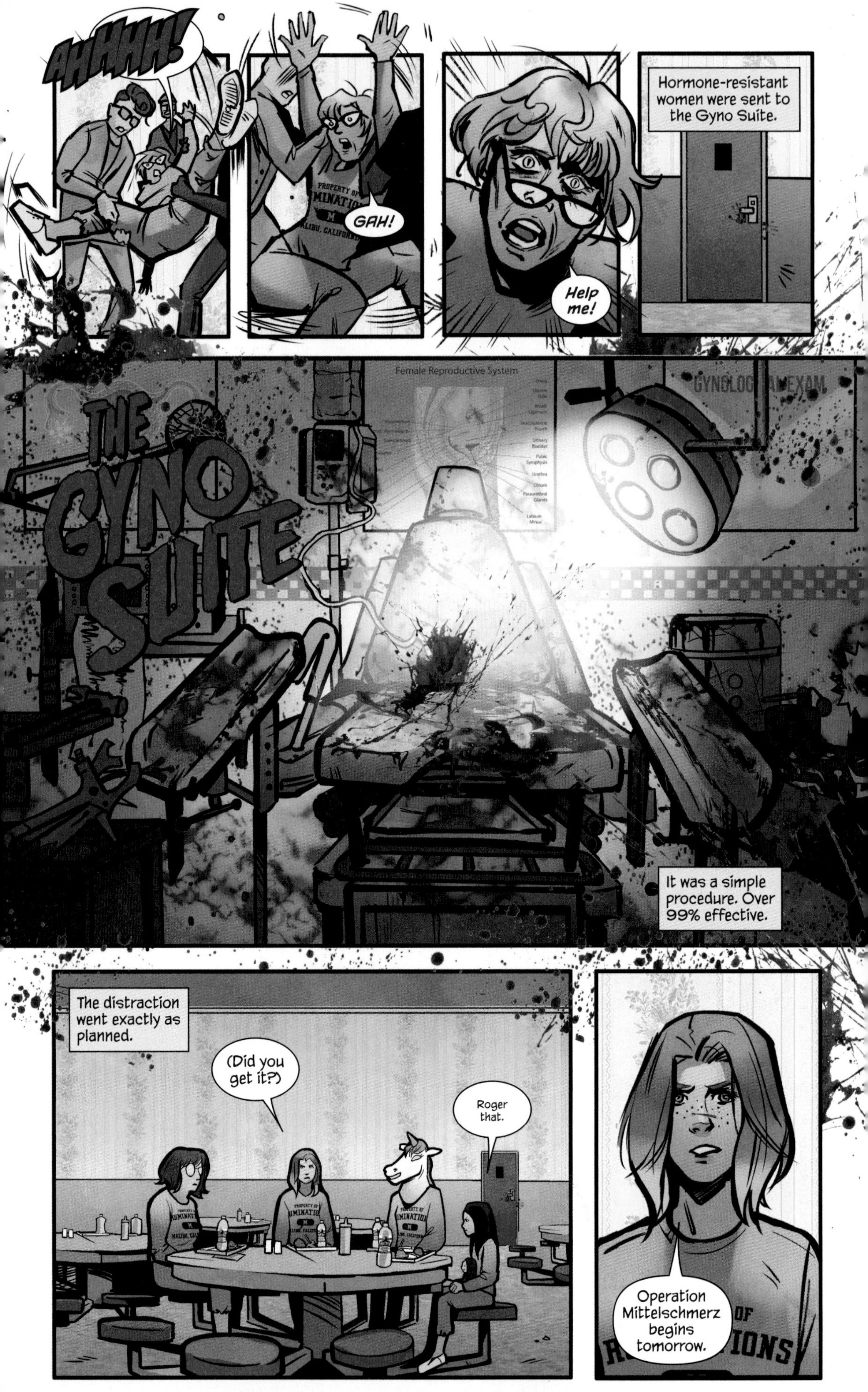
AHHHH!
GAH!
Help me!
Hormone-resistant women were sent to the Gyno Suite.
THE GYNO SUITE
Female Reproductive System
It was a simple procedure. Over 99% effective.
The distraction went exactly as planned.
(Did you get it?)
Roger that.
Operation Mittelschmerz begins tomorrow.

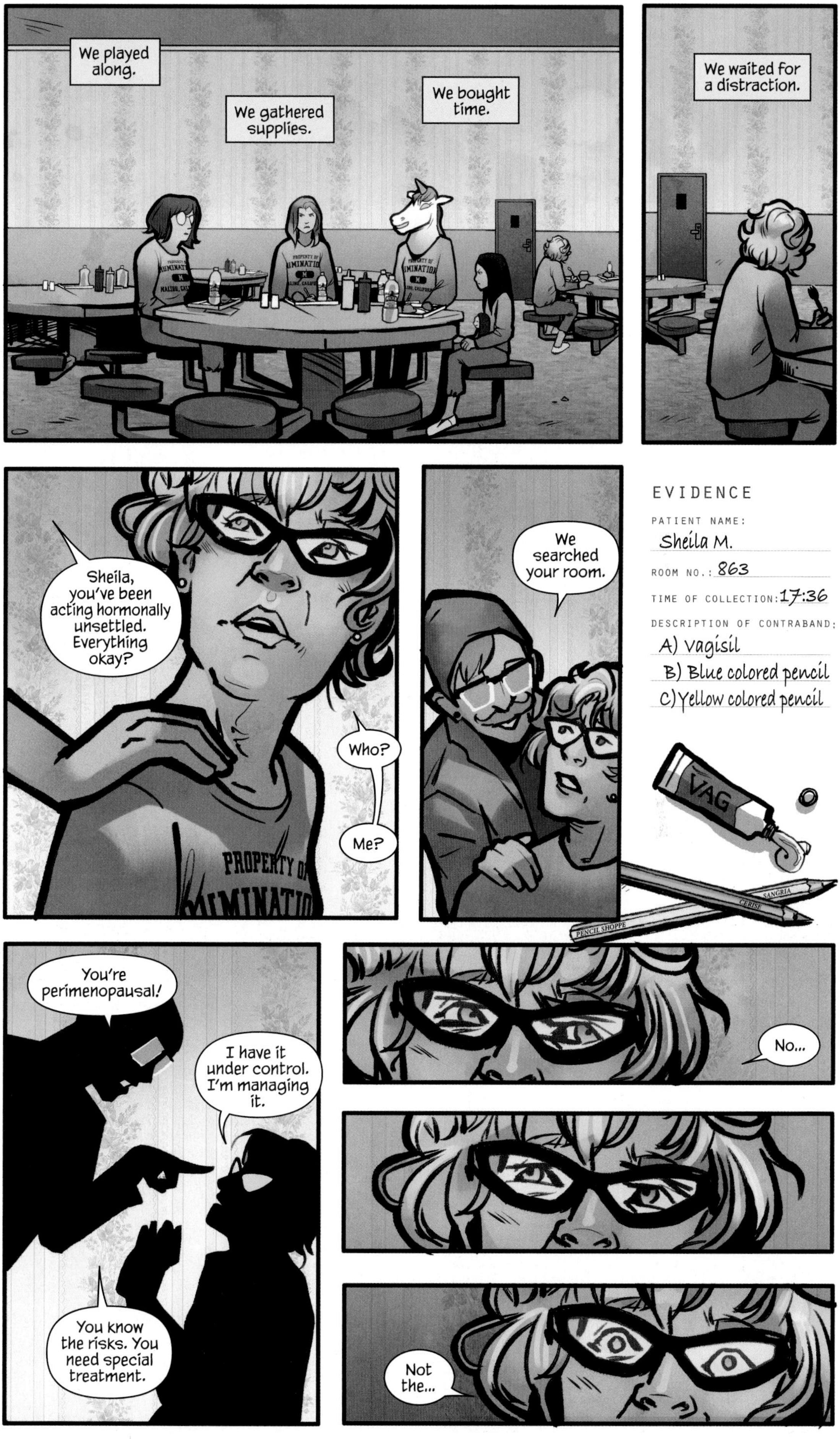

We played along.
We gathered supplies.
We bought time.
PROPERTY OF ELIMINATION
MALIBU, CALIFORNIA
We waited for a distraction.
Sheila, you've been acting hormonally unsettled. Everything okay?
Who?
Me?
PROPERTY OF ELIMINATIO
We searched your room.
EVIDENCE
PATIENT NAME: Sheila M.
ROOM NO.: 863
TIME OF COLLECTION: 17:36
DESCRIPTION OF CONTRABAND:
A) Vagisil
B) Blue colored pencil
C) Yellow colored pencil
VAG
SANGRIA
CERISE
PENCIL SHOPPE
You're perimenopausal!
I have it under control. I'm managing it.
You know the risks. You need special treatment.
No...
Not the...

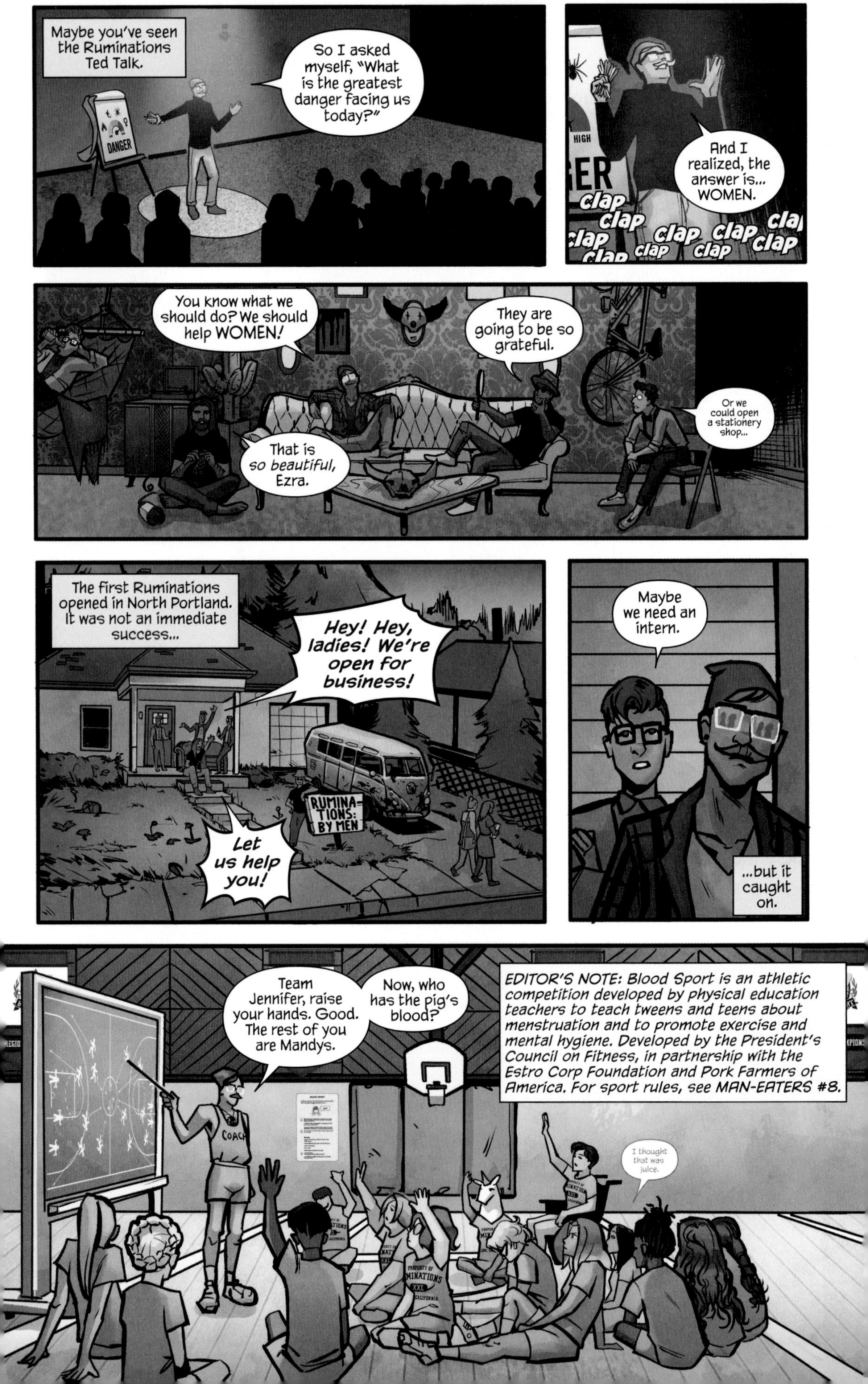
Maybe you've seen the Ruminations Ted Talk.
DANGER
So I asked myself, "What is the greatest danger facing us today?"
HIGH
ER
And I realized, the answer is... WOMEN.
clap clap clap clap clap clap clap clap clap clap
You know what we should do? We should help WOMEN!
They are going to be so grateful.
That is so *beautiful*, Ezra.
Or we could open a stationery shop...
The first Ruminations opened in North Portland. It was not an immediate success...
Hey! Hey, ladies! We're open for business!
RUMINA-TIONS: BY MEN
Let us help you!
Maybe we need an intern.
...but it caught on.
Team Jennifer, raise your hands. Good. The rest of you are Mandys.
Now, who has the pig's blood?
EDITOR'S NOTE: Blood Sport is an athletic competition developed by physical education teachers to teach tweens and teens about menstruation and to promote exercise and mental hygiene. Developed by the President's Council on Fitness, in partnership with the Estro Corp Foundation and Pork Farmers of America. For sport rules, see MAN-EATERS #8.
COACH
I thought that was juice.

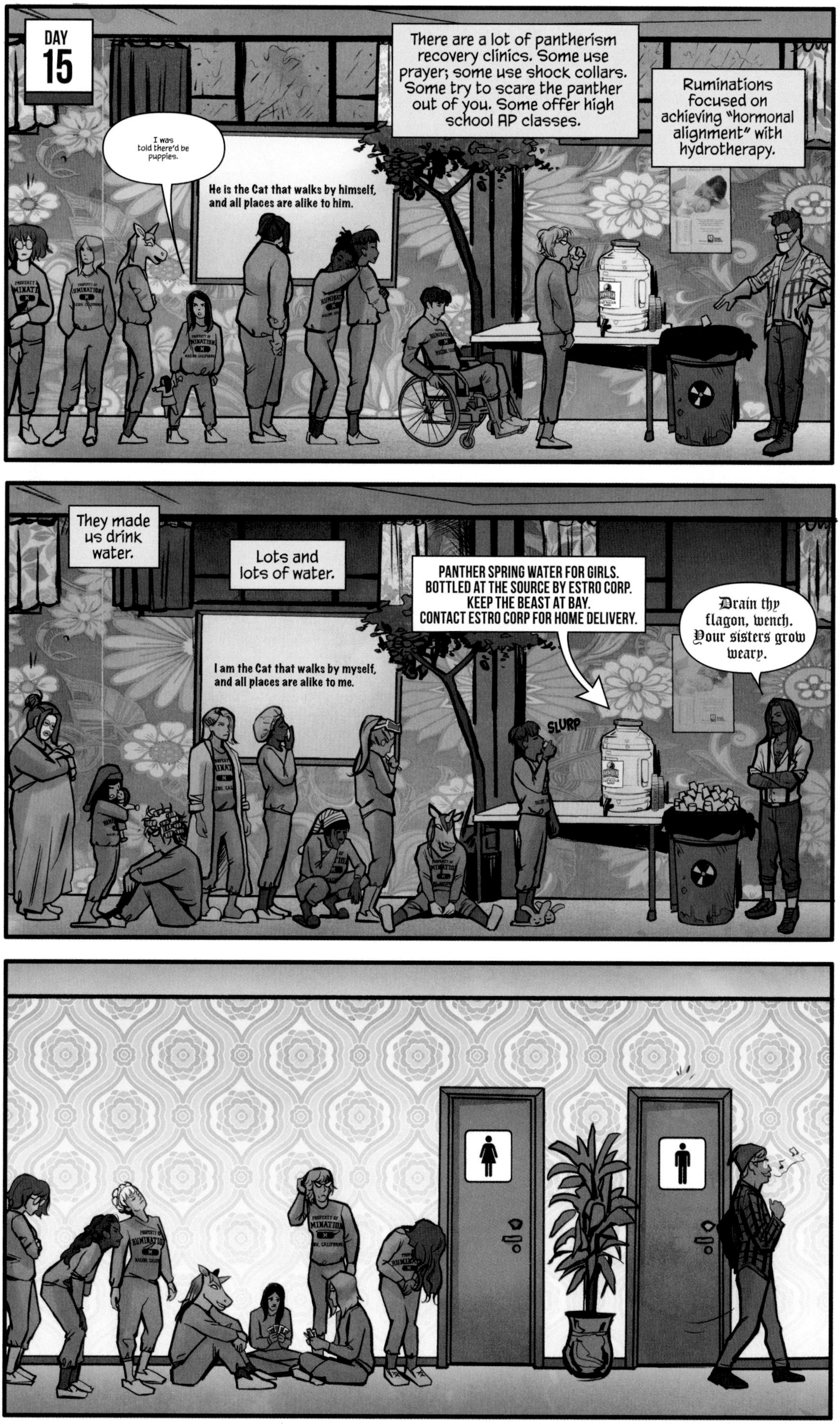
DAY 15
There are a lot of pantherism recovery clinics. Some use prayer; some use shock collars. Some try to scare the panther out of you. Some offer high school AP classes.
Ruminations focused on achieving "hormonal alignment" with hydrotherapy.
I was told there'd be puppies.
He is the Cat that walks by himself, and all places are alike to him.
They made us drink water.
Lots and lots of water.
PANTHER SPRING WATER FOR GIRLS. BOTTLED AT THE SOURCE BY ESTRO CORP. KEEP THE BEAST AT BAY. CONTACT ESTRO CORP FOR HOME DELIVERY.
Drain thy flagon, wench. Your sisters grow weary.
I am the Cat that walks by myself, and all places are alike to me.
SLURP

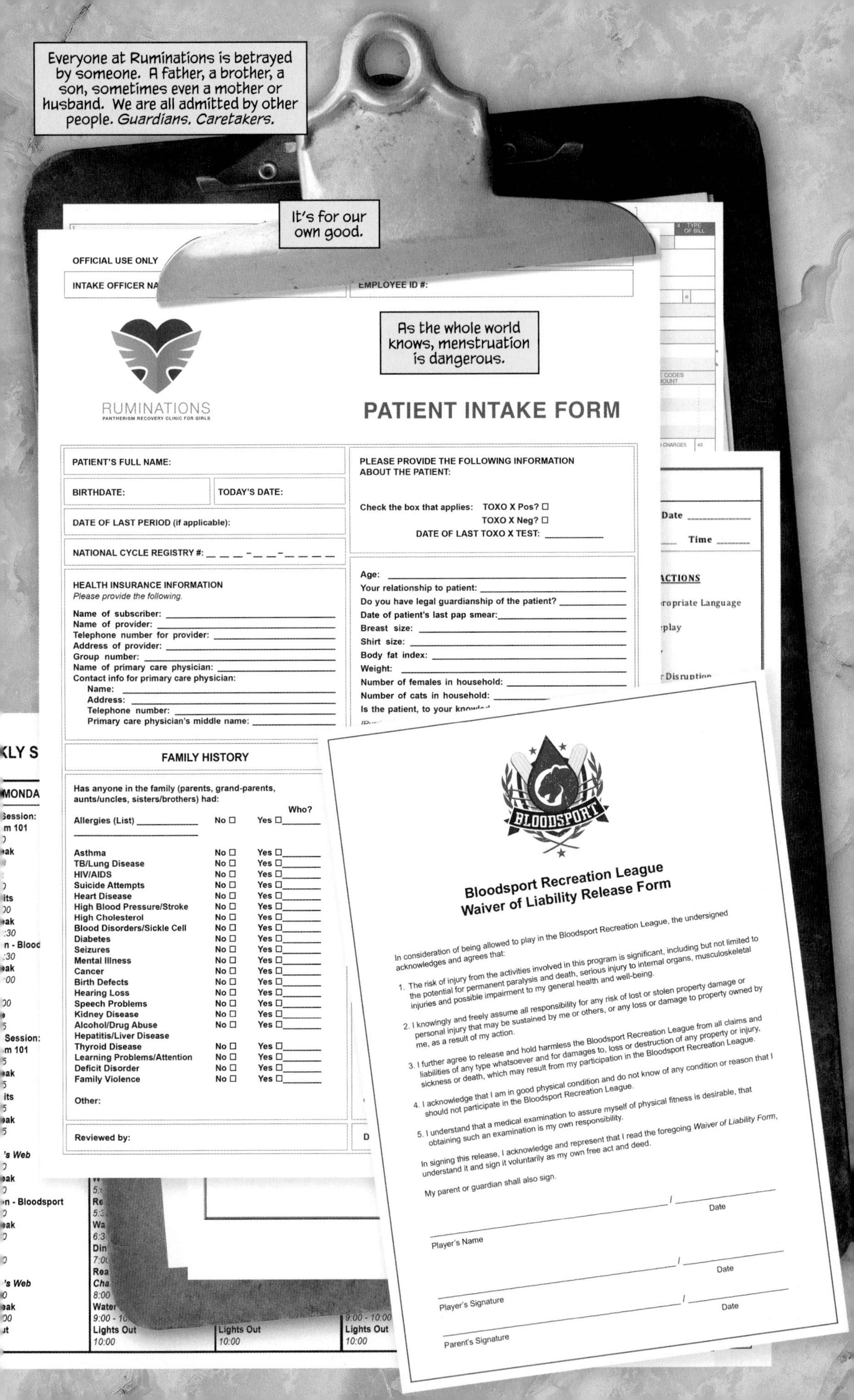
Everyone at Ruminations is betrayed by someone. A father, a brother, a son, sometimes even a mother or husband. We are all admitted by other people. *Guardians. Caretakers.*
It's for our own good.
As the whole world knows, menstruation is dangerous.
OFFICIAL USE ONLY
INTAKE OFFICER NA
EMPLOYEE ID #:
RUMINATIONS
PANTHERISM RECOVERY CLINIC FOR GIRLS
PATIENT INTAKE FORM
PATIENT'S FULL NAME:
BIRTHDATE:
TODAY'S DATE:
DATE OF LAST PERIOD (if applicable):
NATIONAL CYCLE REGISTRY #:
PLEASE PROVIDE THE FOLLOWING INFORMATION ABOUT THE PATIENT:
Check the box that applies: TOXO X Pos? ☐
TOXO X Neg? ☐
DATE OF LAST TOXO X TEST:
HEALTH INSURANCE INFORMATION
Please provide the following.
Name of subscriber:
Name of provider:
Telephone number for provider:
Address of provider:
Group number:
Name of primary care physician:
Contact info for primary care physician:
Name:
Address:
Telephone number:
Primary care physician's middle name:
Age:
Your relationship to patient:
Do you have legal guardianship of the patient?
Date of patient's last pap smear:
Breast size:
Shirt size:
Body fat index:
Weight:
Number of females in household:
Number of cats in household:
FAMILY HISTORY
Has anyone in the family (parents, grand-parents, aunts/uncles, sisters/brothers) had:
Who?
Allergies (List) No ☐ Yes ☐
Asthma No ☐ Yes ☐
TB/Lung Disease No ☐ Yes ☐
HIV/AIDS No ☐ Yes ☐
Suicide Attempts No ☐ Yes ☐
Heart Disease No ☐ Yes ☐
High Blood Pressure/Stroke No ☐ Yes ☐
High Cholesterol No ☐ Yes ☐
Blood Disorders/Sickle Cell No ☐ Yes ☐
Diabetes No ☐ Yes ☐
Seizures No ☐ Yes ☐
Mental Illness No ☐ Yes ☐
Cancer No ☐ Yes ☐
Birth Defects No ☐ Yes ☐
Hearing Loss No ☐ Yes ☐
Speech Problems No ☐ Yes ☐
Kidney Disease No ☐ Yes ☐
Alcohol/Drug Abuse No ☐ Yes ☐
Hepatitis/Liver Disease
Thyroid Disease No ☐ Yes ☐
Learning Problems/Attention Deficit Disorder No ☐ Yes ☐
Family Violence No ☐ Yes ☐
Other:
Reviewed by:
BLOODSPORT
Bloodsport Recreation League
Waiver of Liability Release Form
In consideration of being allowed to play in the Bloodsport Recreation League, the undersigned acknowledges and agrees that:
1. The risk of injury from the activities involved in this program is significant, including but not limited to the potential for permanent paralysis and death, serious injury to internal organs, musculoskeletal injuries and possible impairment to my general health and well-being.
2. I knowingly and freely assume all responsibility for any risk of lost or stolen property damage or personal injury that may be sustained by me or others, or any loss or damage to property owned by me, as a result of my action.
3. I further agree to release and hold harmless the Bloodsport Recreation League from all claims and liabilities of any type whatsoever and for damages to, loss or destruction of any property or injury, sickness or death, which may result from my participation in the Bloodsport Recreation League.
4. I acknowledge that I am in good physical condition and do not know of any condition or reason that I should not participate in the Bloodsport Recreation League.
5. I understand that a medical examination to assure myself of physical fitness is desirable, that obtaining such an examination is my own responsibility.
In signing this release, I acknowledge and represent that I read the foregoing *Waiver of Liability Form*, understand it and sign it voluntarily as my own free act and deed.
My parent or guardian shall also sign.
Player's Name
Date
Player's Signature
Date
Parent's Signature
Date

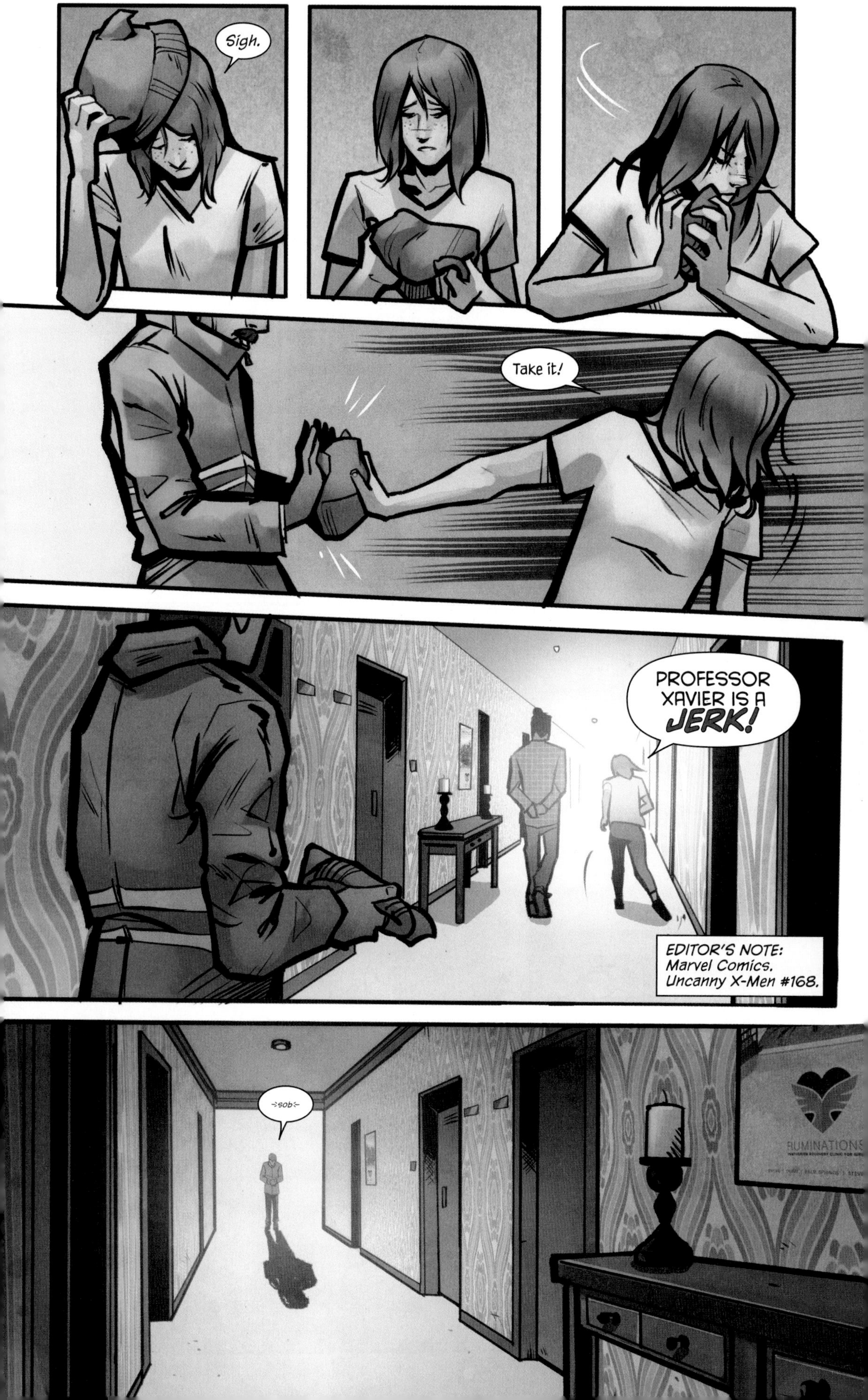
Sigh.
Take it!
PROFESSOR XAVIER IS A JERK!
EDITOR'S NOTE: Marvel Comics. Uncanny X-Men #168.
sob
RUMINATIONS

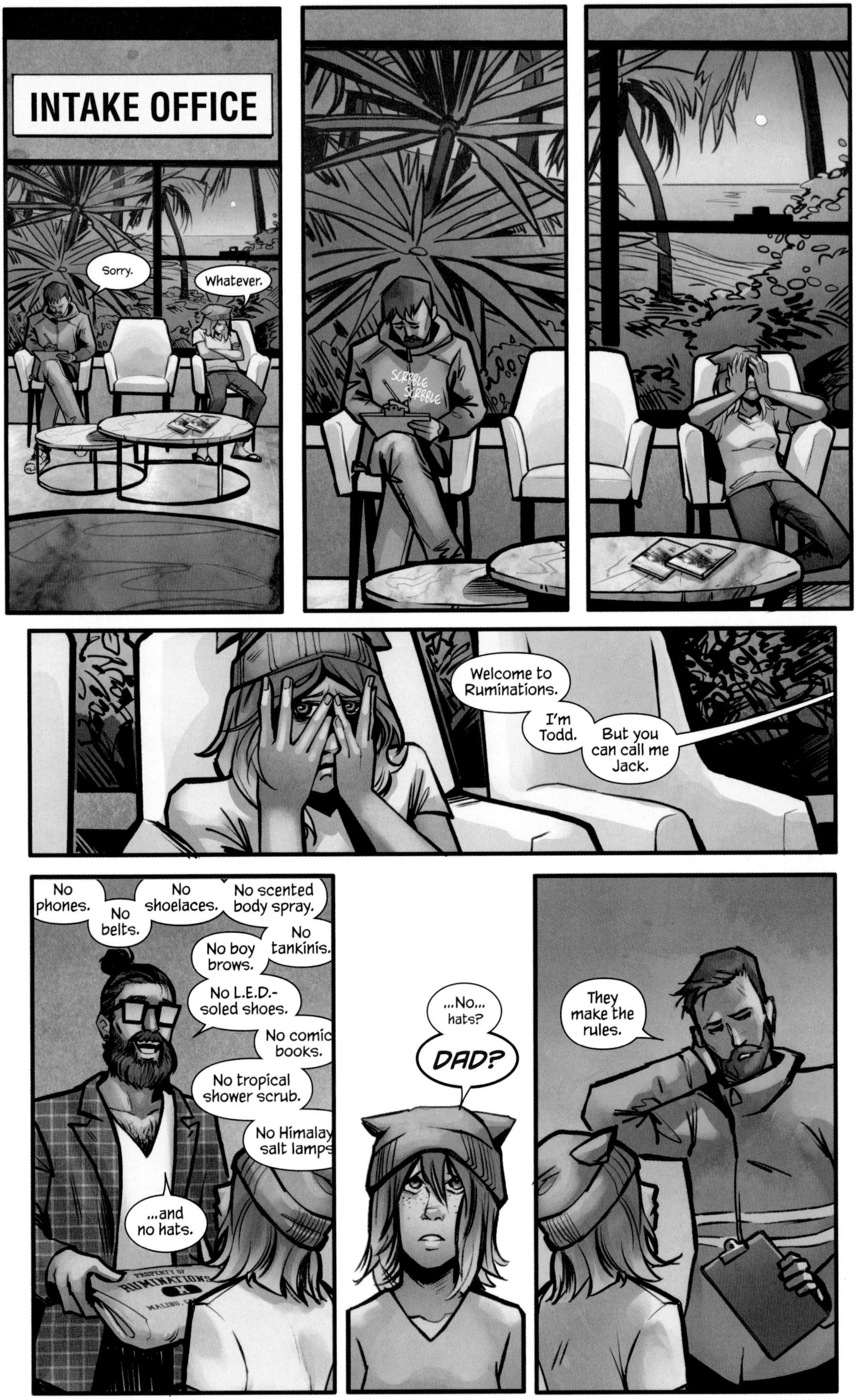
INTAKE OFFICE
Sorry.
Whatever.
SCRBBLE SCRBBLE
Welcome to Ruminations.
I'm Todd.
But you can call me Jack.
No phones.
No belts.
No shoelaces.
No scented body spray.
No tankinis.
No boy brows.
No L.E.D.-soled shoes.
No comic books.
No tropical shower scrub.
No Himalay salt lamps
...and no hats.
PROPERTY OF RUMINATIONS
MALIBU, C
...No... hats?
DAD?
They make the rules.

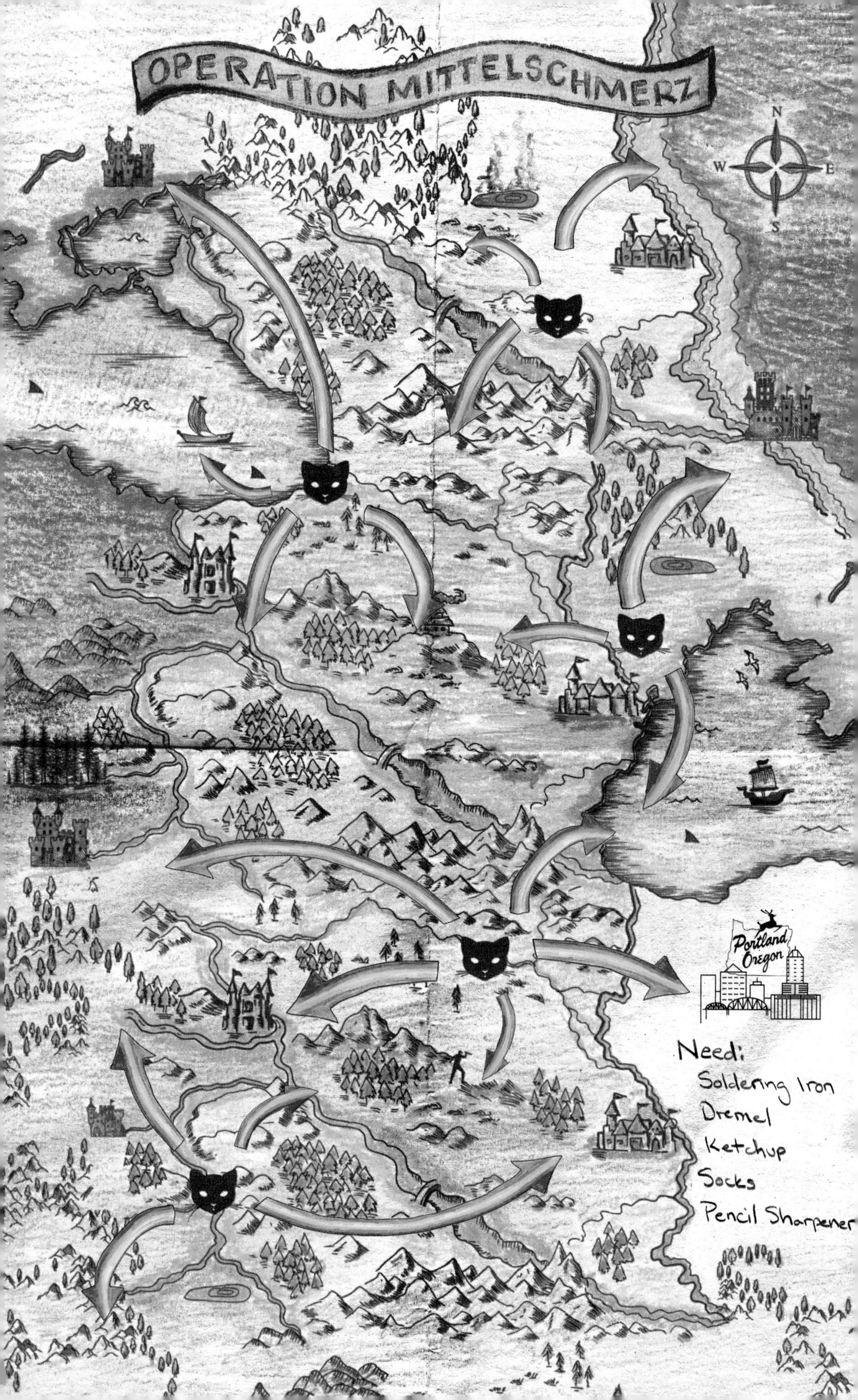
OPERATION MITTELSCHMERZ
N
W
E
S
Portland Oregon
Need:
Soldering Iron
Dremel
Ketchup
Socks
Pencil Sharpener

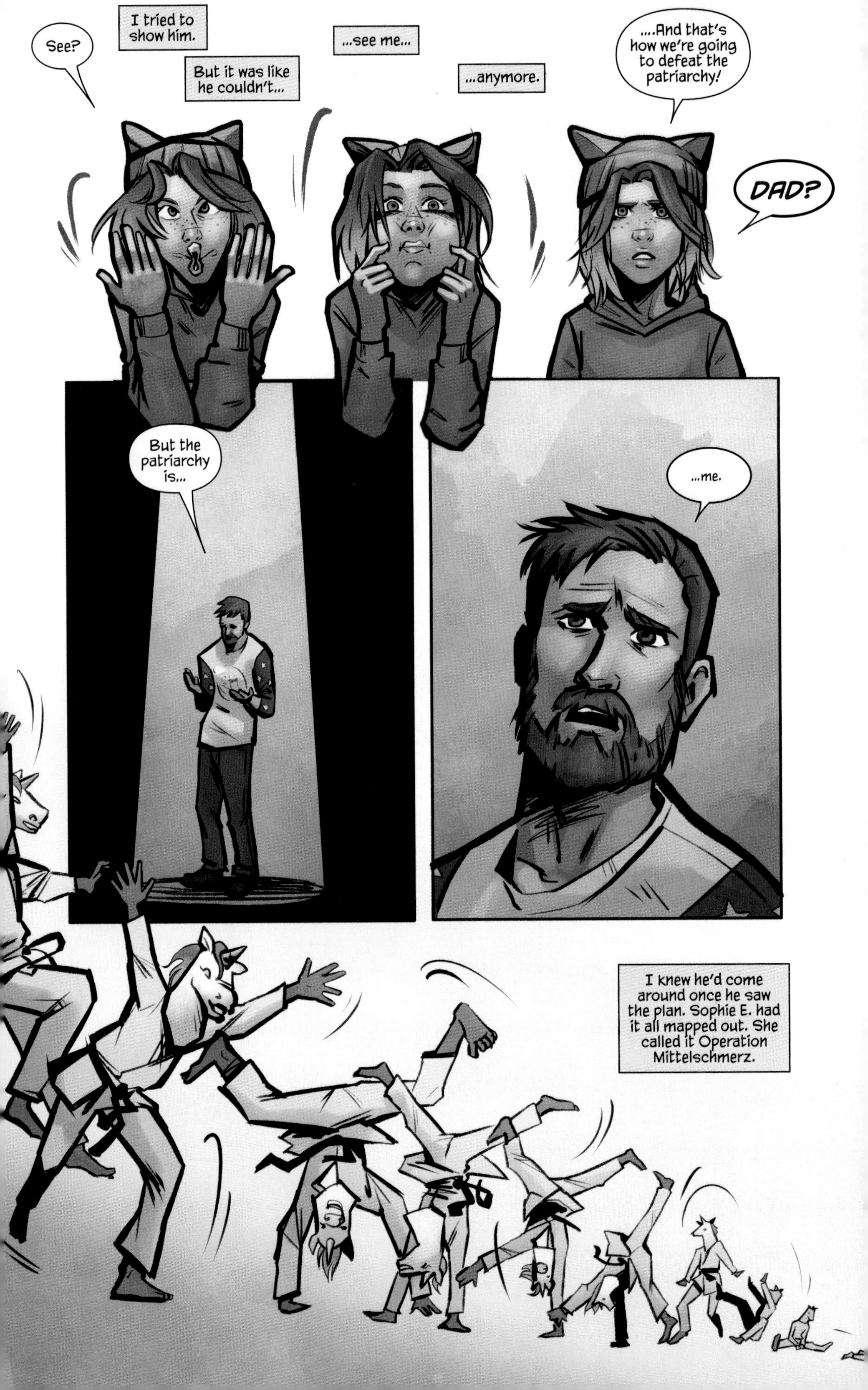
See?
I tried to show him.
But it was like he couldn't...
...see me...
...anymore.
....And that's how we're going to defeat the patriarchy!
DAD?
But the patriarchy is...
...me.
I knew he'd come around once he saw the plan. Sophie E. had it all mapped out. She called it Operation Mittelschmerz.

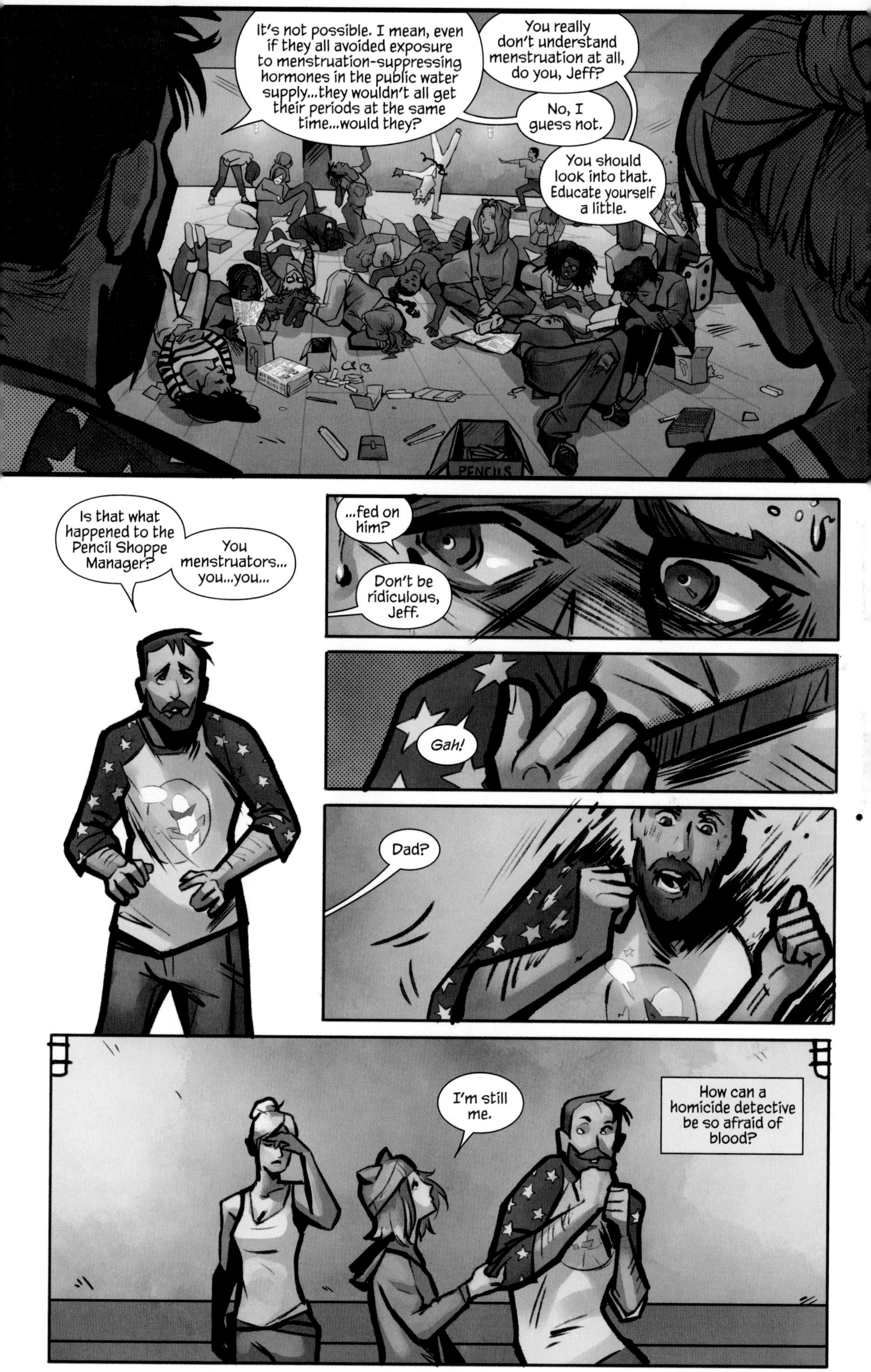
It's not possible. I mean, even if they all avoided exposure to menstruation-suppressing hormones in the public water supply...they wouldn't all get their periods at the same time...would they?
You really don't understand menstruation at all, do you, Jeff?
No, I guess not.
You should look into that. Educate yourself a little.
PENCILS
Is that what happened to the Pencil Shoppe Manager?
You menstruators... you...you...
...fed on him?
Don't be ridiculous, Jeff.
Gah!
Dad?
I'm still me.
How can a homicide detective be so afraid of blood?

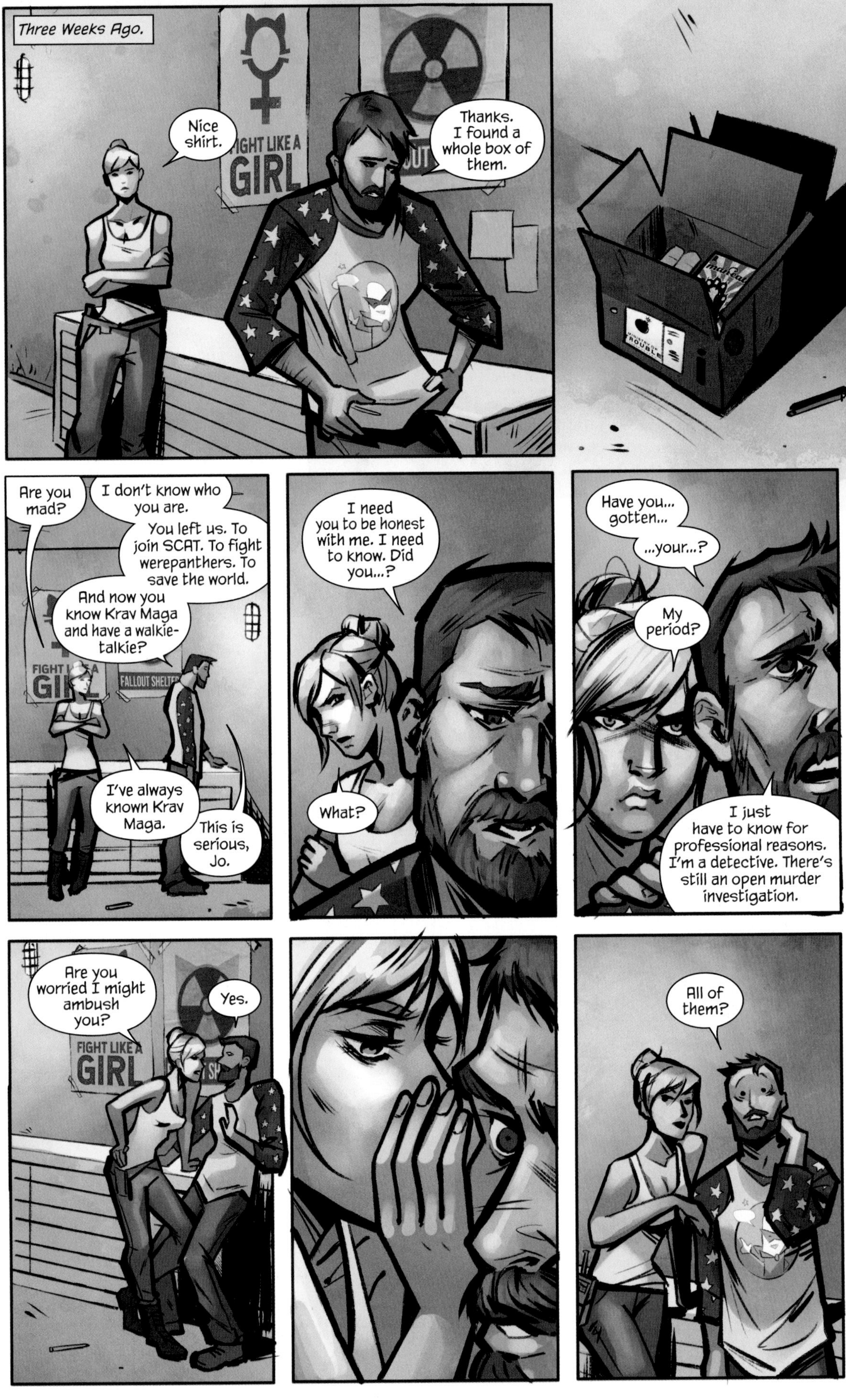
Three Weeks Ago.
Nice shirt.
FIGHT LIKE A GIRL
Thanks. I found a whole box of them.
Are you mad?
I don't know who you are.
You left us. To join SCAT. To fight werepanthers. To save the world.
And now you know Krav Maga and have a walkie-talkie?
FIGHT LIKE A GIRL
FALLOUT SHELTER
I've always known Krav Maga.
This is serious, Jo.
I need you to be honest with me. I need to know. Did you...?
What?
Have you... gotten...
...your...?
My period?
I just have to know for professional reasons. I'm a detective. There's still an open murder investigation.
Are you worried I might ambush you?
Yes.
FIGHT LIKE A GIRL
All of them?

"...and waved one of her front legs at him.

"She never moved again.

"Next day, as the Ferris wheel was being taken apart and the race horses were being loaded into vans and the entertainers were packing up their belongings and driving away in their trailers, Charlotte died.

"...The Fair Grounds were soon deserted. The sheds and buildings were empty and forlorn. The infield was littered with bottles and trash.

"Nobody, of the hundreds of people that had visited the Fair, knew that a grey spider had played the most important part of all...

"No one was with her when she died."

→sniff←   →sniff←   →sob←

→hiccup←

PROPERTY OF
RUMINATIONS
M
MALIBU, CALIFORNIA

We're all alone. In the end.

PROPERTY OF
RUMINATION
L
MALIBU, CALIFOR

You *bastard.*

Gahhh...

Tomorrow, we start *The Diary of Anne Frank.*

Guhhh...
→sob←

→SNIFF←
→sniff←
→sob←

Gahhh...

→snoof←
Gah GAHHH
→sob←

Wuhhh...

OH GOD! Guh!

→snff←
→Hrrk←
→sob←

→hrk←

N-N-NOOO!

Really?? Whuu...

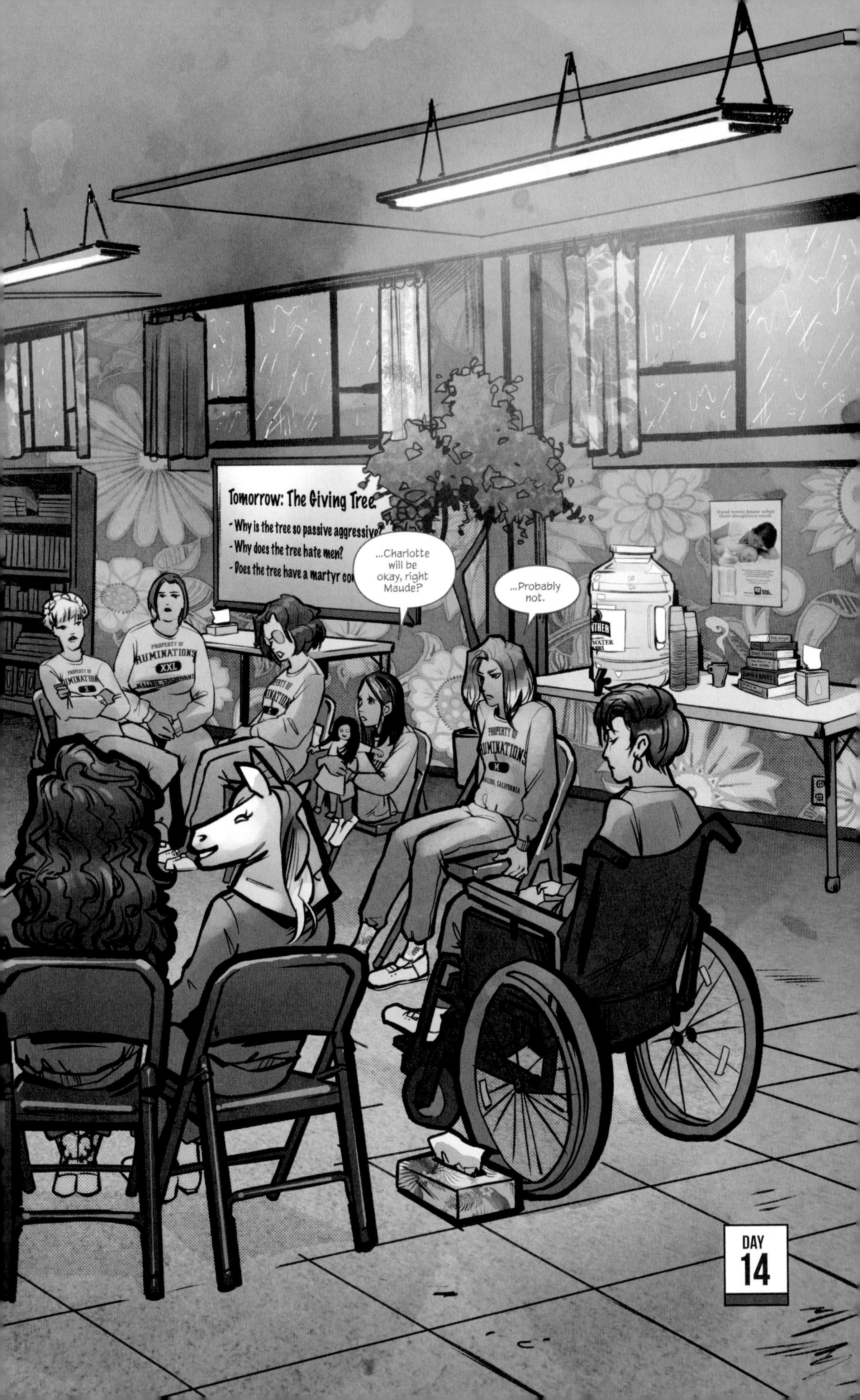
Tomorrow: The Giving Tree.
- Why is the tree so passive aggressive?
- Why does the tree hate men?
- Does the tree have a martyr co
Good moms know what their daughters need.
...Charlotte will be okay, right Maude?
...Probably not.
DAY 14

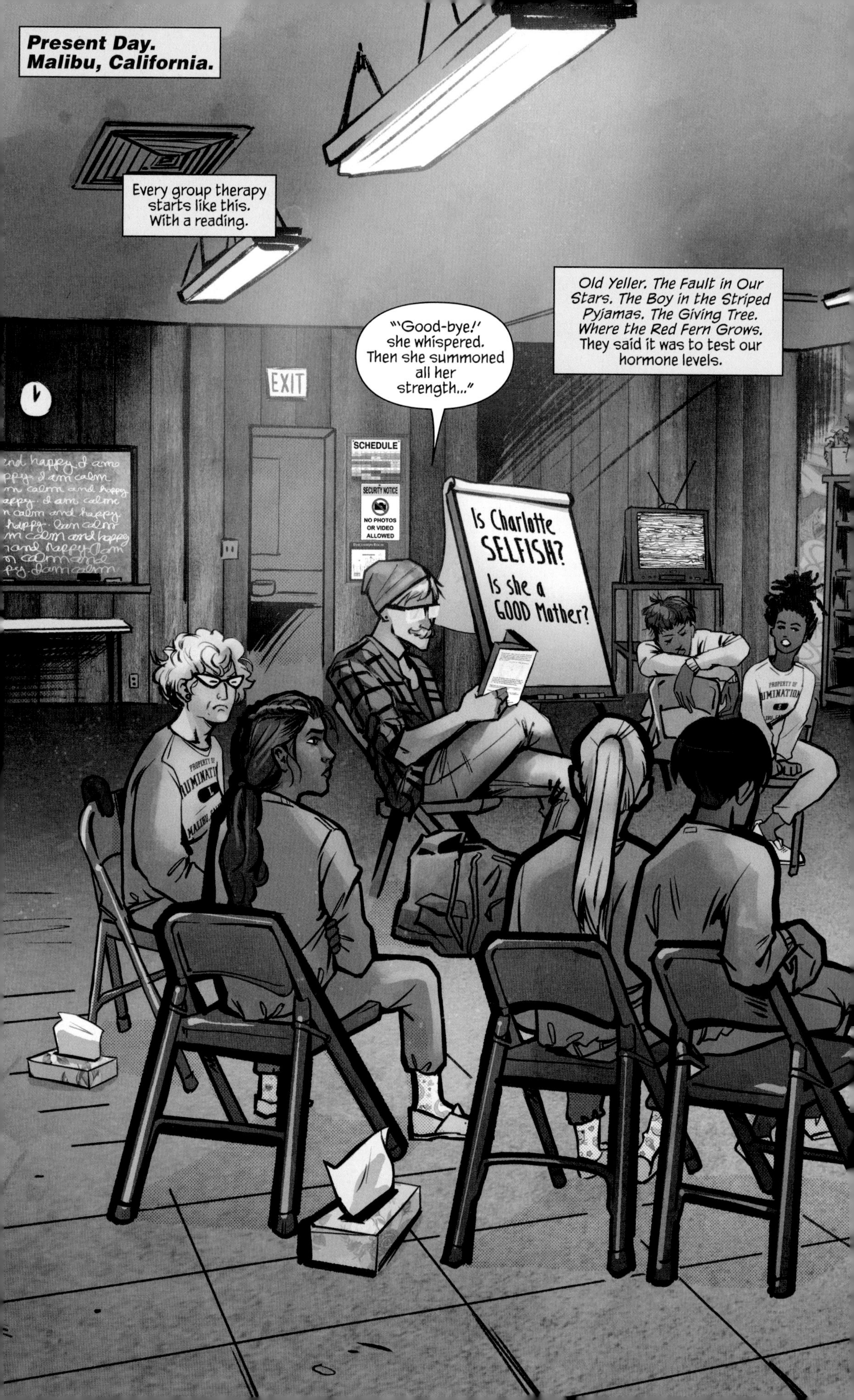
Present Day. Malibu, California.
Every group therapy starts like this. With a reading.
Old Yeller. The Fault in Our Stars. The Boy in the Striped Pyjamas. The Giving Tree. Where the Red Fern Grows. They said it was to test our hormone levels.
"'Good-bye!' she whispered. Then she summoned all her strength..."
EXIT
SCHEDULE
SECURITY NOTICE
NO PHOTOS OR VIDEO ALLOWED
Is Charlotte SELFISH? Is she a GOOD Mother?

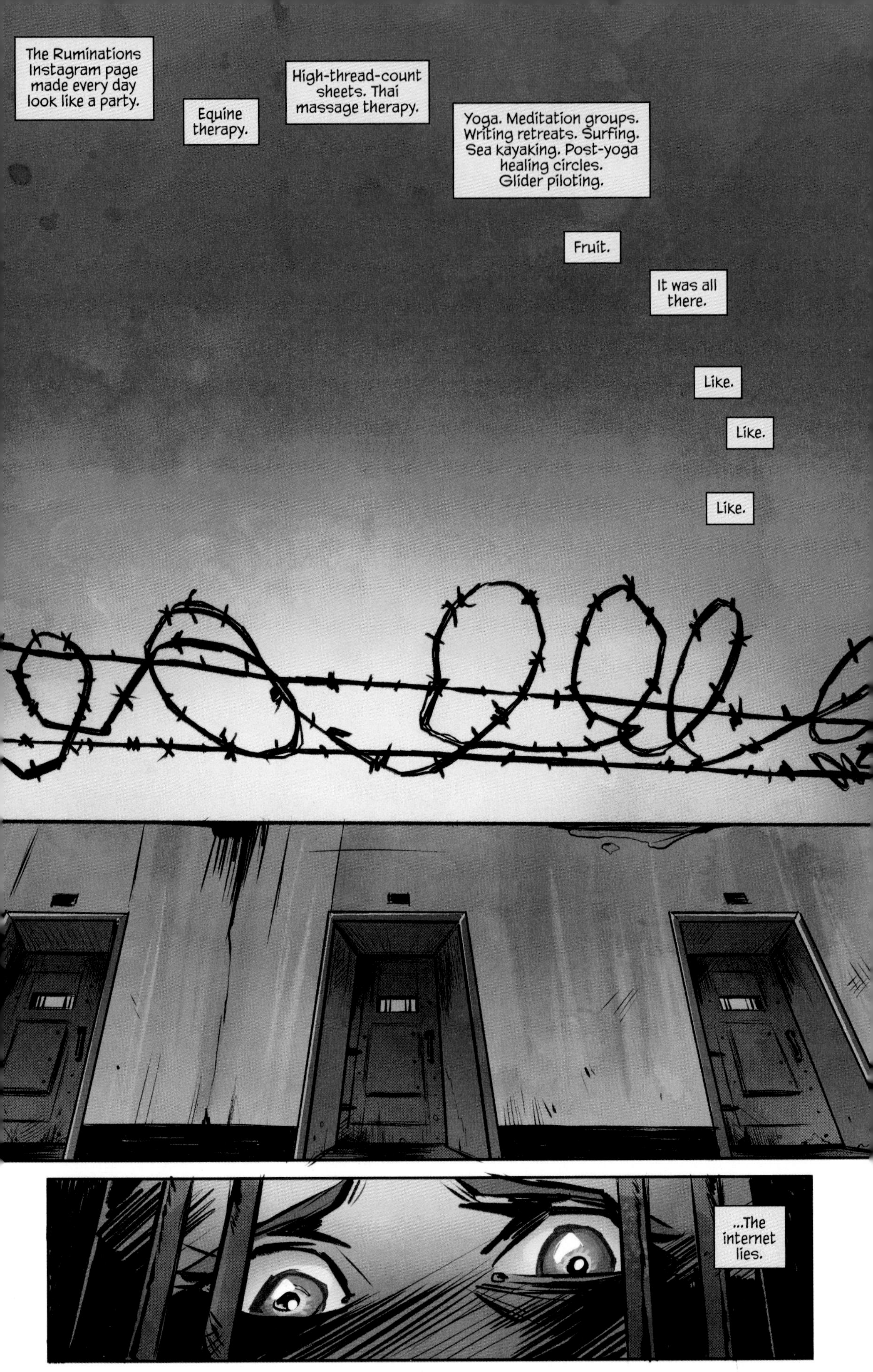
The Ruminations Instagram page made every day look like a party.
Equine therapy.
High-thread-count sheets. Thai massage therapy.
Yoga. Meditation groups. Writing retreats. Surfing. Sea kayaking. Post-yoga healing circles. Glider piloting.
Fruit.
It was all there.
Like.
Like.
Like.
...The internet lies.

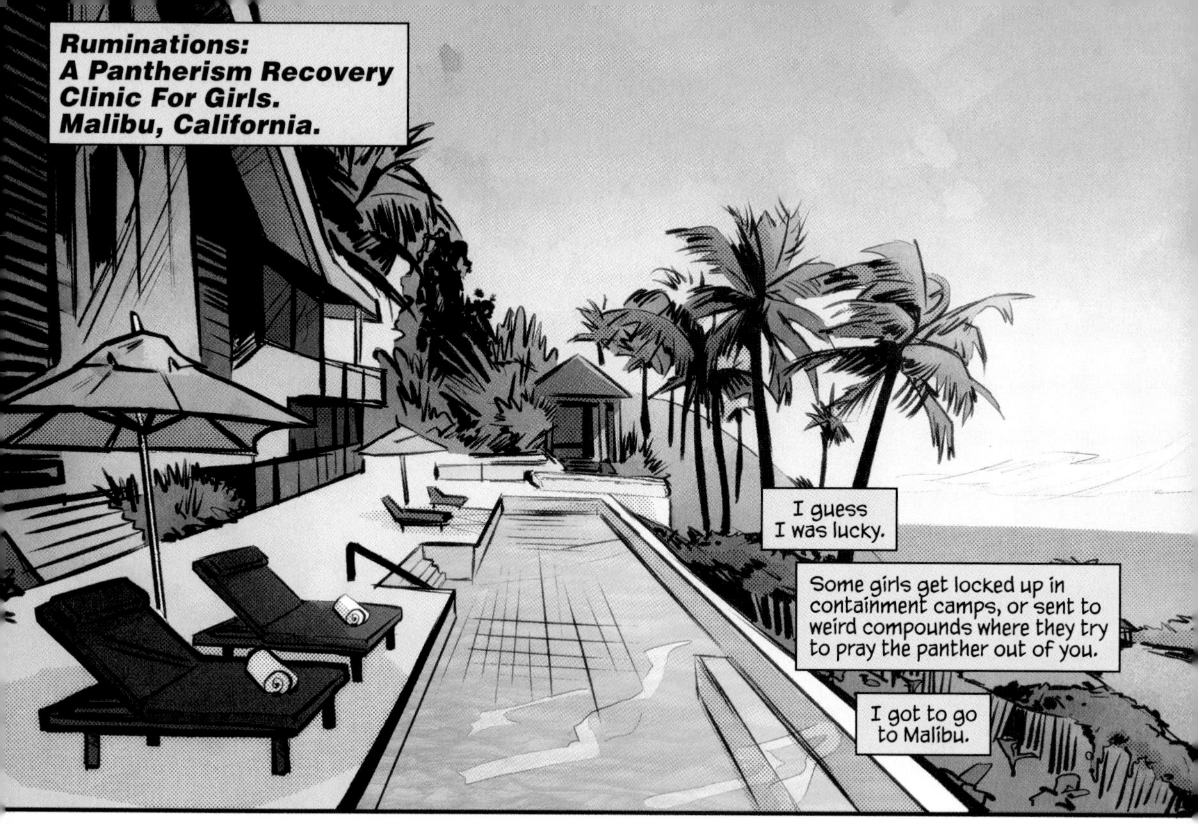
Ruminations: A Pantherism Recovery Clinic For Girls. Malibu, California.
I guess I was lucky.
Some girls get locked up in containment camps, or sent to weird compounds where they try to pray the panther out of you.
I got to go to Malibu.

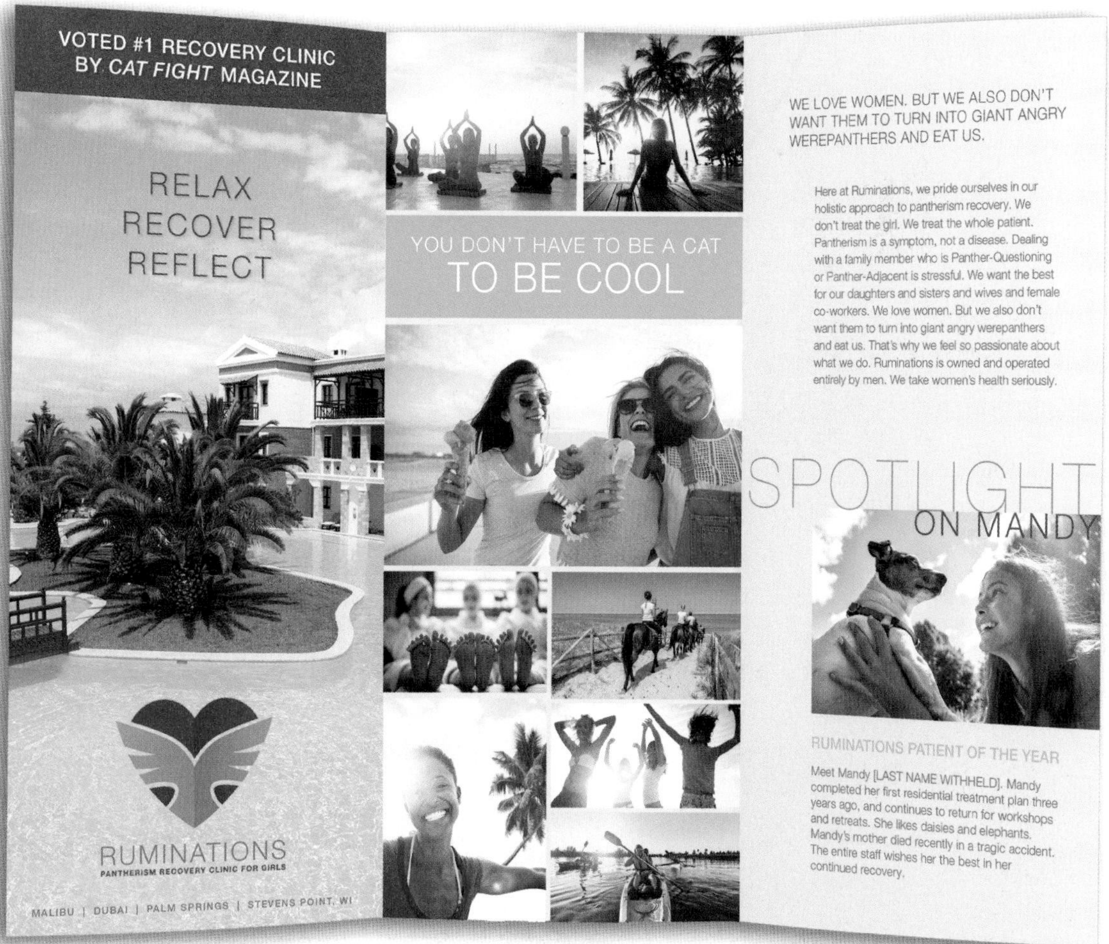
VOTED #1 RECOVERY CLINIC BY CAT FIGHT MAGAZINE
RELAX
RECOVER
REFLECT
RUMINATIONS
PANTHERISM RECOVERY CLINIC FOR GIRLS
MALIBU | DUBAI | PALM SPRINGS | STEVENS POINT, WI
YOU DON'T HAVE TO BE A CAT
TO BE COOL
WE LOVE WOMEN. BUT WE ALSO DON'T WANT THEM TO TURN INTO GIANT ANGRY WEREPANTHERS AND EAT US.
Here at Ruminations, we pride ourselves in our holistic approach to pantherism recovery. We don't treat the girl. We treat the whole patient. Pantherism is a symptom, not a disease. Dealing with a family member who is Panther-Questioning or Panther-Adjacent is stressful. We want the best for our daughters and sisters and wives and female co-workers. We love women. But we also don't want them to turn into giant angry werepanthers and eat us. That's why we feel so passionate about what we do. Ruminations is owned and operated entirely by men. We take women's health seriously.
SPOTLIGHT
ON MANDY
RUMINATIONS PATIENT OF THE YEAR
Meet Mandy [LAST NAME WITHHELD]. Mandy completed her first residential treatment plan three years ago, and continues to return for workshops and retreats. She likes daisies and elephants. Mandy's mother died recently in a tragic accident. The entire staff wishes her the best in her continued recovery.

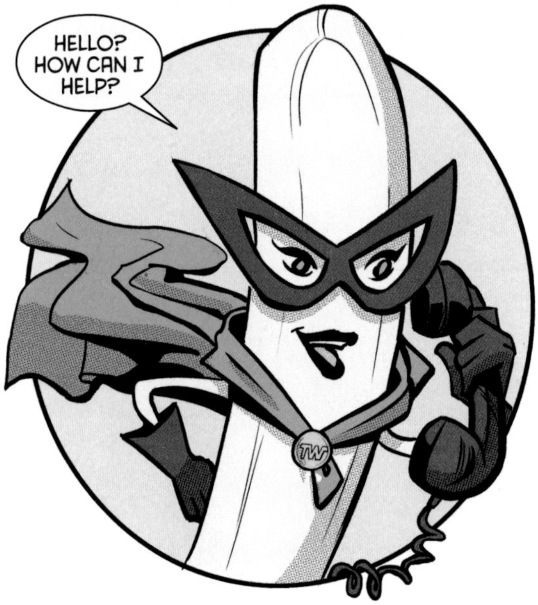
HELLO? HOW CAN I HELP?

MINISTRY OF
TROUBLE
INCORPORATED

WRITER/CREATOR/
COLORED PENCIL ARTIST
CHELSEA CAIN

COVER/CO-CREATOR/
ADS, SUPPLEMENTAL ART
LIA MITERNIQUE

ARTIST
ELISE MCCALL

COLORIST
RACHELLE ROSENBERG

LETTERER
JOE CARAMAGNA

ADDITIONAL INTERIOR ART
STELLA GREENVOSS

YOU HAVE BEEN CONTACTED BY THE MINISTRY OF TROUBLE. AWAIT FURTHER INSTRUCTIONS. ☿

NO. **9**

CHELSEA CAIN   LIA MITERNIQUE   ELISE MCCALL   RACHELLE ROSENBERG   JOE CARAMAGNA